Darkness
AT DAWN

ELIZABETH JENNINGS

BERKLEY SENSATION, NEW YORK

THE BERKLEY PUBLISHING GROUP
Published by the Penguin Group
Penguin Group (USA) Inc.
375 Hudson Street, New York, New York 10014, USA
Penguin Group (Canada), 90 Eglinton Avenue East, Suite 700, Toronto, Ontario M4P 2Y3, Canada
(a division of Pearson Penguin Canada Inc.)
Penguin Books Ltd., 80 Strand, London WC2R 0RL, England
Penguin Group Ireland, 25 St. Stephen's Green, Dublin 2, Ireland (a division of Penguin Books Ltd.)
Penguin Group (Australia), 250 Camberwell Road, Camberwell, Victoria 3124, Australia
(a division of Pearson Australia Group Pty. Ltd.)
Penguin Books India Pvt. Ltd., 11 Community Centre, Panchsheel Park, New Delhi—110 017, India
Penguin Group (NZ), 67 Apollo Drive, Rosedale, Auckland 0632, New Zealand
(a division of Pearson New Zealand Ltd.)
Penguin Books (South Africa) (Pty.) Ltd., 24 Sturdee Avenue, Rosebank, Johannesburg 2196, South
Africa

Penguin Books Ltd., Registered Offices: 80 Strand, London WC2R 0RL, England

DARKNESS AT DAWN

A Berkley Sensation Book / published by arrangement with the author

PRINTING HISTORY
Berkley Sensation mass-market edition / July 2011

Copyright © 2011 by Elizabeth Jennings.
Cover "Couple" © by Vincent Besnault/Corbis.
Cover "Mountain" © by Keenpress/Getty Images.
Cover design by Annette Fiore DeFex.
Interior text design by Kristin del Rosario.

ISBN: 978-0-425-24212-4

BERKLEY® SENSATION
Berkley Sensation Books are published by The Berkley Publishing Group,
a division of Penguin Group (USA) Inc.,
375 Hudson Street, New York, New York 10014.
BERKLEY® SENSATION and the "B" design are trademarks of Penguin Group (USA) Inc.

PRINTED IN THE UNITED STATES OF AMERICA

10 9 8 7 6 5 4 3 2 1

To my dear husband, Alfredo,
and to my wonderful son, David, always.

And to my gang, le amiche di sempre*:*
Athina, Bridget, Diana,
Lorena, Mickey and Theresa.

And of course, to my partners in crime:
Mariateresa, Maria Paola and Giovanni.

ACKNOWLEDGMENTS

Many thanks to my wonderful agent, Ethan Ellenberg, and my wonderful editor, Kate Seaver, and Katherine Pelz of the Berkley team.

I'd like to thank my very dear friend Judith Edge, nit-picker *extraordinaire*, for her careful reading of my books. And another huge thank you to my best buddy, Ellen Cosgrove, who gave me word pictures of Nhala. Thanks to all of you.

$\mathscr{P}$ROLOGUE

NHALA—A SMALL KINGDOM IN THE
HIMALAYAS
NOVEMBER 15

HE trekked painfully forward, in the immense white desert on the roof of the world. There was nothing alive as far as the eye could see—only snow and granite mountain peaks, a brilliant red with the setting sun.

The entire world was red.

He saw red everywhere—the Himalayan valley he knew was covered in snow so pure it glowed, the deep crimson peaks, which had always been white; even the cloudless sky overhead was a lurid purple.

This would ordinarily trouble him, for he was a straightforward, no-nonsense man, the best operative in his section, coming back from a successful mission, information vitally important to the security of his country carefully loaded onto a flash drive tucked into one of the dozen Velcro-zipped pockets of his parka.

Snow was not red, the sky was not purple. He knew this, knew it deep in his bones, but somehow these facts didn't trigger his internal alarm system.

Other things were doing that, such as the fact that he could barely put one foot in front of the other. He was young and strong and smart, had just pulled off an intelligence coup, and all he wanted to do was curl up in the snow and . . . rest. Forever.

The temperature on the digital reader on the sleeve of his parka read—thirty-five degrees, but he was burning up from the inside. Sweat was pouring down his face, down his back and sides under his mountain gear, and he could smell the stench of his own sweat. And of something else, something dark and dank.

The smell of death.

He shook that thought away the second it popped into his head, but it stayed, lingered, like a burr.

He was trekking downhill, but it felt as if he were climbing the peak of Mount Silva, towering overhead at twenty-seven thousand feet, the fourth highest peak in the Himalayas. His legs burned, his lungs burned, he could barely stay on his feet.

He stopped for a moment, swaying, head swimming, heavy sweat making his balaclava stick to his skin. He blinked, blinked again, then kept his eyes closed, the effort to open them too great.

His throat burned and felt raw, as if something sharp had scraped him inside. He opened his eyes with enormous difficulty and looked around him, at the immense red fields. Red, not white. Though he was hot, his entire body shivered.

He swayed, backward then forward, and his legs gave out from under him, plunging him to his knees in the snow, surprised that he wasn't melting the snow around him. His body was a furnace, pumping out heat and sweat.

Goddammit!! He had to . . . He drew a blank. Something was critically important, yet he couldn't think because his brain was boiling.

His stomach hurt, sharp, slicing pain mixed with nausea, rising quickly up his gullet. He tried to swallow it down, but all of a sudden his abdominal muscles tightened and vomit came out of his mouth in a stream that shot a foot out. The taste was vile, the vomit full of clots.

He could hardly breathe, his lungs were on fire, all of him was on fire. His stomach clenched hard again and a red black stream spewed out of him, lasting so long he couldn't catch a breath.

He spat something into the snow and looked at it, uncomprehending. Head swimming, he reached out his gloved hand and picked it up, crushing the spongy tissue between his fingers.

He was a good operative, a brave man, who'd been on a successful mission and had something vital to report. Duty was bred into his bones, and it was duty that had him feebly pressing the commo unit against his throat. He was so weak he couldn't press hard enough. He tried once, twice, three times . . . ah. Finally.

Static crackled in the earpiece curled almost invisibly behind his right ear.

"Mountain bear, come in."

The commo unit operated on encrypted bursts of very low-frequency radio waves. There were two places in the world capable of receiving the messages, one in Langley and one in Fort Meade. Fort Meade was listening, but he was reporting to his bosses at Langley.

He could barely speak, could hardly think, was operating on pure instinct. "Mountain bear, coming back from a walk." *Mission successful.*

At least he remembered the code.

He didn't remember what the mission was exactly. He had to get more information across, even if he couldn't remember much more than the basics. He pressed his finger against his throat again. "Hot zone," he gasped. "Intel . . . Palace."

He couldn't say any more because another fountain of red vomit came out of his mouth before he could take his finger away. A vestige of craft remained in the recesses of his mind, and he knew the signal was bouncing off what was officially a weather observation satellite and traveling down to the other side of the world, and whoever decrypted the signal would also be hearing the sound of his retching.

Didn't matter. He painfully turned his head in the snow, his visual horizon now reduced to a few inches past his face. A chunk of what he'd vomited was right in front of his eyes, and with a last burst of consciousness, he recognized it for what it was. Lung tissue.

He was coughing up his lungs.

He closed his eyes and let the red tide carry him away.

FOUR hundred miles above him, the new Keyhole-13 satellite in geosynchronous orbit received a coded message to direct its SWIR/thermal cameras four degrees north, which in its six months of operation it had never done. It was designed for the Troubled Latitudes, covering Pakistan and India, and had never been given instructions to turn its eye north to the small Himalayan states. But now the cold, pitiless eye moved according to instructions beamed up from fifteen thousand miles away.

Ten photograms a second, the lens caught the infrared signature of a living being in the snowy wastes. A large mammal, perhaps not human, since its temperature registered 101 degrees, then 102 then 104, not normal human temperatures. The mammal stumbled, fell. The instructions were to keep the Eye in the Sky on the mammal, and the lens did just that, taking photographic evidence, indifferent when the mammal fell to the snow and lay there, unmoving, as the heat slowly leaked out of it. Eventually the mammal became invisible to the infrared lens—as cold as the snow on which it lay in a large pool of red.

ONE

SHE smelled him before she saw him—an unmistakable funk of photocopy liquid, good wool, an expensive men's cologne and anxious sweat. She didn't know who he was, but she imagined what he was.

CIA.

She sighed quietly.

Lucy Merritt looked down at a first edition of Emily Dickinson's poems, a lovely illustrated book, which some moron had kept in a moldy garage with leaky pipes. When it had come to her, it had been almost lost forever. Lucy had worked very hard to coax it back to life, for its kind would never come again.

She loved this, loved restoring books and manuscripts, piecing together pieces of human history that would otherwise be lost.

All in all, a highly satisfactory day, and she was looking forward to a very pleasant evening. She had a great apartment just off Dupont Circle, which she'd carefully decorated. Each stick of furniture, the rugs, the artwork on the walls, the kitchen tiles and bathroom fixtures—all just so. A perfect blend of beauty and comfort. She always breathed out a sigh of pleasure as she crossed the threshold and shut the door behind her, closing out the world.

Tonight she had a bowl of butternut squash soup and a slice of rosemary focaccia just waiting to be heated, a half bottle of Sauvignon Blanc chilling in the fridge and two absolutely perfect peaches for dessert. The new CD of Rossetti playing Rachmaninoff just waiting to be cracked open. Fresh, perfumed sheets on the bed. Perfect, just perfect.

Except for Mr. Musty, lurking at the door.

Lucy slowly peeled off her pristine white cotton gloves— bare fingers left oils on delicate pages—and turned around.

There he was, hunched in the doorway, bringing the beauty quotient of her little lab down by several degrees.

Everything in her office had been chosen by her and reflected her tastes. Her coworkers teased her but they, too, liked sitting on the comfortable silk bergère in the corner, sipping her special lemon ginger tisane out of Limoges china breathing in the scent of the homemade potpourri in a small crystal bowl and looking at her watercolors. She wasn't a half-bad artist and had been asked more than once to show, but that would make her private pleasure a commercial enterprise and she already had a job she loved.

Yes, just about everything in her life was perfect, and now look what had come crawling out of the woodwork.

"Dr. Merritt? Edwin Montgomery sent me. May I come in?"

She looked him up and down. More than forty, less than fifty, which would put him at a GS-14 grade, unless he had sold secrets to North Korea or had been caught on film having sex with barnyard animals. Not too unattractive, but exhausted, deep and brand-new grooves carved into his cheeks, with eggplant-colored bags under his eyes. His suit was a Brioni, excellent cut, but looked as if he'd slept several nights in a row in it.

Something was wrong at Langley.

Not her problem.

She'd paid all her dues to Langley, for this life and, if the Buddhism she'd been taught as a child was true, for many more lives to come. Langley had taken everything away from her. What were they doing now, coming knocking at her door?

He still stood there patiently, and she narrowed her eyes at him. "Come in if you want, but I'm about ready to go home. You can go back to Langley and tell them no, to whatever it is they want."

They looked at each other and Lucy broke first. She gestured at her small armchair. "Sit down," she said, clenching her teeth against the automatic *please* that rose to her lips. She wasn't going to say please to a CIA agent. Ever. They'd taken too much from her.

"No," he said, folding his hands neatly in front of his crotch, a little modified civilian-at-ease stance. "I'm fine where I am. And this is a time-sensitive issue. I have orders to take you with me, Dr. Merritt. Whatever it takes."

His voice was polite, firm, unyielding,

Knowing who he worked for, *whatever it takes* could mean forcibly subduing her, drugging her and taking her in shackles to wherever he wanted her to go. These people didn't fool around, and they wanted what they wanted.

She'd had an . . . interesting childhood, under the iron rule of CIA hard-asses. Her first instinct was to refuse, absolutely, but . . . they were stronger than she was. She knew that through bitter experience.

Lucy waited a beat, locking eyes with his, but there was a lot of male will behind those tired brown eyes. Backed up, of course, by over fifty thousand employees, at least five thousand of whom were trained covert operatives who could kill you with a fingernail, and a budget of over sixty billion dollars accountable to no one but themselves.

Yep. Stronger than she was. No contest.

The butternut squash soup, the Sauvignon Blanc, the peaches, the new CD—they'd all have to wait.

"Okay," she told the guy. His face was expressionless, but

he gave a little exhale. Lucy hid a smile. "What? Did Uncle Edwin tell you I'd be difficult? He should know better."

She'd caught him completely by surprise with that one, the man's eyes actually opening wider when she said *Uncle Edwin*. Lucy knew perfectly well that Edwin Montgomery, Deputy Director of Operations, was feared by everyone at the CIA. Grown men, men trained to withstand torture, quailed at his mildest expression of displeasure. He was known for his iciness and control and ruthlessness.

She'd only seen him show emotion once, at her parents' funeral. She'd been fourteen.

Lucy stowed all her restoration tools neatly away, taking her time and doing it right. She was naturally neat, but life had taken that and polished it diamond-bright. Two years of her childhood had been spent in a hut in the Indonesian jungle with a beaten-earth floor. Anything she held dear had to be kept in sealed plastic cases or they'd be destroyed by insects or by the relentless humidity.

When it was done, she took off her lab coat, hung it up on a perfumed padded hanger, hung that on the ornate brass clothes tree, took off her glasses, which she only needed for the very close, meticulous work of manuscript restoration, pulled out the scrunchy that kept her shoulder-length hair away from her face and turned to the operative.

His eyes widened slightly, only this time it wasn't her mention of the Boss of All Bosses. This time it was pure male appreciation.

Lucy knew she was good-looking. Big deal. It had never got her any advantages. In fact, it had been a serious handicap throughout her childhood, spent on undercover missions with her parents. The prime directive for undercover agents was not to attract attention, and pretty little girls are attention magnets all over the world. Her mother used to make her dress in the most drab, unattractive clothing possible, and cut her glossy chestnut hair in a pudding bowl shape, which was why Lucy loved pretty clothes and now went to the hairdresser twice a week.

The man—whose cover name would be Brown or Gray or Smith—hid his male interest immediately, treating her, as she locked her lab door and walked with him down the corridor, with no more interest than if she'd been a seventy-year-old crone with four chins, which was exactly the way Lucy liked it.

She concealed her surprise at finding another operative waiting for them in the parking lot. Two guys to pick her up? Uncle Edwin must have been expecting a *lot* of resistance.

Without a word, Lucy got into the backseat of the SUV. The door closed with that extra special expensive-sounding *whump* that armored vehicles have. No doubt there was a small armory in a lockbox in the back, two pistols in fast-draw harnesses underneath the driver and shotgun seats, and in all likelihood the engine had been reconfigured for extra bursts of power during evasive maneuvers.

There was utter silence in the car as they drove away from the small building housing the restoration section at the back of the monumental Smithsonian buildings and headed south. The guy driving was a clone of the guy who'd come for her, now riding shotgun.

Mr. Black, possibly. Or maybe Mr. White.

The driver broke speed limits on the way, obviously trusting to some secret signal given off to traffic police that Homeland Security was doing its thing and not to bug them. It was also entirely possible that the driver was at times exceeding 90 mph in order to get home in time for a martini before dinner.

You never knew with the CIA.

Lucy was very good at disappearing into her head. The forty-minute trip barely registered as she planned out the various restoration stages for her next project, ten foxed and moldy notebooks by John Steinbeck, arriving tomorrow. Found in a box in the attic of a woman whose great-grandmother had possibly had an affair with Steinbeck. The woman who'd sent the notebooks said that her great-grandmother's diaries had hinted that the notebooks might contain an undiscovered novella, though it would be almost impossible to tell until major restoration work had been done.

Lucy entertained herself with all the possibilities, paying no attention to the landscape dimly visible through the darkly tinted windows.

She knew where they were going.

The entrance took her by surprise, though.

When the SUV finally pulled into the long driveway of CIA Headquarters in the McLean suburb of Langley, it pulled up into the Old Headquarters.

The New Headquarters was flashy—with a four-story curved atrium full of light, elegant and airy. It was the face of the new, consumer-friendly CIA, everyone's best friend, a bulwark against world terrorism.

The atrium of the Old Headquarters they were entering now was low and brutal and businesslike. Stalinesque, even, because that's who they were fighting when it was designed.

The old entrance was cavernous, like some sepulcher of lost lives and lost hopes.

She crossed over the huge star inset in the marble floor, the Agency seal with the compass rose signifying the CIA's worldwide reach, looking neither to the left nor, especially, to the right, to the Wall of Honor.

So when Mr. White or Mr. Brown held open the door, she swept past him and into the building and walked down to the end of the endless lobby to wait for clearance. She looked straight ahead, aware of the security cameras that were following her progress. She wasn't about to give Edwin or anyone at the CIA the satisfaction of seeing her look at the Wall of Honor, a white marble wall with inset black stars, each star representing a nameless CIA officer who had given his or her life in the line of duty.

Nameless, because no one could ever know their names. No information was given as to how or where they died— just the anonymous black star. Often, not even the families knew.

Lucy knew.

She wasn't going to give anyone any satisfaction, so she marched right over the Seal and right by the Wall of Honor, hoping against hope the cameras couldn't pick out the tears in her eyes.

Because two of those anonymous stars were her mother and her father, who had been killed right before her eyes.

CAPTAIN Mike Shafer of the army's Tenth Mountain Division hopped down from the Black Hawk hovering over the helipad at Langley. The roar of the rotors precluded conversation, so he simply gave a thumbs-up and then rotated his index finger.

I'm okay, you guys can get going.

The pilot gave him a two-fingered salute off his helmet, lifted the nose of the helo and angled away fast. The skids never touched CIA soil, and Mike was sorry that his combat boots had to. Ten years army and he'd never been to Langley. He liked it just fine that way. Army pukes and CIA spooks don't mix. And now that he was ready to leave the service, at the last minute the spooks had reeled him in.

It was clear that the spooks at Langley wanted *him*. They'd come for him ten thousand feet up in the Granites in Alaska, on the third week of an intense, six-week mountaineering training cycle, preparing men to take over, combat-ready and acclimatized to the high altitudes, in the Hindu Kush.

Mike had any healthy army man's distrust of the CIA, but he was also seriously annoyed at having to interrupt the training cycle, particularly since it was his last.

He'd hoped to give Uncle Sam at least another four years, but his old man was sick and it was time for Mike to step up for his family and take over Shafer Demolitions. Responsibility for his stepmom and his half brothers and sister and more than 150 employees now fell on his shoulders.

So though he was giving his all to the men he was training in Alaska, there was a part of him that was already gone. He did not want to be reeled back in by Christians in Action.

Yet here he was, having been pulled without any advance notice from three weeks straight in the field, bundled onto a CH-17 Chinook down to Fort Greenley in a raging snowstorm, taken from there by military jet transport to Andrews and from there by Black Hawk to Langley. He was filthy, exhausted and seriously pissed.

As the rotor wash eased up, Mike straightened and turned at the hand on his arm.

"Captain Shafer?" a man yelled. The Black Hawk's powerful engines were still loud even though it was lifting away.

Mike nodded tightly. Something in his face made the man drop his hand, fast.

"Follow me," the man mouthed, and made his way across the parking blacktop.

The man guiding him was a classic bureaucrat—of moderate height, thin, elegantly dressed in an expensive suit by some designer Mike couldn't recognize but his stepmom probably could. Expensive, shiny shoes. Closely shaven, hair recently barbered by someone who knew what he was doing. Cuff links. Fucking *cuff links*. The CIA was known for its snappy dressers.

Mind you, they couldn't find their own asses with both hands and a flashlight. They'd missed the implosion of the Soviet Union and had been dead wrong about WMD in Iraq, but the creases in their trousers were just so.

Next to Mr. Elegant, Mike felt like the Abominable Snowman. He hadn't shaved and he hadn't showered this past week. He'd worn the same fatigues day and night for a week, too. He was hungry, thirsty, sleepy and filthy—and in a lousy mood—as he followed Elegant into a side entrance to a bank of elevators where they went down, way down.

There had been a turnstile and guard at the entrance, but Elegant pulled out a card at a small side door before the turnstile, so Elegant obviously had a top security clearance, probably higher than Mike's own.

In the elevator he could smell himself, and it wasn't

pretty. He could also smell Elegant, who smelled very pretty, of an expensive cologne. The inside of the elevator was lined with brass panels so polished they were like mirrors. Mike stared at their reflection.

Elegant looked like a member in good standing of civilized society, and he looked like a nineteenth-century trapper just in from a winter of murdering and scalping settlers on the plains.

He heard his own teeth grinding.

Finally the elevator stopped dropping and the doors whooshed open onto a plush, quiet corridor with cove lighting along the ceiling. They walked down empty corridors for what felt like almost a mile. Mike walked fast and was delighted to hear Elegant's breathing turn heavy. Finally, they reached the heart of something.

They caught up with three well-dressed men and two very elegant women walking along the corridor, conferring quietly. One of the women greeted the man by Mike's side and froze when she saw Mike. She simply stopped walking. Her four companions stopped, too, startled at the sight of him in their civilized space.

Mike lifted his lips in a feral smile, and one of the women stepped back instinctively. He was swarthy by nature, and the high-altitude sun had baked him a deep brown, almost the same color as his dark bushy beard, so all they'd be seeing is a slash of white in a nut brown face. A none-too-friendly face.

Mike was also armed. No one had told him much, so he'd come loaded for bear. Elegant's special clearance had obviously been extended to him, since he hadn't been disarmed and still had his Glock 18 strapped to his thigh. With this lot he wouldn't need weaponry, though. He was an expert in close-quarters combat. Everyone in this corridor was a paper-pusher. No contest.

He sighed silently. The thought of venting his frustration on these pencil-dicks—even the women were pencil-dicks—was tempting, but of course he wouldn't. Even the CIA had its place in keeping his country safe.

Sort of. When they could get their shit together.

He was frustrated because with each hour that passed, he was losing acclimatization it had taken him time and hard work to achieve.

More and more people were streaming into a room halfway along the long corridor, and that was obviously where they were headed, too. Mike tucked away his frustration and worry about leaving his men ten thousand feet up with no leader. There was nothing he could do about it now.

The room was large, with an enormous polished wood conference table looking at a twelve-foot blank monitor above their heads, covering one entire wall.

The man accompanying him started to take his arm to direct him to his seat, but at Mike's snarl, he lifted his eyebrows and nodded to a chair at the table, near the middle. Mike was surprised to see his nameplate already there.

Captain Michael Shafer, Tenth Mountain Division, US Army.

In front of him was a sterling silver pitcher of ice water, a big water glass, a pad and pen, a netbook and a microphone.

The chair was sinfully comfortable he found as he eased into it. Definitely the most comfortable seating arrangement he'd had in . . . shit, in almost a month. He and his men had been living in Jamesway huts that had lethally uncomfortable tubular steel chairs. He was also massively sleep deprived. If he didn't watch it, he'd drift off if they doused the lights for that huge monitor.

Then any thought of sleep fled his mind as the Secretary of Defense walked in, followed by the Director of the NSA, the Director of Homeland Security and the Deputy Director of Operations of the CIA.

And then any thoughts of anything at all fled from his mind as the DD/O was followed by the most beautiful woman he'd ever seen.

Christ, what was a babe like *her* doing here? Not too tall but long-legged, with shiny shoulder-length chestnut hair, a heart-shaped face with huge blue eyes and an Angelina

Jolie mouth . . . The woman was distraction itself in a room meant for business. Serious business, judging from the top honchos in US security who were taking their seats on the other side of the table.

Interestingly, Hot Babe was seated on the power side, right next to the DD/O, looking utterly out of place.

Mike wasn't a Neanderthal. He worked well with female officers. He'd grown up with a strong stepmother he loved and respected, and he had a half sister who'd kick his ass if he ever showed a woman disrespect. So it wasn't the woman's femaleness that bothered him. Per se. Though that degree of sex quotient should be illegal.

Once he got his mind out of his pants, though, he realized that his first instinct was right. *She doesn't belong.*

There were other women in the room, types he was very familiar with. No-nonsense professional women, dressed well, even expensively, but for the office. They came equipped with BlackBerries, Macs and briefcases the way eagles come equipped with feathers. They scowled and gave off *I'm very important* vibes that were almost palpable.

Hot Babe was dressed for a dinner date with a guy she liked a lot, in a soft curve-hugging sweater with some shiny bits in a blue that exactly matched her eyes, straight black skirt with a flirty little something around the hem, black stockings, black high heels.

Where everyone who wasn't the head of a multibillion-dollar government agency was burdened down with sheaves of papers and communication devices, she was carrying nothing but a purse, though it looked like one of those purses that cost more than his Remington 700.

Above all, she didn't look self-important, didn't check the other people in the room in an instinctive settling of pecking order as everyone else was doing. She looked a little bored and a little amused.

The big door closed. Everyone who was supposed to be here was here. Voices died down as the business of the day was ready to begin.

Something about the intensity of his stare must have charged the air between them because she suddenly looked up and met his gaze from across the ten shiny feet of table.

Mike's breath stopped in his chest. Fuck. She was *gorgeous*. Movie star beautiful. Hardly any makeup, so it was all her. Her look was direct, intelligent and . . . sad? Could that be? He was mulling over what she could be sad about, and why someone who didn't have government agent written all over her should be here in this room, when Secretary Connelly tapped his finger against the microphone for everyone's attention, something Mike hated.

And just like that, his head was back in the game. Whatever it was that they had called him in for, interrupting an extreme training mission, which would cost him in lost acclimatization and leave a group of elite soldiers leaderless, was about to be explained.

It better be good.

"THIS meeting is called to order," Secretary Connelly said.

He was tall, had a shock of blindingly white hair and was as dumb as a rock. Her mother used to say it was a miracle he could tie his own shoelaces. Lucy remembered her parents making fun of his blank expression when he'd been the senator from the Commonwealth of Virginia.

She'd been called away from her squash soup, a lovely wine and two perfect peaches to listen to this bozo?

Lucy tried to wipe the boredom off her face and found it hard. Then she sneaked a glance at Uncle Edwin and straightened up, suddenly no longer bored.

Uncle Edwin looked tense, deep brackets around his mouth, nostrils white with stress. Lucy had never seen him looking even remotely like that. Even at her parents' funeral, he'd looked sad and devastated but not tense and anxious. He'd been a top security official for well over two thirds of his life, and he'd seen everything, twice. Whatever was going on was serious.

She looked around the room while Connelly droned on

about the "grave threats to our way of life" without ever mentioning exactly what the threat was. But then, he had the brains of a cocker spaniel, so it was entirely likely that if it was a complex threat, he had no real grasp of it, as Uncle Edwin obviously did.

The room was full of security types. Not for the first time, Lucy thought how ill at ease her parents would be with the modern intelligence apparatus, staffed almost entirely with officers completely dedicated to climbing a career ladder while looking good. And never mussing their hair.

Her parents, on the other hand, had been serious and dedicated type A's who never shrank from danger or—she had to admit—adventure. They wouldn't recognize the corporate types here as belonging to their business.

Well . . . there was one person here who wasn't a brown-nosing paper-pusher, and he was sitting across the table staring at her. He didn't look like a drone or a bureaucrat.

He looked like trouble.

He was dressed in some kind of ragged battle uniform, otherwise he'd seem like a homeless person, though no homeless person she'd ever seen looked as athletic as he did. Tall and very broad, incredibly fit underneath the grungy uniform, shaggy hair and untrimmed beard. Not homeless, then. Maybe he was what her parents would have called a "snake eater." Special Forces.

He seemed to be fixated on her. In any other setting, she'd take it as masculine interest, but it didn't seem to be that. He seemed surprised and . . . and disapproving. Obviously thinking she was out of place in this room of movers and shakers.

Well yes, Mr. Snake Eater, yes I am out of place. She couldn't wait for the dog and pony show to be over and to finally get back to her peaceful, perfumed apartment.

She suddenly tuned back in to Connelly's droning voice, the pitch having changed: ". . . and so now for a better explanation of the threat to our country, I'll give the floor to Deputy Director of Operations Montgomery."

Lucy focused on Uncle Edwin. Whatever his faults, he

was a serious and intelligent man, and whatever he had to say, she was obviously here to listen to it.

As he rose, the lights dimmed, making the laptop and netbook monitors glow in the dark.

A disembodied voice came over the loudspeaker system. "Ladies and gentlemen, please turn off your computers and cell phones and pagers. It goes without saying that the report you are about to hear is SCI—Sensitive Compartmented Information. Clearance level Majestic."

The entire room took in a shocked breath. Not even the President of the United States was always cleared for Majestic-level intel. It was the level of clearance needed to know that aliens had landed. Certainly she shouldn't be privy to Majestic-level intelligence.

The room was too dark to see individual features, but she could hear a low buzz.

"Quiet please." Uncle Edwin bent down to press a button, and the enormous monitor behind him lit up. At first Lucy thought the projection system was broken, because the screen was blank, white. Then the image came into focus, and she could see granite outcroppings and snow-covered peaks against a blindingly bright turquoise sky.

Something small was moving across the white landscape. The image zoomed, so fast it nearly gave her nausea, and focused on a man, trudging across a snowy valley floor.

Uncle Edwin's voice was clear, calm and emotionless. "This image was taken two days ago at 0600 Zulu time by a Keyhole satellite that was instructed to change the direction of its lens. The man you are watching is one of my operatives, following up SIGINT and HUMINT that a biowarfare laboratory had been set up by Al Qaeda in . . . mountain terrain."

Lucy could hear between the lines. Someone at NSA had picked up a cell-phone conversation or an email—SIGINT—and an operative or operatives had been sent in to wherever to get human intelligence, HUMINT.

Figures were superimposed on the screen, probably geotagging coordinates, and probably encrypted. She couldn't understand them anyway. But on the bottom of the screen in a chyron, the white numbers were easy to understand.

Biodata: temp: 99.7°, BPM: 120, BP: 110/70

The satellite was able to read body temperature, the beats per minute of the heart and blood pressure. The man was running a slight temperature.

He trudged forward, head down, moving as if in slow motion.

Then the man swayed, fell to his knees and, shockingly, vomited. She heard breaths catch around her in the dark as a deep red projectile stream, horrifically bright against the white snow, came spewing out of him. He rose, shaking, to his feet, took a few steps and was wracked by another vicious bout of retching that went on and on, so long Lucy wondered how he was breathing. Bright streaks of red marred the snow.

The man took another few steps, fell to his knees again.

Data was streaming at the sides and across the top, but the most important statistics were along the bottom of the monitor.

Biodata: temp: 103°, BPM: 160, BP: 110/60

The man wasn't getting up. He vomited again, an astonishing amount of material. Surely he hadn't gone trekking in the mountains after a heavy meal? Though most of what he was vomiting seemed to be blood.

There was heavy silence in the room as they watched the man try to get up and fail, and vomit again where he lay, collapsed, on the ground. His limbs were still, the only movements those necessary to retch. Everything that came out of his mouth now was bright red.

It occurred to Lucy, with a hard squeeze to the heart, that she was watching a man die, alone in some frozen desert.

No one spoke; they just watched the monitor as the file speeded up.

Biodata: temp: 104°, BPM: 180, BP: 100/50

Biodata: temp: 104.5°, BPM. 100, BP: 90/50

Biodata: temp: 104.5°, BPM: 80, BP: 80/40

Biodata: temp: 104.5°, BPM: 50, BP: 70/30

Until finally:

Biodata: temp: 104°, BPM: 0, BP: 0

Lucy wanted to look away, but Uncle Edwin said quietly, with that vast authority he had that no one, including her, could possibly resist, "Wait. There's more."

What else could there be? She thought. *The man's dead.*

But, horribly, there *was* more.

Uncle Edwin clicked ahead, the white digits of the chronometer rolling forward faster and faster. What was it he wanted them to see beyond white fields of snow and a dead man, lying in a lake of his own blood, which expanded with each passing minute, deep red close to the body, lightening to a faint pink a couple of feet out?

The minutes ticked by—an hour of film for each minute of real time—and Lucy blinked. The body was . . . she leaned forward, wondering if this was an optical illusion, but it wasn't. The body was shrinking, minute by minute. It was like the death scene of the Wicked Witch of the West in *The Wizard of Oz.*

The man had on thick mountain gear, so it was hard to tell at first, but the clothes flattened out, the head retracted like a turtle's until it was no longer visible. Horribly, a boot fell off and rolled away from the leg, as if the foot had been chopped off.

The film fast-forwarded through sunset, the shadows lengthening visibly in the speeded-up monitor, until the image turned black. But not before an evening wind gusted lightly, blowing gray powder away from the still form.

Lucy suspected that gray powder was the remains of the body, like incinerated ash.

"Your eyes aren't deceiving you," Uncle Edwin's deep calm voice said. "Postmortem, there was a process of early liquefaction, then ultra-fast dessication. The powder you saw at the end was my operative."

A few lights came on, and Lucy could see grim faces around the room. It was a lot to take in.

"We suspect a viral hemorrhagic fever disease. Detailed intel is in a flash drive that was on the person of my operative. We have a senior officer of the CDC here. Dr. Samuels, can you report your impressions on the basis of what we've just seen?"

A disheveled-looking man rose, passing a hand over his overlong flyaway hair and straightening a crumpled jacket. He looked like a caricature of an academic, but the instant his strong voice spoke into the microphone, he held everyone in the palm of his hand. His voice was deep and he spoke with utter authority.

"There are numerous strains of hemorrhagic fever viruses, the most famous of which—but not the most frequent—is Ebola. HFVs are not, strictly speaking, human diseases. HFVs are transmitted to humans by means of contact with infected animals. The virus attaches to host receptors through the surface peplomer and into vesicles in the host cell. The main targets of infection are endothelial cells, mononuclear phagocytes and hepatocytes. Usually, the virus leads to hemorrhagic diathesis through direct damage of cells involved in hemostasis. In other words, vessels can no longer contain blood and the patient bleeds out, dying of hypovolemic shock. Mr. Deputy Director, how long beforehand had your agent been inserted?"

"Two days," Uncle Edwin answered. "But we don't know when he was exposed."

"Well, it must have been an unusually virulent strain. Incubation can typically run up to twenty-one days, after which symptoms develop, including high fever, nausea, abdominal pain." Dr. Samuels pointed a finger at the screen, frozen at the last moment of light—empty clothes in a vast white desert. "No known original cases have been reported outside sub-Saharan Africa, most have occurred in clusters around the equator. HFVs thrive in heat and moisture. Wherever that place is, it is in a mountain range full of snow and the temperature is below freezing. Furthermore, the man in the image seemed normal until affected by violent symptoms. Sometimes humans infected with HFVs have been known to take a week to die. On the basis of what was shown us, I think we could rule out hemorrhagic fever."

Uncle Edwin's voice was clear and cold. "And what about a weaponized HFV, Dr. Samuels?"

Dr. Samuels's bushy gray eyebrows rose. "Weaponized? Hmm. Well, I know the Russians tried it and gave up. There's a working group on civilian biodefense, which includes thirty representatives from academia, public health services and military services, chaired by the CDC. HFVs are twenty-eighth down on the list of possible dangers. It's been said that North Korea might have weaponized yellow fever but doesn't have a delivery system. As I said before, the disease thrives in heat and moisture, which rules out much of the earth north and south of the 30th parallels. Even when someone is infected, during the incubation period transmission of the virus isn't common. These are not highly contagious viruses, and most cases of infection are by direct contact with the mucous membrane of an infected patient."

"Nonetheless," Uncle Edwin said calmly. "I would ask you to posit a mutated form of a hemorrhagic fever virus, airborne, highly contagious, fast-acting also in cold or temperate climates. What would be our position then?"

Dr. Samuels was silent for a long moment. There was no noise in the room at all. Everyone leaned forward a little to hear what he had to say, even Lucy.

"There is, as of today, no known cure for any of the hemorrhagic fever viral diseases. The mortality rate is 89 percent. Treatment is supportive and basically palliative. USAM-RIID, the United States Army Medical Research Institute for Infectious Diseases, has developed a vaccine that is

100 percent effective in monkeys but not in humans. Large-scale contagion of a weaponized, airborne cold-climate virus would require barrier nursing in every single hospital and medical center, all of which would become overwhelmed in less than forty-eight hours. Every infected person would have to be put in immediate quarantine for at least twenty-one days, something clearly impossible if there is large-scale contagion. Every single human being would have to walk around wearing double gloves, an impermeable Tyvek gown, an N-95 mask or at least an air-purifying respirator—which, by the way, cost almost one thousand dollars each—leg and shoe coverings, a face shield and goggles. International, interstate and city-to-city transport would have to be banned, so good-bye food supplies. All planes would be grounded. What would be our position then? I think, Deputy Director, that the technical term for that would be fucked."

$\mathcal{T}$WO

MIKE was beginning to grasp what this was about. A mission, an overwhelmingly important one, at high altitudes. Well shit, he could do that. He'd trained his entire life to do exactly that.

Mike was strictly a boots-on-the-ground kind of guy. And he knew exactly whose boots he wanted on the ground. His men, the men he'd been training at ten thousand feet and who were still there, already acclimatized. So—cut the training mission short and go out in the field.

Fine by him.

Frankly, what he'd heard and seen scared the shit out of him. If someone was about to loose a highly contagious form of Ebola on the world, that someone needed to be stopped, right now.

Montgomery leaned forward slightly into the microphone. "All right, the people in this room below director level now constitute the Committee on Weaponized Hemorrhagic Fever Viruses, code named Stop Cold. Stop Cold will meet on a daily basis until we get the information contained in my operative's flash drive and will report to the directors, who are now the Stop Cold Oversight Committee." He looked slowly around the conference table, eyeing each person coldly. "And remember, you are all under Majestic confidentiality rules, and any breach of secrecy will be treated as high treason."

Jesus. Mike had been on a lot of top secret missions, but never one this secret. Well, he knew how to keep his mouth shut. And he knew how to give his men need-to-know intel. Just enough to do their jobs.

"The Stop Cold Committee will meet in Room 346 right now and start drawing up contingency plans. The efforts will be coordinated by Homeland Security. Everyone in the room is dismissed except for Dr. Samuels, Captain Shafer and Dr. Lucy Merritt."

Mike wondered which of the pen-pusher types was Dr. Merritt when Hot Babe right across from him drew in a shocked breath, opened wide those beautiful blue eyes and turned them on the Deputy Director.

"Oh no," she hissed. "No way!"

Mike was staggered, which was a big sign of how exhausted he was, because he wasn't the easily surprised type. So . . . Hot Babe's name was Lucy Merritt and she was an . . . *operative*? Like Evelyn Salt?

What floored him even more was her saying no to Edwin Montgomery, fucking Deputy Director of Operations of the fucking CIA. No one said no to Montgomery, no one. Mike doubted whether the Defense Secretary or even the Director of Homeland Security would have the nerve to say no to him. Let alone Hot Babe.

If she was in government employ—and she had to be to be here—she'd just committed insubordination.

Mike half expected Montgomery to call in the two mean-looking Marines stationed right outside the door and have her marched out under armed guard.

But then Mike got the second half of the double whammy. Because Edwin Montgomery, who was known to eat newbies for breakfast, merely turned to her with a gentle smile. "Oh yes, my dear."

Hot Babe—Lucy Merritt—crossed slender arms over utterly delightful breasts and sat back, face cold. She didn't have the mulish expression you'd expect of someone crossing a major line. She just looked determined. Despite himself, Mike was a little impressed. Edwin Montgomery was a legend in government. Presidents quailed before him. That a young woman defied him was almost unthinkable.

Montgomery turned to the other people in the room, all of them frozen, mesmerized by the little drama playing out. His glare unfroze them, fast. Inside a minute, the room was deserted except for Mike, Montgomery, Dr. Samuels and Dr. Lucy Merritt.

"Dr. Samuels." Montgomery's face had turned grim again, deep brackets around his mouth, nostrils white with tension. "What else can you tell us, positing a weaponized HFV, based on what we've seen?"

There were now only the four of them in the room. Montgomery had touched a button that switched the screen off and raised the lights. He and Lucy Merritt were sitting together on one side of the enormous table and Mike and Dr. Samuels were on the opposite side, a few chairs apart. Mike swiveled in his chair to see Dr. Samuels better.

Dr. Samuels was looking as grim as Montgomery was. "Well, there are a lot of considerations to be made. First of all, whatever lab mutation has occurred, I'm assuming that the incubation period has been shortened."

Montgomery nodded. "To a couple of hours, as best we can reconstruct."

Dr. Samuels winced. "Okay. If the virus has been mutated to be faster and even more deadly, that's horrible news. In an unaltered form the mortality rate is 89 percent, as I said. So any tweaking would bring it close to a 100 percent mortality rate, which more or less rules out any hospital or medical care at all, as the medical staff will be infected as well. The disease will run its course until everyone is dead. And of course they'd have worked on the medium of contagion. Airborne, you said. So it could be spread by people, by canisters loosed by airplanes, crop dusters . . . you name it. But horrible as all that is, there's another aspect that's terrifying. Unless you're a complete maniac—and though, unfortunately, there are plenty of those around, luckily they tend to be scarce in the scientific community—you don't create a Doomsday Disease that can't be contained. Because you can't be assured the disease won't decimate your own population. It's a little like Cold War MAD. Mutually Assured Destruction. No one wanted to risk it. They'd created something so horrible it was guaranteed to come back to bite them in the ass if unleashed. *However . . .*" He shot an index finger at the monitor. "Can we see that last bit again? The one where it looks like the man disappeared? That's it. Now please fast forward."

The monitor sprang to life, the images crisp and crystal clear. The man lay facedown in the snow, a spreading pool of blood around him and then that astonishing vanishing trick.

"Thank God my mind doesn't work that way," Dr. Samuels said. "But someone's does. What you've just seen unlocks the key to use of highly virulent bioengineered diseases."

"Please explain, Doctor," Montgomery said quietly.

Mike shot a glance at Lucy Merritt, who was looking between the doctor and the screen, face pale. She'd caught on, too.

"Some lab has figured out the perfect off switch. What I said earlier wasn't quite true, it was for public consumption. The fact of the matter is, the Soviet Union did actually manage to weaponize a form of HFV that they were going to deploy in Chechnya. But then some scientist said whoa, think it through. Not only would the soldiers fighting there be infected—though my understanding of the Soviet Union is that that wouldn't have been a major deterrent—but they could never stop the contagion at the border. It would inevitably slip over into Russia and never stop, and not even the Soviets wanted to wipe out their entire population. Most country borders are lines drawn in the sand, not natural borders. And even where there are natural borders, an airborne virus can ride the winds over mountains and cross rivers.

"Another major deterrent to killing off a population if you want to occupy their land is getting rid of the bodies. Humans are many things, but in essence we're just meat. Killing off a nation of hundreds of millions in one fell swoop leaves millions of tons of dead and decaying meat on the ground that's hard to dispose of, not to mention pockets of the disease remaining in the soil, seeping down into the groundwater. But what we just saw—it's genius, though it's horrifying as well. They've figured out a way for the virus to cause the dead body to self-destruct. That ash blowing away won't contain any viruses. So, Mr. Deputy Director, the perfect weapon might be in enemy hands. A virulent airborne disease that kills in a short time span and disposes cleanly of the body. Guaranteed to allow you to empty a country and then occupy the land."

"I think that's just what we're facing," Montgomery said quietly.

"Then my initial assessment was correct," Dr. Samuels answered. "We're fucked."

Mike spoke up, his mind already far along the planning stages of the upcoming mission. "Wherever that scene was, it was obviously at a high altitude in mountain terrain. High-altitude missions are what the Tenth Mountain Division does. I have a team of twenty men who are training right now in Alaska's Granite Range at ten thousand feet. They can be airlifted—"

Montgomery lifted a hand. "Stop, Captain. The team has already been set up. The mission will be carried out by the four people in this room. Two here and two in the field. Dr. Samuels will be the technical advisor, and I will run the field team, made up of you and Dr. Merritt."

That was so outrageous Mike's jaw dropped open. He looked over at Lucy Merritt, expecting to see the same outrage, but all he saw was resignation.

He was so angry he had to steady his voice. Montgomery might be a legend in national security circles, around since the Jurassic, but obviously he'd lost it. Going on a mission where a possible bioterror weapon was waiting at the other end, and in harsh mountain conditions, was bad enough when Mike was infiltrating with his men—the finest mountain troops in the world. Fully equipped, fully trained, with the warrior mind-set to get the job done no matter what.

Infiltrating into a high-risk high-altitude mission with Hot Babe—no way. She was probably some hotshot analyst, probably supersmart, very probably smarter than he was. Fine. So let her stay in a heated room analyzing intel. He and his men would be the point of the spear, and no one more than him knew how deadly it was there.

Maybe Hot Babe had a genius IQ, but she'd last ten minutes, tops, at minus forty degrees.

Mike had a lot of experience talking to shit-for-brains superiors, with crazy-ass ideas that sounded fantastic in a room but were a recipe for death in the field. So he put reason and firmness in his voice, while half his brain was already picking men and packing gear.

"Sir." He flicked a glance at the woman sitting next to Montgomery.

Gorgeous as she was, she didn't have a mountain climbers' physique, lean and sinewy with long muscles. Mountain climbers, men and women, also kept themselves low-maintenance.

She was slender but soft, hair done by a pro, nails short but manicured. Expensive clothes that couldn't just be dumped into a washing machine. The real high-maintenance type.

Nope, she wouldn't last *five* minutes in the field. "Dr. Merritt might have special qualifications, sir, but I can assure you that my men and—"

"Captain Shafer." Montgomery's voice was sharp, cutting right across what Mike was saying. "I am afraid you are laboring under a misapprehension. You're not the mission. Dr. Merritt is. You're just along for the ride as muscle."

IF the situation hadn't been so truly, galactically awful, Lucy would have laughed at the expression on the captain's face, or what was visible of it under all that hair and beard. His eyes widened and he closed his mouth with a snap.

As it was, she could hardly stay in her seat with anxiety. Her heart thudded, and every cell in her body was laden with dread. She knew exactly what was coming next.

Uncle Edwin had put up a photograph on the huge monitor. The Palace in Chilongo, the capital of Nhala, a small Himalayan kingdom, vividly bright against the snowy backdrop. The monitor was so large that it was able to take in the Palace in one view. Lucy knew how huge the Palace was, perched up on the level plain of an enormous outcropping that had been carved out of the face of the rock a thousand generations ago.

The Palace was one of the largest buildings in the world, essentially a small city, and she knew every inch of it. The last time she'd seen it, it had been up in flames, devouring the corpses of her mother and father.

She couldn't do this. She'd spent her life running away from this. She simply couldn't do it.

"Sir," Soldier Boy said, sounding anything but respectful. "That's the Palace in Chilongo, which at the moment is veering toward military rule. Rumor has it that the king is sick, maybe dying, and the country is in the hands of General Dan Changa, who makes Robert Mugabe look reasonable. The streets are patrolled by soldiers day and night, and there's talk of a coup. Chilongo is at five thousand feet, and your agent was probably at eight thousand feet, an altitude that requires acclimatization and training. A mission to retrieve information your agent might have had would be risky for well-trained soldiers, but it is a suicide mission if I have to go in with a woman who probably requires a weekly manicure and can't handle a weapon. Even if she does have a doctorate in political science or immunology or whatever. Sir."

Well. The man needed to be put in his place. Lucy leaned forward into her microphone. "Pedicure, too, Captain Shafer."

The captain turned a blank look her way. "What?"

"Not only do I require a weekly manicure but I also require a monthly pedicure. And I go to the hairdresser twice a week. However"—she lifted her lips in what was meant to be a smile but was really a snarl—"I *am* a crack shot. I will pit myself against you at any moment on the firing range. And for the record, my doctorate isn't in political science or immunology. It's in art history."

"Children." Uncle Edwin raised his hands. "We're in the middle of a national security crisis and I don't have time for pissing contests." He quelled both of them with a grim look. "So settle down."

Lucy sat back, biting her lips against the pressing urge to say *but he started it*.

"Lucy," Uncle Edwin said, turning to her. "My agent died twenty miles from the Palace in Chilongo. And the two agents we sent in before him disappeared. In his last message, he said he'd left some proof with someone in the Palace in case something happened to him. The Palace is closed to visitors. We need for you to go back." He stopped, as if—totally uncharacteristically—he didn't know what to say next. But then he did, because Uncle Edwin always knew what to say next. "Your country needs you," he added softly.

Lucy winced. God. She took in a deep breath and put her shaking hands in her lap where no one could see them, particularly not that snake eater across the table from her, looking at her so critically. So okay, she was not a soldier like he was.

She'd been put in enough danger for a lifetime throughout her childhood. So she liked to live safely and comfortably.

So what?

And yet—her country needed her.

If the man had died in Nhala and they needed to go in, it was entirely conceivable that she was the only American alive with an entrée into the Palace, which in the last ten years had become more and more closed off to the world, as had the country itself. Nowadays, you could only visit Nhala on a strictly planned, government-organized tour, and it cost ten thousand dollars for a visa and a down payment to the Tourism Board.

Uncle Edwin touched her lightly on the shoulder, pressed a button on the remote control of the giant monitor. "You got an email from Princess Paso."

Lucy's heart stuttered. Paso, her childhood friend. Paso, who had disappeared into Palace life years ago.

Then she frowned. She'd checked her email just before leaving her office. "No, I didn't."

"Yes," he insisted. "You did. Here it is."

Up on the monitor was a screen grab of a message from her Hotmail address.

Dear Lucy, It's been so long since we talked! Things are very different now at the Palace. Jomo is very ill and caring for him takes up most of my time. But lately I have been thinking of our time together so many years ago. Do you remember how much fun we had in the days of May?

I'm hoping we will see each other soon. Do you remember the legend of the Snow Dragon? An ancient parchment of the legend has been discovered in a cave in the north and I told them you were one of the best manuscript restorers in the world. So the government would like you to restore it to its original glory.

You will be receiving an official invitation today.

Why don't we Skype? My Skype name is Parachutegirl. Let me know yours and I'll put you on my contact list.

Paso

"The Smithsonian received an official request to have Dr. Lucy Merritt seconded to Nhala for an assessment and possible on-site restoration of a parchment discovered in Darjiba, in the north of the country, several weeks ago. The Smithsonian has already agreed to the secondment."

A familiar anger burned in her suddenly, dispelling some of the vast chill that had invaded her core. The CIA was once again messing massively with her life.

"Of course, no one thought to actually tell me this."

"Because it was—"

"Top secret," she finished bitterly.

"Indeed." Uncle Edwin didn't even make a pretense of an apology. "One thing. Princess Paso only joined Skype yesterday, when she opened an account. She opened a Gmail account at the same time. Our understanding is that she was not allowed to have email and certainly not allowed to Skype. Until now. So, Lucy." Uncle Edwin drummed his fingers once on the shiny teak tabletop. For him it was the equivalent of pacing up and down the room. "What do you make of this?"

She bit her back teeth and tried for a normal tone. "First of all, what I make of that is that I am incredibly resentful that the CIA is reading my email. How long has this been going on? Have you people no shame?"

Her heated words had no effect on him whatsoever. And no, the CIA had no shame at all. They wanted an in to Nhala, and Paso had given it to them. The fact that they'd invaded her privacy was not even a theoretical concern. It was what it was.

She huffed out a breath, feeling suffocated. But . . . her country was in danger, and now it was clear that Paso was, too.

Man up.

She folded her hands on the table, each hand clutching the other to stop the trembling.

"Okay. That message tells me two things. First of all the reference to the fun we had in the days of May means nothing. However, I did teach her the meaning of Mayday as an emergency signal and so she's asking for help. And choosing Parachutegirl as her Skype name . . . She always said that the one sport that terrified her was parachute jumping. So she's also signaling danger. But then we know that."

Suddenly, Uncle Edwin rose. The meeting was at an end.

"Lucy, Captain Shafer, you each have a file in front of you with the information you'll need. I expect you to study it and master it before you leave. Captain Shafer, you are now Michael Harrington, investment banker. In your file you'll find a US passport, credit cards in the new name, salient points of your new identity. You are Lucy's fiancé, and as such you are accompanying her to this new job in Nhala. Your role is to protect Dr. Merritt and to find that flash drive. Both of you will find undetectable receiver/transmitters and a netbook, which has a hidden, encrypted hard disk for comms. A car is waiting for you two outside to take you to Dr. Merritt's apartment, where a team of people will come to turn Captain Shafer into Michael Harrington and deliver other equipment. Departure time will be 0400 tomorrow morning, when a car will be waiting to take you both to Andrews Air Force base. A private Learjet 45, belonging to Michael Harrington's company, EMG Finance, will be waiting to take you to Thimphu, via Rome and Mumbai."

Oh God. Lucy closed her eyes in despair. Flying halfway around the world . . . Her heart would give out.

Uncle Edwin continued as if he'd just said the most normal thing in the world.

"The Chilongo International Airport has been closed for a month, ostensibly due to bad weather. Since the closest open airport is Thimphu, the few people visiting Nhala land there and then drive in. It takes three days over very rough terrain. But Ms. Merritt has been given special clearance, and a Nhalan military helicopter will pick you both up in Thimphu to take you to the Palace in Chilongo. You will be in contact with the Stop Cold Committee on a regular basis, and any intel at all on the virus will be relayed to me and to Dr. Samuels as soon as is physically possible. When you find the missing flash drive, send its contents to me immediately." He skewered both of them with a harsh look. "So. You are engaged to be married and I expect you both to act like it. I will not have this mission compromised because you are squabbling. Do I make myself clear?"

If there was one thing Lucy had learned as the child of CIA operatives, it was to hide her feelings. She could do this. She looked up at Uncle Edwin, then over at the hard-assed soldier who didn't want any part of her. "Perfectly."

Captain Shafer was having a harder time of it. His jaw worked beneath the bristly beard, the muscles at his temple bunching. He looked like a wild man who'd just been told to put on a tux and tap dance.

"Captain Shafer." When Uncle Edwin wanted to, he could make his voice drip icicles. "*Did I make myself clear?*"

Jaw muscles bunched. "Yes. Sir." The words fell like little stones from his mouth. One, then the other.

"Fine. Dismissed."

AFTER Lucy, the captain and Dr. Samuels filed out, Edwin Montgomery rubbed his chest where it hurt. His cardiologist had been saying for years that he should slow down, have a pacemaker put in. Dr. Metz was now making noises about a possible bypass. Maybe multiple. But how to slow down when there was just one goddamned crisis after another?

This was one of the worst, maybe as bad as the nuclear confrontation between Kennedy and Khrushchev, when the world was this close to being blown up. Most bad crises involved hundreds, at worst thousands, of Americans dead. This, potentially, could cause millions of deaths. Could, potentially, wipe America out as a viable country.

Whoever was planning this was ruthless beyond imagining. And here he was, tossing Lucy right in front of them.

God, he remembered her coming home from Nhala, a wounded, traumatized, orphaned fourteen-year-old. She didn't speak for months afterward, and she'd kept her distance from him ever since. In some corner of her heart, he knew, she blamed him for her parents' deaths.

But he'd looked after her because she was the closest thing he'd ever have in this life to a daughter. To a family, even.

Her parents had left her nothing. They'd even neglected to renew their life insurance policies. Coming back home, she'd been destitute. Edwin scared up some black ops money to pay for her schooling and to set up a generous trust fund for her. Later, through a little manipulation and a little blackmail, he'd found an apartment for her to buy at a tenth of its value. Then he'd twisted the arm of a banker who'd been a very naughty boy and he had the pictures to prove it. The banker had given Lucy a mortgage at three points below the prime rate.

It was the least he could do.

"Uncle Edwin" she'd always called him. She'd been a beautiful baby, a beautiful little girl, and now she was a beautiful woman. Sweet-natured, too, though a hard life had forced her to toughen up. She'd deserved better than two neglectful parents who dragged her all over the world. Because what better cover could two covert operatives posing as cultural anthropologists have than a little girl?

Ah. Brad and Marie Merritt. Smart, good-looking, courageous. Adventurous. Two of the best operatives the CIA had ever had, certainly the best within his lifetime. They were legends. Almost reckless in their bravery; smart and efficient and ruthless. They'd almost single-handedly held off proxies of the Red Army in Nhala until reinforcements could arrive, giving government troops breathing room. It was entirely possible that Nhala would now be part of Communist China if they hadn't acted so swiftly and courageously. They'd given their lives for their job and their country.

It was a pity that in their dedication to the job, little Lucy always managed to slip between the cracks. They'd been so busy saving the world that they didn't notice the lonely little girl right under their noses.

She'd barely escaped with her life the last time she'd been in Nhala and had fled from a Palace in flames. And now he was tossing her back into the lion's pit.

Couldn't be helped. The nation's security required it. General Changa had closed the country up tight, but Princess Paso had done an end run around that and brilliantly arranged for an invitation.

Lucy had to go. She and nobody else.

Couldn't be helped.

He just hoped to God he wouldn't have to meet the third and last member of the Merritt family at Andrews Air Force Base as they offloaded the casket.

Another sharp twinge in his chest.

Goddammit, he told his chest irritably. *Not now. You can have a heart attack when this is all over.*

*T*HREE

WHAT *did the damned woman use as perfume*? Mike thought, gritting his teeth. Pheromones?

He had to stiffen his neck muscles so he wouldn't turn his head to stare at her. He'd been in the mountains way *way* too long and had spent way too much time with his men. There was nothing good to look at with his men. In fact, a lot of them were butt-ugly.

Lucy Merritt was the opposite. Everything about her fascinated him, as if he'd never seen a woman before.

Every time he looked at her he just gulped up details. Like how long and thick her eyelashes were. How the hell did she keep her eyes open?

And her neck, long and white and slender. How come he'd never really noticed women's necks before? They were so great. So utterly and completely different from his neck and his men's necks, hairy and rough. No, hers was as smooth as a swan's, rising from delicate collarbones. When the hell had he ever noticed collarbones before? Been fucking *fascinated* by collarbones?

Okay, stop. He was on Op Time right now, no time for

anything but the mission. But once it was over, man, he was going to go to some bar and he was going to get *so* laid. Just stay in bed for a week.

Mooning over collarbones was a sign of something serious.

They were sitting in the back of one of the CIA's armored SUVs with a barrier between the backseat and the driver. It was raining and the windows were as smoked as those in a mafioso's limo. The outside world was barely visible. Staring out the window was not an option, unless he wanted to watch a smoked reflection of himself.

Ordinarily he could sink right into himself, no problem. Just before a mission there was a lot to think about, a lot to plan. He was a good strategist, and he often used the staging period before an op to try to think of all the ways Mr. Murphy could fuck with him and all the ways he could fuck with Mr. Murphy right back.

That wasn't working now. He didn't have men to command, and the plans had already been drawn up without any input from him. His entire team consisted of one girly girl who didn't look the type to follow the chain of command. She'd nearly said no to Edwin Montgomery, something that perhaps only a Medal of Honor winner would ever think of doing. And, maybe, the President of the United States, the day after a landslide election.

Mike had no idea even what equipment he was going to be assigned. All that would be handed over later, at Lucy Merritt's house. There was no mission plan other than to get back the damned flash drive and discover who the Palace mole was, which was too vague to flesh out in his thoughts when he had no idea of the terrain or the actors.

He never went into battle or on a mission without thoroughly studying the terrain, but he hadn't been assigned maps, he hadn't even been given a fucking Lonely Planet guide to the damned country. He knew exactly zip about Nhala. He'd only been once to the Himalayas, on a climbing expedition to Tibet while in college. Tibet wasn't Nhala, that much he knew.

He could, of course, ask Lucy Merritt—who apparently was some kind of expert·on the country—for more intel, but she was looking blindly out the window at nothing, clearly brooding.

One thing was worrying him, and he needed to get it out in the open. The grimace she'd made when Montgomery talked about the long flight over had jolted him. Was she scared of flying? He had to know.

He himself wasn't scared of flying, not in any way. Good thing, too, because he'd flown into a lot of hellholes in a lot of rust buckets, often under fire. He'd been the only passenger to sleep through the twisting, turning, looping landing route the pilots had to take to avoid RPGs at Baghdad International.

But he knew what devastating fear of flying was. His sister, Kathy, had an irrational fear of flying—terror, in the truest sense of the word. When she could be coaxed onto a flight, she descended an utter wreck and had to go to bed for two days.

For someone terrified of flying, a long flight like the one they were going to take tomorrow would be devastating. Mike couldn't afford to have a comatose partner or one who'd expended so much adrenaline during the flight she'd have the shakes at the other end.

So he had to ask.

He cleared his throat, expecting her to turn. She didn't.

O-kay. We were playing the Ignoring Game, were we?

He touched her arm and was astonished when she jumped.

"Hey, sorry." He held his hands up, palms out. Universal sign of harmlessness since humans were protohominids. *No weapons. I come in peace.*

"You wanted something?" The words were harsh, but her face wasn't. Again, he was struck by the melancholy of her expression. He could have expected fear, resentment, aggression. But melancholy?

He tucked that away for further consideration later. Right now there were more urgent things to talk about.

"I need to know something." Might as well jump right in. "When Deputy Director Montgomery mentioned the flight, I saw you had a reaction. And it wasn't one of joy. Are you afraid to fly? This isn't a judgment, but I have to know. I need to know what condition you'll be in once we land at the other side."

"Fear of flying." That luscious mouth turned up at one corner. "There's a wonderful literary tradition of fear of flying. Yes, you're right. I don't like to fly and there is a reason for that. I walked away from a plane crash when I was seven years old. Ever since then, flying terrifies me. Though of course in this world it's impossible to avoid flying, so I have my coping mechanisms. You don't need to worry about me. I'll be operational by the time we land. Uncle Edwin knows that."

Mike blinked, instantly distracted from the no-fly problem. "Edwin Montgomery is your *uncle*?"

He didn't know what surprised him more. That Montgomery used nepotism in such a blatant way or that he had blood relations. More or less everyone just assumed that Montgomery had been hatched from an egg, a fully formed adult, barking orders.

That sad expression deepened. "Not really, I just call him Uncle Edwin. He's my godfather."

Godfather, huh? That was almost as weird as the idea of Montgomery having siblings. That Montgomery could form an emotional attachment to others was . . . wow. Mike found it hard to wrap his head around it.

There was something so wrong about her expression, like that of a unicorn in the forest wounded by a hunter's arrow. Sad and stricken.

Man, she was too beautiful to be sad. Beautiful women were nature's aristocrats. They held the world in the palm of their hands. It was unnatural for someone who looked like her to be melancholy.

Then Mike kicked himself in the ass. The world was big and bad and it bit. What the fuck did he know about her? Nothing. There might be real tragedy there.

And that's when he remembered the second half of her little info-dump. She'd walked away from a plane crash at the age of seven.

"Where?" he asked sharply. "Where did you crash?"

It wasn't an idle question. Ever since his baby sister had required sedation at the age of five for a routine flight, he'd paid close attention to any plane accidents in his never-ending quest to help Kathy cope with her phobia. He thought he knew every crash-survivor story there was, though there weren't many.

He couldn't recall any plane crashes where a seven-year-old had walked away.

She looked him full in the face, gauging something. Coming from a man, that blatant study would have indicated aggression and he'd have bristled. But he wasn't bristling. She was clearly studying him to see whether she could tell him.

And, well, it wasn't exactly a hardship having Lucy Merritt stare at him, because then he got to stare right back.

It was as if he'd never seen a female face before. All that soft, pale skin. Pretty, dark eyebrows that had a lovely, flowing, arching shape like little wings, instead of being a smudge on the forehead. And, of course, that perfume someone had designed to mess with men's heads . . .

"Nicaragua," she said softly, and his entire notion of her turned upside down.

"Fuck," he breathed, shocked. Then—"Sorry."

She dipped her head.

Lucy Merritt was a fucking SpecOps legend. No one had ever known the name of the little girl, but the story had made the rounds.

The daughter of American academics in Nicaragua had been sent from Jalapa to Managua, where she was supposed to be bundled onto a plane for the States as the contra-comandos war was heating up.

The plane crashed in the primeval jungle four hundred miles south of Jalapa. The pilot's Mayday signal had been

picked up by everyone and his cousin. Government Sand-
inista forces and two ragtag competing rebel armies con-
verged on the plane, all intending kidnap and rape. The
Sandinistas to punish the capitalist Yanquis, the contras to
show their displeasure with the Senate hearings on Iran-
Contra up north. The other rebels just because.

Mike's first XO, Larry Gabriel, had been training troops
in southern Honduras and was sent in with his men on what
was considered a hopeless rescue mission. Gabriel told
Mike he'd fully expected to bring home either a small
burned corpse or a small burned, tortured and raped
corpse. But the four groups wandered in the tropical forest
for seven days and seven nights without finding anything
but the shell of the plane and the charred body of the pilot.

Gabriel was about to call it quits when a slip of a girl
walked into his camp at dusk. She was rail-thin, filthy,
dehydrated and had burns all over her body, but she was, by
God, alive. And she'd avoided all the bad guys combing the
jungle for her. Once an entire platoon of Sandinistas had
passed less than five feet from her, she told the captain. She
hid and kept quiet, and they'd continued on down the trail.

"Brave little thing," Captain Gabriel had said. "Pretty,
too, under all that grime."

She was still pretty.

"My former commander was Larry Gabriel," he said,
and her head whipped around to him from where she'd
gone back to studying the rain-slicked streets, shiny hair
belling around her shoulders.

"Captain Gabriel!" Her face turned rosy with pleasure,
which was a lot better than seeing it white with tension.
"Oh my gosh, how is he doing?"

"Fine. Retired to Florida. Fishes and runs marathons. In
the one-hundred-degree heat." Mike shook his head. "He
was a fine commanding officer, but he's also nuts. When
this is all over, I think he'd appreciate a call from you. He
never forgot you."

She had opened her mouth to answer, when suddenly

the driver swerved onto a leafy street. His tinny voice came over the intercom.

"Captain Shafer, Dr. Merritt. We're here."

LUCY studied the captain's reaction to her apartment. Her parents had left her relatively well off, so she'd been able to buy it after college with part of her trust fund. The mortgage had been so reasonable she'd already paid it off. Uncle Edwin had found her the apartment, which had been miraculously cheap for the size and location. It was nice and she loved it. It was her bolt-hole, her refuge, her safe place. Nothing bad could happen to her in her home.

The captain looked in, winced, froze.

Lucy had spent a lot of her childhood in windowless huts, where the only light came from the door. She craved light, in all senses. Though the day was dark, a flip of the switch lit the place up. Lights everywhere, casting out the darkness.

And she liked light colors, too. Pale birch hardwood flooring, pale Kerman rugs, white couches, white lace curtains.

The captain looked down at himself, crumpled and filthy, boots mud-caked. He stopped at the threshold, afraid to enter.

"Shower," he said.

Lucy touched his arm, letting her hand drop immediately. His arm felt like steel under the grungy material.

"Right away," she said gently. The man had obviously been pulled from either a mission or field training. It wasn't his fault he was filthy. "Don't worry. Everything's washable. Apparently people are coming later with your new things. Here, let me show you the way."

She led him to the guest bathroom, peach and cream, with a large array of body lotions, which she guessed he wouldn't be using anytime soon.

He stood in the doorway, nearly filling it, looking utterly out of place. Lucy took pity on him. "Here." She pulled out clean white towels and slapped a rose-scented bar of soap in his hand. He just stood there, and she realized that after the shower he couldn't just put his filthy uniform back on.

She had absolutely nothing that could possibly fit him. Okay. She disappeared into her bedroom closet, pulling out a bathrobe from the back.

"Here." Her voice was froggy and she cleared it as she thrust the bathrobe in his arms. "It was—it was my father's. You're welcome to use it."

He understood. He was filthy, exhausted, probably starving, no doubt dying to step into the shower, but he didn't move. He simply stood there, with her father's ancient dark blue terry-cloth robe in his arms. Those dark eyes held some kind of emotion. She couldn't read him, she didn't know him, but there was something there.

He reached out and ran a long finger down her cheek. Just a touch, but it tingled. She barely stopped herself from stepping back. She wasn't used to being touched.

"Thanks," he said softly. "I appreciate it."

She made a strangled noise and fled the bathroom, closing the door behind her. He'd flustered her.

Lucy didn't do flustered. She could only think that the shocks of the day—discovering that she had to return to the Palace in Chilongo, go back to where she'd lost her parents in a hail of gunshots and a raging fire had made her vulnerable to emotions she'd long since repressed.

The doorbell rang. The intercom video showed a small group of people on her doorstep.

A woman—girl, really—stepped up to the camera, artificially bright red hair sticking out in spikes, bold features distorted by proximity to the wide-angle lens. "Dr. Merritt?"

"Yes."

"We've been sent by—" She consulted a piece of paper. "By a Mr. Montgomery. May we come up?"

Ah. The makeover team, here to transform the captain. Big, sinewy, with rough features and rough hands. Long-haired, bearded, smelling of woodsmoke and sweat and . . . the wild. So Uncle Edwin's team was supposed to turn him into an investment banker?

Good luck with that.

"Come on up," she said. "You've got quite a job in front of you."

They trooped up, filling her entire living room, which was large. She settled them all, told them to prepare their work tools, and closed the living room door firmly behind her.

She went to meet the captain outside the bathroom, enveloped in her father's terry-cloth robe. The hot shower had brought a little red to his swarthy cheeks. His ratty, filthy hair now hung clean and wet almost down to his shoulders.

He had an amazing physique—absurdly broad through the shoulders, unusually lean in the waist and hips. His shoulders strained her father's robe, and her father had not been a small man.

Lucy had no intention of tipping him into the maw of the people camping out in her living room without feeding him first. She knew what the military was like. No one would have thought to feed the man. He was probably going on twenty-four hours without food and without sleep. She couldn't do anything about the sleep, but by God she could do something about the food.

He raised his thick black eyebrows at the noises coming from her living room. The clanking of tools, excited voices. Even a squeal or two.

Lucy smiled up at him. "I'm afraid some hard things await you, Captain, but first I'm going to feed you. A few minutes more won't affect anything either way. No man should have to face what's in my living room on an empty stomach."

He didn't move, just looked down at her. He was very close to her, so close she could smell her own soap and shampoo on him. So close she could feel his body heat. He was very tall. She hadn't appreciated how very tall he was before. As always, she'd slipped off her heels coming into the house and was in flats. He was almost a whole head taller than she was.

"Mike."

His eyes were very dark, with small yellow streaks. So dark they reflected the light of her wall sconces.

"What?" She should step back, she was way too close. If she took in a deep breath, her breasts would brush against his chest. She should step back.

"Mike. My name's Mike." He smiled, the first smile she'd seen from him, besides that feral baring of teeth she'd glimpsed in the corridor outside the briefing room. "Call me Mike. Besides—aren't we engaged?"

Lucy stepped back. It wasn't easy. The man might be whipcord thin, but he exerted a force field around him, like gravity.

"Yes. We are. Follow me." She rolled her eyes. "Honey."

A couple of minutes later she seated him at her pretty cherrywood Shaker kitchen table and watched, amazed, as he ate everything in her refrigerator and started emptying her freezer. The microwave was working overtime. His manners were fine, but he tucked away an astonishing amount of food in an astonishingly short amount of time.

Two bowls of soup, a bowl of leftover tabbouleh, all the rosemary focaccia, a small loaf of whole wheat bread, half a round of brie, a huge slice of pecorino romano, a large bowl of sliced tomatoes, a portion of eggplant parmesan, the half bottle of Sauvignon blanc, some homemade biscotti and her two perfect peaches. The only thing he turned his nose up at was her array of deli yogurts. He drank two cups of fresh coffee, saying that he could sleep anywhere, anytime, even if he had a gallon of coffee in him.

Lucy was amazed, but grateful that he'd cleaned her fridge out. She hated leaving food behind when going away. She'd grown up in some very poor parts of the world, where food was precious. Wasting food was something she abhorred.

While eating, he'd been leafing through the folder Uncle Edwin had given him, his eyes tracking back and forth across the page while he stuffed his face. She was a fast reader, but this beat anything she could do. Who knew if he was retaining everything?

He had to. Their lives depended on it.

Nobody knew more than she did about being under-cover. You had to live, breathe, eat and sleep your cover story. One slip and you could be dead. Or worse.

Whatever they were walking into at the Palace, a wrong word, forgetting something about his backstory, could be disastrous.

All through her childhood she'd been painfully aware of the fact that letting slip the wrong information could cost her parents their lives. And hers.

Lucy would be fine on this mission. No one in Nhala had ever known her parents were CIA. They'd just been two anthropologists whose hobby was target shooting with a young daughter and who happened to be in Nhala during an attempted coup and reacted very bravely. Lucy would have the great privilege of just being herself.

Captain Shafer—Mike—was the one who was going to be under a lot of pressure. Not only for impersonating a part but also for being responsible for sneaking outside the Palace in the Himalayas in winter to find a flash drive in a million square miles of snow.

He turned the last page as he finished up the second peach. Squaring his shoulders, he stood up. "So. Forth into the fray." He winked at her. "Honey."

$\mathcal{F}$OUR

THE PALACE
CHILONGO, NHALA

GENERAL Dan Changa studied the large military relief map spread out on the immense, intricately carved desk in his study. A map he knew so well.

How badly land was distributed in this part of the world. His own people had been apportioned a beautiful but tiny slice of the subcontinent, with very little arable land in the valleys.

He traced his finger along the familiar borders, tracing Nhala's outline. Back and forth, to the north the great upswelling of the mountains that had defined Nhala's existence since the dawn of time, then over the small scimitar that was the inhabitable land and down, across the border to the south, down to Bihar and Gudjarat, the great Gangetic Plains. Millions of miles of arable land, wasted by the Indians, who had no taste or talent for agriculture.

His forefinger tracked along the black line. The border. But was it? Really?

What was a border except an artificial line on paper? Borders were changed every day. Throughout human history the stronger and the smarter went over borders and prevailed.

Men who had the winds of destiny at their backs prevailed, like him. General Changa didn't believe in destiny or fate. He was a soldier, not a priest. But events were definitely converging.

His men had noticed. There was a new deference, fear actually, as the king's disease progressed. King Jomo had wanted to change the nature of the country, which had always had a strong leader. He wanted to be their leader, but he also wanted to "democratize."

The fool.

Nobody cared about democracy. They cared about full bellies and a sense of strength at the top, something Jomo had never provided. The Boy King, who stopped the Chinese, together with two Americans who'd been studying Nhalan culture and who knew how to handle guns.

Or so everyone believed.

Nonsense. It had been Changa who'd saved his country, the Americans had only bought him time. Changa who'd called in his faithful Sharmas, his warrior tribe, the way the Gurkhas had been warriors for the English empire.

The tribe that would occupy the lowlands and turn Nhala into a world power.

He pulled open a drawer, which had a carved dragon's head as its pull. He carefully closed his fist over a tiny transparent cylinder as long as the first knuckle of his little finger and laid it gently on his desk.

Such a small object to hold so much death. Truly almost magical.

General Changa was not superstitious as were so many of his subjects, peasants from the dawn of time. He'd studied at Eton and at Caltech, and he considered himself a man of reason, a man of science. But the small hardened plastic cylinder on his desk, divided into two parts by a transparent plastic barrier, filled him with the awe peasants felt for the forces of nature.

There was nothing natural in what was in that cylinder.

It was the upshot of years of research furtively carried out in mobile labs—nothing more than trucks, really—driving from sandy outpost to sandy outpost to avoid discovery.

It wasn't until he had understood what a world-changer they were working on that he accepted the offer of a Pakistani emissary who'd come two years earlier. For a goodly sum of money, which was even now accruing interest on a sunny Caribbean island, he'd agreed to let them build an underground laboratory in the mountains, beyond the software parameters of spy satellites programmed to control India and Pakistan.

No one would suspect a laboratory above the 45th parallel, at ten thousand feet, and yet there it was, twenty miles north of the Palace.

The scientists were from all over the world, but the money was Arab, the plan was Arab, the head scientist Pakistani.

General Changa didn't care. Arab-Israeli-American. It didn't make any difference to him. Let them all blow themselves up. There was now a weapon to do it, and he was looking at it.

He held it lightly in his hand, knowing that it had been precisely calibrated to initiate a breaching sequence at 150 psi. In the back of a drawer was a compressed-air gun, and he drew it slowly out, delighting in the precisely engineered machinery. It had the look of a gun from the future, only it was very much in the here and now.

The gun shot cylinders into the shoulder or thigh, calibrated to penetrate one centimeter, compressed gas breaching the plastic barrier, imbedding in the other half of the cylinder and injecting a slow-acting acid into it. In precisely twenty-four hours, the second part of the cylinder dissolved, dispersing what the Arabs called the *Ghibli*, the Wind from the East.

The wind that kills.

General Changa knew that the Arabs were planning on sending soldiers on a suicide mission into Israel and New York.

He had no intention of endangering his brave warriors.

He'd had one of his bioengineers in the lab design delivery canisters, like the one the Arabs had designed, only much smaller. Tiny, in fact, so tiny thousands could fit into a backpack.

His men would seed the north of India with them when the Arabs' attack occurred. Whether the first target was Israel or the United States didn't make any difference. His men would slip across the border, place thousands of the canisters and be back well before the twenty-four hours were up.

They would wait out the epidemic, which would burn itself out inside of a day, and march into the emptied out land bringing medical supplies and food.

And then, just stay.

He had recruited hundreds of agronomists, thousands of engineers. The Indians didn't know what to do with all the land they had. Rich, alluvial plains, large, navigable rivers, and they were still poor. Why, Nhala was richer, and they were an isolated strip of land surrounded by granite mountains with only one arable river valley.

The Indians didn't deserve their land. But he and his brave soldiers did. They'd turn it into a garden within a generation.

Yes, the winds of history were indeed at his back. It was as bold a plan as Alexander or Tamerlane had ever dreamed of. Better, even, because no blood would be spilled.

The only blood spilled would be from the infected ones, and it would come out of their own bodies. Neither Changa nor his men would ever touch them. It would be their own bodies that would betray them.

There was even a legend, the Snow Dragon. A Nhalan legend recounted from generation to generation since the dawn of time, until it was in his people's DNA. In the Time Before Time, Nhala had occupied the entire Himalayas and the Indian subcontinent. Nhala had ruled over the peoples of the mountains and valleys with grace and mercy, ensuring peace and prosperity throughout the land.

A thousand generations ago, invaders drove the Nhalan people back into their small valley.

But one day, a Snow Dragon—a creature of immense power and wisdom—would emerge from the north and lead the people into a new age of peace, a new dawn. There were tattered flags on prayer wheels fluttering in the wind, that had been in that exact same spot for a thousand years, replaced every decade or so, calling upon the Snow Dragon to return from the mountains to the valley and to restore the empire. Return the people to peace and prosperity.

General Changa doubted there was even a shred of historical truth to the legend. His people were, alas, ignorant and superstitious peasants. But that was no reason not to use the legend for his own purposes.

So a parchment had been conveniently found in a cave in the north of the country. He'd had it buried in wet soil for a couple of weeks to age it, and the text—written by a scholar in the Old Language—spoke of the return of the Snow Dragon in terms that clearly pointed to him.

When Princess Paso had timidly suggested that Lucy Merritt—the daughter of the two American anthropologists who'd happened to be at the right time at the right place and were legends in the countryside—was a famous manuscript restorer, he'd nearly laughed aloud.

The child of the Merritts, harmless scholars who happened to know how to shoot, would be the agency by which he would rise to power.

Though he didn't really believe in this nonsense, goose bumps had risen on his arms, because having the daughter of the Merritts—whose names were now regularly included in the prayers of half the country—"restore" the document would give it enormous legitimacy in the eyes of the people.

Of course, if she were anywhere close to being competent, Merritt would soon discover it was a fake, but *her* fate was definitely to die young.

Changa would see to that. Just as Jomo's fate was to die young and soon, and Princess Paso's fate was to marry him, so that the new leader of an enormous new country would not only have military credentials, but be part of the line of the Royal Family that had ruled his country for centuries.

He didn't believe in the winds of fate, but nonetheless he could feel them blowing at his back, propelling him into a glorious future.

WASHINGTON, DC

"What's your name?" Lucy Merritt asked, perched on a hassock at his side, looking cool and collected in the middle of the frenzy.

A lock of his hair drifted down onto the floor and Mike winced. It lay there like a long, dark snake on Lucy's pristine light-colored hardwood floor.

"Don't worry, sir, we'll sweep it all up," the guy cutting his hair said behind him, as another lock fell, then another.

He was at the center of five people fluttering around him, one cutting his hair, one preparing some sharp tools, one stropping a razor—Mike was keeping an eye on that one, he'd been sent by Montgomery—one pulling out clothes and one doing his goddamned *nails*.

"Michael Everett Harrington. Born March 6, 1977—which makes me a Pisces—in New York City, of Lorraine Everett Harrington, attorney, currently with the offices of Singleton, Weinstein, Locke and Harrington, and Rupert Harrington, retired banker."

None of that was true, of course. He'd been born on January 19, 1976, of Sally Hughes Shafer, homemaker, who died when he was two, and Bob Shafer, owner of Shafer Demolitions. And Mike was a Capricorn.

"Other hand, sir," the manicurist said, and he looked at his right hand. A manicure. A frigging *manicure*, the first of his life. He kept his nails short and clean, but that was it. Now his nails looked like shiny little works of art. He held out his left hand, resigned.

Lucy was tracking his file, nodding at his answers. "What are your hobbies?"

"Polo and golf, they're my favorites." Mike would rather

have his nuts caught in a thresher than play polo or golf, two asinine activities if ever there were any. Chasing balls around, what the fuck? No, he loved the outdoors, always had, always would. White-water rafting, backpacking and above all mountain climbing, something Michael Harrington would probably never do in his entire pampered existence. "As a matter of fact, I was polo champ—what are you *doing*?" he asked in alarm. Someone was fitting little foam thingies between his fucking *toes*!

The girl at his feet looked up, startled. "Giving you a pedicure, sir." She held his foot up by his big toe in disgust, as if his foot were a big, hairy rat. "No one would ever believe you were anything but a homeless man with feet like these. Sir."

Lucy elbowed him in the ribs. "Be a man. Honey."

"I have no intention of walking around barefoot," Mike grumbled, but it was a lost battle. He looked at her equipment. "Do what you do, but no polish. Hands or feet." The girl's chin firmed in a mulish pout. He put real command in his voice, a tone guaranteed to make his men snap to. "I trust that's clear." She nodded, expression rebellious.

"Where'd you go to school?" Lucy asked, and he turned to her gratefully.

"Yale. Majored in economics, minored in statistical analysis."

"Uh-huh," she said, eyes on the file on her knees. "Where did we meet?"

Mike pulled a blank. Utter and complete blank. Nothing going on up there. Just some wind and lint blowing around in a big empty room.

Lucy's face was bland as she looked up at him. "Darling, don't you remember? We met my last year of graduate school, right after the end of the spring semester. It was a beautiful day in late May. You were playing at Brandywine, and I accompanied my best friend from Georgetown, Carrie Martin, to the match. Her brother was playing, too. I didn't know anything about polo, but you were very dashing on your horse. It was one of those perfect early summer evenings where the shadows grow longer and longer, you know? Carrie introduced us, and you invited me out for drinks that very evening. And dinner the next evening. And the evening after that. We dated for three years, taking turns shuttling between New York and Washington. I learned a little about polo and you learned a little about art history. I started taking riding lessons and you started a small-scale art collection. We got engaged this September." Half that luscious mouth curved up. "Surely you remember, *darling*."

Well, *fuck*. No one had thought to write up their background as a couple. The CIA had as many employees as a small city, supersmart every single one of them, basically undercover work was what they did, and not one had come up with their romantic history. Even though the two of them were going into a dangerous situation predicated on their being a couple.

It was really lucky that Lucy was capable of thinking on her feet. The way she'd recounted the story was absolutely convincing.

As a matter of fact, she'd almost convinced *him*. Because, well, if he were a polo-playing kind of guy, which he wasn't, and a falling-in-love-at-first-sight kind of guy, which he wasn't, well that scenario sounded pretty good. Because Lucy Merritt was exactly the kind of woman a polo-playing investment banker would fall for, head over heels, at once.

He could see it, could almost *feel* it. A summer evening, long shadows playing over the polo field, the distant *thwack!* of the mallet, the smell of grass . . .

"What did we have that first evening?"

Lucy had leaned over and was going through the clothes they'd brought over for him. High-end, high-maintenance clothes. Stiff cotton shirts that for sure required ironing, expensive-looking suits, cuff links. *Cuff links!* Like a spook! Gah.

Lucy was pulling out a pair of shoes, one of several. Shiny, expensive. She peered at the pristine soles in disapproval. "I'll scuff these up for you. What did you say?"

"What did we drink that first evening?" Mike watched her, partly fascinated by her face and partly wondering what her reaction would be.

Perfect. Her face, her reaction.

"I had a Prosecco," she responded instantly, with a reminiscent smile, as if remembering as opposed to making all this up on the spur of the moment. "And you had a beer."

Amazing. No hesitation, no looking slightly up and to the left, nothing. Her answer was exactly as it should be, immediate and relaxed, as if they'd actually had drinks the evening they'd met on a polo field. She'd pegged him, too. He'd have definitely ordered a beer after a polo game.

"And the next evening? Where'd we go to eat?"

"To a Greek restaurant," she answered immediately. "It was delicious. We both enjoy Greek food."

Wow. Mike didn't know about her, but he loved Greek food. She'd somehow tuned into that.

They'd finished cutting his hair, and now someone slapped a hot wet cloth over his face. He breathed in heavily, drawing in steam. It felt real good.

Then lather and a close shave with a very sharp razor, wielded by a man who'd obviously had instructions from Montgomery not to kill the captain.

He kept an eye on the clothes Lucy was pulling out of the packages, relieved to see that there were no jeans and nothing made of cotton. Jeans were death itself in cold weather. Cotton wicked up moisture and held it, creating a wet material that clung to skin. The last thing you needed in subzero temperatures was material that sucked up moisture and retained it. A surefire recipe for frostbite.

What they'd packed looked expensive and elegant, just what an investment banker would wear, but there was a lot of top-of-the-line winter gear there, too. And all the outer gear was Gore-Tex.

He watched as Lucy pulled out a metal canister of an expensive men's cologne, then an expensive shaving lotion and an expensive sunscreen. Each canister had a false bottom with enough C-4 to blow through a wall. The det cord was wound around the explosive, the latest type, as thin as baling wire.

Five meters of rope were wound around the exterior of the suitcase, tucked under the metallic elements.

There were two satellite cell phones, encrypted, both of which could become stun guns at the flip of a switch.

Two of his credit cards would be extra stiff and razor-sharp at one end, capable of slitting a man's throat open with ease.

No doubt if he found he needed firepower, they could airdrop some weapons and encrypt an SMS message with the GPS coordinates.

The one thing the CIA did really well was toys.

Lucy pulled out a long-sleeved undershirt and a pair of underpants made of a thin material and looked at them.

Now we were talking. "Capilene. Thermal underwear. To be worn close to the skin in extreme cold temperatures. It's a synthetic fiber that is hydrophobic, it repels water. *Ow!*" He glared at the girl working on his feet, aggrieved. "That *hurt*! What are you doing?"

Clearly regarding him as not to be reasoned with, the girl turned to Lucy. She held up a strip like one of those sticky things you hang in a room to catch flies. It had black hairs on it. His hairs.

"Just waxing his toes," she said to Lucy, as if it were the most normal thing in the world.

Waxing *toes*? Well, fuck. He had opened his mouth to protest, when Lucy laughed at him.

"Women do that to their, um, private lady parts without complaining. Don't be such a wuss. Honey." She picked up a glove, idly put it on. Her small hand swam in it. She frowned when her index finger poked through a slit.

"Trigger finger," Mike said and her brow cleared.

"Neat." She picked up something else and Mike swallowed. Cylindrical, made of a special felt . . .

She picked it up, turned it over, trying to imagine what it was for. Mike could see the exact moment she figured it out, because she turned rosy pink.

Oh God. Just watching that slender, elegant hand turning it this way and that, full soft lips pursed . . . well, it made him think of sex. Sex right . . . now.

This was payback for all that enforced abstinence. Almost a year in combat in the 'Stan and then the training mission in Alaska. In Afghanistan, more properly known as Nosexistan, and in the wild with his men, there hadn't been one sexual stimulus. His dick had kept itself resolutely down between his legs.

In Afghanistan, the women were covered up in blankets and would be stoned to death for a kiss. No way. And in Alaska—well let's just say his men were strong and smart and tough, but sex was the last thing on his mind with them.

That was probably why he was so susceptible to the luscious Lucy Merritt, with her soft skin and big blue eyes. Why he had swelled erect watching her pretty fingers turn the penis cap around and around. It had been so very very easy to imagine that slender hand holding *him*, squeezing and pulling on him . . .

Down, boy.

She looked at him and he shrugged, very glad that her father's dressing gown was loose around the waist. "It's an appendage, it freezes, too. *Okay!*" He stood up and clapped his hands. His little retinue gaped up at him.

Enough was enough. What was done was done. He was clean, his hair was cut, he was close-shaven, he'd had a goddamned manicure and pedicure. That was it, all he was willing to stand for. The rest was a waste of his time and Lucy's. They'd have to be up at three the next morning to be ready for the 4 a.m. pickup, and they had a long flight and a dangerous mission at the other end.

"Thanks for your work everyone, you can report back to Mr. Montgomery that you did your best to turn me into a civilized man." He walked to the front door and opened it. "And now good night."

Inside of five minutes everyone had put away his or her tools and quietly walked out the door. Mike closed it behind him and leaned his back against it.

Lucy smiled at him. Again, he was struck by how melancholy her smile was. "You must be exhausted."

He sat down on the couch and leaned his head back. It was a comfortable couch, incredibly so. Pure white, but now that he was squeaky clean he didn't have to worry about getting it dirty.

"I'm not exhausted," he said in protest.

Mike didn't do exhaustion. He could go for as long as he had to. He could climb and hike and run until he passed out.

Damn, but the couch was comfortable. He could actually feel himself sinking in.

"Uh-huh." Her voice was so soft, almost a whisper. "I'll go get some sheets and blankets."

"You do that." Why did his own voice sound so far away?

He could hear her rummaging around in the hallway, and then a huge black cloud descended and he heard nothing more.

ANDREWS AIR FORCE BASE
NEXT MORNING

There it was.

Lucy swallowed heavily against the huge, heavy ball of bile rising up her throat. They were on the tarmac in an isolated part of the airfield, quickly approaching the lone Learjet stationed there, steps down, pilot waiting at the top of the stairs.

The plane looked sleek and brand-new, a marvel of modern technology. Designed to glide through the air, invincible.

Except when it didn't—and plummeted through the sky to earth.

Deep tremors shook her body, but she'd long since learned to hide those. She could hide more or less all signs of stress, something she'd learned very early in life. The only giveaway would be the color of her skin. She knew she was icy white. But she'd slapped on a slightly darker foundation, used a light blush and lipstick and just hoped to

God that Captain Mike Shafer—no! Michael Harrington, investment banker—was one of those macho men who didn't really notice women until he needed them for something.

There were lots of those around.

It was still dark. They'd watch the world light up over the sky in a long dawn, traveling east.

The big black SUV slewed to a violent halt so quickly Lucy's seat belt would have tightened painfully. But before it could, an iron arm shot out in front of her, halting her forward movement.

"CIA asshole," Mike muttered under his breath. She would have smiled if she'd had a smile in her.

The driver got out, pulled their suitcases from the back and placed them at the bottom of the plane stairs.

Lucy was so terrified, she was having an out-of-body experience. She couldn't feel her hands and feet and she could barely breathe. It was as if she were watching herself from above, watching as Mike opened her side door, his enormous hand waiting to help her down. Way down.

Why did these vehicles have to be as high as trucks?

Lucy took his hand—they were engaged, after all. But it wasn't to maintain their cover that she took his hand, then the arm he proffered. It was either hold on to him or fall down. Her legs nearly gave way as she stepped down onto the tarmac, and she had to consciously stiffen them.

Oh God, this was going to be bad.

She'd flown after the crash in Nicaragua, of course, but only because she'd been forcibly bundled onto a flight she had to take. Nobody noticed and nobody cared that she shivered violently through each second of each flight. The last long-haul flight she'd taken had been the reverse of the one she was embarking on now. Nhala to Washington—an eighteen-hour nightmare. She'd been too traumatized to remember much about it, just endless hours on a cold, uncomfortable military flight with her parents' caskets in the icy hold beneath her feet.

She never flew long distances again.

An intense smell of jet fuel puffed in her face and she stopped, frozen.

Crawling out through the smoking, twisted door of the plane, tumbling to the damp earth on her back, gasping with pain.

The fall robbed her of breath. She lay motionless, gazing up at the glimpses of bright blue sky visible through the dark green overhead canopy. She hurt everywhere, but she was alive.

Her last memory was of the pilot telling her to fasten her seat belt and lean forward, arms covering her head.

And now they were somewhere in the Nicaraguan jungle.

The pilot!

Lucy turned over and tried to rise, but fell back to her knees. Her head was thumping with pain, her shoulder, too. She looked at her palms and arms, red with burns. She couldn't feel the burns yet, but she knew she would.

It was hot, sultry, the jungle a nightmare of damp earth, wet branches of low bushes slapping in her face as she tried to drag herself around to the front of the plane.

Part of the plane was burning, the stench of burning electronics and plastic wiring rising sharp and acrid in her nostrils. The cockpit was too high to see the pilot. She couldn't tell if he was dead or alive.

Gray black smoke was rising from the body of the plane. If the pilot was alive, she had to somehow help him get out.

A huge tree had been nearly felled by the plane driving into it. Thick branches hung over the cockpit. Lucy knew how to climb trees. Two years in Indonesia had taught her everything about jungle trees. The thick rough bark abraded her burned palms and knees, but she ignored the pain and scrambled out onto the thick branch right over the cockpit.

She clung to the branch swaying with her weight, inch-

ing her way farther until she had a clear view of the cock-pit and the pilot.

McMurdogh, his nameplate had read. He was now a charred mass of shrunken black flesh. The blackened fingers of his hand with the bones showing still clung to the radio attached to the dashboard by a curly cord. His face had burned so badly the eyes were gone, the lips burned back to reveal his white teeth.

She stared at the blackened ruins of what had once been a nice man, now a mass of flesh emitting the stench of charred meat . . .

Lucy broke away from Mike's supporting arm to turn and retch miserably on the tarmac, her stomach clenching in painful spasms so strong she couldn't even straighten up.

Nothing but bile was coming up. Her stomach had been too roiled to even think of eating breakfast, though Mike hadn't had that problem. He'd happily vacuumed up coffee, pancakes, scrambled eggs and the four muffins left in her freezer.

A strong arm went around her stomach, holding her tightly. Lucy straightened, slowly coming up.

Another gust of frigid air and jet fuel and she bent forward again, her stomach trying to crawl out through her esophagus, pumping out a thin gruel of stomach juices.

When she could concentrate on something other than the pain in her stomach, Lucy realized that she had created a little tableau. *Still Life of Mission Launch.* Her partner, dressed like a harmless businessman, behind her, holding her by the stomach, pilot and driver frozen at the top and bottom of the stairs.

Lucy coughed. She felt so chilled, so goddamned cold, inside and out. The only source of heat in the world was Mike Shafer's arm around her middle. They both had on winter clothes, but it seemed to her that his arm not only held her up but heated her up.

Finally, her stomach stilled and she was able to stand upright, head bowed, ashamed and embarrassed. Mike's deep, low voice was in her ear. "Better?" He spoke softly. No one could hear over the gusting wind.

She nodded. A huge cotton handkerchief appeared before her face, and he wiped her mouth with it. Again, a deep voice in her ear. "You can clean up better inside."

She nodded, infinitely grateful for that warm, hard arm around her middle. She could almost feel his hesitation as he said, "Do you want me to carry you up the stairs?"

"No!" A flush of shame ran through her body and she moved away from his arm.

The driver, the pilot and doubtless the cameras watching them were all CIA. She was sorry beyond words that they had caught her weakness, live and on film. Doubtless some young drone in a basement reviewing the tapes would find her vomiting her guts out on the tarmac endlessly amusing.

But she was back in control, and by God, they wouldn't have anything else to report to Uncle Edwin. Certainly not that Brad and Marie Merritt's daughter had to be carried into a mission.

Lucy looked up at Mike's face, dark and grim. She pitched her voice just loud enough for the pilot and driver to hear. Even if the directional mikes couldn't pick up her voice, tapes were habitually reviewed by people trained in lip reading. She even managed a smile. "Sorry about that, darling," she said lightly. "It's either the beginning of stomach flu or those two martinis I had last night."

"Gotta watch those martinis, sweetheart. They're killers." Mike knew full well she hadn't had two martinis the night before. He clearly forced his face to lighten up as he took her arm. It looked casual, but she could feel the strength, feel that he was willing to bear most of her weight, just as she could feel he understood that she didn't want to show any weakness.

They crossed to the steps. The pilot and driver sprang to life like the castle inhabitants in "Sleeping Beauty," suddenly busy with getting their luggage up the stairs and into the cabin.

Mike kept his pace with her exactly, though his legs were much longer than hers. He immediately caught her rhythm as they crossed the tarmac and ascended the stairs.

As one, they turned left to the plane's toilet.

Lucy locked the door behind her, slumping with relief. She shivered and shook with released tension, clinging to the border of the small sink. Finally, she looked up and winced at the ice white face she saw, her lipstick looking like a slash of blood, the blush an unnatural spot of color.

She eyed the toilet, consulting her stomach, but there was nothing left to empty out. Her stomach lay like a cold rock inside her, though fortunately it showed no tendency to clench and rid itself of its contents. Probably because there were none left.

Lucy always carried with her a travel toothbrush and a tiny tube of toothpaste, and she was able to get rid of the god-awful sour taste of bile. She held her wrists under hot water for a full minute and felt warmth at least on the inside of them. She closed her eyes and concentrated on breathing and trying to relax her muscles. In, out. In, out.

When she opened her eyes again, the woman in the mirror had a tiny touch of color to her face. Blotting her lips and applying a lighter shade of lipstick made her look a little less like Dracula's Bride. A quick run of a comb through her hair, a spritz of a springlike scent she'd designed herself, and she felt human again, if not normal.

At the sound of the toilet door opening, Mike turned away from inspecting the darkness outside the windows and moved toward her. It was amazing. His movements were relaxed, easy, but in an instant he was beside her, bending down to sniff. "Hey," he said with a smile. "You smell nice." The words were casual, but his dark eyes were sharp as he scrutinized her face.

"Thanks." Thank God her voice was firm. "I designed the scent myself. I never gave it a name. Now maybe I should call it eau de plane."

He laughed, his eyes still sharp and all business as he accompanied her to the middle of the cabin.

He only released her arm once she took her seat—one of two very comfortable-looking chairs separated by a table. The seats were wide and soft, covered in creamy taupe leather. In no time at all Mike had her coat off, had seated her in the forward-facing seat, buckled her in and taken his place across the table from her.

As if on cue, a garbled message came over the intercom and the plane's engines fired up, a low rumble of vibrations under her feet. The plane started taxiing toward the runway, and Lucy closed her eyes, preparing to endure the next terrible quarter of an hour, immensely grateful that her stomach had already emptied itself.

"Give me your hands."

Her eyes popped open just as she was about to put herself under. His huge, rough hands were extended on the tabletop.

"There's no one to see," he said softly. "Hold my hands."

Oh God. She felt so raw and defenseless. Her terror was so uncontrollable and so damned *visible*. If she'd just been on a plane with anonymous strangers, she could have sat near a window looking blindly out and tried to put herself in that place of meditation she'd been taught as a child.

She'd schooled herself to control as much as possible the trembling of her hands and voice, but she couldn't control her stomach and the color of her face. They were beyond her reach and betrayed the panic boiling inside her.

Of course, what was happening inside her was clear to *him*. To Mike, a soldier, who probably didn't know what fear was, certainly not fear of flying. He belonged to an elite unit. He'd parachuted countless times out of planes, had rappelled out of helicopters, for all she knew was a pilot himself.

And even if somehow the smell of jet fuel triggered the smell of burned human flesh to him, too, he was probably used to it.

Lucy had spent the last fifteen years of her life keeping herself away from these terrible triggers. Enclosed spaces, planes, the jungle, the mountains. Even stress.

She'd been scared witless throughout much of her childhood, waiting while her parents went out regularly on dangerous missions, always hiding the knee-weakening whoosh of relief when she saw them again, safe and sound.

She'd had enough stress for a lifetime. Two lifetimes. So she kept her own adult life low-key, choosing a niche profession where few people could do what she did; she chose her coworkers carefully, keeping complicated people out of her life.

And now look at her. Stepping right into the heart of danger, flying back to where she'd watched her parents mowed down by gunfire in front of her horrified eyes, traveling with a soldier who could probably only feel contempt for her.

"Your hands," he said again.

You can do this, she told herself sternly. She willed her hands steady and slid them across the tabletop.

"Good girl." She looked at him hard, but there was no censure in his gaze, no sarcasm in his voice.

Well, he was going on a mission with her. It was very much in his interest not to antagonize her. She didn't know what he really thought and didn't care.

His huge hands enveloped hers. It was the same temperature in the cabin for him as for her. And yet though she was chilled to the bone, his hands were warm. Hot, even, as if he had some kind of heat generator inside himself.

Of course, not being scared out of his wits probably helped.

The plane swerved onto the runway and stopped, engines revving, waiting for word from air traffic control.

Her hands started trembling in his. However much she tried to hide it, she couldn't. She swallowed heavily, sick and humiliated.

He tightened his own hands around hers. Holding on to the crazy lady, trying to reassure her. For a soldier, going on a mission with a lunatic afraid to fly must seem like suicide.

"I'm sorry," she whispered.

A slight crease appeared between his black eyebrows. "My sister's afraid to fly," he said. "Terrified."

It was totally unexpected. She'd been expecting him to either acknowledge her terror—*Wow, you're a complete whack job and I'm sorry I'm here with you*—or, worse, totally ignore it—*What? What are you talking about? Doesn't everyone shake at takeoff?*

"Your . . . sister?"

"Yeah." His voice had turned grim. "Sweetest kid on earth. Smart and brave. She once climbed a fifty-foot tree to get her kitten back. She was seven at the time. Champion swimmer. Runs like the wind. Can't get on a plane without being sedated. And she's never crashed like you have."

Another garbled message over the intercom, and the pilot released the brakes. The plane rolled down the runway, picking up speed. Lucy's heart thumped wildly. She couldn't breathe through the black terror rising in her chest.

"Look at me." Mike's voice was loud and forceful.

"What?" She could barely catch her breath to say the word.

"Look at me. Watch my eyes. It's going to be okay."

Yes, of course it was going to be okay. Lucy knew that. She was crazy, but she wasn't stupid.

She was split entirely into two personalities. There was the calm, reasonable adult, who knew every flying statistic there was. Knew that flying was infinitely safer than driving—*particularly* driving in DC traffic—safer than almost any other mode of transport. Knew that pilots were dedicated professionals who flew planes for a living and did nothing else. Who understood the mechanics and the physics of flying intimately. Knew, further, that this particular pilot was undoubtedly CIA and therefore one of the best-trained pilots on earth, probably capable of landing in a hurricane on one wing and no prayer.

Then there was her inner Lucy, who was seven years old and terrified and couldn't listen to the adult Lucy because she was screaming too loud.

The engines' thrust was so powerful, the frame began to shake . . . they were a minute from takeoff.

Lucy had been taught meditation by a famous Indian guru in Indonesia. She only found out later that he was world-renowned. To her he was only Uncle Babu. She'd had bad panic attacks when small. Her parents left continually, never letting her know when they'd be coming back, and she never knew *if* they'd be coming back.

With hindsight, of course, as an adult, Lucy realized that her parents couldn't tell her what they were doing because it was top secret. Telling her where they were going and why would not only violate national security but would put her—and them—in danger.

But as a child, Lucy had had no clue. She only knew that her parents disappeared on a regular basis.

Uncle Babu had taught her breathing techniques to overcome the intense anxiety she felt. She grew so good at it as a girl that she could put herself right to sleep. She was sure she could dredge the techniques up out of her memory just as soon as Mike let go of her hands.

Which he wasn't doing.

They took off, in that unmistakable moment of the lifting of gravity that made every stomach in the world swoop. Some barely noticed. Some, like Lucy, broke out in a cold sweat.

She tugged at her hands, uselessly. He wasn't letting go.

The plane banked sharply, leaving her stomach twenty miles behind. There was a low line of red on the horizon, the approaching dawn. It looked like the entrance to hell, yawning open.

Mike leaned forward. "Lucy, look at me. You know, they briefed you on me, or rather Michael Harrington. You know who my parents were, where I went to school, my hobbies. But I don't know anything about you. So—" The plane banked even more steeply and the four molecules of matter that still resided in her stomach crawled up her gullet. She swallowed heavily. He insisted that she look at him, and it helped, sort of. At least looking at his face was more interesting than looking at the land falling away and the imitation of hell on the horizon. "So where do your parents live?"

"They don't."

He had interesting eyes. Dark brown with very faint yellow streaks in them, like the eyes of some jungle predator. You had to be very close to him to see them.

His eyes were warm, the skin around them slightly crinkly with smile lines. His skin was weather-beaten, deeply tanned, with deep lines between his brows and bracketing his mouth. He should moisturize, she thought, desperately keeping her eyes on his, away from the windows.

She realized by his expression she'd said something startling.

"They don't?"

What was he—Oh. Her parents.

"No. They, uh. They died in the Palace in Nhala."

Was he cleared to know her parents had been agents? She had no idea what his clearance level was. Probably Top Secret or maybe even higher, but her parents' standing as CIA operatives was still classified. Some of the agents they'd run fifteen or twenty years ago were still operational.

"There was a coup attempt. In '97. My parents were anthropologists, studying origin myths and language development. They—we—were caught right in the middle. I managed to escape. They were murdered by soldiers loyal to the Chinese Communists. The coup was unsuccessful."

She'd surprised him. He blinked at her, processing this. She could actually see ideas slotting into suitable holes.

She bristled with anger.

They were going *undercover*. His face was an open book. He was going to have to do better than this in the Palace. Nhalans were a lovely people, but it was a civilization well over three thousand years old, and for many of those years they'd lived under foreign rulers.

Nhalans had learned the hard way to read faces. By contrast, a Nhalan's face and voice gave nothing away.

Mike would have to keep up.

"So that's why you know Princess Paso. You lived there, in Nhala. I should have realized that."

She dipped her head, watching his eyes all the time. As long as she watched his eyes, her stomach seemed to hold its place in the center of her torso. Like spotting while executing fouettés.

"Do you speak Nhalan?"

"Yes, I do." And four Indonesian dialects, street Arabic, Spanish and Afrikaans.

He blinked again, and once more his thoughts could just as well have been tattooed on his forehead in glowing red letters: *Maybe she'll be useful after all.*

"So . . . do you have siblings? Brothers, sisters?"

"No." Lucy tried, and failed, to imagine her parents carting around a brood of kids on missions, instead of one very quiet, bookish and obedient little girl. "No siblings, I'm an only child. Only child of only children, too, so no cousins, no aunts, no uncles."

His head reared back a little. "No family *at all*?"

Lucy rarely thought of it that way. Her parents had been dead over half her life now. She was used to thinking of herself as alone in the world. Except . . . "Well," she said, crinkling her nose a little. "Except for Uncle Edwin. But I rarely see him. He's very busy and I'm very busy."

The plane banked again and was hit by turbulence. She closed her eyes and hoped the plane's vibrations hid her shudders. Though it was warm in the cabin, cold sweat trickled down her back. Mike let go of her hands, and she missed the strength, the warmth.

"Here."

Lucy's eyes opened in surprise to find him standing next to her, easily riding out the turbulence, as if standing in a meadow on a bright summer's day. He pressed a cold glass of a golden liquid into her hand.

She bent to smell it. Whiskey. Very fine whiskey. He pressed a small white pill into her hand, too. She raised her eyebrows.

"Whiskey and a special pill. Excellent combo for resting on flights. Me and my men use it all the time. Swallow the pill with the whiskey, atta girl."

Lucy would have objected to being called a girl if she hadn't been on the knife's edge. So she obediently swallowed the pill and the whiskey in a few gulps. They went down nice and smooth and easy.

She handed him back the glass. "I usually put myself out with breathing exercises. Learned meditation as a child."

"So breathe," Mike said easily, sitting back down across from her. He stretched his long legs out, relaxed, completely at ease. Oh, how she envied him. "Close your eyes now and breathe. Do your thing."

The plane shuddered once more and a few minutes later reached cruising altitude, but not before pinging her panic lobe, terror prickling under her skin. It would take about fifteen minutes of breathing exercises to get her hammering heart to slow down.

Might as well start.

In.

Out.

She fell fast asleep.

FIVE

THE PALACE
CHILONGO, NHALA

GENERAL Changa knocked gently on the huge painted wooden door of the Royal Chambers. He didn't need permission to go anywhere he wanted, but it wasn't quite time to make that clear yet.

The servant who should have opened the door didn't, so he pushed it open. Inside, the air was thick with incense. The king had two doctors who'd studied medicine in the West—one at Stanford and one in Munich—at his disposal, but as he felt the life ebbing from him, Jomo was reverting to the Old Ways.

It didn't make any difference.

Old ways, new ways . . . Jomo was going to die soon. One of the brilliant by-products of the underground lab forty miles north of the Palace was a fast-acting form of untreatable leukemia, absolutely indistinguishable from the real thing, though this was induced. Supremely easy. A spray of anesthetic in the face during the night, a syringe full of mutated cells delivered intravenously, and the disease began.

It was useless as a weapon of mass destruction, of course.

The disease was unpredictable and required a direct IV injection, but the fact that it was completely undetectable made it a potential gold mine for assassinations that were not time-sensitive.

Not a warrior's weapon. It was a weapon of stealth.

The fact that the mutated cells had been injected into a formerly perfectly healthy thirty-two-year-old man meant that it was taking Jomo far too long to die, so he was being helped along the way with doses of thallium.

Dr. Deepak Dima had learned capitalist ways together with modern medicine in Stanford, and his bank account was as swollen with money as a blood-saturated tick. Still, it was cheap to kill a king. A mere half a million dollars and Jomo would soon be lying in state.

The two doctors turned to greet the general in the traditional way. One hand cupped within the other, held at heart's height. The deep bow was carefully calibrated to show great respect with a healthy dose of fear.

Princess Paso rose, too, from her usual position at Jomo's side. Gracefully, as she did everything. Her slender hands clasped each other and she bowed. Not at all as deeply as she should.

General Changa frowned, letting his displeasure show. The princess showed no signs of remorse at the slight or even that she'd noticed his displeasure, and yet she'd spent her entire life at court. She knew damned well how to bow to him; she just chose not to.

He ground his teeth. This was one part of the plan that was not coming together as was meant, and it was not acceptable.

Princess Paso had been born and brought up in Nhala, spending her entire life in the Palace, sworn to her royal duties. Unlike many in Nhala, she hadn't been sent abroad to study, her parents preferring to bring in foreign tutors. And ever since Jomo became king fifteen years ago, she'd dedicated herself heart and soul to helping her brother.

That kind of upbringing should have made for a nice, subservient woman who would embrace her duty, and the general. For the good of the country, even if she couldn't bring herself to do anything but snub that pretty nose at him as a man.

Nothing Changa did worked. Whenever he tried to engage her in conversation, she turned out to be hurrying somewhere else, out of duty, of course. At formal events, he arranged to be seated next to her only to find that she'd changed the arrangements, or skipped the event to tend to someone ill in the royal entourage.

She was unfailingly polite, always using the formal form of address. Fifteen fucking years, and he hadn't been able to breach her defenses in any meaningful way.

She hid behind the façade of the king, but once the king was no more, this farce would end. Changa would see to it. He needed her by his side and he needed her obedient.

"General Changa," the princess murmured, eyes downcast, as they properly should be. The princess was following the Old Ways that dictated a Nhalan woman never look into the eyes of a male who was not a family member.

Nowadays, nobody followed that rule. Young women wore Western clothes, looked men in the eye and answered back. Changa would even have approved of the princess's modest behavior if not for the fact that she smiled at everyone and looked even the palace servants right in the eyes.

Just never into his.

Without a word, the princess turned gracefully in an invitation for him to enter the room. Changa could never reproach her for her manners, which were impeccable. Well, soon enough the princess would be by his side. With her brother dead, and no other protector, she would have to turn to him. He would enjoy making her pay for her insolence.

General Changa approached the king's sickbed, keeping his face utterly impassive even at the sight of the bag of bones lying on the monumental royal bed.

King Jomo was the last of a line that had ruled the country for a thousand generations, ever since Nhalans had settled the small, fertile river valley. Nothing but royal blood flowed in his veins, and now it was killing him.

The royal bed dwarfed the king. He looked like a sickly child, shoulders held up by huge silk pillows. His skin was gray, falling off the underlying muscles since he'd lost so much weight. His lips were blue and his nostrils pinched tightly as he tried to pull in air.

Changa barely stopped himself from frowning. Maybe his lab rat had miscalculated the thallium dosage, because it looked like Jomo was going to die any minute. Changa needed him alive, yet incapable of any action, for just a little while more, until the moment came to strike.

If the king died now, the beautiful saffron silk canopy over the elaborate carved wooden bed would be slashed to ribbons, and each and every member of the Royal Guard bedecked with a ribbon. The city and the country would shut down for the obligatory forty days of mourning, during which only the work necessary to feed the population and keep them warm would be allowed.

Travel would be restricted as the country mourned.

The Arabs were going to test run TS-18 soon, and their plan was to unleash it on the world immediately afterward if the test was successful.

Changa would empty a useful chunk of India immediately afterward, using his Sharmas as the first shock troops, followed by the army and then Royal Guard, all stationed in Chilongo for the days of mourning.

The king had to die when Changa said so and not before.

Changa approached the royal bed slowly, head bowed, shoes making no sound on the slate floor, as the Old Ways dictated.

He studied Jomo carefully when protocol dictated he could raise his eyes.

What was it like for Jomo? Did he feel his spirit leaving him, inch by inch? Was he making his peace or raging against his fate?

Jomo was too much the king to show.

The royal bed was covered in a scarlet silk bedspread, Jomo's hands lying on top of the spread. The king shot a glance at his majordomo, who had served the king all his life. The servant, who would never work again after Jomo's death, sprang to the bedside.

"Your Highness," he murmured, bowing low. Jomo gestured up at the heavily carved headboard, with the dragon crest on top.

With another deep bow, the manservant gently pulled the king up as a man would a sick child, placing a mountain of damask pillows against the king's back, holding on to one withered arm so that the king wouldn't topple over.

Sitting up, Jomo was even more pathetic, his sunken chest lost in the elaborate silk embroidered robes. His hand beckoned Changa forward, a clawlike finger curling up.

General Changa stepped to the bed, hiding his disgust at the smell of human waste surrounding the king.

"General," the king murmured, "come closer."

The stench of death hung around Jomo. Changa hid his disgust well. Soon he would inherit an empire. This was a small price to pay.

Jomo beckoned again and Changa bent down, grateful for the incense sticks burning, smoke wafting up to the ceiling fifteen feet overhead.

"Highness." Changa bowed. "I am yours to command."

"General," the king wheezed. His lips had a blue cast. "Take care of my people." The effort to speak exhausted him. He lay his head back against the pillows and closed his eyes.

"Of course, Your Majesty." Changa wondered if the king even heard him. No matter.

Changa bowed again, the deep bow everyone expected, in the secure knowledge that soon, very soon, his bowing days would be behind him.

He backed away still bowing and straightened next to the princess. He opened his nostrils to breathe in her scent, fresh and clean, overriding the stench of putrefaction from the miserable creature on the bed.

"Princess," he said quietly. "May I have a word with you outside? It is a matter of some urgency."

The princess's black eyes narrowed as she studied him openly. Changa repressed his impatience.

The princess bowed, the merest dip of her head. "I would love to, General." Her beautiful eyes were dark and opaque. She waved a graceful hand at the royal bed, where the king had fallen asleep. "But as you can see, a higher duty calls me."

Insolent bitch.

Every cell in Changa's body tightened with rage. She was the sister of the king, a royal princess. Under Nhalan law, he had no power at all to bend her to his will. But soon, very soon, he would. And she would bitterly regret her insolence.

For the moment, however, in a room full of courtiers who had been trained from birth to regard the king as a god, he had to curb his anger. Under the new reign he would institute, under the rule of his mercenaries, this absurd veneration for the royal blood would cease. And Princess Paso would rue the day she was born.

So he bowed his head, knowing that his time was coming.

"As you wish, Princess. I merely wished to tell you that Dr. Merritt will be landing soon."

Changa watched her reaction closely. It was the princess who had put forward Lucy Merritt's name.

Changa had been delighted. Any testimonial by the daughter of the legendary Merritts, who had saved Nhala from Communist domination, would hold great sway over the people. But did the princess have a hidden agenda? Had she summoned an ally? Would this Merritt woman be his enemy?

The princess's face showed only boredom and impatience, her usual expressions in his presence. There hadn't been even a flicker of emotion at the mention of Lucy Merritt's name. The two girls had been friends, but that had been many years ago.

There was nothing there to worry him.

The princess stood before him, slim and beautiful and as remote as one of the ten thousand statues of Buddha in the Palace.

"Please send a servant to come for me when Dr. Merritt

lands, General Changa. In the meantime, I must assist the king."

And she turned her back to him.

To *him*.

Rage suffused his body until he shook with it. Though the room was chilly—it was almost impossible to heat the thousand rooms of the Palace in winter—he could feel sweat running down his back.

The week after Jomo's death, Paso would be his wife and he would exact his revenge, taking it out on her beautiful body. But for the moment, there was only one possible reaction.

"Of course, Princess," he murmured, then bowed and walked out the door, knowing he would have his revenge sooner than Paso could possibly imagine.

FLYING OVER THE MEDITERRANEAN

Nothing like gamma hydroxybutyrate to knock you out, Mike thought, watching Lucy sleep. No breathing exercises in the world would do the trick when you were as stressed as Lucy was. She'd have huffed and puffed for an hour, uselessly.

Whiskey and carefully dosed GHB and she was out like a light.

US soldiers lived off the stuff, just as they lived off dextroamphetamines when they had to stay awake. Particularly fighter pilots who had to fly eighteen hours just to get to the battle zone. Your body needed up time and down time, and they were not always attuned to the US government's needs. The miracle of modern chemistry and the ancient art of distillery kept the two in balance.

He'd gone out like a light himself last night, without benefit of GHB or whiskey. Sheer exhaustion had done the trick. He'd woken up this morning to find that Lucy had put a pillow under his head and covered him with a supersoft blanket that smelled of spring meadows. Maybe that's why he'd slept so soundly.

Well, time to return the favor.

This was a fancy rich man's jet. The seats folded down nearly to beds. Light-years away from the cavernous, freezing cold, noisy cabins of the military transport planes he was used to, strapped into an uncomfortable harness and pissing into a bottle.

He pressed a side button on her seat, and with a gentle purr the back went down and the footrest went up, so slowly and smoothly she slept right through it.

The overhead bin had blankets wrapped in cellophane. He opened a package and found a blanket that was worlds better than the standard stiff airline blanket smelling of plastic, though not nearly as nice as the soft scented one she'd spread over him last night.

He slipped one of those airplane pillows under her head, opened the blanket up and tucked it around her. Then he just stood there, looking down at her. Sleep was putting a little color back into her face. Ice had more color than her face when getting out of the SUV.

Even sick with panic and fear she'd been beautiful, but now that her features were relaxed, whoa.

Beautiful, and brave. Because of Kathy he knew the depth of panic flying could induce in some. Lucy had more reason than most to panic. She'd not only crashed but survived a week in the jungle with hostile groups of men searching for her. That would take major courage for anyone, let alone a seven-year-old child.

Anyone watching her wouldn't have had a clue. Kathy balked every step of the way onto the plane, eyes rolling around in her head like a panicked pony's. Lucy had been white as ice, but other than that, she gave no signs of the terror she must have been feeling. He'd felt the weight she put on his hand and on his arm, but no one else would have had a clue.

She was used to hiding her feelings from others.

She was entirely alone in the world.

That was another piece to add to the fascinating puzzle that was Lucy Merritt. Mike couldn't begin to fathom what it must be like to be completely alone in the world, with no family at all. Not even aunts and uncles and cousins. The closest he'd come had been early childhood with only Dad, though two sets of doting grandparents had lived only twenty miles away. His father was one of four brothers and his mother had had three sisters. He had aunts and uncles and cousins up the wazoo. So though for his early years it had been just him and Dad in the house, there'd been tons of family around, and anyway, his father had been the best father in the world, completely dedicated to Mike. And after Dad married Cheryl, and they had Kathy and Ben and Joe, the house was filled with noisy laughing kids.

Mike loved his stepmother. Nothing step about it really. In every way that counted, Cheryl was his mom and Kathy and Ben and Joe his sister and brothers, nothing half there. He loved them all. Even when away for college and during his years in the military, he took every opportunity to come home. When the kids were small and he came home from college, he'd open the door and brace himself as three warm bodies threw themselves at him like small wriggling puppies. And then Cheryl hugged him and his dad would thump him on the back, beaming.

That's when he knew he was home.

So he returned to the big rambling house in Portland, Oregon, as often as he could manage it and kept in touch with everyone through Skype.

When he'd learned about his dad's illness, there was no question in his mind that he would step in and take over the family business sooner than expected. Cheryl and the kids needed an income, the two boys still had college ahead of them, and Kathy had her heart set on graduate school. He didn't even really consider taking over the business his duty. It was as natural to him as breathing. His family needed him and that was that.

Jesus, Lucy was so alone—and she'd been alone since she was fourteen.

Mike didn't know which idea was more appalling. That a young girl was left orphaned, without any family at all, or that the only thing she had that passed for a family was Edwin Montgomery.

She didn't have a boyfriend, either. The only rings she had on those pretty fingers were on her right hand. She hadn't called anyone to say she was going to disappear for an indefinite period of time.

By God, if she were his, he wouldn't let her walk into danger like this.

The rising sun shot a bolt of bright white light into the cabin, and Mike realized he'd been standing looking at her for over half an hour.

Not good.

Going into a dangerous mission with a beautiful and fascinating woman was . . . well, it was a bad idea. Because you don't go on an op with two priorities, you go in with one.

Get the mission done.

Now his head was divided, and that made him shit scared. Because right up there with getting the mission done was keeping the beautiful woman sleeping in her chair safe.

He shook himself. Standing here mooning wasn't helping anyone. They were walking into a volatile situation and he needed all the intel he could get.

Setting up on the other side of the plane, he opened his laptop on another table. It was a perfectly ordinary laptop belonging to Michael Harrington. It contained several years' worth of financial spreadsheets, and there was a current one, unfinished, dated today. His email address—m.harrington@EBGFinance.com—had 5,547 messages from friends, fellow bankers and financial analysts, going back three years. He had files containing his schedule, personal financial data, bills paid and bank account info.

There were even a couple of emails from lmerritt@hotmail.com. He opened a few. Charming emails, a lot of them planning dinner or an evening out at the theater. Always signed, *love, Lucy.*

On paper, Michael Harrington was worth more than seven million dollars—which was nice. Yesterday he'd lost $103,567 when the Dow took a sharp dip—which was bad.

He did however gain $50,987 back by close of market. Man, he was one smart guy.

His laptop contained the life and times of one Michael Harrington, rich yuppie.

But there was a secret cache, highly encrypted and zipped to within an inch of its life, that was Eyes Only for Captain Mike Shafer of the Tenth Mountain Division, US Army, and that's the one he opened.

He read through the instructions while the theme music of *Mission: Impossible* danced in his head.

Try to identify suspected hidden bioweapons lab somewhere in forty-eight thousand square miles of frozen desert on the roof of the world. In winter. Find dessicated body— basically a set of winter clothes and gear and some dust— and search for flash drive in same frozen desert. Locate and contact possible double agent inside the Palace of Chilongo, even though he'd never been to Nhala before, did not speak the language, did not know the customs and could possibly expose himself as a double agent, in a kingdom which was veering toward a military dictatorship.

Piece of cake.

$\mathcal{S}$IX

"HERE," Dr. Imran Mazari said quietly, finger on the giant detailed relief map spread out over General Goodfellow Mitanga's huge, ornate, highly polished desk. His finger covered a spot far inland from Lagos, in the south of the country, three hundred miles from the border with Cameroon.

General Mitanga nodded wisely, holding on to the edges of his desk. "Animists," he said with contempt. He spat toward a spittoon in the corner and missed. "Infidels."

General Mitanga was nominally a Muslim, but Mazari knew he didn't believe in Allah, the All Merciful. He believed in Goodfellow Mitanga and his bank account.

The general had had the previous president beheaded a month ago, and his troops had declared him President of the Federal Republic of Nigeria and Commander in Chief of the Nigerian Armed Forces an hour later. It had cost him three million dollars, and as long as he kept paying the general staff of the Nigerian Armed Forces, he'd stay president, and he'd keep his head on his shoulders.

His officers had a taste for luxury. The previous president

had left the country's coffers bare, which is why Mitanga had jumped at Mazari's offer of ten million dollars for a quiet little trial run on an obscure tribe living in isolation deep in the equatorial jungle.

That would buy him three years of life at the top. And if he couldn't steal enough in three years to let him retire and live in luxury on the French Riviera for the rest of his life, then he wasn't worthy of being a prominent Nigerian politician.

"Let me run through the plan once more," Mazari said, and President Mitanga nodded his head enthusiastically, nearly falling out of his chair with the movement. He was extremely drunk, Mazari thought with disgust. The general's eyes were completely bloodshot, and he moved with the exaggerated care of the drunk or drugged. He reeked of alcohol and sweat, and Mazari had to use every ounce of self-control not to show his disgust.

But he couldn't. He and his second in command had worked hard to find an isolated settlement of humans where they could test TS-18 in a controlled experiment. It had to be done far away from prying eyes, and it had to be done to people no one would miss.

Harder than one would think.

Luckily, the tribe was situated next to what was suspected to be a substantial copper deposit and the Chinese were very interested in copper. The Chinese were very interested in everything. They would love to prospect for copper without any pesky natives nearby. So getting rid of the small and unfortunately situated Gombi tribe was going to be doubly worth the general's while.

Mazari didn't care at all what happened to the copper. The economics of jihad were not his concern. His brethren in the movement took care of that. There was always money. The world was sick with it.

Knowledge—ah, that was a much more rare commodity. Knowledge was going to win them the world.

He caught the general's eyes, so bloodshot it was painful to look into them. "We start tomorrow."

Had the general even heard? Mitanga sat swaying in his chair and took another drink. The general pulled closer to him the file Mazari had brought, opened it and checked the cover page. It was the original of the bank statement of three million dollars deposited a week ago in the Banque Suisse Populaire, in the name of Goodfellow Mitanga. The general tapped the paper as a sly smile crossed his face.

"Top secret mission, eh? I'll bet it would be worth your while to make sure there's nobody in a hundred-mile radius, eh? No prying UN eyes, no NGOs out in the bush, no journalists. Just the Gombi and jungle. Be worth money, it would." The craftiness of the very drunk lit up his red eyes. "My troops could set up a roadblock at every access road or path leading to the area, make sure you have . . . privacy. I'll bet that would be worth another half a million dollars."

Mazari was disgusted. The man couldn't even stay bought. And the notion that his thugs, who were high or drunk almost round the clock, would be disciplined enough to provide a cordon around the test area was laughable. The general was just trying to extort more funds.

But . . . money was something Mazari had in excess. The test was important to a lot of people, and he reckoned that at least two billion dollars had been spent already on the lab and the salaries of the researchers. Half a million dollars was nothing. If it bought even a little more privacy . . .

"Two hundred thousand," he said firmly. "Half now, half in a week, when the experiment is over."

"Three hundred," the general slurred.

"Two fifty," Mazari answered, and General Mitanga nodded his assent, and on the downward movement of his head, he just kept on going until his forehead hit the desktop.

Mazari looked at him in disgust for a moment, then let himself out of the room.

Let the drunken general put more money in the bank. He'd be shot by one of his soldiers by year's end, anyway.

Mazari didn't care. He had a world to conquer.

IN FLIGHT, DESCENT TO THIMPHU

Lucy came up out of sleep in slow swoops. Unlike most nights, she'd slept dreamlessly. Her dream life was always intense, often with sharp nightmare edges. She was used to sleeping in fits and starts. But now she woke up with an unusual feeling of being rested.

There was a low background hum, constant, so that it wasn't disturbing. And a low-level vibration that almost lulled her back to sleep.

Though . . . since when did she have a vibrating bed?

Lucy's eyes snapped open and she sat up, pushing her hair out of her eyes. A large brown hand reached out, pressed a button, and her seat moved smoothly upright.

Seat, low hum, vibration.

Plane.

Danger.

Lucy gasped, looking around wildly. A man was sitting across from her, watching her carefully. Dark hair, dark face, dark eyes . . .

He put his hands together at chest level, left hand fisted, right hand enveloping the fist, and bowed his head.

"*Nominè*," he said.

Peace.

Lucy breathed deeply. In. Out. In. Out. Since childhood, her calming exercise.

It took a moment for her emotions to settle, which she took to be a huge step forward. Ten years ago, waking up in a plane would have had her choking on a scream.

She replicated the salute, right hand enveloping left fist, bow of head. "*Nominè*." She sketched a smile, feeling her heart rate slowly come back to normal. It was the Nhalan formal greeting, usually of inferior to superior. "You've been doing your homework."

Mike nodded. His dark eyes searched hers. "Interesting place."

A garbled announcement came over the intercom system.

"We're landing," Mike said. "Hold on tight to me."

She didn't even question it. She simply held on tightly to the big, strong hand holding hers and did her breathing exercises while the pilot landed the plane at Thimphu.

A light snow was falling as they exited the plane, still hand in hand. They would be expected, as fiancées, to be holding hands, but Lucy was clutching Mike's as if it were a lifeline thrown to her in a raging river.

She was holding on so tightly, to a lesser man her grip might have been even painful, but she doubted she was hurting him. She doubted she even *could* hurt him. His hand in hers felt like a warm rock.

At the bottom of the stairs were four members of the Royal Guard—the equivalent of lieutenants if she remembered Nhalan rank insignia correctly.

They were lined up two to a side, at attention, and as she stood at the top of the stairs Lucy understood that the easy part was over.

She was tunnel-visioning. The reaction of panic, the therapists had told her. The way to combat panic was to gain control of yourself and your surroundings, and to do that you had to understand your surroundings. Expand your senses. Ground yourself in the here and now.

She pulled in a deep breath. The sun was setting behind a high, snowy peak, a dim milky pale disc in the fog. Tendrils of fog shifted with every movement, a silky white smoke that followed them.

They were in a remote part of the airport. She could see no other planes, only a primitive hangar and a stretch of runway. The airport proper was nowhere to be seen. There were also no vehicles to take them to the airport, so they would be boarding a helicopter very soon. She couldn't even bear to think of that right now.

There were clearly to be no diplomatic formalities, no showing of passports, no border controls at all.

By the time she made it to the bottom of the stairs, Lucy had herself under control.

The mission started here and it started now, and she didn't want to start it with a show of cowardice.

She let go of Mike's hand as her shoes touched the tarmac. The light snow was swirling in the air, so light the wind carried flakes every which way, even up. They might be headed for a storm, so the sooner they got under way the better.

A fifth man joined the military escort, facing the stairs. He was the senior officer, a colonel, judging from the shape of the cap and the bars on his shoulders.

As a matter of survival, her parents had taught her to read military rank in every country they'd lived in.

Lucy and Mike walked up to the colonel, side by side. The four soldiers sprang more tightly to attention, clicking their heels together, fairly quivering with military zeal.

Lucy approached the senior officer. Before she could greet him, he said, "Sampan Merritt. We are honored you are coming back to our country." He used the honorific *Sampan*, usually reserved for high female members of the nobility, irrespective of their marital status.

Calling her *Sampan* was already extraordinary. Then he did something even more surprising. Instead of the usual Nhalan greeting, which Mike had mastered, with his closed fist he thumped his chest over his heart and bowed so low she was afraid he'd strain his back.

Amazing. This salute was one reserved for royalty, and signified absolute fealty—*my heart is yours to command*— and the deeply low bow was a sign of enormous respect.

Luckily, there was a greeting in return for this, which she'd watched Paso and her mother execute a hundred times. And luckily it didn't involve bowing, because she didn't think she could bow from the waist more deeply than he had without giving herself a hernia.

She laid the flat of her own hand over her heart and dipped, back straight, sort of like ladies in waiting did at Buckingham Palace. If she'd been in a formal Nhalan aristocratic gown, the silk of the gown would have pooled at her feet. Paso and her mother had curtsied so beautifully their gowns formed a perfect circle around their feet.

"It is an honor to serve Nhala," she answered in Nhalan.

His eyes widened. He hadn't expected her to answer in his language.

Had she made a mistake? Maybe she should have kept her knowledge of the language a secret. Had she just thrown away a tactical advantage?

No. Paso would address her in Nhalan automatically. And the colonel would know she'd spent part of her early adolescence in Nhala. It might even have seemed strange if she'd pretended she didn't understand or speak the language.

The eternal split-second weighing of choices, the eternal vigilance of being on a secret mission. She'd thought she was rid of this forever.

She turned to Mike, who'd been watching carefully. Good. He was here as a soldier, but the more clued in he was, the better.

She looked him over carefully. She could tell he was a soldier, but could the colonel? His body was combat-hard, not gym-hard. Mike was very well dressed and his heavy winter coat disguised his unusually strong physique.

His hands were gloved, which was good because they were a real giveaway. Though his nails were now manicured, his hands were incredibly strong and hard, covered in nicks and callouses, something no banker would ever have. If someone noticed, she hoped he'd have the presence of mind to slip into the conversation that he was a competitive polo player.

Maybe she should work that into the conversation at the earliest opportunity. Covers had been blown for less. Come to think of it, Scarlett's dire situation had been revealed to Rhett because of the roughness of her hands.

Another thing. Last night's pampering had not been enough to give him that rich-man ruddy spa look. It was a good thing they were going undercover in a harsh mountain climate where all the men looked weather-beaten and older than their age. His looks would be a dead giveaway in London or New York.

"Darling," she said. "This is a colonel of the Royal Guard.

He and his men will accompany us the rest of the way to Nhala."

"Colonel," Mike said in his deep voice. He gave the traditional Nhalan greeting, fist in hand, head bowed.

The colonel nodded his head then looked up at the quickly graying sky. A thick flurry of snowflakes enveloped them. Lucy's long coat swirled around her legs.

"Come," he said in English. "We must go before the storm arrives." He strode off to the side, to an empty stretch of tarmac.

Within a minute they could hear the *whump whump* of helicopter rotors, and Lucy swallowed heavily as a huge black helicopter slowly settled. The mist blanketed them. The rotors gave the mist an almost elegant swirl, tendrils fanning outward in lacy spirals.

This was it.

A helicopter.

She'd known the last leg of the journey would be by helicopter but had repressed it. The plane trip had been bad enough.

But now the moment was upon them. She kept her back straight and her arm through Mike's as they were escorted to the helicopter that waited for them, rotors slowly moving. Mike stopped and spoke briefly to the colonel. She couldn't hear what they were saying over the helicopter's engines, but the colonel nodded gravely.

Lucy's stomach quivered and her knees trembled. She schooled her face to blankness, stiffened her knees. The great lesson of her childhood.

Hide your fear.

𝒮EVEN

THE helicopter terrified Lucy. Mike had flown in helos thousands of times but could understand that for someone scared of flying, the first time in a helicopter could be terrifying.

The light snowfall was intensifying fast and the temperature was dropping. The pilot knew a storm was on the way and wasn't wasting time. He didn't switch off the engines as he put down on the helipad, just powered the rotors down.

Even at minimal strength the backwash was strong. Mike put his arm around Lucy, not a hardship. In hustling her toward the helo, he looked down and saw a pale profile, the strain visible on her face.

But she didn't hesitate, not for one second, where he knew Kathy would have refused outright.

Mike looked down at the ground at Lucy's shoes and frowned.

He was perfectly equipped. He'd had a chance to go through his suitcase on the long flight over, and though he had no idea how they'd done it, some spook three-letter alphabet agency had created an entire winter soldier's wardrobe that was indistinguishable to the eye from the wardrobe of some rich guy who liked the outdoors.

Starting from the skin out.

The underwear—long-sleeved undershirts and longer than usual boxers—was made of a material that looked and felt like silk but was actually a special moisture-wicking polyester designed by NASA, whereby moisture or sweat was moved from the skin to the outer surface of the underwear. All the shirts were made of grid-patterned fleece, which provided another insulating layer. The pants were all elegantly cut to fit his long legs, looked like ordinary trousers, but were made of a material that increased moisture vapor permeability. The jackets and the overcoat were all highly waterproofed, with fur ruffs and hoods that would protect the head from temperatures of up to minus fifty degrees.

His gloves consisted of an outer leather shell and an inner wool-and-polyester lining, designed to withstand extreme cold.

Every single item met the requirements for generation III ECWCS gear—Extended Cold Weather Clothing System—which allowed soldiers to survive and even thrive in extreme environments.

And the shoes and boots, ah, here the maestros of trickiness had outdone themselves, because though the footwear looked normal, even elegant, the shoes had all-rubber uppers that mimicked leather and three layers of insulation that could withstand minus sixty degrees.

So the alphabet-soup guys had kitted him up just fine.

They hadn't even thought of Lucy.

He looked down at her feet. Pretty and slender and encased in ordinary store-bought shoes that would last about five minutes in the kind of snow and cold found in the Himalayas.

She was wearing wool pants, a sweater and a stylish winter coat that was absolutely useless in subzero temperatures. If she ever had to run for it, she'd die in an hour.

Shit, it made him furious. They were putting an untrained

woman into a volatile and highly dangerous situation, with basically a do-your-best brief and little to no backup and no winter gear at all.

She was being thrown into a country and a building where she'd seen her parents killed, requiring a flight traveling halfway around the world when she'd survived a plane crash, and they were giving her zip, the fuckers.

If by any chance she had to go out into the field, she'd lose a limb to frostbite, so her fucking *uncle* wasn't doing that great a job of looking after her, was he?

Mike could feel her shivering against him. She'd probably packed her warmest clothes, but they weren't doing her any good.

He held her tightly, worried. He could already feel the effects of the beginning of altitude sickness, a feeling similar to the flu. He was hardened to it, and altitude bothered him less than it would someone who wasn't trained.

Right now, Lucy would be feeling as if she had a case of full-blown flu, together with a headache and nausea, and she'd be cold.

He looked down at her. All he could see was a pale, perfectly serene profile. But he knew she was freezing, feeling sick and frightened.

And he felt . . . weird.

An op took up everything in you—your head and your muscles and your sinews and your heart. Mike was used to going on missions with other soldiers. Men who'd trained as hard as he did, who were as good with weapons as he was, men who could handle themselves as well as he could.

Most of the other men making up the Tenth Mountain Division had grown up in mountains, understood intimately altitude and cold. They would know exactly what to expect going on a mission into high altitude.

He never had to worry about any of them. They had his back and he had theirs. They zigged when he zigged and zagged when he zagged.

It was unnerving going on an op with Lucy, who hadn't

had his training, who wasn't equipped for this. His mind was split right into two—the op and keeping Lucy safe.

And, well, there was another part of his anatomy that was taken up with Lucy, and it was bad news. The worst.

Man, you were *not* supposed to lust after your teammates. Who knew he ever could? Martinez, Cade, Mantelli and the rest were great guys, but about as attractive as a fart. His head had always been entirely taken up with getting the mission done and bringing back the same number of guys he'd gone in with, with all their limbs intact.

Being distracted by a teammate's profile, long lashes, perfect skin . . . whoa. Wasn't in the manual.

And, well, there was the desire thing, too. Mike was posing as Lucy's fiancé. They'd put them in the same room, the same bed. He didn't know how he was going to do that when he got semi-erect walking with her in an extremely cold environment at the beginning of a snowstorm.

If he had to share a bed with her, what was he going to do? Walk to the bed with a book or a hat held in front of his crotch to hide his erection? How the hell was that supposed to work?

And then Mike saw past her beauty, saw that she was pale, sick, frightened, and he wanted to kick himself in the butt. The only excuse he could give himself was an overlong period of abstinence that was not of his choosing, making all his hormones fire up in her presence, because the last thing this beautiful, scared woman was thinking of was sex.

And just as he'd fashioned a splint for Martinez when he broke his arm and just as he'd held Cade by the back of his jacket collar as he puked his stomach lining after eating fermented goat, he knew he needed to help his teammate, who was hurting. She was a beautiful woman, yes, and he desired her. But she was also walking straight into her worst nightmare and she deserved his help, not his lust.

So Mike forced his dick to go down a little and his head back in the game.

The snow was increasing in texture from talcum powder

to granulated sugar. The fog was starting to hem in the view, closing off the peaks in the distance, disappearing as if by some magician's wand.

The helo was an ancient Chinook. It didn't look particularly well maintained and had rust in spots, like mange. Mike knew the Chinook was a good workhorse of a helicopter with a lot of redundancy and overengineering that would see her through a less than rigorous maintenance schedule, but it looked like your worst nightmare if you were scared of flying.

Like trusting your life to a rusty tin can.

Lucy's eyes widened and she turned even more pale. Mike was about to bend down and reassure her that the Chinook was like Ginger—she could do anything Fred could do, backward and in heels—when he saw that pretty little chin go up and her back straighten and Mike realized that he'd just seen the equivalent of a teammate checking his equipment and walking straight into a firefight.

This was one brave lady.

The helicopter looked as if it had a disease and was on its last legs. Had General Changa been given intel that they were infiltrating Nhala to spy on him, and this was his revenge? If so, they were dead no matter how you looked at it.

They circled the helicopter around to the back, where a big metal ramp was lowered.

Lucy looked at the colonel and the four soldiers who'd formed the honor guard, who were waiting for her to get in first, then looked up at Mike. He'd schooled his face to passivity in front of the soldiers, but his eyes were warm and he had a firm grip on her arm. He gave a brief nod and she gave one right back.

We have to do this.

I know, so let's get going.

She glanced up at the sky, a dull gray that seemingly had been pulled right down over their heads. It was cold, but not the penetrating life-threatening cold it could become at higher altitudes. She was feeling the mild effects of altitude sickness and wondered how she'd react in Nhala, another two thousand feet up.

Everything about this was terrifying. The scabrous-looking helicopter that appeared as though it was going to break apart any second now, the unsmiling soldiers, the hateful noise of the engines, so loud it reverberated in her diaphragm. Thank God she had nothing in her stomach.

Mike had her arm in a strong grip. She thought she could feel the warmth of his hand through layers of clothing. It was an odd sensation, being frightened but having someone on her side, by her side.

She'd always faced her fears alone.

The helicopter ramp yawned in front of her. Lucy looked up, tiny snowflakes melting on her face, and took a deep breath. Her lungs craved air, the first sign of altitude sickness.

She'd survive. She'd survived the last flight, she'd survive this one. She'd survive being in the Palace, with all its memories. She'd go into the Palace and walk past where she'd watched her parents being killed.

It was, however, entirely possible that history was about to repeat itself and that the last of the Merritts was going to her death in the Palace, as her parents had died there before her.

She was walking into a dangerous situation, totally unprepared and untrained. Her entire life since the age of fourteen had been about avoiding situations exactly like this one. She'd studied hard, refined her appreciation of art, learned the exacting science of restoration . . . nothing that would prepare her for danger.

The last time she'd been in the Palace, the floors had been slick with blood, the air had smelled of gunpowder and death. She'd dreamed of those final scenes at least once a week for fifteen years, vowing never to put herself in that situation again, and here she was, walking back into the maw of danger.

Lucy's heart pounded. She hated herself for this. Hated that she was such a coward and couldn't look danger in the face without cringing in fear. A second before the first bullet hit her in the shoulder, Lucy's mother had looked across at her father, face filthy with gunpowder residue and streaks of blood, and had grinned madly. And even after the shot to the shoulder, she'd kept on firing one-handed, brave to the end.

How she wished she were as brave as her mother.

A squeeze of her elbow and she looked up, startled out of her thoughts.

Oh. Of course. Standing there lost in her own head, she was holding everything up, delaying their departure in worsening weather.

Hot shame flooded her. She walked up the ramp, Mike beside her, moving her forward with a hand to her back.

It had to be done and she did it, one step up at a time.

Inside it was cavernous, canvas seats lining the bare metal sheeting sides. Mike moved her forward. They took the first two seats on the right-hand side. The soldiers were filing in, strapping themselves in with a shoulder harness, their breath white in the frigid air.

Lucy took one look and understood the mechanism. She strapped herself in while Mike went to speak to the colonel. He nodded and walked back to her up the length of the cabin.

He looked so much at ease in the helicopter that for a second Lucy wondered how anyone could buy the story that he was some kind of businessman when he looked so very much like a soldier.

It wasn't an idle thought. Any break in their cover could be dangerous.

She'd have to tell him to . . . what? Walk less straight? Slump those broad shoulders? Look soft when he was so obviously hard and fit? In her experience, businessmen were soft and pampered. Getting Mike's physique would take time and effort, time and effort better spent earning money.

Sitting still, it was even colder than it had been outside. Added to the misery of a helicopter ride was going to be the noise and the cold. It was going to take more than breathing to get her through this.

Mike stood over her, then bent down.

"I've got a couple of things that will make this easier." He spoke directly into her ear, voice quiet, though there was no way even someone sitting next to her could overhear. It was like being inside a cement mixer.

He tucked a heavy, scratchy smelly blanket around her. She was instantly enveloped in heavenly warmth. Where he'd managed to scare up a blanket was anyone's guess, but he'd done it.

His cheek had brushed hers. He'd already developed enough five o'clock shadow to scratch her skin. It felt somehow good, solid and reassuring. Warm and utterly, completely male.

He took her hand in his, placed two pills on her gloved palm and handed her a canteen.

"What's this?" One was a transparent capsule with tiny orange pellets in it and the other the pill she'd taken on the plane.

"Diamox. A carbonic anhydrase inhibitor. For altitude sickness." He smiled at her and winked. "It really helps, but you shouldn't operate heavy machinery while under the influence."

No, there was a pilot for that.

"Take them." The smile had gone. His deep brown gaze was serious. "It's not going to be an easy flight, Chinooks are notoriously uncomfortable. You might as well get as much rest as you can."

Made sense. Lucy swallowed both and tried to find a comfortable position, finding it when Mike placed his arm around her shoulders and settled her against him. As a pillow, his chest was too hard, but it had the advantage of being warm. Actually, she was pretty warm all over what with the smelly, scratchy blanket and the man.

The dim light in the cabin turned from green to red, and without warning, the helicopter lifted off in a great swoop.

Lucy would have fallen out of her seat if it weren't for the harness and Mike's arm anchoring her to him.

He bent down close again, his lips at her ear. "You okay?"

A shiver ran down her spine at the feel of his breath at her ear.

The helicopter swooped again, huge rotors making an ungodly roar. The soldiers stationed on both sides of the cabin swayed with the movements, heads down, in Stoic Soldier Mode.

"Yeah," she whispered.

Under her ear Mike's heart beat slow and steady. It was as if his calm transmitted itself to her through their skin. It was almost impossible to feel afraid even though the helicopter was lifting and turning, threading its way through valleys between the solid granite mountains she knew were there, though they were invisible in the night fog.

A human heart was a reassuring thing.

He squeezed her shoulders briefly, bending down again, warm cheek touching hers. "Good. Now rest."

Her eyes closed as the helicopter rose, taking her to a place she'd thought never to see again in this lifetime.

THE ROYAL CHAMBERS
THE PALACE
CHILONGO, NHALA

"They're going to test the disease on an African tribe," said Mohar Thakin, Captain of the Royal Guards. He held her hands. "They're hoping to wipe out the entire tribe."

Paso shuddered. She'd never been to Africa, had never even seen an African, but they had souls. Though she knew that Arabs were behind the horrible things going on in the laboratory, it was Changa who was empowering them. Changa who ultimately would have blood on his hands.

He wouldn't care, as long as it brought him power.

Paso's hands trembled in Mohar's. She looked up at him, at that forbidden, beloved face. "Can we stop them?"

Mohar had new lines in his face, nostrils pinched white with stress.

"No," he said soberly, deep voice steady. "We cannot. The Royal Guards are behind me and would do my bidding, but they cannot command Changa's Sharmas. The Sharmas are mercenaries and would change sides on a dime. They have no love for Changa. But he's paying them and they must obey. To do anything we'd need the Americans on our side. Let us hope your friend Lucy can get a message to the American military."

"Shh!" Paso put her hand over his mouth, then removed it, stroking his strong jawline as she did. "Do not say this, do not even think it! If Changa even suspected Lucy is coming to get information out . . ."

She shuddered.

Changa knew no limits.

For only the second time in the thousand-year history of the Palace, it had a working dungeon, far down, where screams could not drift to the habitable floors. The last time men had been tortured as a state policy had been five hundred years ago, under the iron rule of Tsompa the Cruel.

Changa enjoyed cruelty, grew sexually aroused at pain.

He'd been courting her for two years now and had tried over and over again to get her into his bed. She'd avoided it so far by fighting back, by leaving a room when he entered, by making certain she was always with company in his presence.

But when Jomo died, Changa would come for her. She was part of his plan, she knew that. He had some bigger plan, but the first step was conquering Nhala. And what better way to do it than to marry the only person left of royal lineage, her?

And when he came for her, brave, beautiful Mohar would fight him to the death. If Changa didn't kill Mohar outright, he'd lock him in the dungeon that frightened guards told her was slick with blood, and torture him every day until his heart gave out.

"He won't know," Mohar murmured, bending down to kiss her neck. "He's not as smart as he thinks he is, the general. We will contact the Americans and have them rid the world of that abomination of a laboratory that only brings death." He rubbed his face against her shoulder, and she shuddered again, only not in fear.

Love. Unexpected, unhoped for love. Princess Paso had thought herself beyond love, that her blood had placed her above normal passions. She'd dedicated herself to her brother the king and to her people.

But love had come, in the unexpected form of a brave soldier, who had risked his life to tell her what General Changa was doing in the frozen wastes north of the Palace.

If Paso had been privy to the general's plot, if she was part of it, Mohar would have forfeited his life, condemning himself to a death by slow torture, by telling her.

But she'd been horrified, and they'd worked together to help the CIA agent who'd come posing as a simple tourist. He'd gone to the laboratory of death, been given information by the guard who'd warned Mohar, and had never come back.

Through the horror and anxiety of having her beloved country turned into a charnel house, Paso had fallen in love with the tall, quiet, brave soldier who had risked so much.

And the God of Love had heard, because he loved her back.

They might not survive this trial. Jomo wouldn't survive at all. Changa had somehow poisoned him, and his life was slipping away. All their lives might yet be forfeit.

To stop Changa was going to require much bravery and much help from the spirits. They might fail. Changa might win. They might lose their lives, and a great evil could be loosed upon a world that had already known much evil.

But she'd found love, the most unexpected and greatest gift of all.

She pulled away from Mohar's kiss, reluctant to leave the painless fire of desire. But time was their enemy.

She looked up into his dark eyes. She feared for him so much. One misstep and he would die badly. At times, she felt Mohar walked with one foot in this world and one foot in the next.

Until she shook herself and realized that this was the superstitious nonsense of her nurse that rose in her head in times of stress.

Her parents had believed in education and had brought in the world's finest tutors to teach her the ways of the West—even though she'd driven her math tutor crazy with her lack of interest.

Mohar was not going into the spirit world. He was going to stay in this world, where she could love him. But between now and then many things had to happen, including reconnecting with Lucy Merritt.

Paso drew back from Mohar and looked down at herself. Instead of her usual jeans and Benetton sweater, she had put on the saffron yellow silk robe with the Snow Dragon embroidered in scarlet silk thread on the back that the princesses of the realm had worn for great occasions since the Yun Dynasty.

She hadn't worn it since her father's death ten years ago. Changa had been in England on a training course. He wouldn't necessarily know the meaning of the ceremonial robe, but her retinue, loyal to her and not to Changa, would. The Sharmas wouldn't know, either.

But Lucy would. Lucy would understand that something important was at hand, though she would know that already. Lucy had always been so smart, but also very quiet, so no one realized just how smart she was.

Mohar had pulled out his cell phone and had been talking quietly into it. He finished talking and flipped it closed. His hands, warm and strong, fell gently on her shoulders. "I have just received word from my men that the helicopter with Ms. Merritt and her fiancé will be landing soon."

"Changa will be there," Paso whispered.

"Yes." Mohar dipped his head soberly. "He will."

Paso willed herself to stillness. Every encounter with Changa now was dark and dangerous. He behaved as if in a fever and he smelled of madness.

"But I will be there, too." Mohar's hands tightened on her shoulders.

She looked up into his eyes. As head of the Royal Guard he had every right to be there at the greeting of an honored guest, but Paso knew that he would be there as her paladin.

"If he ever finds out about us," she murmured, unable to finish the sentence. It was too horrible to contemplate.

"He won't." Oh, he spoke with such confidence. Paso wanted to lean into him and simply absorb some of his strength and confidence. Watching Jomo die day by day, trying to stay out of Changa's way—they were trying her nerves until she thought she would snap.

But she couldn't. A princess held fast. Her people counted on her to defend their country, particularly now that Jomo was deathly ill. Changa was much less beloved of the people than he imagined. But then he wouldn't care. He had a powerful weapon, slowly coalescing in a laboratory sixty feet underground, that would give him the power of gods.

Paso knew that he would do away with her, Mohar, even all the Royal Guards, as a man swatted away flies in summer, if he even suspected she knew anything of his plans.

"He mustn't suspect anything about Lucy."

Mohar nodded again. "You must not betray in any way that you care for her or that she has any role here in Nhala, other than restoring a manuscript. Your life, her life, all our lives depend on it."

Paso nodded. Her heart sang at the thought of seeing her friend once more, but they would meet under Changa's cold, watchful eyes. Anything other than the cool, formal, dutiful welcome by a member of the royal house to a foreign professional she'd briefly known as a young girl would be insanity, and lethal.

Paso was going to have to get information to Lucy, and she couldn't do that if Changa suspected anything other than a remote relationship.

So she would have to control her joy at seeing Lucy again after fifteen years.

A rumbling sound came from the rooftops. They both looked out the window at the light snowfall.

"The helicopter," Mohar said. He stepped away from her, a soldier's expression covering the lover's face. His eyes went blank. A foot separated them, but it could have been a chasm. He gave a formal bow. "Princess, we must go."

Paso's back straightened, her face turned blank. She was the princess now, and not the woman.

She swept out the door, not looking back at the captain of her Royal Guard.

$\mathscr{E}$IGHT

MIKE leaned to his left to look out one of the three dusty, filthy portholes on the starboard side of the Chinook. Luckily, they'd left the snowstorm behind in Thimphu and the sky was that of a crystal clear mountain night. An almost full moon shed silvery light over the helipad, though Chinooks had excellent radar.

The Palace was brightly lit, an unearthly marvel against the black mountainside.

Mike thought he'd seen a lot of the world, but he'd never seen anything like the Palace. He'd done his homework on the long flight over, sure. He'd studied the photographs and knew the stats. One of the highest buildings in the world in terms of altitude, six times the surface area of the Pentagon, a thousand years old, yada yada.

But the reality was unexpected, and overwhelming.

The Palace was lit by spotlights and torches along the pathway from the helipad to the body of the Palace itself, which was so huge it filled his field of vision. There was nothing but Palace, as far as the eye could see.

It sat high above the plain below and was accessible through great white swooping staircases and an internal elevator built in the sixties. As large as a small city, it was built of stone made to last the ages, and it had. The rooftops and windows and door frames were made of elaborately carved and painted wood dating to after the Great Fire of the attempted coup, but rigorously modeled after the thousand-year-old originals.

Small wooden temples dotted the terraces. It was said there were more than ten thousand statues inside the building.

Mike was a modern man and didn't hold with superstition, but a shiver of superstitious awe ran through him as his eyes traversed the great, magnificent stone expanse.

This had been built in the mists of time. His ancestors were painting themselves blue and worshipping fire, living in straw and daub huts when this magnificent building was going up.

In its own way, it was more awe-inspiring than any Manhattan skyscraper, since four hundred generations of men and women had lived within its walls.

He stared as the helo flared and settled, rotors raising a cloud of dust and fine snow. Twenty soldiers waited just outside the worst of the rotor wash, surrounding a slender female figure dressed in a long silk robe.

The torches lit the soldiers' faces dramatically, highlighting the sharp, high cheekbones, leaving their eyes in darkness. They looked so foreign, the Palace was so unlike anything he'd ever seen before, that they could have been in a spaceship landing on an alien planet.

Mike felt a gentle touch on his shoulder. Lucy, calling him back to reality. He immediately stopped being fantasy fanboy and morphed right back into the soldier he was.

They weren't in a spaceship landing on a fascinating alien planet. They were on earth, stepping into a dangerous mission where millions of lives were at stake.

And from now on he had to be sharp and stay focused because Lucy's life and his depended on it.

*   *   *

LUCY touched Mike's shoulder to bring him back to earth. The first sight of the Palace did that to everyone. And watching the Palace take shape in the mist from a helicopter almost made her forget her fear. The power and the majesty of the place wiped everything but awe from your head.

How she'd loved exploring it with Paso, all the ancient hallways and forgotten rooms, teeming with history, real and unreal. Paso's *ama* loved recounting legends of the Palace, full of dragons and spirits and the frisky gods that populated the Himalayas before Buddhism, from the dawn of time itself.

She'd had three very happy years there in this quiet Himalayan kingdom, turning from a child to a young girl, taking the same lessons as Paso, studying for her English GCEs, which turned out to be useless when she had to repatriate to the States.

It hadn't occurred to her that it might be odd studying Shakespeare and Wordsworth, cellular mitosis and the Renaissance in a room with stone Snow Dragons looking down on them from every corner. Where the afternoon snack was *momos* and tea with yak butter, where the air smelled continuously of incense and where guards snapped to attention when lessons were over and they left the schoolroom.

Indeed, the straight, unadorned walls, bare hallways smelling of Lysol, and loud, shrill voices of the girls at her boarding school had made her deeply uneasy her first weeks after coming back to the States an orphan.

How she'd longed for the Palace with its miles of corridors lined with colorful rugs, each door a painted wooden sculptural work of art, an altar seemingly every ten feet. The Nhalans had a naturally soft and lilting speaking voice, which she missed, huddling in her bed at night with her pillow over her head, trying to drown out the brash, loud American voices by reciting prayer mantras.

She'd cried and cried over her dead parents, missing

them and Paso and the Palace fiercely. Until, finally, time and distance had made the Palace impossibly far-off and remote, more a dream than a memory.

And now she was back.

The helicopter landed, the big cabin rolling as it settled. Lucy stumbled on the uneven flooring and Mike put his arm around her waist, pulling her to him.

There was no question of falling down while he held her. The earth could crumble beneath her feet, and if he was holding her, she'd stay upright.

She marveled at how incredibly *hard* he was, like warm steel. And grounded. For a second, as she lost her balance, she'd leaned her entire weight against him, totally unexpectedly, at the moment the helicopter was shifting its massive bulk.

Any other man would have staggered a little at having the weight of an adult woman suddenly press against him on uneven footing. But Mike held her, completely steady, his legs compensating for the uneven footing like an old sailor at sea.

He was holding on to her very . . . tightly.

She was plastered up against him, like being up against a warm wall. One arm was around her waist, the other on her shoulder. He lifted the hand on her shoulder and tucked a lock of hair behind her ear, smiling at her warmly.

His body, the smile . . . they heated her up nicely and she smiled back. A perfect little moment out of time, enveloped in warmth and strength. A little human connection that was slightly more than simply from one human to another.

It was very definitely a male-female kind of moment, and she leaned her head against his shoulder, smiling. She felt a kiss against her hair and could almost feel his smile in the invisible gesture.

Nice. Very nice. She closed her eyes and snuggled for just a second, emptying her mind of everything, simply letting go. It had been a long time since she'd been held like this.

And then she remembered—it wasn't real. He wasn't her fiancé or boyfriend or even a friend, really. He was a soldier on an undercover mission, and part of the cover was acting like they were lovers. So obviously, a man would hold his fiancé closely after a tumultuous flight in a helicopter, would comfort her and kiss her.

Mike was playing a part and she wasn't. She'd genuinely bought into the embrace and welcomed it, and though a part of her could congratulate herself on sticking to her cover story, the other part of her, the real part that couldn't fool itself, knew that she'd reached out because of neediness.

Though the cover had to continue, the neediness had to stop. Right now.

She pulled back, gave Mike a big smile that had him narrowing his eyes, and reached up to kiss his cheek. "Thanks, darling," she said in a slightly overloud voice.

The ramp at the back lowered with a metallic thud that shuddered through the entire frame. Frozen air swirled into the cabin. If it had been chilly before, it was freezing now.

The soldiers in the helicopter filed down the ramp, lining up outside to form another honor guard for them.

Lucy pulled her coat more closely about her, put her arm through Mike's. "Let's go," she said.

Walking down the ramp, into the gelid winter mountain air, with the south wall of the Winter Palace right in front of her . . . Lucy let out a held breath.

With each step, it was déjà vu, only she wasn't eleven, the age she'd been when they first landed in Chilongo. She was seeing the scene before her through a woman's eyes and also through a young girl's eyes. The dizzying beauty carried the adult away almost as completely as it had the young girl.

The white walls of the Winter Palace rose so high they were lost in the mists settling gently down from the mountains. The curved gilded wooden rooftops were invisible from here. They had to be seen from down on the plain, from the central marketplace, in the sunshine, when the entire rooftop, several acres in size, glowed golden in the sunshine.

Even the Winter Palace's south terrace was outsized,

like everything else. Lucy felt dwarfed as she walked past the honor guard, now standing at attention, hands touching their ceremonial hats with the palms out, like the British. A hundred yards away stood a small group of people under a painted wooden portico, the gleaming temple with the golden Buddha barely visible in the darkness behind them.

Sensations bombarded her, almost overwhelmed her. The pungent scent of sandalwood incense that would be forever associated in her mind with Nhala. The biting, invigorating dry cold. The effects of the altitude, which were often described as a sickness, but actually just felt like being high, in all senses of the word. The faint sounds of the city, barely audible so high up.

Lucy walked slowly forward, Mike keeping pace with her. She moved at a ceremonial pace, quite aware that she was now in a traditional society, meeting a princess and under observation.

The Nhalans had an unusual capacity for joy, but in public and in ceremonial situations, they observed a quiet dignity that Lucy respected.

Any emotions running through her had to be tamped down. She was here for a reason, and it had nothing to do with the joy she felt at seeing Paso again.

There she was!

As they slowly crossed the huge stone expanse, as big as a city square, Lucy could make out individual figures waiting under the portico. Two men in military uniform, several attendants and . . . Paso.

Lucy's heart took a wild leap in her chest. If this hadn't been a formal occasion, she would have broken away to run to Paso and hug her tightly.

Thank God she didn't. Because as she slowly traversed the square, arm in arm with Mike, Paso's hand lifted slightly, palm up. A universal sign for *go slow*.

Okay. Lucy was close enough now to make out individual expressions and she was not reassured. Paso's lovely face was blank, completely void of any expression at all, well beyond the serenity a woman of the royal blood should show in public. She could have been a stone statue and not a beautiful, warm-blooded woman.

Keeping her own face blank, walking at a stately pace, Lucy drank in every detail of her friend. She'd been a lovely girl and she was now an extraordinarily beautiful woman. She was Lucy's height, exactly. They'd often joked about that. Being Lucy's height meant being taller than average in Nhala, while Lucy was just average in the United States.

The Nhalans were a small and graceful race.

It had shocked her so much, those first weeks in boarding school back in the States, to be surrounded by kids so tall they seemed alien.

There was nothing small and graceful about the man standing next to Paso. He was tall, powerfully built, face a series of granite slabs beneath a peaked khaki cap with a white dragon on the crown. General Changa.

Lucy watched him as she approached Paso, slowing surreptitiously so she could have a chance to study him. Mike slowed, too, naturally matching the pace of his long legs to hers.

Paso stood straight as a rod but slightly facing her right, away from the general, who kept flicking irritated glances her way. His face was cold, eyes colder. Reptilian eyes that didn't reflect any light. The few accounts of political events in Nhala that had escaped the general lockdown spoke of the general reopening the dungeons hundreds of feet beneath the ground. Dungeons that had been used five hundred years ago for unspeakable cruelty, then sealed off ever since.

Now open again.

Lucy had no trouble at all believing that. The general looked as hard and as dangerous as a cobra. She'd met a number of third world dictators in her childhood. They frightened her then and he frightened her now. They all shared a look of cold inhumanity, as if they were another race.

Lucy stopped ten feet from the Nhalan delegation and Mike stopped, too. He still held her arm, as if wanting to make a point of their engagement. She looked up at him, sketched a small smile and made an imperceptible movement with her arm. He dropped his hand, letting his arms drop naturally to his side. But Lucy noticed his fingers were curled, like a gunfighter's, ready for the fight if it came to that.

Lucy faced Paso, waiting for her lead.

Paso nodded to her, face blank, and sketched a light curtsy, ceremonial robe kissing the ground briefly as she dipped.

"Lucy Merritt," she said softly, in the perfect, lightly accented English Lucy remembered so well. "Welcome."

Hmm. Not welcome *back*.

Lucy curtsied. "Princess Paso. It is an honor to be in Nhala."

There was utter silence on the great terrace, the only sound that of the great torches crackling. The flames cast flickering shadows over Paso's face and the hard planes of the general's face.

Lucy stepped back two precise paces and gave the traditional Nhalan greeting, arms out, fist in fist, and bowed deeply.

To her utter surprise, Paso stepped forward, pulling something from her sleeve. A flower with white, fragile petals. Paso held it delicately by its stem and offered it to Lucy. "By Buddha's birth, my country thanks you for your service." Once Lucy took the flower by its stem, Paso dipped more deeply than before in a curtsy, her robe belling about her feet.

Lucy blinked, not knowing how to answer.

The general stepped forward. "Welcome to Nhala, Dr. Merritt. I am General Changa. We have set up a laboratory for you in the Summer Palace. We followed the instructions given by the Manuscripts Department of the Smithsonian, and I understand you have brought some tools of your own. You will let me know if you need lab assistants. I am certain you wish to see the manuscript. Two of my men will accompany you there—"

Mike held up a big hand. "Wait a moment, General

Changa. My fiancée has flown halfway around the world to help you restore this manuscript. I understand it is important to your people, but I must insist that she be allowed to rest. She is tired, cold and hungry."

The general's cold eyes snapped to Mike. His features tightened, his deep voice cold and commanding. "I am certain that Dr. Merritt—"

"Wishes to rest. Yes, she does." Mike's voice turned cold and commanding as well. "I am glad you understand that."

The two men stared at each other in a test of male wills. Mike wasn't backing down. The two all but sprouted antlers. The general inclined his head. "Of course, Mr., er . . ."

"Harrington." Mike beamed, morphing right back to clueless, genial American businessman. You could almost forget that a couple of seconds ago he'd sounded dangerous. "Michael Harrington. Call me Mike. Everyone does." He looked around at the torchlit scene, up at the walls disappearing into the misty sky, down at the brightly colored rugs laid down for the princess. "Beautiful place. Glad I decided to accompany Lucy, never been to this part of the world before. Farthest east I've ever been is Greece."

He grinned.

The general spoke softly and two officers came forward. "You will be escorted to your room." He fixed Lucy with his obsidian stare. "Dr. Merritt, I trust you will be rested enough to come to your laboratory tomorrow morning."

Paso's face tightened every time the general spoke.

Lucy pasted a smile on her face. Mike wasn't the only one who could be a clueless American. "Sounds fine, General. Around ten o'clock, say? I'm wondering whether Princess Paso—"

"The princess has little time for social activities. Her brother is very ill. I will escort her back to the King's Chambers. She insisted on being here to greet you, but her time is limited." He bowed, watching Paso's face. "Princess. It is time to rejoin your brother."

Paso's face was unreadable. Lucy noticed that she avoided having any part of her touch the general.

The general turned briefly to Lucy. "Dr. Merritt."

Lucy bowed her head. "General."

So that was the way of it. Not only was the general reducing a happy country to a state of sullen misery and harboring a bioweapons lab, he was threatening her friend Paso.

Lucy turned slightly and inclined her head again. "Princess."

Paso looked back at her out of opaque, unreadable eyes, and Lucy understood perfectly.

Whatever General Changa planned, it was going to be over her dead body.

*N*INE

NDOUMA lay in wait behind the huge bole of a cashew tree, spear at the ready. Across the leaf-strewn clearing, the branches of a small papaya plant shook as the bushpig rooted around for the sweet fruits that had fallen to the ground.

This was a very good day. Two hours before, Ndouma had skinned another bushpig caught in a snare an hour's walk away. He'd quartered the animal and stored the meat in netting hung from the branches of a eucalyptus tree. The meat from that bushpig and this one would keep his village fed for a week.

He was a master hunter, just as his father and his father before him had been. It was a gift of the gods. His head was filled with mental maps of animal hunting grounds, trails leading to watering holes, hidden valleys where roving herds of antelope could be culled.

His father had taught him all the invisible signs to follow prey and had taught him how to interpret his dreams. Last night Ndouma had had vivid dreams of dying animals and he knew today would be a good day for hunting.

There!

For a second, the bushpig's fleshy snout had peeked between the leaves. The bushpig turned back, and Ndouma could measure its size by the displacement of leaves. A big animal, as high as Ndouma's upper thighs, good for three days of eating. Together with the other bushpig, it represented so much meat they'd have to smoke some of it to keep the maggots out.

Now Ndouma could hear the snuffling sounds the bushpig was making as it ate. A good moment for the kill, as the animal would be paying less attention to its surroundings and could be taken unaware.

Ndouma rose from his crouch in a slow, seamless movement, as his father had taught him, bringing his spear arm back.

At the last second, in which his spear would fly across the distance between him and the bushpig and pierce the pig's heart, almost as a foreordained event, Ndouma was distracted by a small sound at his feet, like a person exhaling after holding his breath for a long time. A puff of air that shifted the leaves on the ground and distracted him just long enough for the bushpig to sense his presence and escape, squealing.

Ndouma downed his spear, disgusted, knowing that he'd be bringing only one bushpig into his village. He looked down at what had cost him several days' worth of meat and frowned. He crouched and studied it. Made by man, and men of the city at that. There were no handmade marks. This was made by machinery.

He'd seen machined artifacts before, but nothing like this. A glass cylinder held together by a shiny metallic clamp. Part of the cylinder had exploded; shards of shiny glass littered the ground. He poked around with his finger, careful to avoid the cutting edges of the glass. His grandfather had been thrown through a window on one of his rare trips into a city and had nearly bled to death.

These shiny things *cut*. They didn't stab or tear, they cut. Deep and sharp.

There was an odd smell in the air, something he didn't

recognize. That had to be man-made, too, because he knew all the smells of the jungle and could identify them easily. He didn't have a category for the smell; he only knew it wasn't natural. Like the smells of the copper mines, or the trucks that lumbered through roads at the edges of his tribe's territory.

Ndouma sighed and looked up at the sun. It would take him until late afternoon to get back to where he'd hung the quartered pig from the tree, cut the nets down and haul the meat into the village. He didn't have time to track another animal down.

Unease crept through him. This was not right.

The second pig should have been his.

In his mind's eye he'd seen it. The straight, powerful throw of the spear, the animal's squeals of surprise, then pain, the sounds tapering off quickly because Ndouma had been aiming directly for the heart. He was known far and wide as a marksman with his spear, and he and his family were always given the heart of his kills, with the sharp slice through the heart, to honor the accuracy of his throw.

It hadn't happened.

And yet—he'd dreamed of dead animals, always a harbinger of success in the hunt. It troubled him to have clear dreams in darkness that weren't echoed in sunlight. It was wrong. He'd followed his dreams all his life and trusted them as he trusted his eyes and his hands and his feet. He was even wearing his special ivory hunting amulet.

Troubled by the missed kill, Ndouma turned and made his way back to the first kill. At least he wouldn't be going back to the village empty-handed.

But it turned out to be more than an hour's walk. The sun had passed the treetops and was moving back to the earth when he finally tracked down the meat that was still hanging from the netting.

Ndouma's steps were dragging. He was sweating so hard drops were falling off him when he reached the tree. Chunk of meat were swaying from the branches.

He was hot, burning. He could hardly breathe from the

exertion of making his way back here, though he knew in his heart it was an easy walk.

He knew what he had to do—climb the trunk, crawl out onto the big tree limb and use the knife sheathed at his hip to cut the nets and let the chunks of meat fall to the leaf-covered ground.

But it was beyond him. He leaned one-handed against the huge tree trunk and looked up. And up and up. It seemed as if the treetops brushed the sun, higher than the buildings his cousins said existed in Lagos. Higher than the mountains.

It was impossible to climb.

Maybe he was bewitched. That was it. His amulet was no protection against witchcraft, which was the only explanation for his weakness. He fell to one knee and stayed there, head bowed, drops of sweat falling so quickly from his brow he could hear the spatter on the leaves.

All of a sudden, the world turned from the deep green of the forest and bright blue of the sky to red.

The Devil's work. This was clearly the Devil's work. Ndouma had to hurry back to the village and get his most powerful amulet, perhaps ask the medicine man for a cleansing ceremony. It involved bloodletting and was painful, but so was this.

His stomach hurt, as if he'd swallowed knives.

There was no question now of carrying the meat back. He'd be lucky to make it back himself. He knew the location and could describe it to his brothers. Seventy paces in the direction of the setting sun from the monkeys' watering hole. They could get the meat themselves.

He needed to be cleansed of the evil spirits. Now.

It was an hour's walk back to the village, and it took him three. The sun had long since disappeared behind the trees and almost all the light in the sky was gone when he stumbled into the central clearing. He'd long since lost the strength to wipe the sweat from his eyes and had made it by sheer doggedness, because he could find his way home literally blindfolded.

He stopped in the middle of the clearing, right outside

the chieftain's hut, hands on thighs, head down, panting. Sweat poured off his body and he felt as if he were on fire. His knees trembled and he tried to straighten them. A hunter like Ndouma didn't simply collapse to the ground. He had to stand straight, yet he couldn't.

For a moment he was able to get outside himself, outside the horrific spell that was burning him up inside, and wonder why no one came. The village was used to him coming home from a hunting expedition with precious bush meat, the kids capering around him, the elderly women looking up from their chores and smiling.

No one.

He opened his eyes, blinking against the sweat, and turned his head painfully. Any movement felt like turning his head inside thornbushes.

It was close to dinnertime; the entire village should be outside their huts, the women cooking, the men in conversation. Yet there was only silence.

He scanned as much as he was able, every movement of his head sending a red hot spike of pain through his brain.

No one. Emptiness.

Had a rival tribe come along and slaughtered his people? There had been no war with the Mbekeli since his grandfather's father's time, but perhaps that was the meaning of his dream?

Had all the animals been killed? Because there were no human sounds and no animal sounds. No sounds at all.

Only smells. The smell of meat cooking, only unlike any meat he'd ever smelled before.

Ndouma looked again and saw them. On the ground. His wife and mother, his daughters. His son, belly down in the dust, unmoving. He stumbled to his wife, gathered her lifeless body in his arms and called to the gods above to tell him why this had happened. No one responded.

He looked around desperately, seeing more bodies.

The chief and his wife. Beyond their hut, to the right, was a campfire, a body he couldn't recognize over it, as if he or she had fallen suddenly and had been unable to get up.

Blood around the heads, though he was unable to see any wounds. What could have done this? What kind of evil spirit could bring blood without wounds? What—

Ndouma suddenly jerked, his limbs flailing, completely outside his control. His stomach clenched mightily, as if he had been punched by a strong, invisible man. Maybe the same man who had killed his village?

He fell to his knees. An uncontrollable fountain of vomit spewed from his mouth, deeply red and thick. He could hardly breathe. His knees gave out and he kneeled in the dust and vomited again, the taste vile. The taste of death itself.

Even kneeling became too much for him, and he fell face-first into the dust, small puffs rising as his arms slapped the ground. He vomited directly onto the ground, so fast and thick the ground couldn't absorb it. He found himself breathing in the foul liquid and coughed it out. The cough turned into another bout of vomiting. He barely had the strength to turn his head before more hot, sour liquid poured out of his mouth.

It felt as if he were vomiting life itself.

This, surely, was a curse. Someone had cast a black magic spell over his village, which was already dead.

It was his last thought as his body convulsed once more, taking his final breath with it.

THE PALACE
CHILONGO, NHALA

Palace attendants dressed in rich, fluttering silks walked before them, leading them to their room.

Mike had been in the Pentagon plenty of times, but this building made the Pentagon look like the morgue of Corn Fields, Iowa. The Palace was enormous, of course, but he'd known that. Even a roughneck from Portland, Oregon, could figure out that a hundred acres of building was a lot of real estate. But where modern office buildings were spare and repetitive, it was as if the Palace were made up of a thousand buildings, each one different. Each corridor was painted a different vivid color, with temples or something temple-like every fifty feet or so. So much incense burned it gave him a headache.

He'd read the Palace had ten thousand statues, and he believed it, absolutely. There were statues everywhere, small, big, made of painted wood and brass and terracotta. Some of the Buddha, some of what looked like warriors of days gone by, some couples doing things he couldn't slow down enough to check out, but that was definitely on his to-do list. Looked interesting.

Looked like sex.

Don't think of sex, he told himself sternly. This was a mission and sex was off the table. Though sex *on* the table sounded pretty damned good. On the table, on a chair, on any of the billion and one garishly painted wooden trunks that lined the hallways.

Hell, even the braided cotton rugs lining the slate floors looked pretty good. Oh yeah, lay Lucy right down and . . .

He wrenched his mind back to business and was surprised at the real effort it took, like turning a rusted lug.

It seemed amazing to him that he was thinking of sex constantly, and at the same time it seemed amazing that he wouldn't. No one should have to withstand the temptation of Lucy Merritt. It went against every single rule in the US Army Manual.

Maybe this wasn't a mission at all. Maybe it was a new training hell. God knows the army had a shitload of dangerous training exercises up its sleeve, most of them with live fire.

So suppose they were testing his resolve, to see if he could resist temptation, and suppose he failed? They'd haul him before a court-martial, and he'd turn to the judge and point at Lucy and say—*Judge, what man is going to resist that? I rest my case.*

And of course the judge would dismiss the case.

Christ, pay attention to your surroundings, he admonished himself. He had an excellent sense of direction, but even he was getting lost. His watch was a GPS system, and he knew they were generally headed north, but that was it. There was no floor plan of the Palace existing on earth, the briefing he'd read on the flight over said. None. Or, it said primly, none that the NSA could find. Which meant none. Zip.

The NSA could map out the intestines of the Chairman of the Chinese Communist Party if it wanted to, and when the NSA said no plans were available, that's what they meant.

So Mike had to look sharp, keep his head and stay oriented, even though he had temptation itself by his side.

He chanced a look at her, saw how tired she was, and mentally kicked himself in the butt for his thoughts. Well, they weren't *thoughts*, really. More like images. Bright, Technicolor images, high-def. Just like his dad's brand-new plasma TV.

The images were crystal clear. Lucy smiling at him, kicking off her shoes. Lucy slowly taking off her sweater and sliding her pants down those long, slender legs. Lucy in bra and panties, which he just knew would be these frothy lacy sexy confections, reaching to unhook the bra and . . .

He gritted his teeth and willed all the blood rushing to his groin to go right back up into his head so he could think straight.

Now was not the time for this. And anyway, Lucy was looking dead on her feet, and anything but a shower and a meal was off limits.

He bristled when he thought of that two-bit dictator fuckhead Changa wanting her to start work right away, after having flown halfway around the world.

At the time, Mike had reacted strongly, pretending to himself that it wasn't good for the op for her to be setting off so soon for the lab; they needed to regoup inside the Palace, there were things to discuss, he needed to sweep their room first . . . yada yada yada.

Noise.

The truth was that a white-hot flash of pure rage had

shot through him as Changa made to escort her to the lab. He'd bit back the words he wanted to say—*Touch her and I will break your fucking arm, you son of a bitch*—so hard he'd nearly cracked a tooth.

If the fuckhead had touched her, Mike would have taken him down in a second and probably been shot, certainly arrested. So it's a good thing he had won that staring contest, because otherwise, given what he knew about Changa's gentle democratic rule, he'd probably be shackled to a dungeon wall right now, pissing into the rushes at his feet.

Not good for the op.

He looked back down at Lucy, who somehow seemed right at home here in the Palace. She was holding that white flower the princess had given her, twirling it under her nose.

They followed their guides around another corner and Mike was officially lost. "Do you know where we are?"

She looked up at him, and he nearly stumbled over a lump in the carpet covering an irregular slate. God, her eyes were so fucking beautiful, a light blue gray, a darker blue around the rim of the pupils.

Shit, she'd said something while he'd been mooning. "What?"

"I said, we lived in the Summer Palace section, about a mile away, but still part of the building. This is the Winter Palace. Mostly bureaucrats and palace attendants lived and worked here. We stayed on the other side. But to answer your question, yes, I know where we are."

"How far do you think—" he had begun, when the two attendants stopped in front of an enormous, garishly painted door.

"We're here," she said.

One of the men took out a huge iron key, like one of those that opened the castle in a Disney movie about princesses, inserted it into an enormous lock with a back plate as big as a table mat and turned it.

For such a huge door, it had good hinges, which was going to be useful if they had to sneak in and out. Mike had been prepared to steal some yak butter if necessary to oil the hinges, but it wasn't going to be necessary.

The attendant indicated with a graceful wave of his hand. "Dr. Merritt. Mr. Harrington. Your quarters."

Mike was nearly blinded by the colors of the room visible from the corridor. "Mike," Lucy said quietly, and he stepped inside.

Every color on earth was in the huge room, bigger than most apartments. All the walls were covered with colorful frescoes. There were Buddhas, yes, sitting and standing and thinking and smiling in elaborately painted golden frames, but also dragons, dragons everywhere, and mythical beasts and flowers and fantastical landscapes.

The floors were covered in brightly colored rugs, the windows had deep yellow silk curtains. Intricately carved wooden furniture everywhere and . . . Mike gulped. Against the opposite wall was a huge bed. Enormous bed. The biggest bed he'd ever seen, big enough to put Hugh Hefner's to shame.

With a carved and painted headboard, gilt frame, huge silk pillows, painted birds, carved dragons and acres of embroidered silk bedspread.

And the instant he saw it, every other aspect of the room fled from his mind because he could see, so clearly, Lucy in that bed, dark shiny hair spilled over the silk pillows, slender arm out, beckoning to him . . .

Mike closed his eyes and swallowed because dammit, he had just swelled erect. This was so bad on so many levels it wasn't even funny.

He was on a mission, a highly dangerous one. True, he was here basically as muscle, but he was necessary muscle. He was here to protect Lucy, and he wasn't going to be able to do that if he was going to get a hard-on every time he thought of her.

She was gorgeous and he liked her. Actually, he liked her more the more time he spent with her. It would be better if he liked her less.

This unexpectedly powerful effect on his libido was

dangerous and could get her killed. She deserved better muscle than someone who got erect every time she breathed. He was going to get her killed if he didn't watch out.

She wasn't some pretty woman he met in a bar. She was his op and she was doing something hard and dangerous for her country. It was his job to keep her safe.

His eyes roamed once more over the room, this time avoiding that bed. Someone was very fast. Their suitcases had been delivered and emptied, the clothes hung neatly from hangers in a big wooden closet whose doors had been left open. A royal courtesy, as in Buckingham Palace. And, of course, an opportunity to go through their bags.

Lucy walked the servants to the door and bowed. They bowed back, and one of them said something to her in a low, musical language. She answered back in the same language and closed the huge door behind them.

"What did they say?" he asked.

"Dinner's coming soon."

She smiled at him and reached up on tiptoe to kiss his cheek, whispering inaudibly, "Can you sweep for bugs?"

He smiled back, tucked a lock of her dark, shiny hair behind her ear and kissed the soft skin just under the ear. "Yeah," he breathed without moving his lips.

She pulled away just in time, because the temptation to let his lips just linger there was enormous. "I'm going to take a shower and there'll be time for you to take one, too. Wash the trip off us."

When she disappeared behind a huge, carved wooden door, Mike sniffed himself and winced. This was one of those female-male mysteries he was never, ever going to solve. They'd taken the exact same trip, spent the exact same number of hours in a plane or helicopter. So how was it that she smelled like spring and he smelled like a goat had died in his crotch?

He was going to have to solve this some other time. Now he needed to know if Changa had bugged the room.

Mike picked up his empty suitcase, stored it in a corner as if simply getting it out of his way, and casually palmed what looked like a decorative element in the handle. It was a miniature, very powerful signal detector with a radius of a hundred feet. If it found a signal source, it vibrated instead of beeping.

Mike walked slowly around the room, picking up objects, fingering silks and sweeping for bugs. The device in his hand remained inert. At the end of fifteen minutes, he was as certain as he could be that there were no listening devices in the room. There wasn't even a phone.

As far as vidcams were concerned, he was also certain that there were none. Covert vidcams were harder to install than people thought. The walls here were thick and ancient, one solid block without any modern ports of egress such as air-conditioning or heating vents. As a matter of fact, there weren't even radiators. Heat radiated from a green enameled wood-burning stove in the far corner, and several braziers lit with coal and some aromatic herbs emanated warm, scented air.

He'd just finished his third visual inspection of the walls when the bathroom door opened and fragrant steam billowed out.

Then Lucy appeared, lit by the bathroom light from behind, as if on a stage. Oddly enough, she hadn't put on a nightgown. She was dressed in black from head to foot. He'd been looking forward to seeing her in a nightgown.

Her dark, shiny hair had curled up from the steam and fell to her shoulders in glossy ringlets. Her ivory pale skin had a rosy undertone now from the hot water, and she simply looked luscious enough to eat.

As if picking up on his thoughts, a knock sounded at the door and two servants rolled in a stainless-steel cart, looking incongruously modern in this ancient room. Steel domes covered big earthenware plates, and the fragrant scents of good food filled the air. Silently, the servants carted a big heavy wood table to the center of the room, brought two carved wooden chairs, transferred the food to the table, bowed and left, having never spoken a word.

Lucy crossed her arms over her pretty breasts and looked at him and then, pointedly, at the bathroom.

Okay, he got it. No food while smelling like he did. He would be allowed food once he'd washed.

Obediently, he loped off to the bathroom, grabbing the toiletry kit someone at Christians in Action had packed for him back in Langley.

When he opened the door he had an *oh, fuck* moment. Steam still billowed, soft and fragrant, and it arrowed straight to all the male lobes in his brain and pinged them. Hard.

On a wooden shelf was the reason why. An ungodly number of lotions and creams and perfumes and things he didn't even recognize were lined up in a neat row.

For some reason, they entranced him.

For most of his adult life he'd traveled with toothbrush, toothpaste, soap, a straight razor, shaving cream and brush— his beard was too heavy for an electric shaver, and anyway, he was often in places where there was no reliable source of electricity. That was all he carried. And often, as in the Granites training cycle, shaving went by the wayside.

This was an entirely different life.

He fingered some of the lotions curiously, his hands feeling big and awkward as he touched them. Every bottle was pretty and, even stoppered, smelled nice. Everything in the bathroom smelled nice. Smelled of woman.

All the blood in his body rushed right back down to his dick.

Oh, God. He quietly bounced his forehead off the tiles, hoping the tiny bite of pain might take his mind off the idea of Lucy in here, naked. Washing under the shower. Smoothing on lotions, bending, turning . . .

Naked. Oh, Jesus.

Every cell in his body was alive to her ghostly presence, as if her womanhood were still here, something she'd left behind to torment him. If she had, she'd done a really good job of it. He could hardly think of anything else but her.

To distract himself, he opened his own elegant blue leather toiletries kit, packed for him by some CIA flunkie, and simply stared inside.

Apparently, Michael Harrington was the male version of

Lucy. He rooted around inside the neatly packed bottles and tubes, having had no clue that they existed. But they did. He didn't know any man who'd have the *time* to use all this crap. Jesus. Moisturizing pre-shave gel, moisturizing post-shave gel, plain moisturizer, one for day and one for night. *Eye moisturizer.* What the fuck was that? It was a cream. Were you supposed to squeeze it in your eyes when they got dry? Hand lotion. Perfumed shower gel. Body lotion. Foot lotion. Teeth whitener. An amazingly full manicure set with scarily sharp implements. Three kinds of aftershaves, one for morning, one for daytime and one for the evening. He opened that one and his head reared back.

Jesus. He could fell livestock if he put too much of this crap on.

He brought out a bar of very expensive-looking elegantly wrapped soap. The tasteful beige wrapper assured him it was hand-milled and made of the finest natural ingredients. He also took out a shampoo that assured him that it, too, was made of the finest natural ingredients and would enhance the color of his hair, leaving it soft and shiny.

The bathroom, like the bedroom, was huge and ancient. The fixtures were simple and modern, but not über-modern like those bowl-shaped sinks stuck on top of slabs of marble you found in hotel rooms nowadays. There was an old-fashioned white porcelain sink, a toilet and a shower that had been attached to the ancient walls. White tiles had been applied to the walls up to about a foot below the ceiling, obscuring what were probably priceless frescoes, which would have been a real pity if the whole palace hadn't had about a billion acres of priceless frescoes. So maybe a few feet could be spared to allow Captain Mike Shafer—aka Michael Harrington—to have a hot shower.

The shower stall was even more insidious. He could smell Lucy everywhere in here; the hot water felt like fingers caressing him. It was sensory overload and further proof if he needed it that he'd spent way too much time in the field these past few years.

Mike looked down at himself, the water making the

thick hairs on his chest flatten out and aim down to the one part of his anatomy that wasn't flattening out and definitely wasn't aimed down.

What the hell could he do?

He could take care of it himself, of course. His fist usually did the trick just fine when there wasn't a woman around. But this time it wasn't a question of just getting an itch out of his system, thinking about some generic woman.

His dick wanted *her*, Lucy. Just thinking about her, here where the very walls seemed imbued with the smell of her, made him swell even bigger. There was no way he could go out into the bedroom like this. He'd taken into the bathroom with him the very elegant and very expensive navy blue silk pajamas the nameless CIA bureaucrat had so thoughtfully provided. Those pajama bottoms would stick out like a tent if he went out in this condition. About the only thing that could keep his dick down was his tightest pair of jeans, a useful fact he'd known since junior high. Pity his tightest jeans were back in his duffel bag in the semi-empty apartment right outside Fort Hood.

Fist no. Jeans no.

The only thing left was to think his hard-on down.

Okay, that's easy. Think of General Changa, that motherfucker who was turning his country into a military dictatorship. Think of those cold, black eyes. Think of rumors of the ancient dungeons in the Palace being reopened because they were so deep, and the walls were so thick, screams went unheard.

Okay. We're going right down, now.

Now think of this motherfucker either alone or in tandem with another motherfucker operating a bioweapons lab that had basically discovered a Doomsday Bug that had killed one US operative in a horrific way and that was about to be unleashed to the world.

And now take all that and imagine all that evil aimed at Lucy, at that beautiful woman who had accepted walking into this situation. Imagine Changa with a trembling Lucy in his hands . . .

It worked. He went down like a deflated balloon.

Feeling grim, working out his schedule for the next couple of days, Mike dried off and put on the superexpensive pajamas. They felt weird, but he knew he wasn't going commando in bed as he usually did.

Mike pushed open the bathroom door and the smells of food now invaded the room. Fine. If he couldn't satisfy one appetite, he was going to satisfy another. He was starving.

Lucy smiled at him and started serving him.

Her own plate was still empty.

"You didn't have to wait for me." She must be just as hungry as he was.

"That's okay. I liked the idea of company for a change."

Hmm. So she didn't usually eat with company? That just confirmed Mike's considered opinion that American men had all turned into wusses and idiots. You don't let a woman like this get away.

He looked down into his bowl, recognizing it instantly. Rice and lentils. Gah. He'd once dated a vegetarian, and he'd overdosed on rice and lentils. But—it was warm food and he was really hungry.

One bite and he smiled. This was miles away from Sarah's "food preparation," which was what she called cooking. What she did with food was a crime.

"Good?"

"Yeah." Surprisingly good.

"*Do bhat.* It's a staple dish here."

"Do they use yak butter?" Mike asked, looking into his soup. In his weeklong Himalayan climb years ago there'd been yak butter in everything, including the tea. One of his climbing mates had puked when he found out, which Mike thought was really dumb.

"Probably." She ate beautifully, manners delicate. She looked up suddenly, gauging him. "Does that bother you?"

He nearly snorted, stopped himself just in time. "Nah. When I'm hungry, I'll eat just about anything that's not poison. And don't forget I've spent years in Uncle Sam's

service. I've survived months on MREs. If that didn't disgust me, nothing will."

She lifted her eyebrows. "MREs?"

"MREs. Meals Ready to Eat. They all taste like sh—"
His lips clamped shut. "Er . . . terrible. The chicken tastes
like beef and the beef tastes like mildly burned rubber."
And they all gummed you up but good. When you were out
in the field dining on Uncle Sam's finest cuisine, you could
forget the regular dumps of home.

"Well, try this." Lucy reached over and ladled something else into his bowl. She sat back and watched him, the
way you'd settle back for a good film on TV.

Curious, Mike lifted a spoonful to his mouth, sniffed it.
His eyes met hers. "Chili peppers, eh?"

She smiled, the first genuine smile of amusement he'd
seen from her and it nearly bowled him over. Man, for a
smile like that he'd eat a ton of chili peppers.

"You think I'm not going to be able to take it?"

Her head tilted, studying him. "Well, you're very tough,
anyone can see that. But Nhalan chili peppers are hot, and
this particular dish, *sha phon*, is, um, known for its spici-
ness. Beef stewed in butter and garlic. And, of course,
chilis."

"Makes strong men tremble?"

The smile was a grin now. Man, he needed to make her
smile more often.

"Indeed."

"Okay. But I'll have you know that one of my best
friends is a Texican, and he says his chili is off the charts.
Literally. Apparently there's this scale to measure the hotness of chili peppers, and his chili gets to a couple hundred
thousand. But I eat it regularly, no problem."

"Okay." She nodded at his spoon. "Dig in then, macho
man."

Mike really liked spicy food. He was looking forward to
this. He happily put a spoonful in his mouth, and the top of
his head came off.

He didn't even chew, he just swallowed in self-defense,

and felt a nuclear explosion go off down his gullet and into his stomach.

Lucy was calmly eating the dish, showing every sign of enjoyment. Mike was sure his face was red and his eyes were bulging.

"The first bite is always the hardest," she said, though she didn't show any signs of distress at all. "Just take a little rice to soak up the capsicum oil," she moved a small bowl of white rice to his side of the table, "and let the taste settle in your mouth. Each bite gets easier, and you'll love it by the last bite. If you're still conscious."

Let the taste fucking *settle*? When his mouth was burning up? Trying to be cool and smooth, trying not to gobble the rice, Mike found that the taste did sort of . . . settle. And it wasn't half-bad. There were some other tastes in there, too, he didn't recognize. Something minty or peppery. And maybe some cloves?

He only knew he had to take at least another bite or he'd lose face with Lucy. Daintily and prettily, she'd almost finished her bowl.

He put another bite in his mouth and found that he could actually chew a couple of times without detonating.

Lucy picked up some rice with her chopsticks and dipped a sticky ball in the chili sauce. "You were talking about the Scoville scale." He looked at her blankly. "The scale that measures the hotness of chili peppers? These peppers come from Bangladesh and they measure one million on that scale. I grew up eating this stuff. Congratulations, Mike. You just passed the Tough Guy test."

He had. By the time his chopsticks hit the bottom of the bowl and, contrary to expectations, his mouth hadn't blown up, he was enjoying it.

They shared a small bottle of excellent wheat beer, pale yellow and delicious. Mike was feeling replete, tired in a good way, ready for bed. Or the floor.

There was a pot of strong green tea. He poured some in a glass with a metal handle and slid it over to Lucy. "I can bunk down on the floor, no problem."

"Nonsense," she said and sipped.

Despite himself, his heart pumped a little faster. "No really. There are rugs. I've slept on worse, believe me."

All amusement had fled her face. She leaned forward and spoke softly. "Firstly, you're not going to sleep as well on the floor as on that bed, and I need for you to be rested and alert. We're in a difficult position, and at some point you're going to have to make a trek up in the mountains to retrieve the flash drive and come back alive, and it has to be done right under the noses of General Changa's men. That's not going to be easy. Secondly, there are going to be cleaning ladies reporting back, and they're going to be able to tell whether two people slept in the bed or not. No sense arousing suspicion unnecessarily. And thirdly, that bed is big enough to grow corn in. We'll be sleeping with about five feet separating us."

Not if I have anything to say about it, Mike thought, then was instantly ashamed of himself. Lucy Merritt, girly girl, manuscript restorer, was being more professional on a mission than he was, and he was a professional soldier.

"Well, I'm about ready to turn in." He eyed her clothes. "What about you?"

"Not yet. I still need to meet with the princess this evening."

"What?" His voice had been too loud. He lowered it. "What? What do you mean? She barely spoke to you out there on that terrace."

Lucy examined his face carefully. "Did you see the way General Changa was watching her? Like a mongoose watches a rabbit? She was protecting me in the only way she could, by pretending coldness and distance. He wouldn't have any reason to believe that we were friends. When—" she hesitated a moment, then continued. "When the Palace burned, he was a lieutenant stationed in the north. That's part of his myth—that he comes from the north. There's an old Nhalan legend called the Snow Dragon. Nhalans believe that thousands of years ago they ruled over all the Himalayas and were slowly reduced to living in what is essentially a small valley. So the legend is that one day a great dragon, the Snow Dragon, will rise from the north and restore Nhala to its past greatness."

"That's what the manuscript is about, right?"

She sighed. "I imagine. It's undoubtedly a fake, but I can stretch out its 'restoration' for as long as you need. Anyway, Changa is trying to wear the mantle of the Snow Dragon. Marrying the last of the royal blood would help a lot in that."

"Paso," Mike said.

"Yes. If Jomo passes away, she will be the last of her line. If Changa marries her and they have sons, they will be of royal blood." Her beautiful face was somber. "I don't know what he thinks he'll get by using bioweapons; it doesn't make sense. But he's got a hot lab, and a manuscript tailor-made to suggest he's the Snow Dragon. If he marries the princess, no one will be able to stop him."

"What does Paso plan?"

"I have no idea. That's why I need to talk to her."

"Whoa, whoa." Mike held his hands up in a time-out gesture. "Just where are you meeting her and when? Did she slip you a piece of paper or something? As I recall, the two of you never touched."

"We didn't have to. Do you remember she greeted me 'by Buddha's birth'?"

Mike nodded.

"It might have sounded like a traditional Nhalan greeting, but it wasn't. I'd never heard the expression before. But Buddha was born after a ten-month gestation, so she wants to meet at ten o'clock. And that flower she gave me? It's a fairly rare kind of snowdrop that only grows above a certain altitude and under the branches of a Himalayan yew tree. It's cultivated in the Palace Orangerie, a sort of greenhouse. So she wants to meet at ten in the greenhouse." Lucy checked her watch and stood. "I'd better get going if I want to be on time. You stay here, I should be back in about an hour."

"No, no way." Mike stood, too. "There's no way you're going to that meeting alone."

Lucy's face stilled, her tone was cold. "I beg your pardon? Why not?"

Mike's brain froze. Simply stopped functioning. He couldn't think above the clanging warning bells in his head. There was no way he was going to let her step into possible danger, but he needed to say that in a way that didn't push her buttons.

He tried frantically to reason it out, but the cogs weren't working. His mind simply whirred emptily, no words occurring to him. But there were pictures in his head, oh yeah. Very clear ones, the worst one of a dead Lucy in a pool of blood with a coldly triumphant Changa standing over her. That one messed with his head so much he couldn't even talk.

The silence stretched out. With a sound of impatience Lucy moved toward the door, and Mike stepped in front of her, getting right into her face. She was wearing flat shoes, and he towered over her, using his height deliberately to intimidate her.

"Mike," she said quietly. "Get out of my way."

"No." He set his jaw.

"Get. Out. Of. My. Way." Each word was punctuated by a sharply tipped nail of her index finger poking holes in his chest.

She could fucking punch holes in him with an ice pick. He wasn't moving.

He drew in a deep breath and willed his head into action.

"No," he said. "Think about it. If you're found wandering the halls alone, it's going to look suspicious. But if you're found sort of strolling around arm in arm with me, it will just look like we're jet lagged and you're showing me around the Palace. We weren't told to stay in our rooms. No one will think twice about it."

She blinked. "That makes sense," she said slowly.

Mike let out his breath. He'd been very stupid and he wasn't a stupid man. He'd been around women long enough to know for a fact that smart women did not like being told what to do. He *knew* that the way he knew the sun rose in the east. So why had he just issued his order like some tinpot dictator, knowing it would raise her hackles?

That image of a hurt or dead Lucy had just switched the thinking part of his head right off, and he'd been left with instinct. And his instincts now were those of a warrior. He'd stepped in front of her exactly the way you'd push a comrade out of the line of fire.

Act now, explain later.

That didn't usually work too well with women.

He was very lucky that Lucy was not just a smart woman but a sane one, too. A lot of women turned mildly insane when they felt an obey-me-or-else button had been pushed. Not Lucy, thank God.

"Yeah," he said quickly. "So let's go for a stroll that will just happen to take us past the whatever it's called, the greenhouse, just two clueless tourists. Give me a minute to get dressed, okay?"

She nodded and he lunged for the closet, dressing fast just in case she changed her mind, because he knew one thing and that was that she wasn't walking out there alone in the middle of the night with possibly trigger-happy guards around. Not an option. He'd tie her to the bed first. So he was really happy this was going to be done peacefully.

His second instinct was to tell her to stay put and he'd go to the appointment, but that was a guaranteed butting-heads moment. And, if he was honest with himself, he knew that he'd accomplish less than she would. It was entirely likely that the princess wouldn't even talk to him. And they needed intel.

Mike found himself in a dilemma that had never happened to him before. Soldiering was a really straightforward business. At least the kind that he did was. He rarely went in undercover. He went into the field in uniform with a brief to wipe out the bad guys. Not easy to do but easy to understand.

There were never any countermanding considerations,

except for the pissy rules of engagement, and they were written out. He commanded men who were well trained, well armed and who knew how to look after themselves

This kind of situation was brand-new to him and he didn't like it. Because while he absolutely understood the imperatives of their mission—he would never forget the sight of that poor man literally vomiting his guts out then disappearing in a cloud of dust—he also found himself unable to accept danger to Lucy. To this beautiful woman who could rise above her fears.

Jesus, he was a mess.

But a chic mess, he found, as he dressed quickly in some dark-colored clothes he pulled out of the closet. Designers duds, *très* elegant. In seconds, he was back at the door where Lucy was waiting for him, having turned her back to allow him privacy as he dressed.

She looked up at him. "Smile," she ordered.

What the . . . He scowled.

"Smile," she repeated firmly. "Remember at all times who you are. You are Mike Harrington. You are a successful investment banker. You are rich, your job is secure, you're healthy, engaged to me. You're on an adventure in this country you've never been to before. So that's your persona—rich, contented businessman. Clueless, nice, happy." She reached up to smooth out the lines on his forehead. "*Happy*, I said. If you go out right now, looking like this, you're endangering the mission and you're endangering me. So look the part. Empty your mind and fill it back up with the personality of Michael Harrington."

She was absolutely right. They were out on a limb, way exposed. In enemy territory without backup. Looking for clues to a mortal danger that was going to be well guarded by soldiers led by a strongman.

Lucy opened the door and smiled up at him. He gave her a blinding smile in return, trying to look as if he'd suddenly been able to Botox all his worry lines away.

"Well, if we can't sleep, we might as well go for a walk, don't you think, darling?" Her voice was light, amused.

He schooled his own voice to lazy pleasure. "Absolutely, honey. Let's explore a little. Never lived in a palace before. My partners are gonna want a complete rundown."

They walked out at a leisurely pace, arm in arm, barely glancing at the soldier who'd been stationed outside their door. Surreptitiously, Lucy directed Mike to the right, and he followed her.

Mike hadn't even glanced at the soldier, but he had excellent peripheral vision and he was reassured by what he'd seen. The man was sitting in a chair, which was good news in itself. No soldier posted to serve serious guard duty would do so sitting down. Just wasn't done. Mike had seen a thousand Marines guarding prisoners and potentates and they never sat, never. They hardly even blinked.

The guy outside their room had been dressed in some kind of male sari belted kind of thing, lots of yellow and green silk. A ceremonial guard. Mike hadn't even seen a weapon besides a small dagger in a silk sheath.

Good. So Changa wasn't taking them seriously.

He and Lucy strolled arm in arm down the corridor. He murmured nonsense words in her ear and she gave a light laugh, as if he'd said something amusing.

He glanced at his watch. Nine forty p.m., local time. Two forty p.m. Zulu time. They had twenty minutes to make it to the greenhouse. And he was expected to file a report, encrypt it and send it via his special comms unit as a single burst of ultra-low-frequency waves at 4 p.m. Zulu.

They turned the corner into a magnificent, enormous, empty corridor. Lucy dropped his arm and speeded up.

She kept herself in shape, that was for sure. A quick walk was nothing for Mike, he could walk fast forever, but most people he knew who weren't soldiers were out of shape and got winded easily. Not Lucy. She was speed walking, moving toward what seemed to him to be the heart of the building.

"You know where you're going?"

They were at a sort of intersection. The corridors were so huge they were as big as small town streets. Lucy glanced down the left corridor and then the right, hesitated just a second then turned left. "Yeah, I know where I'm going. Paso and I spent a couple of years running wild through the Palace. They've made a few changes, it sometimes throws me off. But we're headed in the right direction, don't worry."

"To the greenhouse?"

"The Orangerie," she corrected. "Built by a Frenchman in 1737. It's going to be really warm in there. We're overdressed."

"Well, we're not overdressed for out here."

"No."

Unlike their quarters, the corridors were unheated and chilly by normal standards. Mike wasn't bothered by the cold, and neither did Lucy appear to be.

They'd been walking for nearly twenty minutes. It was almost ten o'clock. Lucy was standing still at a corner, checking all the features, when she saw something she recognized and took off again.

She seemed to have taken minor routes. The only person they'd encountered had been an elderly lady carrying a tray, who hadn't even glanced at them.

"We're almost there," she said and Mike tensed.

Lucy seemed to be absolutely convinced that Princess Paso was still her friend, but Mike hadn't seen anything that convinced him of that. Her gaze had been as cold and as opaque as the general's. And the hidden message might not have been a message at all. Lucy knew Nhalan, but she hadn't been in the country for fifteen years. Maybe *by Buddha's birth* had become some kind of common greeting in the meantime, like, say, *yo*. And maybe that flower was cultivated everywhere now.

And maybe they were walking into a trap. Goddammit, he didn't even have a weapon.

Lucy stopped outside a set of truly huge doors. They'd moved generally in a southern direction, though with frequent deviations, and by Mike's calculations they were now at the outer southern wall.

If only they'd been able to find a floor plan, he could

have pinpointed their location to within a foot with GPS. But the only map they had was in Lucy's beautiful head.

She knocked lightly at head height on the right-hand panel of the enormous door stretching at least twenty feet high. Before he could stop her, Lucy bore down on an enormous brass handle, opened the door and nearly ran inside. Mike followed right behind. He moved fast when he heard Lucy cry out.

$\mathcal{T}$EN

"FOR you, sir." A young assistant left a piece of paper on his desk and exited quietly. Christ, he looked about twelve, and yet he was probably the same age as Montgomery had been when he'd been recruited right out of college. Ten thousand years ago, it felt like.

He rubbed his eyes, making them even redder. They felt as if his eyelids were made of sandpaper. He was on his fifty-sixth hour straight without sleep, and it didn't look like sleep would be on the agenda any time soon.

As DD/O, his office came equipped with everything—including a well-appointed bathroom and a very comfortable sofa bed. A closet held several changes of clothes, including several sets of pajamas and tennis outfits. He could lift up his phone and order an excellent meal with a decent French wine, a massage, or he could drop down to the spacious in-house gym and go for a swim or relax in the steam rooms.

He'd done them all in his time. Sometimes crises lasted days. He was fully equipped to face even weeks without leaving his office, but also without roughing it.

He was roughing it now, never leaving his desk, simply

because there was no way he could leave it. Intel was streaming in on an hourly basis.

And now this.

He looked down at what the courier—who undoubtedly had a PhD in either political science or contemporary history or Arabic studies—had left him. A flash drive and a small piece of paper on which was printed a series of numbers and a message.

This was sent to us by the South African National Intelligence Service.

Montgomery frowned. The US didn't have close relations with the South African NIS. Maybe, and the thought chilled him, the intel was too much for NIS to handle.

He inserted the flash drive into the USB port at the side of his Powerbook, and when the field came up, he carefully typed in the twelve-digit code. Instantly, there was a beep and a file name came up.

Stop Cold. Nigeria.

Nigeria? Montgomery thought. Christ. He rubbed his tired eyes again and clicked on the file.

A video file opened crisply. Some kind of surveillance monitor, panning slowly over the canopy of an equatorial forest. Underneath were latitude and longitude data and the date and the time. Three p.m. yesterday. He had no idea if that was local time or EST. The camera moved slowly, on the underbelly of a drone.

Did the NIS operate surveillance satellites? He made a note to ask.

And then everything else fled his mind and he looked forward, eyes locked onto the screen.

A large clearing. He estimated it at five hundred yards across. Small, well-maintained huts on beaten earth. Several campfires burning.

And bodies, everywhere.

At least a hundred corpses fallen to the ground, heads ringed with red. Looking more closely, Montgomery could see that one of the bodies had fallen into a small campfire and was burning. The quality of the video was first-rate, and Montgomery thanked whoever arranged these things up there—he'd long ago stopped believing in a benevolent God—that they still couldn't reproduce smell together with vision.

He forced himself to study the screen carefully and saw signs that the men, women and children had dropped suddenly. He could see dark clouds of flies congregated over the masses of vomited blood.

A few held something in their hands. He peered more closely, touched the screen for a zoom shot. The picture went out of focus then focused in again, more tightly. Several of the tribesmen held small crystal cylinders in their hands. Montgomery couldn't tell how long they were until he noticed several glints on the ground.

He zoomed in even closer, frowning. More cylinders, scattered around on the beaten earth. About an inch long. Some had a pattern of streaked dust around them, as if a small air explosion had gone off.

Undoubtedly then, there was a release mechanism that was air fired, shooting the virus into the air.

He could feel his heart pounding heavily in his chest, could feel the individual cardiac muscles pulsing, as all the permutations of what he was seeing occurred to him.

This was a test run, on a circumscribed population. And it was successful.

A man came stumbling into the clearing from the north, a tribesman. He staggered, looking around with wide eyes. The resolution of the screen was so good Montgomery could clearly read his expression—one of absolute terror. He kneeled next to a woman, perhaps his wife, and held her in his arms, looking up at the sky, his mouth a perfect O of horror, his sweaty face shining under the African sun.

He was shouting something and Montgomery was glad there was no sound. There would be no intel to be had, just raw human pain. The man wasn't talking. He was screaming his despair at the sky, and there was nothing to be got out of him but sadness.

Montgomery felt that out of humanity he should turn his

face away to preserve the man's dignity, but it was war-time, and human dignity is one of the first luxuries to go when man raises his hand against man.

The only live man left, possibly the last of his tribe, rose to his feet and roamed through the camp. Montgomery watched as he stumbled his way from corpse to corpse, desperation clear in the strong, slumped shoulders, big arms held listlessly to the sides.

Suddenly, the man dropped to his knees and Montgomery's heart skipped a beat.

That was happening more and more lately. 'Extrasystolic arrhythmia' his cardiologist called it, a symptom of an ailing heart. Though this time it wasn't a physical phenomenon but a reaction to what he was seeing. For he knew what was coming next.

And, indeed, the African's head bowed and a bright red stream of vomit spewed from his mouth, soaking instantly into the dust. It was painful to watch. Another bout of vomiting and the man fell face-first into the dust, vomiting again. His movements were now weak, more twitches than gestures.

Montgomery watched, face impassive, as the man died.

There was a counter at the bottom of the screen giving the percentage of time elapsed in white numerals. He'd only watched 10 percent of the video. He clicked onto the counter and scrolled it slowly to the right, the white numbers flicking rapidly.

10%-20%-35%-50%-75%-90%-100%.

As green filled the field from left to right, the bodies on the ground in far-off Africa began to shrink, as if being mummified. Within half an hour, all the bodies were dust the wind whisked away, leaving only red circles in the dirt, some scraps of cloth and various implements.

In the end, at the very last, Montgomery watched as the last man's body started to shrink. The video was over, but he knew what the man would shortly become. Dust.

It was as if no one had ever lived in the clearing.

Montgomery had been in the intelligence business for a long, long time. For all of his life, his greatest fear had been of a Broken Arrow, a nuclear incident. He'd thought of it daily, been woken up gasping from a nightmare of a mushroom cloud. He'd dedicated himself heart and soul to ensuring that a Broken Arrow never happened, and so far, it hadn't.

But now, he had a new, far more terrible fear. It was real and it was coming soon.

NHALA
THE PALACE

Lucy rushed into the room, straight into Paso's arms, and hugged her tightly. Paso was holding her just as tightly, and they rocked together.

Oh, it felt so *good* to hold her friend again! They were both babbling in Nhalan, nonsense words of affection. Lucy rested her forehead against Paso's and whispered how much she'd missed her. Paso stroked her hair, then wiped the tears from her eyes and then the tears from Lucy's eyes. Lucy hadn't even realized she'd been crying.

A soldier of the Royal Guard, a captain, was standing behind Paso. Lucy recognized his face. He'd been the head of the Royal Guard at the welcome ceremony. He stood behind Paso stolidly, at parade rest.

Finally Lucy pulled back and held Paso by her shoulders at arm's length and looked at her. Oh, how she'd missed her!

Her friend was still a beautiful woman, with the clear, smooth, golden olive skin Lucy had envied so much as a girl. But Paso also had swollen eyes with deep circles under them. Instead of the elaborate ceremonial robes she'd worn at the greeting ceremony, Paso was wearing slim jeans and a white shirt, her uniform as a girl. Lucy was happy to see that she could shed the princess persona that had so chafed her as a girl.

"I am so happy you could come, my friend," Paso said

softly, in the musical tones Lucy remembered so well. "I need you so much."

"Of course I came," Lucy said. "You knew I would."

Lucy released Paso and took Mike's arm, walking forward. "My fiancé insisted on coming with me. Mike, meet my dear friend, Princess Paso of Nhala. Paso, my fiancé, Michael Harrington."

Lucy looked briefly at Mike, the merest flicker of a glance. It was never a good idea to give away more information than necessary, even to friends and allies.

Would he understand?

She'd underestimated him. He held out his hand to Paso, body language casual and relaxed. "Princess Paso, it's a real pleasure. I sort of invited myself along. I hope that's okay with you."

His face was unsmiling, though, and there was a very strong subtext. *If it's not okay with you, that's too bad.* His tone, his entire demeanor, was immensely protective. He put a heavy arm around Lucy's shoulders and squeezed.

It was playacting, Lucy knew that. But it felt so incredibly *good.* She'd never had a protective boyfriend, and her parents hadn't been the protecting kind at all. For the first time, Lucy understood the appeal of chivalry. Of having a strong man at your back. She was filled with warmth and strength. She told herself she was a fool, but she felt the warm mantle of protection settle over her. As if it were the most natural thing in the world, she leaned against him, her entire left side heating up, soaking up the warm, steely strength of him.

Paso looked up into Mike's face, studying him, her own face troubled. She switched her gaze to Lucy. "Is he trustworthy?" she whispered.

"Yes," Lucy answered firmly. "He's very trustworthy. I'd trust him with my life." That part was true, because she was trusting him with her life. His hand on her shoulder tightened.

"All right." Paso gave a tentative smile up at Mike.

"But I don't know about this guy behind you." Mike's

deep voice held suspicion. "Isn't he one of Changa's guys? I don't know what's going on, but it seems to me that Changa isn't one of the good guys here."

The princess dipped her head in acknowledgement. "No, indeed. He is definitely not a good guy." And then Lucy was surprised when Paso stepped back and the soldier put his arm around her, mimicking Mike's stance. It surprised her doubly because Paso hadn't given any sign at all that the captain was special to her. Paso looked up into the captain's face, smiling faintly, and his arm tightened.

"Lucy, Mike. This is Captain Mohar Thakin, of the Royal Guard. And if General Changa had any idea that he was here tonight, with me, he'd have him immediately executed."

Lucy believed her, absolutely. "Don't worry," she said gently and met the captain's dark eyes. "Your secret is safe with us."

Paso sighed. "There are many things I must tell you. Let's find a place to sit down."

The Orangerie was huge, warm and green, the air fragrant and fresh, filled with all sorts of exotic plants. The Frenchman who'd designed it had torn down one entire south wall and filled it with glass panes, letting in as much sunlight as was possible.

The plants were thriving and provided perfect cover for a meeting. A minute into the huge Orangerie and they were completely hidden from view, both from the entrance door and from the outside. Here and there were benches where the greenhouse workers could sit down and work.

The lights of the Orangerie were refracted by the thick, dense leaves of the plants. It looked as if they were meeting underwater.

The scent of all the plants in the overheated steamy air was almost overwhelming, all the smells of Nhala concentrated and intensified.

They sat down, Paso still in the captain's embrace. She was pale and tense, and she clearly derived strength and comfort from his touch.

Odd that, Lucy thought. She understood completely now, but wouldn't have even just two days ago. She realized that she touched very few people, and never for comfort. The touch of friendship, the touch of desire, these she was familiar with, though they were infrequent in her life.

But the touch of comfort? Before Mike, she'd never really thought to seek comfort and strength from someone else. Mike's touch was fictitious, the embrace of a man playing a role. And yet even that was delicious, a bulwark against the world.

Clearly, Paso had found her bulwark, and she needed it. Her world was as treacherous as shark-infested waters. If General Changa needed her for his plans and discovered that she'd already given her heart, he wouldn't hesitate to take his revenge. He might have to be careful with a princess and couldn't hurt her publicly, but the captain . . . Lucy shivered. Changa could have the captain accused of treason and hung, all in the space of an hour.

Or worse.

"I'm so glad you're here, Lucy," Paso said, reaching out to clutch Lucy's hand. Her skin was cold and clammy. Her hand trembled. Lucy held Paso's hand between hers, trying to warm it up.

"I'm glad to be here. Now, tell me everything that's happened. Where'd this Changa come from, anyway? He wasn't around when we were together here."

Holding Paso's hand, Lucy felt the slight jolt at hearing Changa's name, saw color drain from her face. Paso was terrified of him.

"No, you never met him. He was just a lieutenant in the regular army fifteen years ago. He wasn't even in Chilongo during the coup. Lucy . . ." Paso's grip tightened even more. "When all that happened . . . when we almost lost the country to the Chinese, when your parents lost their lives . . . Well, it was all such a mess. My father sent Jomo and me away to the Summer Palace in Bhoktu. The Americans immediately came and took your parents' bodies and you away. I never got a chance to say good-bye. Never got a chance to thank you on behalf of the Royal Family. I don't even know whether my father thanked you."

It had been a terrifying, chaotic time. The gunfight, her parents' deaths, Paso disappearing, grim-faced men coming for her, forcing her to identify her parents' bullet-ridden bodies before watching them put into a casket and the cover nailed over . . .

She remembered it mainly in her nightmares, chaotic chiaroscuro flashes of blood and violence.

"It doesn't matter," she said gently, and leaned forward to kiss Paso's soft cheek. "What matters is that I'm here now, and I want to help. So tell me what's going on."

Paso looked at her, at Mike, then back. Her body language betrayed indecision.

Lucy smiled. "You know, Paso, you can consider me an . . . emissary of my government. I am here to help the Nhalan people by restoring a manuscript, but—"

"Pah!" Paso cried out. "The manuscript is a fake! Changa is not the Snow Dragon! He created the manuscript so he'd have acceptance from the people when he has himself crowned the new Khan, the Snow Dragon of legend! It's why he's killing my brother and why he wants me! And why he's planning something terrible. So terrible I can hardly understand it!" Paso looked up into the handsome, still face of the captain. "You tell them, Mohar." She shuddered, her entire slender body shaking. "I cannot believe such evil exists in the world."

Lucy remembered that until Changa's appearance in her life, Paso had led a very sheltered existence in the Royal Palace. She'd been the joy of her parents, the king and the queen, and Jomo had always been a protective older brother. It was entirely possible that what was happening now was her first glimpse into the evil at the heart of the world, an evil Lucy had seen and known from earliest childhood.

Paso's love, the captain, however, was a soldier and clearly had no trouble at all believing in the evil of the world. He turned Paso's head into his shoulder and absorbed her shudders. He met their eyes over her head. "You tell them," she mumbled.

The captain gave a sharp nod. "Two weeks ago, one of my soldiers came to me. He is a cousin of mine and he has a friend who is a member of the regular army. You understand that the first loyalty of the Royal Guards is to the Royal Family?"

The captain's English was clear, though heavily accented. Lucy nodded. The Royal Guard was an elite group protecting the Royal Family, much as the Secret Service protected the president of the United States.

"As such, we are not always aware of political currents in the armed forces. But what my cousin's friend said was very troubling."

Lucy leaned forward a little and so did Mike. She glanced up at his face, grim and focused. "Yes, go on," she urged the captain.

He hesitated. "You are a friend of Paso's, Dr. Merritt," he said, looking at Mike. "And you said you were an emissary of your country. But your fiancé . . ."

"Is a former soldier," Lucy said firmly. "And he was briefed by our government before coming here, as was I. My government is aware of the fact that something is happening here in Nhala."

The captain's eyes sharpened. "Soldier? What kind of soldier? CIA?"

Mike said the truth. "No, not CIA. Tenth Mountain, army."

The captain's eyes lit up. "Elite mountain troops! Excellent! I trained with Major Khalid Aslam himself."

Mike's mouth lifted slightly. "I met him once. It was an honor." He looked down at Lucy. "Major Aslam wrote the book on mountain warfare. Literally. We used his book as a basic textbook. He really knows his stuff."

Men. Lucy nearly rolled her eyes. They were in a desperately serious situation, and here these guys were, bonding over another soldier who was good with crampons. "That's nice. But we need to find out what's going on."

The captain nodded. "The army man said that a year ago, a man came. He was a Pakistani. A man of science, but also a member of Al Qaeda. He stayed for a week in General Changa's home. Shortly afterward, work started on a secret underground laboratory north of Chilongo, in the Begwal Mountains."

She touched Mike's arm. "The Begwal Mountain Range is in the foothills of the highest Himalayan ranges. It's desolate country. Year-round glaciers, almost completely uninhabited." She turned to the captain. "Did your source tell you anything else? Any specifics about the lab? Did he give an indication of what they were producing? How many scientists were working there? What kind of timetable they are on?"

His head was shaking slowly. "All I know is what I told you. It's a bioweapons lab and has a level-four section. I do not know how many scientists work there. The Pakistani scientist was here a few days ago. They tested a disease on some political prisoners. They died terribly. That is why one of the soldiers spoke to my cousin. He was horrified. He said something bad was going to happen soon, but he didn't know exactly what. That is when I contacted a man in Thimphu that I knew was either CIA or had worked for the CIA. I know nothing further."

"We need to speak with your cousin, as soon as possible. And his friend." Lucy clutched Mike's hand.

The captain shook his head. "I am afraid that is impossible."

"He has information that might be vital," Lucy said tightly. "If we plan the meeting carefully—"

"You can't plan a meeting with dead men."

Lucy covered her mouth with her hand.

Captain Thakin nodded grimly. "My cousin met with an accident. While training. Or so I was told, though no one actually saw the accident. His friend has just disappeared. The general has reopened the dungeons. If he took my cousin there and tortured him, then the general knows my cousin talked to me. And I am already a dead man."

"No!" Paso's voice rang loudly. She lowered her voice. "No," she whispered fiercely. "I will not let him take you."

A look of tenderness crossed the soldier's handsome face. He ran the back of his finger down her cheek. "And I will not be taken, *dosha*. I will kill myself first. He will not get to you through me."

"How many men do you have who are loyal to you?" Mike asked.

"About four hundred."

"And how many men are loyal to the general?"

"On paper, the entire army. But only because the general rules with an iron fist. He is not loved. Any subordination is punishable by death. There have been many killings by firing squad in the last six months."

"My father would never have allowed this," Paso said harshly.

"No, my *dosha*, he wouldn't. Nor would your brother have allowed it. But he is dying."

Paso hung her head. "General Changa poisoned him."

"What?" Lucy started. It hadn't even occurred to her, but it made sense for a man planning on taking over a country and who had a bioweapons lab available to him. Take out enemies from the top down. "I thought he had leukemia."

Paso lifted one shoulder. "My brother was perfectly healthy until six months ago, when he had a series of routine tests done. Several required taking blood. The next day he fell ill, and all the doctors in our country cannot cure him. I called in a French oncologist, and he said it was leukemia, fulminating leukemia, of a type he's never seen before. I would have taken him out of the country, but he is so weak, I don't think he'd survive the trip. Then Changa closed the airport. For repairs, he said. But the fact is that Jomo would never survive the helicopter ride down to Thimphu, nor would he survive the road trip in an ambulance." A lone tear ran down her face. "Changa killed Mohar's cousin, he's killing Jomo and now he's going to kill who knows how many people before he's done."

"Absolutely not." Lucy felt an electric pulse run down her spine, looking over at Mike. His hand in hers was hard, tough, and that was great because she needed him to be hard and tough. And she needed to be hard and tough, too, because they were going to stop this monstrous man. Her parents hadn't died to keep Nhala from the Chinese Communists only to see it fall into the hands of a monster. "He's not going to kill anyone else, is he, Mike?"

"No. He must be stopped."

Oh God. Just the sound of his voice, deep and calm, reassured her. She saw Paso, bright, vivacious Paso, gentle and funny and kind, almost completely beaten down by this man, the general. And her lover, risking his life just to be with her.

They were going to stop him. She and Mike and Paso and the captain, backed by the US military. Changa was planning on killing millions and they'd stop him. They had to. Anything else was unthinkable.

Her parents had died because they wanted and were willing to fight for a world in which the General Changas didn't win. Lucy remembered them talking quietly in the evenings. Her parents had had an unusually close relationship and had shared everything in their lives, including a hatred for bullies, which spilled out into a hatred of dictators.

There were faint noises from outside the big door, muted by the door and the plants. Lucy could feel Mike tense up against her side, his arm tightening around her shoulders. They all fell silent until the noise passed.

Lucy lowered her voice. "I think we need to get back, Paso. There was a ceremonial guard outside our room, but I don't know if he reports back to the general."

Paso frowned. The captain answered. "They don't report directly to the general, but the guard will file a report that the general will have access to. You've been gone about an hour. Any longer would raise suspicion. Do you need anything?"

Lucy looked up at Mike then back to the captain. She was treading carefully here, unsure whether they could trust the captain completely. He was here with Paso and he loved her. But love never precluded betrayal. "Would it be possible for Mike to have use of a Jeep or an off-road vehicle without anyone knowing? He's . . . a former soldier. Maybe he can find something out. I'd like for him to have a look around while I'm working on the manuscript."

She ignored Paso's soft grunt of disgust at the mention of the manuscript.

Mike needed to find that flash drive. He had the GPS coordinates of the last place the flash drive had been.

The captain glanced at Mike, a frown between his eyes. "All right," he said slowly. "I'll leave one of our vehicles in a small clearing just behind the South Gate tomorrow morning."

"I know where that is," Lucy said.

"With a full tank," Mike added. He was right. It would not be good for a *shishin*—a foreigner—to stop at gas stations.

"With a full tank," the captain agreed.

"Just . . . hurry," Paso whispered. "I think something terrible is going to happen."

"Do you have a timeline?" Mike asked the captain.

"A . . . timeline?"

"Some kind of schedule, an idea of when General Changa is going to make his move, whatever it is."

"Ah." The captain's brow cleared. "No. I don't think my cousin knew. But not before the Dragon Feast, he said. General Changa wants to make a big announcement then. And show off the manuscript then, maybe." He bowed ironically to Lucy. "General Changa is counting on you to present it and its tale at the festivities, which start the day after tomorrow."

A tale that would undoubtedly be of a Snow Dragon looking remarkably like General Dan Changa, whose life history would be magically intertwined with the Snow Dragon myth, coming to restore Nhala to its lost greatness. Well, if it bought time, she was willing to do anything. If it was written on toilet paper with a Sharpie, she would be willing to swear it was the long lost manuscript that was so important to Nhalan mythology, if she had to.

The captain made a sound, and they all looked at him. He was clearly struggling with something. Lucy and Mike gave him the time to work it out in his head. Paso watched him, puzzled.

Finally, the soldier came to a decision.

"Here." He pulled something from a bag on the ground. "If anything happens to me, I think your government needs to know about this." He held out what looked like a pistol, though not any kind of pistol Lucy had ever seen.

It was small, for one thing. When Mike took it in his big hand, it looked tiny. It was precisely engineered, barrel small and without sights, with a shiny metallic sheen. It looked like an alien artifact or a gun from the future. Mike turned it over in his hand, then looked up. "It's not a weapon."

"Indeed it is, only not a firearm." The captain's face was grim and pinched. "It is for injections. It injects a tiny cylinder into the human body. The cylinder is divided into two parts with a wall between them. Depending on the amount of acid in one half of the cylinder, the wall will dissolve in twenty-four hours, releasing a disease. My cousin didn't tell me the nature of the disease, he only said it was horrible. He saw . . . tests carried out in the lab. There are many of these guns to shoot the cylinders into people, who then will become—" He stopped and turned to Paso, speaking in Nhalan.

"Carriers," Paso said.

"Carriers." The soldier nodded. "Yes, indeed. They will have something terrible inside them, and that something will explode and they will carry the disease."

"You said there were a number of these pistols." Mike turned it over again in his hand, so well engineered it was almost a thing of beauty. "Do you have any idea how many cylinders have been manufactured?"

"Tens of thousands," Mohar answered. "Maybe even hundreds of thousands."

There was utter silence in the huge Orangerie. The

living plants absorbed all sound; the lights reflected off their tense faces. Lucy exchanged a quick glance with Mike. They'd both seen the devastating effects of the weaponized disease the cylinders would be carrying.

"Then we'll have to stop him," Mike said steadily, tucking the injection gun into his waistband at the back and pulling a sweater over it. "I'll see that this gets to the right people."

Absolutely. They would do absolutely everything in their power to stop this man. She and Mike had the might and the brains of the US military behind them. And they were on the side of the angels. She'd seen too much to believe that the angels always won. They didn't. But this time they would, because the alternative was simply unthinkable.

"Paso, how do we stay in touch?" If she needed to communicate with her friend, she couldn't very well walk around the palace asking where she was. Not to mention the fact that if Paso was nursing her brother, she would be in the Royal Chambers, closed to those not of direct service to the Royal Family.

Paso frowned. "If we need to contact one another, let us leave a message under the foot of the Dancing Buddha. You remember where that is, don't you, Lucy?"

Lucy swallowed. Yes, she remembered exactly where the Dancing Buddha was. The Palace was full of statues of Buddha—serene Buddhas, smiling Buddhas, laughing Buddhas—but there was only one dancing Buddha. In the Summer Palace, not ten feet from where her parents had been killed.

"Okay, Paso, we'll leave each other messages there."

Mike looked at her sharply. Oh God. Had he noticed a change in the tone of her voice? She wasn't used to being read so easily.

"Let's go, Lucy," Mike said and helped her to stand, hand under her elbow. He turned to Paso and gave a credible imitation of the Nhalan greeting, fist held in hand, elbows out, arms at chest height, head bowed.

Paso gestured toward the huge doors. "You two leave first. Then I'll go. Mohar will follow."

Lucy took a deep breath, filling her lungs with the clean fragrance of a thousand species of plants. The corridors outside smelled of ancient dust and, now, treachery.

*E*LEVEN

"DO you think you can find the body in all that snow?" Lucy asked, her anxious face turned up to his once they'd made their way back to the room down a thousand different-colored corridors. Even pale and frightened, she was still so beautiful it hurt the heart.

The sixty-four-million-dollar question.

"Yeah." Mike reached out and tucked a lock of shiny hair behind her ear then put his hand in his pocket, because the temptation to continue round, cup the back of her head and bring it to his was almost irresistible.

She was worried sick. He was worried sick.

Let's have sex.

Sex as stress reliever—sounded real good right about now. Her eyes searched his, looking for—what?

God, she looked so very lovely in this room, exotic and remote, somehow fitting right into the lush richness of the décor, like a unicorn in a brashly colored forest. She also looked scared, which put the kibosh on the little sex fantasy that had bloomed instantaneously in his head, a little explosion of sensory input.

He'd been able to see it, almost taste it. Damn straight. They'd had a nasty jolt, something filthy was in the works, and since they couldn't do anything about it right now, getting sweaty between the sheets would be a great way to work it all off, wake up refreshed in the morning, ready to do battle.

She wouldn't have to get undressed, oh no. He'd do that for her, nice guy that he was. Up and off with that sweater, down and off with the pants. Taking a long moment to savor her in just bra and panties. Lucy was definitely the kind of woman to have really frilly frothy underwear, oh yeah. He didn't even particularly care for frou frou, but in this case . . . mmm. She'd be all slender curves, dainty arms and pretty breasts.

Speaking of which, after a moment to admire, he'd help her with bra and panties, by which point he'd be frothing at the mouth, barely in control. He'd want to carry her to the bed, but there wouldn't be time for that.

No prob. The floors were covered in carpets, thick, multicolored carpets. He'd be a gentleman and go on his back. Watch her ride him, fast the first time, slower the second. And third. Make sure she doesn't get carpet burn on her knees.

Just move in her slow and easy . . .

Jesus.

Mike pinched the bridge of his nose, to bring himself back to earth.

All those images of a naked, happy Lucy vanished like smoke because the real Lucy, the flesh-and-blood woman, brave and exhausted from having traveled halfway around the world when she was terrified of flying, was standing right in front of him, arms around her waist, looking lost and lonely.

Well, of course she was lonely. She didn't have him here in the room with her. She had a jackass version of him, drooling over the idea of sex with a woman who was swaying on her feet.

He should be shot.

She was watching his face carefully, pale and exhausted, bruised flesh right under the beautiful blue eyes. Thank God telepathy didn't exist. He knew that for a fact because if it did, she'd have rightly smacked him in the face.

But she must have sensed something, caught maybe the intense sexual vibes he must have been throwing off, because she was looking at him warily, as if he could jump her at any second.

This was wrong. He was better than this.

He banished every thought of sex from his head, just wrenched those hot images right out, stomped them to the ground.

"You're tired," he said gently, and her eyes widened at his tone. Some of the tension left her body, and he felt like even more of a shit. He'd made her uncomfortable and tense. Jesus.

"Yeah." She was hugging herself a little less tightly. "I am. All of a sudden it all hit me. The trip, what we're learning here. It's a little . . . scary, isn't it?"

"Very." He did her the honor of not messing with her and not lying to her. It was scary, no use ignoring it. "But we've got our backs covered. We've got help here in the Palace. It's not our job to stop this. Our job is just to get as much intel as we can and then scram. So far no one suspects anything. Actually, if I understand the situation correctly, you're really valuable to Changa. He's not going to hurt you."

Or he'll answer to me.

Jesus, she was messing with his head, big-time. Instead of concentrating on Changa, running over in his head tomorrow's op, he was flashing on sex with Lucy and then, perhaps even more emotionally intense than the sex, flashing on pulling Changa's fucking head off if he hurt Lucy in any way.

This was not a good head space to be in, not while in a huge building full of a few friends and many more potential enemies. Not while somewhere up north bad guys were concocting a hellish witch's brew that could destroy whole peoples.

He needed to keep his shit wired tight.

"We should be getting to bed." Lucy's huge eyes never left his face.

"Yeah. While you're changing, do you want me to ask that guy outside if he can get you some tea? Something warm to drink?"

She smiled, a slight uplifting of her mouth but still a smile. "Already done." She pointed to a conical cloth on a sideboard, two bowls beside it. He lifted the cloth and found a steaming teapot underneath. He opened the lid and sniffed and closed the lid once again. Gah. Smelled like fermenting hay.

"Come, Captain," Lucy said, teasing him. She poured them both a bowl and placed one in his hands. "It's good for you. Detoxifies the system, promotes sleep."

And ruins libido, he thought. Hard to think of sex while you were sipping a noxious brew. He brought the cup to his lips and sipped gingerly. It was boiling hot and tasted like crap.

Lucy delicately finished her bowl, clearly tougher than he was.

"Tastes like fermented hay," Mike complained.

"That's because it *is* fermented hay. But no yak butter. Promise." She laughed and went into the bathroom, trailing behind her something that looked pretty and peach and frothy.

God. Better get in bed first so when she came out, she wouldn't see him standing there like a dork with a hard-on.

So he was in his pajamas, lying flat on his back in bed, when she came out of the bathroom, and oh God, she was so fucking pretty as she lifted the heavy blankets on the other side of the huge bed and slipped in. She was incredibly beautiful without makeup, skin fresh and clean, shiny hair brushing her shoulders, as silky as the peach-colored nightgown.

He'd left a small lamp on in the corner of the vast room, a tiny glow in the darkness. It shed just enough light to see her by.

"Can we keep the light on? I don't like sleeping in the dark in unfamiliar rooms. Can you sleep if there's a little light?"

"Sure." He could sleep through a firefight in the blazing sun.

"Okay." Her voice was growing drowsy. Her eyes drooped. "Good night, then."

"Good night."

Inside of a few minutes, Lucy was sleeping soundly. He turned, leaned his head on his arm and watched her. She was a quiet sleeper, barely moving the blankets as she slept. In sleep, the wariness with which she faced the world dissipated, and he could see the girl that she had been. She looked so young, so vulnerable, so pretty. Completely alone.

Tomorrow was going to be a busy day. He needed to sleep, too, but for one of the few times in his life, it eluded him. His mind just kept churning like some vast steam engine.

He tried counting sheep, got to a thousand, and quit. It wasn't working.

Then he started counting Lucy's breaths, got to fifty, and fell into a deep, dreamless sleep.

TWENTY NAUTICAL MILES OFF THE LIBYAN
COAST
MIDNIGHT, LOCAL TIME

She was the *Star of Orion*. A one-hundred-ton oceangoing fishing vessel. She no longer carried fish in her hold, though. She carried death.

She was anchored twenty nautical miles offshore, Bengazi a sparkling blur on the horizon.

The men arrived in four batches of ten in military Zodiacs. The way was clear, they were not stopped. The Libyan government wasn't sponsoring this act of jihad, but it wasn't preventing it, either. The same for the governments of Pakistan, Syria and the Palestinian Authority.

Dr. Imran Mazari was on his own here. His wasn't a movement or a political party or even an organization. Just a handful of superior biochemists, security provided by mercenaries, backed, of course, by all the money in the world.

If he was successful, any number of organizations and countries would boldly claim credit. If he was unsuccessful, well, there would be no telltale clues Western authorities could use to trace the attack back to anyone at all.

Jihad as a virtual company, all elements outsourced.

Mazari loved that idea.

The first of the men from the lead Zodiac started climbing up the rope ladder. When they reached the gunwales, most of the men stumbled. God had granted them calm waters this evening, another sign of grace. Jihad's warriors were the bravest of the brave. No Western military organization would be able to find so many men willing to die a terrible death as his martyrs were. They were the bravest of the brave.

But they were no sailors.

Mazari and one of the crew remained on either side of the rope ladder on deck to steady the unsteady bodies of his warriors, many of whom had never been on board a ship before.

That was why Mazari had spent a lot of money on stabilizers. He had four of them, the most expensive in the world. And belowdecks was completely refitted for all the needs of a *shaheed* warrior. White and calm and quiet. He couldn't offer the peace and space of the desert, but he could, *inshallah*, offer the maritime equivalent.

Quiet, sound-insulated rooms, pristine bunks and prayer mats, fresh fruit and tea. Pure surroundings for the pure of heart.

The last of the men were offloaded onto the ship, registered to a consortium of shell companies, flying a Panamanian flag.

The load was complete. He had taken on thirty men in Nicosia, thirty in Algiers and now forty in Bengazi. They now had one hundred warriors, voted to martyrdom.

Mazari ushered them quickly belowdecks. He wanted to get under way as soon as possible. There was a deadline and it was fast approaching. Before following the men down the ladder, he gave a sign to the captain impassively watching from his perch high above the deck. Immediately, he could feel the powerful thrum of the engines beneath his feet.

The captain was good at his job, as was his crew. Quiet and reliable and efficient. Well worth the hefty sum Mazari had paid them.

His martyrs were ushered into a large room where barbers and tailors awaited them. Each man would receive a haircut in line with the new persona that would be attributed to him. Some would have a sleek short businessman's cut, some a longer student's cut. Some would have their hair lightened, some would have streaks put in.

All would be carefully shaved clean. No beards, no mustaches, no facial hair at all. All would have manicures.

Next door was the wardrobe. Each man would be issued an outfit, carefully chosen by a brother sensitive to the cause who worked at Harrods in London. Rich businessman, dowdy professor, casual student—they would all be represented. Every single style carefully chosen to be nondescript and nonthreatening.

Most of the men would be issued glasses with clear lenses. Men in glasses looked less threatening. Each man would have an accessory of his trade—from an expensive Gucci leather briefcase to a student's casual backpack.

Each man had some form of identity—driver's license, credit cards made out in his name, company ID, university ID, US passport. All would survive a superficial examination.

Mazari withdrew to his quarters on deck and went over his material once more. Weather forecasts, epidemiological studies, virological reports, blood analyses . . . he had about four kilos of paper, and he patiently went through it one more time.

This was going to be one of the greatest medical experiments in the history of the world, over and above being the greatest blow ever inflicted against America. Every detail needed to be perfect.

He studied through the night, the powerful engines thrumming away under his feet and carrying the ship eastward, until Mazari saw the faintest lightening of the sky ahead of him. He closed his computer and stood up, stretching. He was sometimes so immersed in his work he lost all knowledge of the world outside his head.

That was dangerous now. He had to be alert, alive to his surroundings. He was going to do something that had never been done before, and he was going to strike a blow to the enemy so devastating it would take generations to recover, if the enemy ever did.

He went down the ladder and along the corridor to the rooms where his brave martyrs were being transformed into the enemy. He opened the door and looked, pleased. "Ah, my brothers." He walked around, hands behind his back. "You have all done remarkably well."

And they had. The barbers had done perfect work. Every single man had a different haircut, perfectly suited to his look and the style of his clothing.

Mazari had given orders that all the clothes be expensive, even the casual student outfits, and that all the haircuts be attractive. It made a huge difference. Each brave *shaheed* who came on board had the heart of a lion, but his body betrayed a lifetime of privations. There was nothing he could do about their teeth, there was no time, but he could coat their bodies with the sheen of Western prosperity.

It was the one thing guaranteed to stick out in Manhattan. When he was going over the plan with his financial backers, they had resisted the cost of the expensive clothing for men who, after all, would die a gruesome death soon after. But Mazari had insisted, and he knew he was right.

The martyrs were to blend into the crowd of a great festive occasion. The crowd of hundreds of thousands weren't trained to notice anything out of the ordinary. But their senses would alert them to the man who smelled bad, whose hair was long, dirty and greasy, whose fingernails were black, whose clothes were cheap, all-synthetic—there would be subtle warning bells ringing.

His men now would fit in perfectly. Tomorrow they would receive instructions in Western body language.

But for now, there was another operation to see to. He went quickly back up onto the deck and leaned against the railing, pulling in his breath, breathing in the sea air.

He had been born in Lahore and had never even seen the ocean until he was twelve years old. It had astonished him—the limitless blue ripples edging out to as far as the world went, the briny smell, so unlike the smells of the city, the sense of unfettered boundaries.

His life had been the life of a student, made up of books and then, later, laboratories. Cold, sterile environments. An environment of the mind.

This was the physical world, made for a life ruled by God. Not the Americans' world, a world of conquering infidels, with outsized appetites for everything—food, sex, money. If it had suited them and they could do it, Mazari had no doubt the Americans would have sucked up the oceans to feed their appetites. They were already destroying the land.

He was doing God's earth an act of mercy, ridding the world of as many Americans as science would allow.

He pulled in another deep breath, the slight smell of civilization that had underlain the air in the Mediterranean gone. They had passed the Azores an hour ago and were now on the open sea.

A light line on the horizon gradually grew lighter. Day would soon be upon them, and they had to hide from the Americans' prying eyes in the sky.

The engines suddenly shut down.

A low horn sounded, and like a well-oiled machine, the crew emerged from below the decks and began a practiced routine. Something they'd done every morning for six days and undone every evening for six nights.

It was a fascinating sight. Mazari stayed on deck to watch it.

Four crew members, two on each side of the back of the ship, disengaged a mechanism and a huge blue cylinder emerged from the planking of the deck. With the push of another button, the huge cylinder began to turn, unfurling an enormous blue canvas tarp.

As the cylinder kept turning, the agile crew pulled it over the entire ship, from stern to bow, and just like that, the ship became completely invisible to military satellites overhead during the day.

For the rest of the trip, the *Star of Orion* would travel by night and cover itself by day.

It was effectively lost to the world.

*T*WELVE

SOMETIME during the night, the huge space in the middle of the enormous bed shrank.

Lucy found herself lying on a very hard, very warm surface. Very hard, very warm, very *hairy* surface. She came awake in a sudden panicked rush, turned her head and met amused dark brown eyes.

"Good morning." His morning voice was a little hoarse. One big hand was on her shoulder. If she was going to bolt out of bed, she'd have to knock his hand off.

"Good morning." Her own voice was a little hoarse, too. But she was wide, wide awake.

The entire front of her body was plastered against him, from her head resting on his hard shoulder to her toes brushing against his hairy shins.

He felt absolutely delicious.

Heat pulsed through her in a blinding flash, and it wasn't menopause. A heat so intense her skin tingled with it. She had very fair skin and she just knew she was blushing. She might as well have had a red bulb on her forehead flashing. *Turned-on woman.*

"Did you sleep well?" Though he kept his voice low, it was so deep it reverberated through her diaphragm, like the bass lines of overly loud disco music. She could feel the vibrations.

Everything about him was amazing. She'd slept with a few men in her life, though sleeping was a misnomer. She'd had sex with a few men, and had tried to avoid sleeping through the night with them.

She was familiar with the male body, with how it differed from the female body. Men smelled different, for one. They had more body hair. Their hands and feet were usually bigger. But, in the main, the differences weren't all that enormous, except for that penis-vagina-breasts thing.

They had four limbs, one head. Slept. Ate. The differences had always seemed less important than the similarities.

Mike seemed like . . . like another species. Maybe a species that had evolved on a heavy-gravity world, because though he was lean, his muscles were incredibly thick, with no give in them at all. And he smelled wonderful, too. Not that gamy smell of the wild he'd had when they'd yanked him out of the field, but a musky scent ripe with pheromones, absolutely designed to lure women to their doom.

The bits of him that she could see—such as his huge, dark sinewy hand on her shoulder, the strong jawline covered in early morning beard—the feel of an enormous body exerting a heavy gravity against her, the smell of a healthy male animal . . . it was almost too much.

She had to think to come back into herself. And remember that he'd asked a question.

"I slept very well, thank you."

It was the polite response, but to her amazement, it was true. Lucy was a light sleeper and rarely slept an entire night through.

Last night she had slept like a rock, an intense, deep sleep she hadn't experienced in years.

He was watching her carefully, so carefully she was afraid he could read her mind. She couldn't think of the last time someone had been so close to her, so close his breath moved a few strands of hair, so close she could follow the exact line of demarcation of his heavy beard, see the slight striations of yellow in his pupils. His eyes moved, watching hers, and that sense of him being a heavy planet with gravity increased, pulling her to him.

"I'm glad," he said softly. "You needed it."

What was he talking about?

As when a planet pulls a moon, the distance between them grew smaller, not as if he were lowering his head to hers but as if some universal force stronger than they were was at play, rolling her over onto her back.

His mouth settled on hers and there was an explosion of feeling inside her. Her heart gave a startled leap in her chest, and she could almost feel an electrical crackle as their mouths met.

It was too much, for both of them. Startled, he lifted his mouth and looked at her narrow-eyed, as if something had happened that he wasn't sure he liked.

But he was willing to try it again.

This time his mouth stayed on hers, opened. Helplessly, she opened to him, too, and that same electrical charge ran through her at the touch of his tongue against hers. They both drew in shaky breaths and she breathed him in.

The Nhalans believed that some people—mothers and their children, lifelong lovers, close friends—have bits of their souls embedded in each other, so that over time you become a little bit your loved one. She felt this strongly, right now, as if parts of him were flowing into her, as if she were breathing in Mike,

It wasn't just *his* body that was strong and tough—hers became strong and tough, too. Some of his fearlessness and courage flowed into her.

She wanted more. More of that heat and strength.

She arched up against him, lifting her head from the pillow, but that wasn't necessary to get closer to him because he was pressing down on her. His whole body had shifted and now he was on top of her, his heavy weight pushing her down into the plush mattress. It felt so incredibly natural that her body automatically accommodated him, her arms and legs opening to receive him, her hips forming a cradle for him.

All his muscles were so tense it also felt natural that his penis pushed against her, hot and hard, in slow, rhythmic pulses, like the tides of the sea. Her arms were around that impossibly broad back, but couldn't meet. Her fingers traced the ridged muscles along his spine and singled out thick scar tissue, two big round puckered scars and one long one along his side, her palms slowly making their way down the long planes of his back to rest on the small of his back, riding the movements of his hips.

She could feel everything he was feeling. Except of course, she didn't have a penis.

But she had something better, a blossoming of red hot heat in her groin, exactly where he was rocking against her, pulses of feeling so intense she thought her heart would knock its way out of her chest.

"Someone's knocking," Mike murmured and she opened her eyes. His face was changed almost beyond recognition. Arousal suffused it with blood, making it even darker. His lips were red, swollen and wet from her mouth.

"My heart," she answered. "I think it's going to blow."

"Okay. Makes sense." His eyes narrowed, face tightening. He had started to lower his head again, when both of them heard a distinct knocking at the door.

"Should I tell him to go away?" Mike asked. "After all, we're engaged."

And that was when her head caught up with her body. Clearly it had gone on a spin around the Palace while she'd been making out with Mike like a high schooler in her boyfriend's backseat.

"No, no." Lucy pushed at Mike's shoulders, and with a sigh he rolled over. She caught her dressing gown on the way to the door, the thick silk rippling behind her as she all but ran across the large room.

Outside was a Palace servant, an elderly man with deeply engraved wrinkles in his nut brown face, smiling widely at her, holding a huge wooden tray.

"Blessings upon you this morning, Father." Lucy greeted him in Nhalan, and his mouth fell open, showing a nearly toothless mouth. He almost dropped the tray in his surprise.

"You speak the Dragon Language, my child? How is this possible?"

"I lived in your beautiful country when I was young, Father. My parents came to study your beautiful language." She swallowed. *"They died here."*

The old man's eyes widened. "Merr-itt," he whispered.

Lucy bowed and pulled the door open.

The old man moved quickly across the room, leaving the heavy tray on a sideboard, then turned to her. *"It is an honor to meet you, Lady Merr-itt. Your esteemed parents are legends in this country. Please consider me your humble servant."* It was said in one breathless stream, fast, in a choked voice.

Lucy bowed again, and the old man bowed back so low his forehead nearly touched his shins. He backed away, much as courtiers used to back away from the Sun King, and closed the door quietly behind him.

"Well, that was interesting. I think you've just made a new friend," a deep voice said from behind her. She turned and had to fist her hands so hard her nails bit into her palms to keep from throwing herself at him.

Mike was just so incredibly, impossibly sexy, sitting up cross-legged in bed, bedclothes tumbled around him, head leaning against the brightly painted headboard. By some wild coincidence, his head covered the round orb of the sun and bright yellow rays emanated from his head like an old-fashioned halo. But he was no angel. Not the way he was looking at her.

"Do you, um . . ." She coughed to clear a dry throat. "Do you think that *that*," she pointed at the tangled covers, "might be due to the altitude?"

It was one explanation. She didn't remember a craving for sex as the body's reaction to high altitude, but then the last time she'd been here she'd been fourteen years old.

"No, ma'am." A corner of his mouth lifted. He looked like sex on a stick, a comma of jet black hair hanging down over his forehead, morning stubble darkening his cheeks and what had been a remarkable erection probably still alive and kicking beneath the sheets. "If anything, high altitude is a libido-killer. Nope. *This*—" His voice mimicked hers as he swept his hand over the tangle of bedsheets covering his groin. "This is all us."

Oh, God.

This was not good, on so many different levels. She couldn't even begin to list the reasons why this wasn't good.

They were here on very serious business. Dangerous business. Undercover, too. It was one thing for two perfect strangers to pretend to be engaged. It was all playacting, none of it real. But if they became lovers for real, some truth would seep in, muddy the waters. When your emotions were involved, it was all too easy to zig when you should zag.

Lucy met Mike's eyes. Something of what she was thinking must have seeped through into his consciousness, because he'd lost the grin. She could only hope he'd lost the erection, too.

"I think we should eat breakfast and then plan the day." To her surprise, she was wringing her hands. She stopped, could feel a flush rising in her cheeks, and clasped her hands behind her back.

From childhood she'd been taught to control her emotions. Cool, calm, collected. It was second nature to her.

Somehow, coming back to Nhala, the strong shock of being back in a country she'd never thought she'd see again, reuniting with Paso, the enormous danger they were facing—they'd all worked to jolt her out of her usual headspace.

She thought she heard a sigh coming from the bed, and

Mike threw back the covers and stood up. At some point during the night he'd lost his silk pajama top but the pajama bottoms were thin silk. Sure to show everything. Lucy raised her eyes to the ceiling.

"It's okay." Mike's voice was wry. "I'm okay. Back to, um, normal." He walked to the big tray, studying its contents with interest. "Why don't you go first to the bathroom?"

"You just want first whack at the breakfast tray," Lucy said accusingly.

"Busted." He grinned again, a faint simulacrum of his earlier, sexy grin on the bed, watching her face.

All of a sudden it occurred to Lucy that he'd noticed her floundering, seen how unsettled she was and was trying to put her at ease.

How odd, the feeling of being looked at and . . . and understood. She was so used to gliding through life keeping her thoughts and feelings to herself.

It made her feel unsettled. The bathroom sounded like a really good place to be right now. She grabbed her clothes and fled.

It had been touch and go, there.

What had he been thinking? Well that was the problem. He hadn't been thinking at all. Just feeling. Feeling Lucy's slender body beneath him, a flash of immense heat prickling under his skin wherever he touched her. And the taste of that Angelina Jolie mouth . . . God, he'd forgotten everything.

This was not like him at all. Mike liked sex as much as the next guy. More, even. But he liked doing his duty even more than getting laid. Except right now.

Right now he was sorely tempted to march into the bathroom where at this very moment she was undoubtedly naked—the sound of the shower started up and he groaned, because now she was naked and officially *wet*—grab her and finish what they'd started. Get this prickling feeling out of his system, because it was annoying him, like a huge itch you couldn't scratch. He wasn't used to unrequited lust. He made real sure he didn't get the hots for the wrong kind of woman—no crazies, no druggies, no working girls. And above all they had to be single—no messing around with another guy's life. That still left a lot of women. When he latched on to a woman, she usually wanted him back. Just like Lucy.

So holding it back right now felt unnatural. What was the problem? Why not just go for it?

Well, there was this pesky fact that they were on a mission to stop really bad guys from doing really bad things. There was that.

But if he had to be honest with himself, and he always made a point of knowing himself, he'd admit it was the expression in her eyes that stopped him.

She'd just looked so lost.

If he pushed, she'd fall. He knew that. Taken unawares just after waking up, her body had been totally welcoming. It had been unmistakable and, well, pretty damned wonderful. Her arms had opened up, her legs. He'd never felt anything like it, like some rare flower blossoming.

But right now? She'd gone back into her shell, back behind that beautiful, untouchable mask she wore. She wasn't ready for sex. He was—he was raring to go. But he didn't want to persuade her, he wanted her to come to him on her own, because she wanted it as desperately as he did.

So, he thought as he dressed, if he couldn't have sex, he could at least have breakfast. Someone in the Palace kitchen had prepared enough food for ten stevedores. There were three kinds of omelets, several kinds of biscuits, a big bowl of something warm and sweet that looked like oatmeal but wasn't, four kinds of bread and about a thousand different tiny bowls with various flavors of chutney, a big platter of fruit and an enormous teapot with enough tea to drown a horse. It was all good, and he was hungry.

She stayed a long time in that shower. More than long enough for him to have finished everything on the tray. However, though it cost him, he scrupulously left her half.

Lucy stuck her head out of the bathroom door, cautiously, as if uncertain of his mood.

He kept his voice casual. "You better get here quick before I finish everything off. Because I don't know if they have a coffee shop in the Palace."

Lucy smiled faintly. "No, there's no coffee shop, and not much coffee, either. But I imagine all we'd need to do is ask for more tea and biscuits and they'd bring it." She sat down in one of the huge carved wood chairs and poured herself a cup of tea.

She'd put on her Serious Woman uniform. Dark blue turtleneck sweater, tailored dark blue trousers. She'd draped a blindingly white lab coat over a chair, just waiting. She had on minimal makeup, her hair was pulled back into a tight ponytail, and she was wearing black, severe Marian the Librarian glasses.

It was a message. Mike read it, loud and clear: *No fooling around*.

O-kay.

"I want to go with you to where they've set up your lab. I want to see where it is." He tried to keep command out of his voice, so as not to get her back up. But he had to know where she'd be all day while he was up in the mountains looking for a dead man's flash drive.

He wouldn't be able to concentrate unless he knew she was safe. So he put mildness in his voice, though he wasn't about to take no for an answer.

But he underestimated her. She sipped at her tea and put the cup down gently. "That's a good idea. And I'll wait there for you to come to me this afternoon so we don't end up chasing each other all over the Palace."

Man, he really liked it that she didn't make a big song and dance about her independence. This wasn't a man-woman thing. They were teammates, and the first rule in the field, after staying alive, was to keep track of your teammates.

"Okay, it's a deal." He waited for her to put a jacket on, fold her lab coat and fit it into her purse, and pick up her heavy briefcase. Or toolbox, more like it. She listed slightly to one side, so it must have been heavy. "Need help with that?"

"No, I've got it."

Don't push your luck, he thought. "Okay. Let's go."

The ceremonial guard outside their door must have had instructions, because he silently turned and beckoned them to follow.

Down huge hallways, up staircases, down staircases, every wall painted a different brilliant color, gilt statues everywhere, every door and window with a painted and carved frame or casement—it was ADD paradise.

Mike tried to keep track in his head, trying to fix the route by color—left green, right red, left yellow . . .

After they'd been walking for what seemed like hours, they descended stairs into a more modern part of the building. The colors were the cool gray and beige of Western modernity. Even the smell of the air had changed from ancient mustiness to the modern smell of neon and electricity and fax toner and central heating.

Lucy slowed down imperceptibly, and he followed her lead. She stared straight ahead and spoke in a low voice that wouldn't carry. "I know that felt like a labyrinth, but essentially we crossed the north-south axis of the building and are at the opposite end of the Winter Palace from our room.

Mike instantly oriented himself in his head, as if pondering a map that made no sense until it was turned around the right way. She was right, and now he knew he'd be able to find this part of the Palace again. He gave an unobtrusive thumbs-up, staring straight ahead. They caught up with the guide as he stopped outside a white laminated door and opened it. Mike and Lucy walked through, and the door closed behind them.

They were alone in the room. It was windowless, the air close and sterile. Lucy shook out her lab coat briskly, put it on, then hauled out that heavy briefcase and started removing things. Jars and bottles and steel instruments and every single size of brush known to man.

When she was completely ready, she looked around. "I wonder—"

The door opened suddenly, without a knock. General Changa stood in the doorway; he looked around coldly then entered the room. He said a word in a low voice, and a soldier behind him snapped to attention, took two steps forward and handed a long and beige roll of parchment to the general.

"Dr. Merritt," he said, handing it to her. The manuscript.

Lucy smiled enthusiastically. "My, what an honor!" She put on cotton gloves and unfolded it reverently, the very picture of a scientist with something new and interesting. "Hmm." She hummed a little as she touched the rough, dirty surface reverently with a gloved finger. "Now, I don't wish to be hasty, and of course I'd need to run some tests, but I think we have some polyphenols here, together with epigallocatechins plus some minor catechins." She bent over to look at the manuscript more closely. "Very exciting."

She came across as an adorable nerd, pretty nose almost stuck to the parchment.

The general simply stood there watching her impassively, eyes cold and dark.

Lucy's eyes rounded. She turned enthusiastically to the general. "General Changa, this is partially written in the Old Language! This dates it back at least five hundred years, perhaps more. As you know, the Old Language died out five hundred years ago, but remains to this day in formal speech, much as demotic Greek remains embedded in modern Greek." She glanced up at his face and smiled. "I am so sorry. My enthusiasms do get the better of me. My parents were anthropologists but they had a strong interest in the semiotics of language and—"

"When will the manuscript be ready?" That cold voice, interrupting.

"Oh." Lucy pushed her glasses up to the bridge of her nose. "Ahm . . . well, let's see. I'll need to do mass spectrometry. I'll need to take a fragment of the manuscript, but I assure you it will be a minute amount. I can actually shave some fibers off with a razor, that will give me enough material to put into the mass spectrometer. And of course, it will require an initial cleaning, and once I've determined the exact composition, I can get down to a more careful cleaning, and then—"

"I want a readable copy to present to the people on the day of the Snow Dragon Feast."

"Oh!" Lucy blinked. "Well. Well, uh, that's the day after tomorrow, and I don't know—"

The temperature in the room was falling rapidly. The general hardly seemed human. He looked more like some ancient evil god who could summon death from the sky at any moment. Which, of course, he could.

Lucy placed fist in hand and bowed. "Of course, General," she murmured. "It will be ready and mounted on a Plexiglas stand for the people to admire by the Feast of the Snow Dragon. You can count on it."

When she rose from her bow, her face was calm and serene. Did she understand the situation? Understand what kind of danger they were in?

General Changa stared coldly at Lucy for an entire minute. Lucy stood calmly under his gaze.

The general spat a command, and the soldier behind him sprang to attention, walked briskly to the door and opened it. The door closed firmly behind them and Mike heard an explosive exhalation.

Lucy, needing air. Bending forward. "God," she said in a strangled voice.

"Yeah. That was creepy." He placed his hand on her back and felt her shuddering.

Lucy rose, and he saw how pale she was. She hadn't underestimated the danger at all. She'd understood it yet kept her cool. "You did good, Lucy Merritt."

"Yes." She sketched a shaky smile. "I did. Particularly considering that that manuscript is a complete fake. The ink will probably be chemically the same as ancient ink— which was usually burnt bones, tar and pitch—but everything else will be inauthentic, and the parchment will prove to be modern. Someone buried it in the ground to give it a false patina of age. It's an old trick. Together with staining the pages with tea."

"And you're going to have to pretend you have no idea it could be fake."

"I will, yes."

"That chemistry stuff sounded pretty damn convincing. What was that stuff anyway? You really blinded him with science."

Lucy gave a smile the Mona Lisa would have envied. "I gave him the chemical composition of tea."

$\mathcal{T}$HIRTEEN

DR. Imran Mazari stretched out his maps on the tabletop. His quarters were very small, but that was fine. He'd grown up in four cramped rooms in the Galwandi, the oldest part of Lahore. His only knowledge of the West was through television programs, and more than the otherworldly wealth, the brazenness of the women and the unfathomable social mores, what had astonished him was the space.

How big the houses and the squares and the buildings were! And inside the buildings and the houses—huge rooms, in succession. It seemed that each person living in the West had more room than ten Pakistani families.

Imran had never said so to his strict Muslim father, who railed against the godlessness of the West, but Imran had secretly dreamed of living in empty spaces. Having a room of his own, one of those enormous rooms on TV as large as a house, instead of the cramped room he shared with his three brothers.

The TV programs also showed broad, empty avenues, tree-lined, inviting. Public squares that instead of teeming with merchants screaming their wares had only a few men—

and women!—strolling about, the women with their heads uncovered, unaccompanied by a male relative.

And when he'd won his scholarship to study microbiology at Stanford, he secretly wondered, as he embraced his stiff father and weeping mother, whether he would ever come home again.

But he had. Because although the spaces in America were beautiful, enticing, they were filled with evil, godless men and women, who didn't deserve their country.

How could Allah have given such an evil people such a beautiful and empty land, when his brethren throughout Islam could hardly breathe in their crowded spaces?

Look at Cairo or Damascus or Lahore or Dhala. Or the Camps. The reeking camps, forty to a tent, sewage running through the muddy alleyways . . .

And the Americans, with hundreds of millions of square miles, empty.

And yet the Americans were befouling the land Allah had bequeathed them, so quickly you'd think they were in a race to despoil their country, all in the name of trinkets. Cheap clothes, cheap TVs, cheap toys, cheap sex.

In the four years he spent at Stanford, Mazari had watched as orchards and olive groves tended for generations had fallen to the bulldozer for yet more shopping malls.

Appalling. They didn't deserve their land because they didn't tend it. They wanted more and more and more, in an ever-expanding cycle of waste. Mazari had had two sets of clothes throughout his childhood, his mother carefully washing and hanging out to dry the set he wasn't wearing. Had they had the money to buy new clothes, there would have been no space for a closet in their home. Each morning, he awoke to find his clean set carefully folded on a chair, yesterday's clothes already hanging on the line in their living room.

Once in California, he had accepted a fellow student's invitation to visit his home in Chico over the weekend. The house was as large as a palace. His friend's closet was larger than their apartment in Lahore. Mazari had actually felt nauseous seeing that enormous closet filled with enough garments to clothe an entire village.

No, the Americans didn't deserve their spacious country. It was why he had spliced in the extra mutation, to rid the earth of the bodies fast and cleanly. His backers had been enthusiastic, because, of course, it was a way to clear out Israel, once and for all.

By the time any international authorities could act, his brethren would have filled the empty cities of Zion. The borders would go down instantly, manned only by empty clothes and dust that had once been human. A great dam holding back a tide of humanity, dissipated in a cloud of dust.

And America, with all its Zionists, would not react, because they would have their own huge tragedy to deal with.

There would be chaos, a thousand times greater than the chaos following the great victory of 9/11, the repercussions spreading from the center of the financial world outward.

No, it would be years, perhaps decades, before they could turn their eyes outward from the tragedy that had taken place in their world. And by that time, Israel would be occupied, permanently a part of Greater Palestine.

But first, Manhattan. Then America.

Mazari looked at the detailed map before him, following his finger along the predestined route of the great event. Hundreds of thousands of people in the city and, all of it broadcast live to the entire country. And to much of the world.

He could envision it easily, *see* it, in his mind's eye.

Locals and tourists, in their hundreds of thousands lining the streets, jammed against the barriers, in colorful winter wear, noses red, holding balloons, waving to the TV cameras. Happy and relaxed. There would be police officers, sure, but they would be happy and relaxed, too. There for crowd control, though they knew from eighty-four years of experience that no one would get rowdy. It wasn't that type of crowd. The morning duty would mostly consist of rounding up lost kids and restoring them to their parents and carting away anyone who had a heart attack.

Mazari's men would fan out, fitting right in. College students, business executives, ad men, writers, professors, office workers—all would have different looks, different accessories. But with one thing in common—a tiny cylinder shot into a shoulder twenty-four hours previously, containing the most virulent form of the virus. They'd have thousands of tiny cylindrical canisters in their backpacks and briefcases, to be scattered wherever possible, in trash cans, bathroom wastepaper baskets, down grates. Left in Starbucks and Saks Fifth Avenue. Behind trees and bushes in Central Park. Dropped casually on the ground in the crowd.

Mazari had timed it, too. If all went well, the first victims would start falling to the ground in the first hour of the parade, between 9 and 10 a.m. The first would be his men, of course. They knew they would be in paradise by noon. They were all volunteers. And their families would be compensated until the end of time. Their families would be given large land holdings in the new Greater Palestine, their mothers honored. None of the *shaheed* had wives or children. They'd been chosen for that.

But they wouldn't need children to perpetuate their memory. It would live on in eternity.

Mazari could visualize it clearly. One man down, spraying bloody vomit. The crowd would back away fast. Overhead helicopters, filming the festivities, would see something happening, veer that way.

And another would fall, and another. Half the people there inside of an hour. The other half by noon. The overhead helicopters would be filming perhaps a million people dying. If the news anchors were outdoors, they would start dying, too, in front of the cameras.

America, then the world, would be riveted, then appalled, then terrified.

No troops would dare enter what was clearly a place of

contagion. It would take time, finding enough Level A hazmat suits, suiting up.

By the time troops entered Manhattan, encased in what looked like space suits, with closed-circuit air, they would be entering a charnel house.

It took America, with all its wealth and military might, two months to begin retaliation for 9/11. That had been trifling in comparison. Two buildings, several thousand dead.

This would leave Manhattan *empty*. A wasteland. With no clue who to retaliate against. There were no advanced biowarfare labs in the Middle East or the East Asian Islamic countries. None. The West could try to invent one, but after the fiasco of the missing WMD in Iraq, who would believe them? Who would think to look for a lab in a neutral country in the Himalayas?

Mazari's finger retraced with pleasure the route of Macy's Thanksgiving Day Parade, in four days. The last one ever, in the history of the world.

CHILONGO
DUSK

Mike parked the Jeep exactly where he'd found it, at the rear of the Palace, and hurried into the Palace through the nearest entrance. The place was so amazing. Even this relatively insignificant entrance was elaborately decorated, painted, gilded, swathed in silks, flooring covered in precious rugs.

At any other time, he'd have stopped to admire it, but he was anxious to get to Lucy, and he knew there would be at least another half hour's trek through the vast building before he got to the lab, even walking fast. He could run it. He was a fast runner and could run for hours. But why on earth would Michael Harrington run?

Shit, it was hard being undercover. He hated it. War was bad enough when you could do what had to be done. But this—this constant weighing of what he should do as Mike

Shafer with what Michael Harrington would do—it was nerve-racking.

So he settled for a brisk walk, trying to pretend it was the brisk walk of a man hurrying to make a million bucks, when it was actually the walk of a man trying to get to a special woman as fast as he could without triggering an alarm among the many soldiers in the building.

Last night and this morning he hadn't seen many soldiers at all, but now the building was lousy with them. At every door there was an alert soldier, it seemed. Certainly one in every corridor.

Armed.

Fuck, had something happened while he'd been scrabbling in the snow up in the foothills of the vast mountain range hovering over the country? Had something happened to *Lucy*?

His heart rate decelerated. His vision sharpened. He was aware of every limb and of exactly where his body was in space.

Time slowed down. His lungs pulled in more air. He was getting ready for combat.

He walked with a hand in his parka pocket, as people do in cold climates. The hands are the first to feel the cold.

He kept his hand in his pocket because the flash drive he'd been looking for was in his fist.

The GPS location had been correct. He'd discovered it four hours after starting off. He'd driven to within five miles of the location, parked the Jeep behind a giant spruce and taken off straight uphill. The snow had turned firm, making for relatively easy walking.

He'd uncovered the site where the CIA operative had died fairly easily, a little after 1300, as the sun was just starting its descent behind the western range of the Delahari Mountains, exactly where his GPS locator had said it would be. The CIA had programmed the last known location of the body into his GPS to tell him where the death had occurred.

The area around where the head had been had lost its almost violently red tinge and was now only faintly pink. There was a high-tech balaclava, fleece-lined Carhartt cargo trousers with long underwear inside, mountain boots with the socks still in them. One boot had rolled two hundred meters down the hillside.

No parka.

Mike had checked every single inch of the clothing for the flash drive, fingering the linings, turning the clothes inside out. Checking the boots carefully.

Nothing. The operative had clearly put the flash drive into one of the pockets of the parka.

He buried the clothes in case a stray peasant came across them and reported that a crazy Westerner had stripped naked in the snow, then stood for a moment, thinking.

He looked up at the heavy, blindingly white glacier seven thousand meters above, a great white spill between two mountain spurs. A fierce katabatic wind flowed down the glacier, carried by gravity. It was very likely that the parka had caught in the wind and been driven downhill. On the other hand, apparently there was rich wildlife in this area, the Himalayan Frontal Thrust, and it was also entirely possible that an animal had carted it away.

Mike studied the terrain carefully, but if there were animal tracks, the wind had ablated them away.

He'd opted for downhill simply because in the hours of daylight left, he'd be able to search a wider area than he would have been able to trekking uphill. And he was right. He found the parka and the flash drive four hundred yards downhill.

When Mike pulled the flash drive out, his heart sank. The flash drive was bloodstained and the metal USB connector was twisted.

It wasn't usable in any way. They'd have to wait until they got back to Langley and the technoweenies could fix it.

He and Lucy had to leave immediately; the intel on that flash drive was time-sensitive. But the damned general had locked them into being here for that Dragon whosis, and he wouldn't be amused if they left early.

If they *could* leave early. The airport was closed, and if they made a run for it in a stolen vehicle, they'd be picked up well before they reached the border five hundred miles away. And the white hats were not going to make an incursion five hundred miles into sovereign territory without permission to pick them up. Urgent as the intel was, no one was going to provoke an international incident over a flash drive whose contents were unknown.

No, they had to stay.

The concentration of soldiers grew heavier the closer he got to the area where Lucy was working. His heart rate slowed down even further, blood rushing to his hands and feet. His reaction to danger.

Something was wrong. Something had happened to Lucy. She hadn't called him all day. They both had satphones and a verbal code. If she was in danger, the code word was "sunset," and if he was in danger, the code word was "birthday."

She hadn't called once.

Maybe she'd gone to see her friend the princess, and the general had caught them talking; maybe he had some other reason to suspect her; maybe she'd tried to send an email to her uncle Edwin and it had been intercepted . . .

There were several soldiers outside the lab, and by the time Mike got to the door he was so worked up he just rushed by them and slammed the door open, body entirely ready for combat.

Lucy looked up, startled, from her workbench. The manuscript was rolled out to its full length and she was working on it. She was safe, unharmed.

He'd been so crazy with panic he'd even left the door behind him open, which was not smart. Not something he'd have done ordinarily.

"Michael." Lucy rose, smiling, completely natural, as if a wild man hadn't just slammed into her lab. She went up to him, kissed him on the cheek standing on tiptoe and then, just as naturally, closed the door.

An engaged couple wanting some privacy after a day's separation. Most natural thing in the world.

Mike felt like an idiot.

"You okay?" Lucy asked with a frown.

He nodded. For some strange reason, his throat was too dry to talk.

"Did you get it?"

He silently pulled the bent, bloodstained flash drive from his pocket and held it out to her in the palm of his hand. She winced.

"That's not good."

Mike shook his head. No, it wasn't good.

"Let me see if I can do something here." She took the flash drive from him and stared at it for a moment, then met his eyes, sorrow on her face. That blood was the blood of a good operative, who'd done a very brave thing and had died for it. "We need to get the information in this out as soon as possible."

She took it over to her workbench and examined it carefully. Though she already had a pair of very serious black-framed glasses on, she took out what looked like a jeweler's loupe.

"Hmm. We need to get rid of the blood first. The casing's cracked. If the blood gets in, it can destroy the internal mechanism." She tilted her head. "Do you know what the inside of a flash drive consists of?"

Mike shook his head.

"Neither do I. So let's just hope it hasn't been hopelessly compromised."

She took a small jar from her work case and unstoppered it. The heavy scent of solvent filled the air. Next, she took a tiny brush, dipped it into the jar and very slowly and extremely carefully cleaned the outer casing of the flash drive.

Her movements were careful and delicate. She didn't rush. Finally she looked up, holding the drive in the palm of her hand. It was immaculate.

"I checked the casing carefully. It's cracked but intact, so with some luck the blood hasn't penetrated the workings."

They both stared at the little plastic device with the bent metal USB connector, completely unusable. And so very important.

"I think I can straighten the metal bit, the port," Lucy said quietly, putting the flash drive back on the counter. "But I'm not certain. If I make a mistake and the metal breaks, the information inside will be lost until we can get back home." She looked up at him, waiting for his decision.

Lucy had placed her technical expertise, including her knowledge of the language and customs of Nhala, at the disposal of the mission.

The tactical mission decisions were his to make. She'd made that clear, just as she'd made it clear that she would abide by his decisions. She didn't try to horn in on his part, just as he didn't horn in on her area of expertise. He'd followed her lead with Paso and the general instinctively, and she was waiting calmly for his lead in this matter.

Partnership at its finest. No ego, no tantrums.

He looked at her hands, slender and competent. Cleaning the flash drive, her movements had been delicate and sure.

The decision settled within him.

"Straighten it out now."

Without another word, she pulled a gleaming steel instrument from her work bag. It looked like a space-age pair of pliers. She bent over the flash drive, holding the metal connector delicately by the pliers, and exerted a little pressure, utterly concentrated on the task.

There wasn't much Mike could do to help her, so he simply stood there, watching her. The bright overhead light made her hair shine, picking out blond and red glints in her chestnut hair. Standing over her, he admired the dark, lush crescent of lashes over the curve of her cheekbone, the delicate play of tendons and bones in her hands as she operated on the flash drive with the skill and dexterity of a surgeon . . .

The door crashed open and General Changa stood in the doorway, three soldiers behind him.

Fuck. Fuck fuck fuck!

The general would find the flash drive. If some tech guy in his army was able to replicate what Lucy was doing, open the drive, he'd understand immediately what was going on. The intel was heavily encrypted, but the general would want to know what they were doing with files with sixteen-bit encryption.

Mike moved immediately in front of Lucy. If anything was going to happen, it was going to have to happen through him.

But she rose smoothly, brushing his arm as she stood, and he read the message loud and clear.

Stand down.

She'd felt his tension and she wanted him to know she'd handle this.

Well, they were partners. Okay. She'd know more about how to behave in front of a Nhalan dictator than he would.

"General Changa," she said warmly, walking up to him, giving him the Nhalan greeting. However hard Mike looked, he could see no sign of the flash drive. "How kind of you to visit. I know how busy you are, but it's a pleasure to show you the progress that has been made on the manuscript. Such an interesting document, too. It's an honor to work on it. Come in, please."

And she beckoned him into the room, cool as you please.

One soldier followed the general closely, basically walking in his footsteps. The other two took up stations on either side of the door. They all carried their weapons at port arms, ready to fire at an instant's notice.

Mike was unarmed. Any move on his part and he'd be dead and no use to his country and, above all, no use to Lucy. The only thing he could do was stand ready and try to disguise the gnashing of teeth.

The general stood so close to Lucy that Mike imagined the fine hairs of her body were standing up. His sure were.

The general was an observant son of a bitch. He quartered the room carefully, checking everything out, making no pretense that he was casually looking around. His gaze eventually made its way back to Lucy.

"I came to see how the restoration is proceeding."

"Oh, it's so exciting, General Changa." Lucy was smiling, cheerful, as she led the general to her workbench. "Great progress has been made, as you can see."

The general bent down to look at the opened parchment, standing very close to Lucy. She would be unable to make the slightest untoward movement without him noticing.

Where the fuck was the flash drive? It had to be in her lab coat pocket.

The general grunted, looking down at Lucy. Mike's hackles rose at his expression, cold and calculating. He was looking for an excuse to accuse her of something, but there wasn't any. A dead man could see that she had been working hard all day.

Whatever the nature of the parchment, whether it was real or fake, it had arrived in bad shape. Now it was stretched out to its full extent, Lucy's work clearly visible. Half of the parchment had been carefully cleaned, the underlying material the tawny glow of a lion's mane instead of spotted with dirt.

"Good," the general grunted, almost in spite of himself.

Lucy beamed. "Oh, thank you, General! That is very kind of you. It is not an easy job. The parchment was quite friable, so I started out by using an ultrasonic mister, and then I used methylcellulose instead of gelatin as a consolidant, because of course—"

"Enough!" It was possible that the soldiers didn't understand English, but they understood tones of voice. Their hands tightened on their weapons at the general's tone.

"Oh, sorry!" Lucy shook her head at her own foolishness. "I do get carried away. I apologize, General. It's just that it is such an interesting document from all points of view."

Her tone was breezy, a little chagrined that she'd let herself go on about technical issues.

Mike was amazed. She was giving an absolutely word-perfect imitation of an unworldly academic, completely immersed in her own narrow little world, with no interest in anything else. A nerd, and completely harmless.

Her body language was perfect, as well. Open, a little overenthusiastic. Puppy-like, even.

Only he could see the vein pumping in her neck, the faint sheen of perspiration on her forehead.

She was magnificent.

The general looked around again, cold and suspicious.

"The princess recommended you." Something in his voice suggested that the recommendation from the princess was in itself a reason for suspicion.

"Yes. That was very kind of her." She smiled up into his dead, black eyes. The eyes of a cobra. "I am surprised she even knew that I studied restoration. We haven't been in touch in *years.*"

The general studied her face for a full minute. She stood still under his gaze, beaming cheerfully. He looked down at her workbench, picking up the pliers she'd dropped onto the countertop when he'd marched into the room. "What is this? You need this to restore a manuscript?"

Mike tensed. It was not anything you'd associate with paper restoration, yet it was something she had clearly been using.

"Oh, that." Lucy picked up a sharp, short blade. "This is to scrape extraneous matter such as dirt or dust off the surface of the parchment. Even minute imperfections in the blade are intolerable, can cause irreparable damage. This one has a slight indent. If I were back home, at the Smithsonian, I would have sent the scraper back to the manufacturer to have it reground and resharpened, but since this is a time-sensitive restoration, I decided to straighten the blade out myself. I have a fairly steady hand."

The general listened impassively, heavy features absolutely still. "Have you seen the princess today?" he asked suddenly.

Lucy blinked, the very picture of puzzlement. "The princess? Why no, I've been in the lab all day. As a matter of fact, I haven't even had lunch and I'm starving. I wonder whether—"

"A meal will be brought to you, to your quarters. I suggest you retire there now." He held his hand out, and Lucy's smooth brow furrowed. "Your lab coat," the general said impatiently.

Mike's blood froze. Shit. The flash drive was in one of the lab coat pockets, it had to be. The general was suspicious of something, that was clear. Mike readied himself. Lucy was going to refuse, perhaps play the modest lady card, the general would insist, and then those bastards behind him would bring up their assault rifles . . .

Lucy removed her lab coat and handed it to the general, as if he'd asked the most normal thing in the world. "Here. I'd be really grateful if you could have the meal sent soon." She flashed a flirtatious smile at Mike. "We'd like to retire early, wouldn't we, Michael?"

The only thing to do was play along in their established roles. Lucy, cute little nerd. Mike, clueless rich guy. "Sure thing, honey." His voice boomed. "I'm a little tired, too."

Like the Eye of Mordor, the general's eye alit on him. "Ah, Mr. Harrington."

Mike smiled broadly. "General."

The general's malevolent attention was like a cold hand passing over him, almost a palpable thing. "Did you have a good day?"

So what the fuck was he supposed to answer to that? *Shit yeah, General. I went out to find the corpse of a murdered countryman of mine you poisoned with one of the most dangerous viruses on earth, which you are planning on releasing into the world. There is nothing remaining of my fellow operative but clothes and bloodstains. Luckily, inside this poor man's clothes was something that I will*

*sacrifice my life to ensure will bring down the wrath of the
entire US military onto you.*

Great day, thanks for asking.

"Very enjoyable, General."

"I understand you appropriated a military vehicle for
your . . . sightseeing."

The temperature in the room dropped about twenty
degrees. There was no doubt the general was angry at the
thought of Mike running around in a military vehicle. Even
back in America, letting a civilian have a military vehicle in
a high-security situation would be a court-martial offense.
God knew what it would be in a dictatorship. And the vehicle had been made available by a top officer—the Captain
of the Royal Guards. There was no way they could betray
his name. Mike was running scenarios through his head
when Lucy coughed discreetly.

"That was me, General." She smiled. "We were talking
about how Michael could get around Chilongo and where
we could hire a car. An older soldier recognized me, said
he knew my parents. Said it would be an honor to lend his
vehicle for the day. I do hope that was okay? I wouldn't
want him to be in any trouble."

The general turned to her. "What was his name, this
soldier?"

"I'm sorry," she said simply. "I have no idea. We didn't
even think to ask. It was a generous offer and we didn't
want to be churlish—be impolite—and refuse. So Michael
accepted the offer."

There was utter silence in the lab as the general, Lucy's
lab coat in hand, absorbed this. There was absolutely nothing Mike could do. Changa would either accept the explanation or not.

It was a good thing Lucy was able to think so fast on her
feet. His admiration for her went up another notch.

The general looked at them both carefully, taking his
time, without even trying to dissemble what he was doing.
Lucy's expression remained friendly, turning to slight puzzlement as the silence went on. Perfect reaction.

Mike was having a little more trouble with his reaction because he wanted to tear the general's balls off and feed them to the dogs, but there were three weapons in the room, in the hands of men who knew how to use them, and he had none.

Right now, Mike's main weapon was Lucy's brain.

Finally, the general laid Lucy's lab coat slowly on the back of a chair and gave a slight bow. Considering the depth of the bows Mike had seen so far, this one was an insult.

"Dr. Merritt. Mr. Harrington. Let me accompany you to your room."

Where I will post a guard and from which you will not emerge until tomorrow morning was the unspoken subtext.

Lucy didn't even try the *oh but we couldn't possibly impose* gambit. He wanted to make sure they were locked up for the night and she got that.

"Thank you, General," Lucy said softly. "We're honored."

Outside the lab, the general took the lead, Mike and Lucy followed, and the three soldiers took up the rear. It was really hard not to think of themselves as being under arrest.

The general took an entirely different route back to their room, one Mike wasn't familiar with. He didn't think much about it until he felt Lucy stiffen at his side.

What?

He looked around for danger, but all he saw was a huge hall with an enormous staircase leading down.

The general stopped in the middle of the hall and looked back at them. "So this is where your parents died, Dr. Merritt."

She swallowed. "Yes."

Son of a bitch. The fucker was trying to throw her off balance, catch her out in a weakness, by using the place her parents had been murdered to upset her. Mike wanted to tear him limb from fucking limb.

General Changa watched her carefully, but Lucy gave no sign of an emotional reaction, so he turned again and walked forward.

Mike glanced down at her. She kept a serene expression, but she had turned pale.

They walked for another fifteen minutes, then Lucy gave an exclamation. She stopped in front of a massive brass statue of Buddha, one of about a billion in the Palace. This one was of the usual fat happy man, one foot raised.

"Oh! Mike, look! This is a famous statue. The Dancing Buddha." She reached out and touched the tip of his toes. "Touching him brings good luck. Here, you touch him, too."

He reached out and touched the toes, which were shiny from being rubbed over centuries. Goddamn if she hadn't palmed a small piece of paper, done perfectly, right under the nose of the general and the three soldiers. If Mike hadn't known to look out for it, he would never have seen it.

Finally, they were at the door to their quarters. The general gave a brief bow. "Dr. Merritt, Mr. Harrington, I hope you have a pleasant evening. Dr. Merritt, the Feast of the Snow Dragon begins tomorrow at seven in the evening. I trust the manuscript will be ready."

"Certainly, General." Lucy smiled up at him, friendly and calm. "I'll mount it for display. We're honored to be here for the Feast. Good night."

Once they were inside the room, Lucy's face crumpled. She leaned shaking against the door and let out a long, shuddering breath.

Mike grabbed her and pulled her into his arms. He couldn't wait another second to hold her. She was trembling. He could feel her heart racing when he put the palm of his hand against her back. She was terrified. She hadn't given any sign of it, but she was terrified.

"That was *awful*," Lucy gasped.

"Yeah." He just held her against him, absorbing the tremors, one hand holding her head against his chest. He wasn't trembling, but he wasn't doing too well himself. If Lucy hadn't kept her head so well, they could be in the Palace dungeons right now.

"Where the hell did you put the flash drive? I thought we were blown for sure."

She clung to him for a moment, gave one final shudder and pulled away. "Never underestimate a woman."

Mike thought of his stepmom and half sister. "No, ma'am," he said fervently and watched, fascinated, as she pulled the flash drive from between her breasts. She also conjured up a tightly folded slip of paper, the one she'd invisibly palmed at the Dancing Buddha.

She carefully unfurled it, frowning as she read the message.

"What does the princess say?"

"She wants to meet with me. Tonight. In the Royal Chambers. It's urgent."

"How can—" Mike began then stopped when he heard a grinding noise from the huge wooden door to their room.

The sound of a key turning in a lock. They were locked in.

$\mathcal{F}$OURTEEN

LUCY sat trembling in a chair while Mike swept the room. When he gave her a thumbs up, she let out a huge breath.

"You were so great," Mike said, and Lucy rolled her eyes.

"Yeah, right." Lucy Merritt, Superwoman.

"No, no." Mike actually looked a little shocked at her reaction. "You were incredibly brave. You didn't show any fear at all. You were just amazing."

It seemed impossible to Lucy that the huge freight train of terror that was in her hadn't shown. "Mike. I was terrified. Every second he was in that room I thought I was going to die of a heart attack. I was scared out of my mind."

"Well, of course you were," he said, frowning. "You'd have been crazy not to be frightened."

"You weren't." And he hadn't been, not at all. The waves of anger and aggression coming off him had almost been palpable, no fear in there at all. Lucy was a connoisseur of fear, knew all its permutations and flavors. There hadn't been any in Mike. She was surprised the general hadn't had him shot.

The key ground in the lock again and Mike shot to the door. A Palace servant stood there, surprised to see a very large Westerner right in front of him. Mike took the huge tray from his hands. His voice boomed loudly in the enormous corridor outside.

"That's great, thanks so much, appreciate it."

His big, fatuous smile faded as the door locked loudly behind him. He placed the tray on the table.

"Four soldiers stationed outside," he reported grimly. "Armed."

Lucy looked at him, dismayed. "How on earth are we going to get out and get to the Royal Chambers? And I'll bet you anything the Royal Chambers are fully guarded, too. Something is happening, Mike. Something really serious."

"Well, I've got some ideas, but first let's eat. I didn't have lunch, either, and we've got to fuel up if we're going to do anything."

When Mike talked about fueling up, he wasn't kidding. The amount of food on the tray was enough for a small platoon. When Lucy had eaten her fill, Mike looked a question at her. When she nodded, he finished up everything else. It was true that he'd spent the entire day out in the snow, looking for dead bodies. Or rather, the remains of dead bodies.

Lucy sat back. "Do you want me to try again with the flash drive?"

Mike stilled, fork halfway to his mouth. "You can do that?"

"Maybe. I always carry a mini kit of tools with me. I can certainly try."

Neither of them needed to be told that the information needed to get into the right hands as fast as possible.

In case they never made it back.

"Go for it."

Lucy pulled out her little tool kit, a very expensive one that almost exactly replicated her large briefcase-sized one, except all the tools were beautifully engineered miniature ones.

When she sat on a carved wooden chair directly under a wrought-iron lamp, she picked the bent and misshapen flash drive up and was instantly lost to the world.

It never failed. She was constitutionally built for this kind of long-term focus, for intense, exacting, highly detailed work. Sometimes she'd sit down to an ailing manuscript in the morning and come, startled, out of a dream trance in the late afternoon, having worked steadily and without interruption for eight hours.

The pliers were tiny, but powerful and precise. Millimeter by millimeter, Lucy straightened the small bits of alloy metal until finally she sat up straight, pleased. The flash drive looked perfect.

She pushed her glasses to the top of her head and held the drive out to Mike in the palm of her hand. "Here you go. I think it'll work."

Then Lucy saw his expression and blinked in surprise. Every single plane of his face was stark, skin tight over high cheekbones, eyes blazing darkly.

"What?"

He swallowed. "You are incredibly sexy when you concentrate."

She swallowed, too, because it was very clear that he was intensely aroused. Enormously . . . greatly aroused. Oh God.

"Um . . ." Words deserted her, utterly. There was absolutely nothing to say.

"Don't pay any attention to that."

He opened his laptop and gently, gently pushed the flash drive into the USB port. It slid home smoothly and he pumped the air with his fist.

"You're a genius, Lucy." He was typing away furiously at the keyboard, filing his report. He pressed the enter key and sat back. "There. No matter what happens, the info will get into the right hands. I think we should be planning on getting out of here, pronto."

"We can't know whether the information on that flash drive has been compromised or not." She hated to say it because the idea of staying under General Changa's rule for even a moment more than necessary made her skin crawl. "We need to get confirmation that the CIA and the Stop Cold committee received it and that it was readable. In the meantime, Paso wants to see me, urgently. I don't know how to do that, how to get away from the guards outside our door, make our way through the halls and get through security into the Royal Chambers. Did you notice that there were many more soldiers out tonight than last night?"

"Yeah, I noticed." The muscles in Mike's jaw were working overtime.

"What do you think has happened?"

"I don't know, but it's nothing good. Soldiers stationed in cities and government buildings are never good. I have an idea. We couldn't find a map of the Palace anywhere on the net. Do you think you could draw me a map of the Palace? Floor by floor? And an especially detailed map of the Royal Chambers?"

"I imagine I could," Lucy said slowly. She was a decent draftswoman and she knew the Palace inside out. "But my information would be fifteen years out of date. They might have put a gym where the kitchens are, for all I know."

"But they won't have changed the Royal Chambers."

"No. No, they wouldn't." There were hidden rules governing the Royal Family and the Royal Chambers Lucy had never understood. Her parents had told her that they were the precepts of an ancient religion that predated Buddhism.

As youngsters, she and Paso had been exempt from all royal protocol, and Lucy had been able to run wild through the Royal Chambers, which would have been closed to her as an adult.

"Here. I'll use this." She pulled out her artists' sketch pad. It was always with her when she traveled. It pleased her and relaxed her to sketch things—an interesting face, an architectural detail—when away from home.

It took her an hour and ten pages of her sketch pad, but she put what were essentially floor plans to the entire palace in Mike's hands. "Now what, O Great Leader?"

He slanted a glance at her, amused. He had himself under control. She hadn't looked up from her furious sketching to see him looking at her as if she were a cream puff he wanted to eat. As a matter of fact, he'd basically ignored her, prowling around their huge quarters, pulling odd objects out of his suitcase and hand luggage. He'd also dressed in a very sexy ninja-like jumpsuit.

"Now I do what I do best," he replied, finger on the page where she had sketched their floor of the Winter Palace. "I climb."

"What?"

Mike was placing the sketches all together on the floor, taking in the layout of the Palace as a whole.

"They did us a favor locking us in. We'll send the tray out and say we're retiring for the night. I think I can make it over to the south windows of the Royal Chambers without being seen. The rooftops are steeply pitched, but it's not snowing. Should be okay. Wooden shingles, right?"

Lucy nodded.

"I have essentially a full climber's kit with me, all the gear I need. I think I can make it there and back in an hour or two."

She swallowed. "That's great. When can we leave?"

"What the hell are you talking about?" Mike stared at her. "What do you mean 'we'? Are you crazy?"

Lucy stared at the rope and grapple lying on the bed, knowing the years and years of training required to be able to use them, and nodded. Yes, yes she was crazy. No question.

"I don't want to do this, Mike. Believe me. I'd rather just stay here and wait for you to do your thing. But Paso's note . . . well."

She smoothed out the small crumpled piece of paper, forcing her hands to stillness. The note was very short. Very clear.

Meet me in the Royal Chambers after ten. I need you.

Lucy could almost hear Paso's voice. She looked at

Mike, feeling miserable. "What else can I do? I have to go. Maybe she has information she'll give me and not you. I'd give anything to be able to stay here. But we can't afford for me not to go, Mike. Surely you can see this? The choice isn't mine to make."

He stared at her, face tight.

There wasn't anything she could do to convince him, either way. He didn't want her with him, obviously. She didn't want her with him, either.

He was an expert mountaineer, he knew what he was doing. She'd be pure ballast. Her presence would make his mission harder, more arduous, possibly even expose them to discovery.

He was an athlete, his very body spoke of years using that gear, going up and down mountains. She wasn't an athlete in any way. Her idea of a perfect day was a couch, a book and a cup of tea.

But she had to go.

Whether he saw that, understood that, was entirely up to him. He was much bigger and stronger than she was, and she couldn't force him to take her along.

She waited for his decision.

He nodded.

"Dress in dark clothes. Wear rubber boots or at least shoes with rubber soles if you have them. Put on two pairs of gloves. Tie your hair tight." He watched her for a second or two, judging her. She knew what he was seeing. A total wimp, someone who knew nothing about climbing. "And you obey me, instantly. You do what I say at all times. Is that clear?"

"Absolutely."

She went to change her clothes, praying she wouldn't let him down.

Christ, that's all he needed. Lucy along. Not because she was a silly or difficult woman, not at all. He could absolutely count on her to stay quiet, keep her head, do what he said.

But *fuck*.

She wasn't a climber, not in any way. In his head, following Lucy's clear sketches, he'd mapped out a path to the Royal Chambers. Out their window and over the rooftops. Easy stuff, certainly easier than his usual climbs. No granite cliff faces, no treacherous avalanches, just a quick climb up, crossing the roof, rappelling down into the windows of what Lucy told him were Paso's quarters. Piece of cake. He just had to avoid detection by Changa's guards, who presumably wouldn't be patrolling the sharply pitched roofs.

Lucy added an entirely new factor of danger. He could haul her up and down, no problem. He'd just give her the harness. But she couldn't walk on those tiles. No one who wasn't a climber could. The rooftops were cold and icy and steeply pitched.

He'd have to rope her to him, and if she slipped and fell, he'd make a racket trying to save her.

So it was Plan B: a series of under the roof corridors she said were never used.

He hated this. He hated exposing her to danger. The soldiers would shoot on sight. He knew enough of her to know that she would control her fear, which was all that anyone could ask. But she wouldn't know what to do, instinctively, as he did. Her body would be stiff, unwieldy, slow to react.

She wouldn't stay behind, though. He was beginning to understand that pale, determined look, and he couldn't do anything but admire it. Her friend Paso wanted her, and she would literally swing from the rooftops to be with her.

Okay. His job, then, was to get them there and back safely.

She'd finished changing and stood before him, clad in black, short boots with rubber soles, her hair not only tied back but under a black watch cap.

Mike went to the door, listened carefully. From his gear belt he took a tiny, flattened metallic tube and inserted it between the ancient slate floor and the even more ancient wooden door. Even if the two had been an airtight fit originally, over the past thousand years feet had worn the floor down, creating a space.

He inserted the tube carefully, stopping when he gauged that it was just past the barrier of the door. The eye of the snake was a wide-angle-lens camera that transmitted to his cell phone. He watched the display carefully for five minutes.

There were three men stationed outside, all armed, but their body language was relaxed. Two were leaning against the wall, across from the door, talking. The third crossed over to them and lit a cigarette.

In the US Army, they'd be court-martialed, or at least harshly reprimanded and demoted, for this kind of behavior while on guard duty. They were distracted from their primary focus, and as for the guy lighting the cigarette—well, you smoke with your dominant hand. Which is also your gun hand. Crazy-ass dumb.

On the other hand, it meant that he and Lucy were not considered dangerous. To the guards, standing watch over their door was simply a wasted night when they could be in their beds.

Satisfied, Mike put the snake camera back in his webbing and turned to Lucy. "So—you have any music in your computer?"

She didn't hesitate. "Yes, do you need it?"

"Yeah, turn some on, they'll think we're relaxing, and it'll mask any sounds we make as we go out the window."

In an instant, the pretty strains of the Peasall Sisters sounded from her laptop speakers.

"Okay," she said, looking up from her laptop. "I've got my music on a loop. It'll just start over again when it's played all my MP3 files. The loop lasts about an hour and a half."

"We should be back by then. Let's go."

The windows opened out onto a wooden terrace. Dark, deeply carved wood, heavy wooden plank flooring, big dark wood carved posts dividing the space up into frames. One floor down was a courtyard, hemmed in by high walls. On the far end of the courtyard was a series of brass dragon heads jutting out of the brick wall, water spouting from the open, fanged mouths into a stone trough.

Good. The rustling water would provide more cover if they made noise.

Leaving the doors just slightly ajar, Mike played out the thin rope that had been wound around the perimeter of his Samsonite suitcase and attached a grapple to the carabiner at one end. He leaned out from the balcony, looking up, gauging distance. Right under the eaves was a wooden portico Lucy said ran around the building. It was dark all along this wall. Two stories up. Doable. As long as the balcony itself was strong. Well, it had lasted a thousand years, so it must be.

"Here." He adjusted the harness around Lucy's chest. If they were in the mountains and he had to climb with a complete newbie, he'd have insisted on the full harness— chest and upper thighs. But there wasn't much choice here. He hooked a simple figure eight onto the harness, leaned out, gauged and threw.

The grapple engaged with the wood of the portico balustrade. He tugged, then pulled himself up easily, jumping lightly down into a crouch, listening. There were sounds coming from the Palace, but distant. A soldier's barked orders, a woman's laugh, instantly stifled, some kind of light gong. But nothing close. And very few lights on this side of the Palace. They'd been put into a half-empty wing. Good.

He leaned over the balcony, looking down into Lucy's pale, anxious, upturned face.

"Stand on the balcony," he called out in a low voice, and she did. He threaded the end of the cable through an ATC device. It was there to stop the second climber from falling, but in this case it was going to have to be used to pull Lucy up as a deadweight.

He could do it. He and his team sometimes pulled up hundreds of pounds of gear and food when planning on staying in the mountains for weeks. Lucy was easy.

She stayed loose on the way up, which was good. Pulling a wriggling, panicking woman up would have been a nightmare.

Her hands landed on the top of the balcony, and Mike

pulled her up and over, into his arms for a quick hug. "Good girl! Now let's go."

"Let me go ahead," Lucy whispered. "I can orient myself better than you."

Mike's teeth gnashed. He had a superb sense of direction, thank you very much. But more than anything else, the idea of Lucy taking point went against every single instinct he had. They had no guarantee that they wouldn't run into patrolling soldiers, even though the portico seemed deserted. And if they ran into trouble, Mike wanted trouble to find him first.

But if there were no soldiers, Lucy should be in the lead because of her superior knowledge of the Palace and its layout.

Mike was an officer. He was used to making decisions and making them fast. In the field, indecision could get you killed. Sometimes even a wrong decision was better than no decision at all.

He knew this. He knew it in his bones.

But the rational part of his mind that told him calmly that Lucy should go ahead because she was more familiar with the terrain clashed violently with the crazy part of his head that could only see Lucy lying on the wooden boards in a lake of her own blood, having taken a bullet because she was in the lead.

Yes, no, yes, no . . .

Lucy watched him carefully, the anxiety slowly draining from her face, replaced by exasperation. She huffed out a breath, turned and started walking. Mike followed, right on her heels.

They worked out a system. At corners, Mike sent his worm camera around the edge and studied the long corridors of the portico. Open to the elements, lit only from below. When he saw the corridor was empty, he let her go ahead.

Twice she turned right when he would have turned left. Lucy on point turned out to be a good idea. It didn't stop him from grinding his teeth, though.

The longest corridor was the entire western face of the Palace. That side overlooked the huge esplanade where they'd been welcomed to Nhala only—God, was it only thirty hours ago?

Mike lightly touched Lucy on the shoulder and she stopped immediately, looking back at him with a question in her eyes. He stepped to the balcony and studied the view below.

There were at least double the soldiers in view than there'd been at their arrival. They carried MP-5s in slings. Everyone had a sidearm. They also looked very fit and alert—elite troops.

A dull roar came from the south. Mike watched as a helicopter appeared out of the mist, hovered, then settled onto the helipad. Twenty soldiers, fully armed, hopped out.

These soldiers—and all the soldiers on the huge plaza— were from some separate force. Their uniforms were completely different from those of the Royal Guard and of the regular troops he'd seen guarding the corridors and their rooms.

"Who are they?" he asked Lucy. "Not the Royal Guard. Not the regular army."

"No," she whispered back. "They're mercenaries. Sharmas, a warrior tribe from a small neighboring country. Their main export is soldiers, and they're good. If Changa is planning a coup, he won't be able to count on the Royal Guard or even the regular army, which is recruited from the peasantry and loyal to the Royal Family. The mercenaries' only loyalty would be to Changa."

He looked up and Lucy took off again. More corners, more long walls, until finally she stopped. They looked down over the edge. This was another long wall, along the back. No soldiers in sight.

Many rooms, many balconies, separated by about five feet. One balcony was particularly large. Lucy pointed. "The King's Chamber," she murmured. "The room next to his is Paso's. This entire section comprises the Royal Chambers."

The King's Chamber was well lit, the room next to it dark. Almost all the rooms along this wall were dark, except for the king's and a corner room about two hundred yards away.

Mike and Lucy looked at each other.

Paso's note had only spoken of the Royal Chambers, not which room. If they rappelled down onto the wrong balcony, they'd have to either pull themselves back up to the under-roof portico or hop from one balcony to another.

"Which?" Mike whispered.

"The King's Chamber," she whispered back. "The lit one. She'll definitely be there."

Mike took one look at her face. She was sure of what she was saying. Good enough for him.

"Okay, this is how we'll work it. I'll rappel down and see if I can look inside the room, see who's there. See if the princess is in the room, too." He fitted the harness to her, drove a nail deep into the ancient wood, affixed a figure eight, ran the rope through it. "When I give the signal, get on the railing of the balcony." He watched her carefully. "Do you trust me?"

"Absolutely," she replied quietly.

"Good. Because you're going to have to step off the balcony and trust that I'll be guiding you down safely. Do you think you can do that?"

She nodded.

Rappelling down was easy. He landed lightly onto the balcony of the King's Chamber and studied the window. Yellow silk curtains covered the windows, but the silk was thin. He could make out a figure inside as its shadow played on the silk.

The curtain didn't quite cover the window on the left-hand side. He placed his face close to the glass pane, being careful to ensure that his breath didn't fog the pane up.

The room was enormous, the ceiling lost to shadows, magnificent with gilt furniture, huge colorful tapestries, outsized carpets, lit partially by a huge wooden chandelier. Everywhere were tables with brass statues of the Buddha, candles lit at the base, surrounded with vases of fresh flowers, small bronze and brass statues of animals and large necklaces of jade and coral with long, brightly colored silk tassels.

A huge carved bed, the largest bed Mike had ever seen, stood high off the ground, fierce dragons carved at the top of every bedpost, under an enormous yellow silk canopy as big as a sail. A thousand brightly colored pillows sat against a carved headboard at least five feet high, and an enormous, heavy, thick comforter covered the rest.

And lost in the huge bed was a tiny figure. More like a child than a man. A bald, emaciated child. An IV tree was next to the bed on the side closest to the door, holding a clear solution in a Baxter bag, the line running to the bed, under the covers.

Next to the tiny man Paso sat on a chair, holding one of his clawlike hands. She was completely concentrated on the man in the bed. Her body language spoke of deep distress but not fear.

Mike waited five minutes, watching the little tableau, and at the end concluded that the two were alone in the enormous room. No attention was in any way directed elsewhere.

He could wait some more or he could go ahead.

He tapped on the window. Paso looked up, wary. The figure on the bed didn't move. Paso picked up a heavy candlestick and approached the window slowly.

Smart lady.

Mike took a step forward and remained unmoving when the curtain twitched. A second later, the huge heavy curtain was pulled back and the door thrown open.

"Mr. Harrington!" She looked around the long balcony. "Where's Lucy?"

First things first. "Are you alone in the room with the king?"

"Yes."

He leaned his torso out over the balcony, looking up. Lucy's face appeared immediately. Mike stuck his thumb out.

It's okay.

Without hesitation, Lucy stood on the balcony, waited until the cable tightened and, at his nod, stepped off. Mike brought her down, nice and easy, caught her and brought her onto the balcony. He had barely had time to set her on the ground and unhook the carabiner, when Paso shot into her arms and they hugged each other fiercely.

Paso's face was wet with tears. "You came! You came! I was so worried that you couldn't make it! There are soldiers everywhere, I couldn't imagine how you'd get here."

They moved indoors, Mike following. Lucy unbuckled her harness and handed it to him without looking.

Paso held Lucy's hands in hers as she guided her to the king's side. She looked down at her brother, wiping at her cheeks.

His eyes were closed, moving rapidly behind the lids, as if he were awake but couldn't find the energy to open his eyes.

Jesus, Mike could believe that. He'd never seen anyone look as bad as King Jomo. Mike had seen soldiers die, often. Soldiers died messy, violent, bloody deaths on battlefields. Strong young men, at the peak of their powers, blown apart.

This was somehow worse. This was the body blowing itself apart. Though Mike knew that the king was a young man, barely in his thirties, he looked ancient. Mike remembered reading a book on Greek mythology as a kid. He never forgot the Fates, holding life by a string. The king's string was frayed, weakening by the minute.

Every few breaths, there was a burbling sound in his chest, and Mike knew he was hearing the death rattle. He doubted the king had more than twenty-four hours to live.

Paso's voice was low and strained. "This morning, my brother heard two guards discussing something, something terrible. They thought he was unconscious, but he wasn't. He has refused pain medication ever since and begged to have you brought to him." Paso dropped her forehead onto Lucy's shoulder. "I knew what I was asking of you when I left that note at the Dancing Buddha. General Changa has filled the Palace, and from what I've heard the entire city, with troops. But Jomo wanted so much to see you."

They both looked down at the young/ancient king. He looked as if he'd crossed some kind of boundary. Maybe they'd arrived too late.

"Did he give a hint of what he overheard?" Mike asked. Both women jumped as if they'd forgotten he was in the room.

"He tried." The princess's voice wobbled and then she steadied it. "He tried to talk to me. He ordered the nurses to remove morphine from his drip." She drew in a shaky breath. "He's been in terrible pain all day. I didn't know what to do for him. This past hour he's just been lying there without responding."

Mike hated having to do this. But it was likely the king knew something of vital importance. His hand hovered over the king's shoulder and he looked at Paso. "May I?"

Fresh tears filled her eyes and she bit her lips. But finally, she nodded.

Mike shook the king's shoulder, very gently, trying to keep the pity from showing on his face. God, the man was all bones. He barely stirred. Mike shook his shoulder again.

Suddenly, the king's eyes opened, and for the moment they were clear and knowing. He swept the room without moving his head, and his eyes lit on Lucy.

"Lu-cy."

Lucy moved to the bedside. Mike could see her long, slender throat working as she swallowed. Her face was pale, but she didn't cry. "Jomo." She sketched a shaky smile. "You remember me."

"Of . . . course. Listen, Lu-cy." The king's free hand clutched hers so tightly his knuckles whitened under the golden skin. His head lifted slightly from the huge embroidered silk pillows. "Bad men. Very bad men." His eyes were fixed desperately on her face. "Changa . . . your government . . ."

His head dropped back onto the pillows. The sound of his wheezing as he tried to draw breath into his dying body was loud in the huge, silent, shadowy room.

Paso was hugging herself tightly, tears leaking out of the edges of her black eyes.

Lucy's face was gentle as she bent over the king. "Jomo," she said softly, as she touched his shoulder. "You are so brave. A true king. You shall live in your people's hearts forever. Let us know how we can stop these bad men. Help us save your people."

It was exactly the right thing to say. King Jomo's eyes fluttered open. "Changa is planning to . . . attack India. Deadly . . . disease. Millions will die." His eyes went to his sister, rocking back and forth in pain. "He plans to . . . marry Paso after I die . . ."

Mike leaned down again, "How—" he had begun, when he heard boots in the outside hallway.

Fuck.

He tackled Lucy, taking her to the floor with him, rolling them under the high, ceremonial bed just as the big doors slammed open and soldiers marched into the chambers of the dying king.

FIFTEEN

LUCY was on her back, Mike's heavy body completely covering her, head to toe, his big hand over her mouth. When he saw that she understood, he removed his hand and turned his attention to the direction of the door, listening intently.

Lucy knew he was unarmed, but the expression on his face was frightening, a warrior's face. Even unarmed against guns, she'd bet anything he'd take down several soldiers before falling himself. He felt like stone on top of her, every muscle tense and ready.

The heavy silk cover of Jomo's bed fell halfway between the bed and the floor. If she looked to the left, she could see some of the room reflected in an enormous silver-backed mirror in a heavy wooden frame hanging at an angle. Lucy tapped Mike on the shoulder. His head turned to the left where she pointed.

General Changa stepped into the frame of the mirror, and every hair on Lucy's body stood up. Menace emanated from him as he walked slowly to the right-hand side of the bed, looking down at the dying king.

Behind him, four soldiers stood at attention, assault rifles held across their chests, completely blank-faced. The Sharmas. The mercenaries. Fierce and brave warriors, famed throughout the Himalayas. But true mercenaries. They'd fight to the death for their sponsor, but the instant he lost power, they'd turn their backs on him, ready for their next paymaster.

Lucy watched in horror as the general stared down coldly at the king and pinched the hand where the IV went in. The king didn't move. Lucy couldn't imagine anyone conscious not reacting instinctively to the pain. The general grunted, satisfied that Jomo was passed out.

Paso went wild. She screamed and launched an attack on the general, scrambling at his hand to dislodge it. The general backhanded her without taking his gaze from the king's still form.

Mike jerked, muscles moving as he prepared to attack. Lucy immediately locked her arms and legs around him. His movements had been instinctive, that of a male unable to stand a woman being slapped around, but he wasn't going to help anyone, Paso or the king, by revealing their position. He'd only get them killed.

Mike understood this. He stilled. His face got even grimmer, eyes as cold as the general's as he watched events unfolding in the mirror.

Paso had been knocked to the floor but was unharmed. She scrambled to her feet, screaming.

The general put his big hand around her throat. Mike's jaw muscles danced and his hands clenched. Lucy put her hand on the side of his face and turned it to hers. She shook her head sharply. *Don't interfere.*

Changa wasn't strangling Paso, he was establishing control.

"You silly woman. Your brother is almost dead. The only way you can become queen is to marry me. And you will, if I have to drag you to the ceremony. You are crazy to oppose me, for I am planning on great things for Nhala."

"You son of a bitch!" Paso spat in his face. *"I would*

rather die than marry you! The only great thing possible for Nhala is for some brave soul to put a dagger through your black heart!"

Mike looked at Lucy, but she didn't dare translate. She was surprised the general didn't hear the frantic tattoo of her heart, beating so hard she thought it would beat its way right outside her chest.

The room went white with a bolt of lightning, followed by a window-rattling rumble of thunder.

The general tightened his grip around Paso's throat, stilling her.

Behind the general and Paso, however, the soldiers exchanged wary looks. They were the general's mercenaries and, by their own code, his soldiers. But they didn't have to like the sight of the princess being manhandled, hurt.

The general bent down to Paso, his face very close to hers. *"I don't like your attitude, Princess. Perhaps you have been coached in rebellion by your American friend, eh? I'm going to go tell her to mind her own business. You should know better than to listen to outsiders. After tomorrow night, she'll be gone. And you will be my wife."*

He released Paso suddenly. She staggered, gasping.

The general turned on his heels and left the room, his soldiers following. A cold, evil wind blowing out the room.

The instant the huge heavy door closed behind him, Paso ran around the bed, falling to her knees. "Hurry!" she cried, tugging at the black sleeve of Mike's jacket.

Lucy felt the same remorseless bite of urgency. She pushed at Mike's shoulders. He rolled out from under the bed, pulled her after him and stood.

"What?" Mike looked from Paso to Lucy. She took a split second to look at the king, lying on the bed unconscious. Jomo. At seventeen, he'd felt keenly the weight and responsibility of being a future king. He'd treated the two girls, one his sister and the other a beloved foreigner, as children.

But he'd always been kind, and she was certain he'd

been a very good and responsible king. This was the last time she'd see him on this earth.

"No time, Lucy!" Paso gasped. "You must go, now!"

Lucy ran to the windows, Mike on her heels. She turned to him on the enormous dark balcony. Rain started spitting out of the black night sky. "Changa's on his way to our room. We have to hurry! He can't catch us out of the room!" Lucy translated the Nhalan for him.

Mike was already throwing up the grapple, tugging when it bit. "No time for belaying." He bent at the waist. "On my back."

She didn't hesitate, climbing onto his back, twining her arms around his neck, trying very hard not to choke him.

"Legs around my waist."

Lucy's heart was pounding. *Hurry hurry hurry!* drummed in her head. How could they possibly make it in time? If he found an empty room, Changa wouldn't execute them—would he? But he would certainly imprison them.

It was freezing out on the balcony. The temperature had dropped, and a harsh, sleety rain had begun, pounding so hard she could hear the heavy drops splash on the stone tiles below. When Mike swung out over the balcony, they were exposed to the full force of the sleeting rain, falling so hard the drops actually hurt the top of her head and her back.

"Hold on tight." He started climbing, slowly, steadily. Against her front, she could feel his steely muscles at play as he climbed the narrow rope as steadily as a machine.

She couldn't even imagine the strength it took to pull them both up an entire tall story, hand over hand. She hugged him more tightly, head tight up against his neck, knees and thighs hugging his hips, on the theory that anything that anchored her to him would help.

Hand over hand . . .

Surely the rain made the rope slippery, made his job harder? And yet he gave no sign of distress, just kept climbing.

What could she do to help? Nothing. Nothing physical,

at least. Mentally, she mapped the route back so they could take it at a dead run instead of checking corners.

The general was walking the internal corridors right now, warm and dry, arrowing straight to their room.

She sharpened her ears, sent her senses out for any hint of danger. Two soldiers' voices rang out, one a command, one an answer.

"Check this wall."

"Yes, sir."

"Mike," she murmured directly into his ear. "Soldiers coming around the corner."

He gave only a grunt in answer, but speeded up, muscles bunching. Though the rain was freezing on her back, Lucy was warm wherever she touched Mike.

Five holds to go. Four, three, two, one.

With another grunt, he reached the top of the portico balcony and heaved them both over. They tumbled to the floor, splashing in a pool of icy water.

Down below, the soldier reported back. *"All clear, sir."*

Mike lay on his back, eyes closed, breathing heavily, big chest bellowing, rain bouncing off the dense, complex material of his ninja suit. His eyes opened, stared into hers.

Lucy reached down and gave him her hand. He grabbed her hand but got up under his own steam, without pulling at her at all.

He lifted the grapple from where it had stuck to the ancient wood, and quickly coiled the rope.

"We have to run now," Lucy said. "He's on his way." She met his eyes. "I'll go first. We can't stop to check at corners. If we come across someone, I'll duck."

Mike's jaws worked as he bit back the words that were undoubtedly burning in his chest. He wanted to be first, "take point" as he called it. But only Lucy could actually lead them back at a dead run. Mike would hesitate, check his bearings.

Lucy took off.

She didn't even try to run quietly, she simply pounded down the long wooden corridors, sleety rain blowing in her eyes, soaking her jacket, her pants. Somewhere she'd lost her knit hat. The wind whipped wet strands of hair around her head. Mike was behind her, but though he was much heavier than she was, he was making a lot less noise.

She was gasping by the time they finally made it to the spot just above their room. She bent over, hands on thighs, struggling to breathe. With a sharp downward slash, Mike stuck the grapple to the top of the balcony, the dark wood swollen with rain.

Now that she wasn't running flat out, Lucy was freezing, the very core of her chilled. She didn't have gloves on and her hands felt numb. Her face was numb, too. Her brain was obviously numb as well, because when Mike crouched at her feet, she simply stared at him stupidly, wondering what he was doing.

He caught her hand and turned around, still crouching, that hugely broad back to her. "Come on, honey. Hop on. We don't have much time."

He tugged, and her mind unfroze for just a second, just long enough to understand what she had to do. Nothing much, really. Just hang on to Mike like a barnacle. She was so cold she couldn't possibly have done what he did, which was step up onto the top of the balcony and cast himself off into the cold, sleeting darkness in what felt for a horrible second like a free fall.

The scream of terror died in her throat when she realized that it wasn't an uncontrolled fall at all. That he was simply going down the rope as fast as was humanly possible, faster than she'd imagined it could be done.

In an instant he had them on their own balcony. A huge gust of wind blew rain over them. It was like being pelted with buckets of ice water. Mike made it over the balcony and rushed them into the warm room. Lucy stood, frozen and trembling violently, the sudden heat painful.

Outside, the rope swung gently.

Mike was moving fast. He stripped her of her wet clothes, stuffing them into a nearby cabinet, and rushed her to the bathroom door. "Hop into the shower, honey. When Changa comes, we need an explanation of why you're wet."

His words came from far away, from another country. She wasn't sure she understood, but then he was nudging her into the hot bathroom, grabbing a towel, turning on the shower. Steam rose almost instantly. When he pushed her under the shower head she nearly screamed at the sudden heat on her frozen skin.

She was standing under the shower, turning slowly, feeling heat returning to her body, thoughts starting to resurface in her head, when there was a loud rap on the door to the room and General Changa and his soldiers marched in.

Goddamn! Mike thought. He'd stripped in an instant, freezing sodden suit, wet boots, socks kicked under the bed, but his hair and face were dripping wet.

Pretend you've just come out of the shower.

Nothing to do but bluff it out. He brought the towel he'd grabbed from the bathroom and draped it around his hips, knotting it as the general walked toward him.

"General Changa!" He put some bite into his voice. Nice American guy, usually friendly and polite. But really—charging into someone's bedroom was very uncool. "I'm sorry . . ." He lifted his hands, looked around. "Did you forget something? Because we're ah, well, we're about ready to go to bed."

Thank God he'd had cold weather gear on. He'd been protected from the cold. Otherwise, he'd have started steaming the instant he stepped into the warm room. Steam had already started rising from Lucy when he'd shoved her toward the bathroom.

The general would have instantly recognized the source of the steam. A body that had been out in the cold suddenly come into the warmth. He'd have been suspicious, started questioning Mike and Lucy.

General Changa was *not* going to slap Lucy around. It had been bad enough watching him with Paso. It was not going to happen to Lucy. Mike would fight the entire fucking Nhalan Army if Changa so much as touched her.

The bathroom door opened, and perfumed steam billowed from the open doorway. Lucy stepped out, wrapped in a big towel, another big white towel around her hair. She looked rosy and beautiful, the towel showing just the tops of her soft breasts.

The eyes of the four soldiers behind Changa widened.

"General Changa!" Lucy exclaimed. She looked bewildered, a half smile on her face. Trying to be polite, but embarrassed. She tightened the towel around her breasts, but in order to do so, she had to loosen it for a second, showing a touch more of her breasts. "This is . . . most unusual. Has something happened? To the king or to the princess?"

Shit, she was *perfect*. No one on earth could have possibly guessed that only a few minutes ago she'd been frozen and terrified and winded. Anyone looking at her would take the situation for exactly what it looked like. A beautiful young woman emerging from the shower, a little upset, a little exasperated.

"The princess is well," the general growled. "Have you spoken to her recently?"

"The princess?" A perfect frown creased the smooth skin between Lucy's eyebrows. "No, I haven't General. You asked me that at the lab. After which you yourself accompanied us to our room where," she let a little anger show, just a little, "where we were locked in."

Lucy waved her hand at the huge tray holding the remains of their meal. To wave her hand, she had to let the towel slip for another moment. The four soldiers were focused like laser beams on her.

"We ate our meal and took our showers because we are both very tired. We. Are. Ready. To. Go. To. Bed." Each word emphasized, tone severe, the closest a lady could get to telling a boor to fuck off.

General Changa didn't budge. Which was lucky for him. One bad move and he was dead.

If Mike had to, he could take them all down before they could draw their firearms. The soldiers' sidearms were holstered, and the holsters were snapped shut. He mapped it all out in his head.

First step—the brass letter opener embedded in the general's eye.

Mike was good with knives. The letter opener wasn't a knife, but it would do. If he could hold the general still, he'd be able to find the exact spot to slip it into the man's black heart. But at a throwing distance, the chances of it bouncing off a rib were too great.

So letter opener to the eye, where it would penetrate the cortex. Before the general even hit the floor, Mike would hurl any of the ten heavy bronze, hand-sized statues of Buddha straight at the heads of the men behind him, using both hands. He'd once had a baseball he'd thrown clocked at 90 mph. Once they were down, he'd grab their weapons and make sure they stayed down.

Then a fast exfil from the Palace with Lucy. Dress, rappel down, quietly make their way to the motor pool. Hot start the engine of an all-terrain vehicle, drive away.

Doable.

He didn't want to do it, because there could be a firefight and he wanted Lucy far away from anything even resembling a firefight. But if it came down to it, if they were fighting for their lives, he could do it. He could get himself and Lucy to safety.

The general stared down at Lucy for a long, long moment, gaze black and hostile. The only sound in the room was the icy sleet pinging against the windows. *Please God, don't let him see the rope hanging outside the balcony*, Mike thought.

Then all thoughts flew out of his mind as the general stepped closer to Lucy. A danger alarm clanged in every cell of his body. He became an animal made up exclusively of instinct. Only one thought in his head. *Do not touch my female*.

Mike had taken a step toward the general to rip his fucking head off his fucking body, when Lucy shook her head slightly. *Back off.*

He clenched his jaw, breathed heavily, didn't move.

Fucking general made one move to touch her, all bets were off.

The general looked down at Lucy, eyes narrowed, skin tight over his cheekbones, nostrils flared. Cold, aggressive, commanding.

"You will finish restoring the manuscript by tomorrow evening, Dr. Merritt, when you will present it to me and to the princess at the opening ceremony of the Feast of the Snow Dragon in the Great Hall. At the ceremony you will speak to no one, especially not to Princess Paso. You will be escorted back to your room after the ceremony, and the next morning, you and your *fiancé*"—he spat the word— "will be accompanied to the heliport and flown back to Thimphu. Is that clear?"

Lucy drew herself up, completely unintimidated. "Perfectly clear, General. And now I will thank you if you and your soldiers leave so we can get some rest."

Christ, she deserved an Oscar.

The general turned on his heel and strode straight to the door without breaking his stride. Either someone was going to open the door or he'd slam right into it. His soldiers scrambled to open it for him and he marched through. Mike wished they'd been less quick on the uptake and let the fucking general break his fucking nose against the fucking door.

The door slammed shut behind the general and his men, and the key turned in the lock from the outside.

Lucy let out a long, shaky breath. "Man, that was—" She stopped when she saw him. "Mike? Is something wrong? You look—"

He had no idea what he looked like. Crazy, probably.

All he knew was that he had to have her, right now, or die. He pulled her to him, roughly, and his mouth came down over hers.

Instant kiss, a real one. No fluttering little busses around the mouth, testing her out, seeing if she liked it, if he liked it. Swapping a little spit, seeing if they liked each other's taste. Playing the game.

This wasn't a game. This was so far from being a game it wasn't funny. Mike held the back of her head with his hand and dived into the kiss, zero to a hundred in two seconds.

He twisted his mouth, opening hers farther, and took his first big taste of her, his tongue licking hers. His body turned into a huge electrode, buzzing with energy. The kiss lasted so long he forgot to breathe; then, when his lungs protested, he just breathed from her, as if they were one entity.

Some dim bell in the back of his head rang, its vibrations shaking a few thoughts loose from a brain completely seized up by proximity to Lucy, fried from holding her so close, having her under his hands.

He was kissing her hard, holding her hard against him, everything hard, particularly what was under his towel. Hands gripping her hard. He had strong, tough hands. A climber's hands and—Jesus—maybe in his excitement he was hurting her.

He loosened his grip a little, though he had to think consciously about it. *Open those fingers, that's right. One at a time . . .*

Because the last thing his hands wanted was to let go of Lucy, stop touching all that soft, soft skin. It was as if he'd become one of those dinosaurs whose brains were too small to control their bodies. Those dinosaurs had a second brain in their tails. He knew where his second brain was.

Every single body part seemed to be on its own, doing what it wanted. Touching her, holding her, kissing her.

He pulled his head back, gasping, astonished at how hard it was to do. Loosened his grip, tried to step back.

Looked down. Man, you'd have to be dead to resist her. Lucy's face was rosy, lips wet and slightly swollen from his mouth, beautiful gray blue eyes dazed, pupils dilated.

"Am I hurting you?" His voice sounded rough, as if he hadn't spoken in days.

"No," she answered and pulled his head back down to hers.

So that was that.

He swiped his hands and both their towels fell unnoticed

to the ground, and ah, Jesus, she was naked in his arms, warm and soft and *Lucy.*

He pulled her tightly against him, so that every possible inch of his body could be touching every possible inch of hers. Hands over the smooth, sleek planes of her back, down to the swell of her backside, her own arms around him, fingernails digging into his back. She leaned into him, warm and tender, each breath bringing her close up against him, thighs rubbing against his.

Oh, man. Couldn't do this standing up. Nope. Knees wouldn't hold. Mike went straight to the floor, pulling Lucy down with him, without breaking the kiss.

Luckily the floor was covered in a million rugs, huge cushions scattered everywhere. He rolled them both onto an enormous silk-covered cushion the size of a car, kissing her wildly, coming to rest on top of her. Their hands met, entwined above her head. Her hands were slender, fine, delicate. Everything about her was delicate.

This evening he could have lost her, in a second. In the princess's room, on the way over, on the way back, in their own room.

They weren't out of the woods yet, not at all. Anything might happen, and though Mike's new imperative was keeping Lucy safe, shit happens. No one knew that more than he did.

Lucy was smart and worldly, but she was also gentle and kindhearted, and this world isn't kind to the kindhearted. It is brutal and cruel.

In this far-off kingdom, with a dying king and a tyrant-in-waiting with an army of mercenaries behind him, Lucy was in deadly danger every second.

It drove him a little crazy.

He wanted to be inside her, because sex with Lucy right now seemed like the most desirable thing in the world, but also because if he was with her, inside her, holding her, he could keep her safe. Cover her body with his, shelter her. Hold her, have her.

As long as he was touching her she was safe.

He moved his mouth from hers to nip at her jaw, the soft skin under her ear, her neck. His thighs moved, opening hers. His penis nudged against her opening. He shook with restraint.

"I don't think I can wait," he said roughly.

"No." Her voice was a mere whisper, right against his ear, soft, warm breath coming with the word. It raised gooseflesh all over him. "Don't wait."

Mike entered her, an electric flash of pleasure bursting through him, like slotting his body into a warm, welcoming place that had been awaiting him all his life.

It galvanized him. He lost all control, barely registering his heavy breathing, the sound of their bodies slapping together, the warm, wet sound of their kisses.

Oh God, it was too much. So much hot pleasure, from so many different places, Lucy holding him tightly with her arms and legs wrapped around him, as if to keep him from leaving her, as if that were even a remote possibility.

The heat grew, incandescent friction, bubbling up irresistibly from some secret place inside him. He was helpless to check the wave of pleasure crashing over him, unstoppable, uncontrollable. He shook, teeth clenched, as he emptied himself inside her.

It took forever. It was over in a second.

He lowered himself over Lucy, forearms bracketing her head, facedown on the cushion next to her head, breathing hard and sweating.

His brain was absolutely wasted, not a thought in his head, just physical sensations, all of them good. Fantastic, in fact.

Then, as he slowly came back to himself, the thoughts were not so good. He had no idea if Lucy had come, he'd been so concentrated on the wild riotous things rolling around inside him.

This wasn't like him. He thought of himself as a considerate lover, careful and controlled, solicitous of his partner's pleasure.

He did not consider himself a warthog in heat, but that

was how he had behaved. To *Lucy*. And he, Mike Shafer, elite warrior of the Tenth Mountain Division, was scared to death to ask how she felt.

Do the hard thing. What he constantly told his men.

"Ahm." He turned his head and cleared his throat. He was so close to her he could have seen the pores of her skin if she'd had any. She didn't. Her skin was utterly smooth, like marble. She was looking up at the ceiling, her face impossible to interpret. Was she mad? Upset? Disappointed? He studied her profile, tender and mysterious. "How you doing?"

That earned him a smile. Good. Smiles were good. She turned finally and met his eyes. Hers were so beautiful and unreadable.

"I'm fine. And you?"

Something garbled came out of his mouth. He'd just had the strongest orgasm of his life. He thought at one point during it that his heart would explode.

He smiled. Her smile grew.

She lifted a hand and traced the outline of his face, from his eyebrow, over his cheekbone, to his mouth. He could feel his lips curving. Her touch felt wonderful.

Make amends. Get it right.

"I'm sorry if it wasn't . . . great for you. I'll do better next time." Which would be very soon, because he was still hard as a rock inside her. "Promise."

"Sex is a great stress reliever, isn't it?" she asked softly, and his smile disappeared. Wiped right off his face.

"No," he snapped. "It's not. My stress hasn't been relieved at all."

Is that what she thought this was about? Relieving fucking *stress*? He'd thought that himself a day ago. Now everything had changed.

He levered himself up on his forearms so his face was right above hers, nose less than an inch from hers, staring her right in the eye so she got the message.

"This wasn't stress-relief sex, and it wasn't comfort sex, and it wasn't getting-to-know-you sex. It was . . ." Mike's mind whirred, looking for the exact right term, maybe something with a little science behind it. Lucy was basically a scientist herself, so it would be something she'd understand. "It was bonding sex."

He nodded sharply. Good term. He was proud of himself for making it up when his brain was mostly cream of wheat sloshing around in his skull.

The corner of Lucy's mouth lifted. "*Bonding* sex? Is that a real concept or did you make it up?"

"No, no, I, um, I read an article about it. In a magazine." Her smile was widening. "It's like, when your pheromones come together and . . . mate."

Lucy sighed. "Mike, pheromones don't mate. That's like saying the insulin from your pancreas mates."

Mike looked at their hands together. He had his father's hands—big and tough. The hands of a man who worked with them, mostly outdoors. One morning when he was seventeen he'd woken up and there they were—his father's hands at the end of his arms.

How often he'd seen his father twine his hand with Cheryl's, and it looked exactly like Mike's hand twined with Lucy's.

It was as if something in the universe slowed and settled within him. This was exactly as it should be. He felt connected to every single Shafer man since the dawn of time, the first Shafer entwining a hairy paw with his mate's hairy paw up a tree.

His father had found his mate and now Mike had found his.

So he needed to start treating her like a lady. Starting now.

"We need to do that again. I need to show you I can do it right."

"I don't know," she said, smiling, eyes starting to droop. "Felt fine to me." Lucy stretched lazily, and every hair on his body stood up because she was stretching underneath him and he felt it all, sleek belly rubbing against his, thighs stretching under his, small perfect breasts against his chest . . .

He swelled even harder inside her. Lucy's eyes opened wide, startled.

"Yeah," he said roughly. "I'm ready for round two. Really ready."

"I can see that. I can feel it, too. But . . ." She gave a gentle smile, cupped his chin in her hand. "You need to give me some time to recover. Please."

Startled, Mike looked at her. Really looked at her. Saw beyond the beauty who messed with his head. Saw beyond the off-the-charts sex. Saw *her*, Lucy Merritt.

Saw a woman who'd been under enormous stress yet had kept herself together, but at a steep price. Saw the slight bruises under her eyes, saw the drooping eyelids.

She was tired.

His dick could just take a hike.

"Okay." He slid out, rolled off her, kneeled and scooped her up.

"Whoa!" Lucy emitted a half scream, half laugh and clutched his shoulders. "What are you doing?"

"Taking you to bed." Her eyes rolled. "Not that way. I mean that way, yeah, sure, but not right now. Later. First you rest."

He pulled back the covers and lay her down on the bed that wasn't much smaller than the landing strip–sized bed poor Jomo was dying in. The enormous silk-covered comforters were warm and heavy and nearly a foot thick; it was like sleeping under a silk-covered mountain.

Mike slipped in after her, putting his arms around her and pulling her close, resolutely and heroically keeping his mind centered above his navel. A second later, they'd found the perfect fit, all her bits fitting against his bits.

The sheets and comforter were warm and soft, Lucy was warm and soft.

They were in a building where a king was dying, where deadly conspiracies were brewing, bristling with soldiers who would turn on them at a shouted command.

But here, in the cozy, dim room, with only a small night-light for illumination and shadows filling the dark corners, here he and his Lucy were safe and warm. He tightened his arms around her.

Once when he was about twelve, he'd camped out in the Rockies with his dad. It had snowed most of the day, but the night was clear, with a full moon. Restless, he'd gone exploring and had chanced upon a wolf pack in the night. A thick snow muffled sounds, and he was downwind from the pack. The sky was completely cloudless; the full moon bathed the uplands with an eerie silver glow. He'd rounded a corner and there they were—a pack of gray wolves asleep in a natural den under an overhanging cliff.

He watched them for almost an hour, fascinated. They were magnificent creatures, silver-stippled, with long, elegant muzzles, the males thick-chested, a few females with balls of fur curled against their bellies.

It was freezing cold, at least twenty below, but the wolves slept comfortably, protected by their thick fur and by the heat of all the members of the pack. Even in a raging snowstorm, they'd be safe.

Mike had envied them, sleeping so comfortably with their kind, warm and safe, snuffling through the night, dreaming of the hunt, in a complex geometry of bodies, each part fitting beautifully and perfectly to create a magnificent whole.

Lucy's head turned slightly to find a better fit on his shoulder, and he smiled down at her. Her eyelids were at half-mast.

"I'm not as sleepy as you think," she protested. "I'm just going to rest my eyes."

"Uh-huh." He didn't even smile when she yawned. "Absolutely."

Inside a minute she was gone.

Mike moved a little, found an even more perfect position and closed his eyes.

It was good to sleep with his pack.

$\mathcal{S}$IXTEEN

EDWIN Montgomery rubbed his chest, where it burned. Acid reflux.

This was it. This was his last mission. Once the bio-weapons lab that threatened to unleash a terrible plague upon the world was closed down, the threat eliminated and, above all, Lucy brought home, he was going to retire. Just stay home. Stay home and . . . what?

His mind pulled a blank.

The intercom pinged. DS&T. "Yes?"

"Deputy Director, we're sending the results of Stop Cold Essence," the contents of the flash drive, "to your computer."

Ah . . . the geeks. He'd been told it might take three days, and they'd done it in less than one.

"Is the intel intact?"

Silence. "Not quite, sir. There's a section that is only partially recovered."

Everything was coming online now.

"Have them continue. Get NSA involved if necessary."

"Yes, sir." The voice was gelid. He'd just told his own

people that he thought the NSA techies were better than the CIA techies, which would have been cruel if it weren't true. Montgomery didn't give a shit about hurt feelings. He wanted results.

He read through the contents of the flash drive, dread rising in his system. Christ. A two-pronged attack—Manhattan and Israel. Maybe three-pronged, depending on what was in the destroyed part of the flash drive.

Analysts had even given some preliminary estimates of casualties and consequences.

Manhattan, during the Macy's Thanksgiving Day Parade. Estimated casualties: at least 8 million. Manhattan closed down for years, maybe forever, as Hazmat-suited officers combed every single building, floor by floor, for containers of the virus, going very slowly, because it would take very little to put in place trip wires that would trigger new outbreaks.

The entire island, and a buffer area of miles into the neighboring boroughs, would be no-man's-land for generations. Maybe forever.

A large chunk of America's wealth was in Manhattan, in every sense. The companies, the banks, Wall Street, real estate. A loss of several trillion dollars just in economic terms alone. Over and above the 8 million lives. And that was a lowball estimate.

A devastating blow, from which the country would never recover.

The cost to Israel: another 8 million, wiping the country out. Plus at least another 1 million from the neighboring countries and Palestine. Montgomery was very clear on the mind-set of his enemies. The fact that maybe a million of their people would die an agonizing death meant less than nothing to them.

So Israel would be taken out and America wouldn't lift a finger. Once the attack on Manhattan was unleashed, all troops stationed around the world would be brought home immediately to deal with massive security issues, the country closing in on itself. It would be torn apart, martial law declared. The military would be necessary to contain the violence.

The United States as an expeditionary power would be gone, maybe forever.

Certainly no troops could be spared to help the Jewish diaspora. They'd be on their own.

Israel was well armed, and generations living in the midst of crazed fanatics had hardened its resolve. Before it died, Israel would have its revenge.

In its dying throes, someone in Israel's security establishment would pull the nuclear trigger, and the crazed jihadists would be indirectly responsible for the deaths of even more millions of their coreligionists.

The horrible thing was, Montgomery reflected, some wouldn't even mind. Pakistanis were behind this plan. They wouldn't care if the entire Middle East were taken out. More power for them.

And General Changa? What did Nhala have to do with this plan? Nhala was a peaceful kingdom with no known hereditary enemies and no terrorism, whether homegrown or imported.

So what was Changa doing? Was he just the conduit? Offering a site for the biolab where no one would think to look? It was the third element of the plan, if there was one, where the intel was degraded. Though what had been preserved was horrible enough.

He lifted his receiver. Thanks to Captain Shafer and Lucy, maybe millions of lives could be saved.

"I want to talk to the Chairman of the Joint Chiefs of Staff, the Director of the NSA and the head of Mossad. And patch this all through to DHS. Now."

"Yessir," the smooth voice of his assistant said.

One by one, faces appeared on his monitors. The Director of the NSA, Admiral Robert Larsen, face as ascetic as any monk's. They said he ran ten miles a day, every day, and never ate. It was entirely possible he wore hair shirts and cilices.

Then the Chairman of the Joint Chiefs of Staff, Admiral

Keith Ripley, came up. No asceticism there. He was at least thirty pounds overweight and ruddy. And very smart.

Finally, after five minutes, a third monitor lit up and the face of the head of Mossad appeared, surrounded by a wreath of smoke. Dov Zamir, the world's greatest pessimist. He had deep lines in his face and looked as if his best friend had just died.

When they were all online, Montgomery folded his hands and leaned toward the tiny camera at the top of the central monitor.

"Gentlemen. I have just received news of the greatest import. Several days ago, one of our operatives, acting upon intelligence, retrieved information from a hidden bioweapons laboratory in Nhala."

The three men facing him were immune to surprises. Their entire professional lives had been spent juggling huge problems thrown at them from nowhere. But even they allowed themselves the barest minimum of a surprised expression. He could almost hear the cogs in their brains whirring. Bioweapons lab—there was a place in their heads for that, unfortunately. A dark, scary place. But a bioweapons lab—in *Nhala*? That took a second to compute.

And he could see in their faces the immediate *oh, shit* reaction. Up until now, the small, peaceable Himalayan countries had been outside the circle of the War on Terror.

If Nhala was joining world terror, then the other Himalayan countries might, too. And the entire intelligence community would have to man up—recruit new types of agents, add those languages to the mix, immediately change the curricula of most of the faculties of political science in the West to create new areas of expertise, change the latitude parameters of the spy satellites . . . It didn't bear thinking about.

If they managed to save the world once again, this time he really was going to retire.

Now the second half of the double whammy.

"Part of the information our operative retrieved concerns this nation, and part of it concerns yours, Mr. Zamir." Dov's puffy eyes remained steady, one more vital threat to his country. But first, the threat to Montgomery's own. "Director Larsen, General Ripley, there is a ship crossing the Atlantic right now, which will land somewhere along the Eastern Seaboard sometime in the next thirty-six to forty-eight hours, and which is carrying an unspecified number of jihadists in the hold. At some point before offloading these terrorists, they will be injected with a bioweaponized form of a mutated viral hemorrhagic disease which is fast-acting and airborne." The two tough soldiers, who'd survived any number of crises, blinked. It took a lot to make them blink, but this did it. "It is our belief that they intend to land, make their way one by one to Manhattan and be on the streets in time for the Macy's Thanksgiving Day Parade."

Montgomery gave them time to digest this.

"It goes without saying that the ship must be found and stopped at all costs. We must find this ship and destroy it and everyone on board. We don't have a name and we don't know where landfall will be. All we know is that it stopped in the port of Bengazi and that it is headed for somewhere along the Eastern Seaboard and, ultimately, for Manhattan. Details have already been sent to you. So NSA will use all its resources and work in close conjunction with the navy and air force to find this ship and neutralize it. As of this moment, every single resource of the United States government is to be concentrated on this task, and this one alone. There is no higher imperative. Is that clear?"

He waited for the murmurs of assent from the director and the chairman and then turned to Dov Zamir.

"Mr. Zamir, our intelligence leads us to believe that there are a number of jihadists already in your country, in a safe house in Tel Aviv, waiting to spread the disease. This bioweaponized form of hemorrhagic fever burns itself out within twenty-four hours, reducing the contaminated body to dust. It is, essentially, a weapon to empty a country, and that is what we fear is planned. To kill every single Israeli citizen, plus some collateral damage along the neighboring borders." Montgomery stopped for a moment, heart heavy, telling a man that perhaps his whole country was about to be wiped off the face of the earth. "We are talking about the annihilation of Israel as a state, and its subsequent repopulation by Israel's enemies. This is scheduled to occur two or three days after the elimination of Manhattan, in the certain knowledge that no US forces will be deployed for the protection of Israel, as we will have sustained a lethal blow ourselves. You would be entirely on your own. Do I make myself clear, Mr. Zamir?"

"Very." Dov's cigarette-roughened voice was steady.

"We will make available to you the precise intel we received, and it will be up to your agents, using whatever means they can, to discover the exact location of the safe house and to deal with its occupants. How many Level A Hazmat suits does your country have, sir?"

Dov Zamir's mouth tightened. "Ordinarily that would be confidential information. But this is an extraordinary situation. We have about one hundred Level A Hazmat suits."

"You're going to need more for your soldiers. I'll order three thousand to be airlifted to you, immediately."

The head of Israeli intelligence bowed his head briefly, in thanks.

Montgomery didn't mention the corrupted files. There was no point, until his geeks could restore them. The intelligence services and military already had their hands full dealing with the disasters they knew about.

He put his hands on the table. "Gentlemen, that is it. We have already sent all of you everything we know about what our agent discovered. We all now have one priority and one alone—to find the ship carrying a mutated virus to Manhattan and to find the safe house where terrorists are about to unleash that virus on Israel. Everything else takes a backseat. I'll expect updates from all of you, and rest assured that the full resources of the CIA are at your disposal. That's all."

Montgomery pressed the button that cut the connection off, thinking hard, rubbing his chest. Maybe . . .

He called the head of NORAD, the North American Aerospace Defense Command.

"General Sharinsky."

"Montgomery. Do you have drones with IV capability?"

"Yes, sir, we do. Not many."

"I want nighttime flights over the Atlantic, throw every asset you've got at it, retrofit some drones if you can. Count every ship in the Atlantic that gives off a heat signal."

"Yessir. What are we looking for?"

"A plague ship. Headed straight for us."

A pause. Then—"Yes, sir."

Montgomery sat at his desk quietly, thinking hard, feeling each heavy heartbeat like a dull, throbbing pain. When his monitor lit up, his heart squeezed, hard, when he saw the origin of the message. DS&T. He didn't know if he was up to any more news. He read, barely breathing, switched his monitor off and sat, head bowed.

The last words were still in front of his eyes in glowing white. The last piece of intel that had been decrypted from the flash drive, concerning Nhala. An attack on India.

And the last words were: *Estimated deaths: at least 100 million.*

THE PALACE
CHILONGO, NHALA

Cold. Darkness. The lights had gone out. Light snow was falling, slightly muffling the sounds of army vehicles gathering in the huge courtyard. She got up from her bed, shivering, and looked down into the flagstoned courtyard, eyes wide as she watched men spilling out of military vehicles. Hundreds of them.

They were all dressed in black, the color of their weapons. She recognized AK-47s because they'd been present in all the places she'd ever lived. She also recognized what was happening immediately.

Insurrection.

Trembling, she went to the simple dresser that held her few clothes and started dressing. In layers, for warmth.

Shots. Women screaming . . .

She was just tying the laces of her snow boots with shaking hands when her mother burst into her bedroom.

Her mother took in her room in a glance. "Lucy. You're getting dressed. Smart girl." She slapped a pistol into Lucy's hand and moved to the window. A Smith & Wesson .38.

Lucy's hand curled around the gun with the ease of long acquaintance. She'd fired it thousands of times and had the calluses to prove it. Her mother had tossed two magazines onto the bed as she passed. Lucy slipped one into the butt and put the other in her jacket pocket.

Her mother was already armed herself, with a Glock. She was a superb shot. At the window, she looked down at the courtyard, watching the men's movements.

Lucy saw that her mother was completely calm. Her hand holding the Glock down alongside her leg was utterly steady, and her expression was pensive rather than shocked as she looked down.

"Mom?" Lucy whispered.

No one down in the courtyard could possibly hear her over the rumbling of the transport vehicle engines, men shouting and running. But Lucy had been taught to be quiet in emergencies, and this was an emergency if ever there was one.

The last big emergency had led to her being bundled onto a plane late at night and crashing in the Nicaraguan jungle.

"It's okay, honey," her mother said. She had that faraway voice when she was thinking of something else. Lucy suddenly knew, with a child's abrupt rush into adult wisdom, that it wasn't okay.

"Mom? Who are they?"

"Genza's men," her mother answered absently, focused on the courtyard below. Genza was the leader of the NLP, the Nhala Liberation Party, a hard-line Communist party funded by Beijing. "He's making his play. The king must be dead. And by sheer chance, half the Royal Guard has been sent north."

Lucy pulled in a shocked breath. King Noram. Jomo

and Paso's father. He was an aloof figure, in the pocket of the prime minister. He made ceremonial appearances several times a year, and the rest of his time was spent in the Halls of Meditation.

Lucy had listened to her parents speculate about this moment when they thought no one was listening.

Lucy had also heard guards talking about Genza's cruelty. She shivered again.

"Mom?" Lucy whispered.

Her mother turned away from the window and chambered a round, the snick of the slide loud in the room.

The Palace was made of stone, and the deep boom of the men's voices in the courtyard echoed off the walls.

"Come," her mother said abruptly. "Don't forget your gun." No, she wouldn't forget her gun. Lucy had trained with her father and her mother—who was the better shot—since she was eight. They'd lived in some scary places, and her parents made sure she knew how to take care of herself.

The noises from the courtyard were louder, trucks moving in. Army vehicles, she could tell. Men's voices, shouting. Not the sound of men out of control, but the sound of disciplined men, on a mission.

The Palace was waking up, but the lights were still out, throwing everyone into confusion.

"Marie?"

Dad! Lucy wanted to run to her father but in the dim light she could see that he was tense, combat ready, not in the mood to calm a frightened girl. So she stood silently while her parents went to their room and came back with combat rifles.

Her father checked out the window and turned away. "Hurry," he said over his shoulder.

The whole Palace was in an uproar now. There was another noise, and a terrible smell . . . Her parents had their heads together as they quietly conferred. They were good at strategy, Lucy knew. She kept very still so she wouldn't bother them.

There was a yellow glow lighting their profiles, though the lights were still out. Smoke billowed in the hall. The Palace was on fire! Though the Palace walls were made of stone, the ceilings and door frames were all made of ancient, painted wood, as were the thousands of small altars.

Her parents peeped out into the corridor, nodded at each other and rushed out of her room, firing. Now that her heavy wooden door was completely open, she could see the chaos outside: Palace servants streaming by, screaming, a few soldiers kneeling by the balustrade, firing down into the Great Hall, where what looked like hundreds of soldiers in the unfamiliar black uniforms were flooding into the Palace.

Heat, the crackling sounds of a vicious firefight, yellow flames licking greedily at the ancient tapestries lining the Great Hall. Lucy trembled in the darkness of her room, cold pistol in her hand feeling heavy and alien despite the thousands of practice rounds she'd shot.

She jumped, terrified, when a Royal Guardsman crumpled, dead, over her threshold, half his head blown away. There was something wet on her face, and she swiped at it, looking in horror at the bits of blood, bone and brains of the dead soldier.

She wanted to scream but clapped her bloodstained hands over her mouth. No distracting her parents, who were fighting for their lives at the top of the stairs.

The battle was raging outside her room, huge flames now eating at the big painted wooden banisters, the smell of smoke overpowering the stench of gunpowder.

She stood, shaking, inside the room, hidden in the darkness, pistol up in a two-handed grip, as her mother had taught her, waiting for the insurgents to come swarming up.

Lucy poked her head outside the door and gasped. The huge ceremonial staircase was littered with bodies, blood dripping through the balusters onto the stone flagging below. The battle raged with a ferocity she'd never seen before, a battle to the death.

And there were her parents, at the top of the stairs, holding off the insurgents. She moved out into the hall and saw her father recoil, his shoulder blossoming red. Her mother's shirt was red, one of her arms hanging uselessly at her side, blood dripping to the ground. Lucy ran to her mother, but her mother dropped to the ground, a pink mist around her head.

Lucy screamed and screamed . . .

A strong hand pulled at her arm, a voice boomed. "Lucy!"

Lucy jerked, coming awake on a wave of choking panic, heart racing, terrified, the smell of wood smoke and gun smoke in her nostrils, still seeing her mother's head exploding . . .

She swiveled her head, eyes wide, trying to take in a foreign environment, huge room in darkness except for a small, dim light illuminating a space around the huge bed. Colorful tapestries, the smell of incense, frescoed walls . . . the *Palace!* Oh God, she was back in the Palace. Flames, gunshots, soldiers . . . danger!

There were techniques to breathe down the terror, but they weren't working. *She couldn't breathe!* Oh God, she was dying! Trying to pull in a breath, but it wasn't working, her chest wasn't working, her throat wasn't working, *she couldn't breathe.*

Her throat was making horrible clicking sounds, her chest bucked as she tried to suck in air. The edges of her vision were blacking.

A large brown hand covered her chest, from between her breasts to her neck. The warmth and weight of another hand pressed against her back.

"It's okay," a deep voice said. "It's okay. You can breathe, there's nothing wrong, your lungs work. You just need to relax a little so you can pull in a breath. You can do it." The hands, front and back, pressed harder, she was sandwiched between them, those warm and solid hands. The hand on her chest circled lightly, massaging her. "Now, wait just a second," that deep voice said, "and breathe . . . *now.*"

As if her chest had burst a steel chain wrapped around her, she drank air into her starving lungs on a great, desperate whoop.

"That's right," the voice said calmly. "Perfect. Now again."

Her head hung low, hair around her face, as she pulled in another wheezy breath, let it out. Coughed.

Her heart was still hammering. Everything was focused in her chest: the pain and the fear and the nightmare. All there, right in the center of her being.

"That's right, good girl," the deep voice said, the calm in it somehow calming her, too. Nothing horrible could be happening if he could be so calm. "You're here, with me. You've been sleeping really well until just now, when you had a nightmare. It's okay. Breathe."

His voice lulled her. At the quiet command, she breathed again, and found that her lungs worked once more.

And that's when the reality crashed into her.

The nightmare.

Mike had seen it all.

All her deepest fears were right out there, like exposed nerve endings. She was scraped raw, down to bedrock, with nowhere to hide, nowhere to go, too shaken to gather her dignity around her.

It was why she never had a lover stay the night. The first time she'd had sex was in college, when her roommate was away for the weekend. A sweet guy, a jock who read. The sex had been . . . okay. He'd certainly seemed pleased. Without wanting to, Lucy had fallen deeply asleep, only to bolt up screaming at three in the morning, shaking and crying, terrified.

He'd held her until she went back to sleep, then he'd slipped out of bed before dawn. He'd avoided her all that semester, turning on his heel if he saw her in the corridors.

Who could blame him? Who wanted a lighthearted college romance with a raving lunatic?

After that, she never allowed her few lovers to see her in anything resembling a vulnerable state. Or anyone else, for that matter.

And here, horribly, she had no choice. Nowhere to run, nowhere to hide, just like the song said.

So horrible to have someone witness her wild panic and grief, all the years of careful construction of herself gone in an instant, yanked back in a heartbeat into being the terrified fourteen-year-old, screaming as she watched her parents shot to death.

Lucy struggled to get away, she didn't know to where, just *away*. Away from the smoke of panic still clouding her mind, away from the raw humiliation, away from here, away from her life, just . . . away. Maybe rush into the bathroom, pretend to be sick to her stomach, stay there awhile, until she could face the world again in the shape of Mike Shafer.

Now that she was breathing, she'd been pulled by strong arms against a solid, rock-hard chest and held there tightly. The hold wasn't painfully tight, but it was unbreakable, she found, as she tried to wedge her hands against his chest and push.

Wishing he'd let go, wishing she could just disappear. Just wipe herself out, press the restart button, start over.

But she couldn't. She knew that through bitter experience. She was what she was, and though she could hide her demons most of the time, so much so that she had a reputation for being a calm, even bland woman, she knew the monsters hiding under her bed and in the closet and above all in her mind were real. They had fangs and claws. They'd bitten huge chunks out of her and had claimed the only family she had.

Who could possibly guess that cool, calm Lucy Merritt woke up screaming in the middle of the night several times a month? That she had to hypnotize herself to get onto a plane?

Well, now Mike knew.

She was plastered up against him, one big hand covering the back of her head, the other around her waist.

She moved her head forward an inch, until it rested more comfortably against his chest. He smelled wonderful, and she smelled of the cold sweat that was pouring off her face, down her back, between her breasts.

"Let me go. I have to go to the bathroom." Maybe she could just stay in there until morning. By then, surely, she'd be herself again. Do some breathing exercises. Get rid of the aftermath of the nightmare.

"No," he said calmly and his hands tightened.

Lucy drew in a sharp breath. The inability to breathe had been terrifying. Though the left lobe of her brain understood clearly that she hadn't been in anaphylactic shock and that her throat wasn't swollen and that she could, in fact, breathe perfectly well, the right lobe of her brain, the animal part of her, couldn't *breathe* and was sure she was going to die.

The terror of that still pulsed in her.

She pushed at his chest and met an immovable wall. "I said let me go!"

"In just a moment. I want you to warm up first."

So much had been taken from her. She'd had to put herself back together piece by miserable piece. Now even her dignity had been stripped away, and she was left raw and naked and shivering, all her weaknesses right out there in the open, visible to him.

She couldn't stand the thought, simply couldn't stand it.

She began struggling wildly, a low sound of distress coming not from her throat but seemingly from her stomach, from her viscera.

Now the sound rose up within her and became a wild keening, the sound of an animal in pain, as she struggled with the immovable object.

"Jesus. Stop that. You're going to hurt yourself." He loosened his grip and her right hand shot out, began pummeling him. She was writhing in his grasp, sobbing, face completely wet. Tears weren't falling from her eyes, they were spurting from them, little fountains of salty wetness welling forth, as if they'd been bottled up and someone had pulled the cork.

She didn't even know why she was fighting, or even who

she was fighting. All she knew what that her body craved some kind of release, physical release, and he provided it— an absolutely unyielding wall she could beat herself against.

The struggle was silent, ferocious, lopsided. Of course. Her entire life her struggles had been entirely lopsided. There was no way she could prevail, no way to keep her dignity, no way to disappear. She could just endure.

In the end she simply lay against him, spent and dazed and ashamed.

As calm seeped back in, she burned with shame. In all the years since the crash and the Palace fire, she should have learned how to cope. And she'd thought she had, until today.

Apparently, there was still a long way to go.

There was no strength to fight anymore. So she simply lay against him, her head tucked up under his chin, his chin resting on the top of her head.

It was an animal kind of comfort he offered, the most basic kind. The kind early humans must have found in caves. Skin contact, body warmth, the reassuring sound of the steady heartbeat of a living creature under her ear.

"Bad nightmare," Mike said quietly.

There was only one possible answer. "Yes."

"About the Palace?"

"Yes."

"You have them often?" Oh God. The moment of truth. She could lie. *No, of course not. I never have nightmares, nightmares are for crazy people. I sleep soundly every night, the sleep of the just. This was a one-off. I have no idea what happened.* How she'd love to say that.

Then, of course, there was the Truth Option.

He might as well know what kind of lunatic she was. She couldn't guarantee she wouldn't have another nightmare. She swallowed heavily. "Yes."

Silence.

"I'm sorry," she whispered miserably.

His arms tightened briefly, then relaxed.

"You know," he said calmly, his voice a reassuring deep rumble in his chest, "when I was a kid, nothing bad ever happened to me. I lost my mom to cancer, but I was two when she died. I don't remember anything about her. My dad was the best father in the entire history of fatherhood and I was a real happy kid. I got myself a wonderful step-mother when I was eight. She's not really step anything, she was the best mom a boy could have. After they got married, she started popping out kids, my sister, Kathy, then Ben and Joe. Great, great kids. So. When I was fourteen, I was small and scrawny—"

He must have felt her eyebrows rise. He was a full head taller than she was. Her arms were around an incredibly broad chest, packed with dense, hard muscles.

He chuckled. "Yeah, I know. I got my spurt of growth around seventeen. At fourteen I was a real runt. But I loved track and at fourteen qualified for the regionals.

"I trained for that sucker day and night, for months. I wanted that medal so bad I could taste it. On the big day, Dad and Cheryl and Kathy were in the stands, rooting for me. Ben was a baby, but he was rooting for me, too. I could feel it. Joe wasn't born yet, but later he was my biggest fan. Anyway, when the big day came I was so excited I couldn't eat. I was popping out of my skin with nerves. When the gun went off, I thought my heart would explode. I ran as hard as I could, and I was catching up with the front runner when I slipped and fell, two hurdles from the finish line. Afterward, Kathy cried for me. I was devastated. I was depressed for two whole months. Didn't eat, grades dropped. So, there it is. That was my big tragedy at four-teen. A skinned knee and a lost tin medal worth maybe a buck fifty for a regional championship nobody cared about. I don't think that can compare with watching your parents gunned down in a firefight."

"You're a soldier," Lucy murmured. "You've been in your own firefights." Unlike her, he actually ran toward danger, not away.

"Oh yeah," he said softly. "I've been in my own firefights.

I've spent the past six years in the Land of Bad Things. But as a full-grown man. Trained to process what was happening, and even then it's not easy. I can't even begin to imagine being in a firefight as a kid and watching your parents killed. So I guess you've earned your nightmares."

It was a nice thought. Lucy was listening to his words, but more than anything else, she was letting the tone of his voice seep into her. Low, deep, calm. Lulling. A real Ambien voice.

Sleep came like a warm, soft, dark blanket gently settling over her.

$\mathscr{S}$EVENTEEN

LUCY put down her brush and looked at the manuscript of "The Legend of the Snow Dragon." It was perfect. It looked brand-new, and it should, because it was. She estimated the paper parchment to be a year old, at most. The ink, ditto. Someone had done a decent job with the calligraphy, however, and if you squinted your eyes and didn't understand antique manuscripts, you could very well believe that you were looking at an ancient parchment from the dawn of history, foretelling the rise of a great warrior who came from the north. As happenstance would have it, Dan Changa was born in the northernmost province of the country.

Placed under Plexiglas, with a direct light on it creating glare, and kept from the populace by a cordon ten feet out, it was more than enough.

Particularly if General Changa was willing to ensure that the "prophecy" was fulfilled, at the point of a gun.

Lucy rubbed her back. She'd been "cleaning" that damned thing all day. Mike said to wait for him. He was spending the day reconnoitering as quietly as he could.

She missed him. Fiercely. Missed everything about him, his smell, his touch, his warmth.

How surprising. She had always prided herself on her self-sufficiency and here she was . . . *pining* for a man. Longing for him.

It was, of course, sex. That potent weapon nature had devised to bring perfectly sane women to do crazy things. Sex with Mike was just off the charts. Her body heated solely at the memory.

So . . . sex was okay. There was a place in her head for that, or at least the concept of it. But, over and above the sex, she missed *him*. The sound of his voice, deep and reassuring. The spark of intelligence in his dark eyes. Not once had she had the feeling that he didn't understand what she was saying to him. He *got* her. She also had the feeling he understood her background, certainly more than most men she dated.

She missed his physical presence, like an ache.

Bonding sex, indeed. She smiled, remembering the utterly serious expression on his face as he put forward his little theory that their pheromones were mating.

Maybe they were.

If only he were here . . .

"Lucy?"

God, that deep voice. She'd recognize it anywhere. In the dark, in a room full of men, all he'd have to do was say her name and she'd know him.

She turned around and forced herself not to leap into his arms. There he was, filling the doorway, strong, reassuring, sexy as hell. She could practically see her pheromones reaching out to his.

Calm, Lucy, she told herself. The mission first. How frighteningly glad she was to see him was something she'd simply have to tuck away. Think about later.

She watched him walk into the room, over to her, and noticed for the first time that gunslinger's walk, all hips and long legs, eyes focused on the horizon. Or rather, she thought as he drew near, eyes focused on *her*.

"Hi." Her voice sounded breathless. Maybe because it was hard to breathe, as if someone had sucked all the oxygen out of the room. "Did you—"

He kissed her. And kissed her and kissed her.

What she was about to ask, what he might have found out during his scouting, what the plan was for this evening— it all just flew from her head, like startled birds at a hunter's shot.

She was plastered up against him as close as she could possibly get and tried to get closer. The slight melancholy and loneliness she'd felt all day working alone in the lab dissipated like morning mist under a hot sun. Mike made a very good hot sun, and he was melting her bones.

They both needed air at the exact same second. His mouth lifted from hers, his face harsh, eyes narrowed, as he pulled in a quick breath, and then his mouth descended once more.

A gong sounded, a mournful vibration of the air. Deep, low. The air had scarcely stilled when it sounded again. And again.

"Oh God." Lucy pushed at Mike's shoulders, stepped back.

He straightened, watching her face, understanding that something was wrong. "What?"

"Jomo," she whispered. "The king is dead."

Lucy took off. Mike was so startled it took him a second to react, by which time she was at the door, flinging it open.

Goddammit! There were guards outside that door, who'd looked him over carefully when he'd walked in. Any guard is trained to react instinctively when the person he's keeping tabs on takes off at a run.

Mike reached her just as the startled guards shouldered their rifles. His blood ran cold. Lucy stood still, four rifle muzzles pointed at her, a thin drizzle of smoke rising from one of the guard's cigarettes thrown to the ground.

Mike stepped right in front of her, facing the rifles, and heard four snicks as the guards thumbed their safeties.

Fuck! He wasn't armed and he was facing four weapons,

aimed right at him from three feet away. Not even Granny Shafer, who suffered from Parkinson's, bless her heart, could miss.

The young soldiers facing him weren't elite. They were probably country boys, not many months off the farm. They didn't want to shoot him, they'd rather be shooting the breeze with their buddies, but they would if they had to, that was clear. Two of the muzzles trembled slightly, and Mike looked their owners in the eyes. Determined and scared.

And incapable of missing at that close range.

Lucy said something sharp behind him and stepped to the side, exposing herself. What the hell was she doing? He had reached out to thrust her back behind him, when she touched his arm. "Stand down, soldier," she murmured and walked right up to the guards.

Right fucking up to them. The muzzle of one of the rifles touched her chest, right at the sternum. One pull of the trigger and the soldier would blow her heart right out of her chest.

Mike vibrated with tension.

Goddamn. He hadn't signed up for this. He had signed up to fight beside other warriors, men who could take care of themselves and who, like him, were trained to fight. He could do that.

But *this*—he couldn't do this. Watching Lucy walk right up to the rifle muzzle, knowing she was a breath away from death. Man, no, couldn't do it. His nerves couldn't take it.

He was about ready to jump her, take her to the floor, flatten himself on top of her, hoping the bullets wouldn't go through him to her, knowing they would, when she started talking.

You'd think that a woman talking to four armed soldiers who were pointing their weapons right at her, well, you'd think she'd talk to them in cajoling tones. Soft, gentle voice. Beseeching.

But no. Lucy's voice was sharp, commanding. She wasn't persuading, she was ordering. Soldiers. Armed soldiers.

Mike prepared to take her to the floor.

Another gong sounded three times and Lucy said something else, sharp and angry.

Fuck, this was not going to end well . . .

And then the soldiers took a step back, bringing their rifle muzzles up. Two of the soldiers were sweating. All of them stared at the floor. Classic submission behavior. The two middle soldiers moved, one left, the other right, opening up a path in the solid wall they'd presented.

And Lucy took off again. Mike kept pace easily.

"Damn, what did you tell them back there? I thought we were done for. Was already writing my obit and had just got to the part where it said *died a valiant death because his lady got into a fight with armed soldiers.*"

She wasn't smiling. "I told them that I was going to be with my dear friend Paso at the moment of her greatest grief. I told them that their king had just passed away and that he was looking down on them from the spirit world. I told them the king was ashamed that his soldiers would hold a gun on a defenseless woman. I told them that the Merritt family had always been a friend to Nhala and that my parents died for their freedom."

Well, the guilt trip had certainly done the trick. He'd thought they were going to die back there outside the lab but nope. She'd fucked with their heads and here they were.

He looked around as they speeded down another corridor. "Are we going to have problems with other soldiers? There were lots posted around the entrance to the Royal Chambers."

"No. I told them to alert the other guards in the Palace, otherwise they'd be in trouble and have to answer to a higher power."

"Buddha?"

"The princess."

Another corridor, bright yellow this time, with altars every five feet or so. At the far end, almost a hundred yards away, two huge carved and gilt wooden doors with an enormous brass dragon head for a knocker. The entrance to the Royal Chambers.

And about twenty soldiers. Mike tensed by Lucy's side as she slowed down, approaching the enormous doors. If they were going to have problems here, they were in deepest shit, because not even in super-Ninja mode could Mike hope to defeat twenty soldiers in an enclosed space. Unarmed.

But Lucy was in warrior mode. She marched right up to the door and the soldiers parted for her, like the Red Sea for Moses.

She reached up to that huge brass knocker in the shape of a dragon's head and brought it down twice, two sharp cracks of sound. The door opened slowly.

Mike walked in behind Lucy, senses on alert. Again he was struck by the sheer size of the room. Soldiers were everywhere, though not standing to attention. The soldiers were evenly divided between the Royal Guards in their yellow and scarlet ceremonial uniforms, large swords sheathed at their sides, MP-5s on slings, and another group of soldiers, all with a similar cast to their faces, in black BDUs. The Sharmas. The mercenaries.

Grief filled the air, together with enough incense to fell a bull. Long sticks burned in elaborate brass holders at every altar and on the large table beside the bed. A group of women in bright traditional dress stood huddled in a corner, weeping.

A tiny figure swathed in saffron yellow silk lay like a cocoon in the middle of the Royal Bed, dwarfed by the proportions of the bed.

The king, dead.

All the members of the Royal Guard looked sad, except for the captain, who looked pissed. And dangerous. The Sharmas were stoic and expressionless. They found themselves, as is often the case with mercenaries, duty-bound and honor-bound to serve an asshole.

General Changa was holding the princess's arm. She was arguing with the general in a low voice, unheeding of the tears that poured down her face. She turned at the huge doors opening and saw them coming in.

"Lucy!" she exclaimed and wrenched her arm free from General Changa's grip. He started after her, and the entire Royal Guard snapped to attention, heels together, hands hovering over their sidearms.

Tense moment.

Lucy and the princess were embracing, both women crying. From somewhere close, the gong sounded again, three slow tolls. Like the mournful cry of a wounded animal.

Mike watched the two women for a second, then checked the soldiers again. The Royal Guard soldiers had all moved more closely together. So had the Sharmas.

There were ten sets of windows in the huge chamber, like the nave of a Gothic church. Nine of the windows had been covered in white silk, as had all the mirrors. Only one set, at the back of the room, was still uncovered. Needles of sleet pinged the windowpanes and Mike gritted his teeth.

He'd received a weather update. A huge snowstorm was headed their way. He'd hoped to get himself and Lucy out of Dodge before it hit Nhala, but it looked like they might be shit out of luck. Already, ice spicules were interspersed with the sleet. Heavy snow would be arriving soon.

There was enormous tension in the air. With the king dead, Changa was going to make his move to take over, backed by his mercs, but it looked like the Royal Guard, headed by the captain, was going to try to block that.

They were a minute away from being caught in the middle of a civil war, and the only way out was through a snowstorm.

Lucy and the princess were standing, foreheads together, conferring quietly in Nhalan. General Changa watched for a moment, then strode to them, soldiers scattering before him.

Mike came to attention in an adrenaline rush, super-alert, combat-ready. The general's body language signaled violence, and Mike was prepared.

All the details of the physical room faded, and what was

left in his head was the position of every single soldier, the distance of every single hand from its weapon, and every detail of General Changa. His hearing became super-acute. He could hear the pinging of ice on the window and the dull roar of a rising wind. He could hear the rustling of the general's uniform as he walked toward Lucy and the princess, the creak of the leather of his holster.

Mike edged closer to a Royal Guardsman who had his sidearm holster unsnapped; he calculated the time it would take the guard to draw from the holster. Half a second. Doable.

Changa gripped the princess's shoulder, and every single Royal Guard watched while the captain stiffened. The general bent low and gave a command in Nhalan to the princess.

He looked at Lucy, his head turning like a reptile's yellow brown eyes unblinking. He started speaking to her and she put up her hand.

"English please, General. You're speaking much too fast for me to follow."

It was nonsense. Words had come pouring out of the princess, and Lucy hadn't had any problems. She wanted Mike in the picture and wanted the general at a slight disadvantage.

Smart girl.

The general's mouth tightened, hooded eyes flat and cold. "The commencement ceremony of the Feast of the Snow Dragon will begin in an hour. The princess will be on the royal platform, and she will officially announce the death of her brother, the king, and her engagement to me. You will then come up on the platform and present the newly restored manuscript of the prophecy of the Snow Dragon to the princess and to the people of Nhala. And then you will go back to your quarters."

The princess's eyes flashed, dark yet full of light. She glanced briefly at her captain and drew herself up. "When the official mourning month is over, General Changa, I will become queen of Nhala. I will never marry you. You

can kill me, but you will never become the Snow Dragon of
Nhala through me! And as for Dr. Merritt, she will bear
witness to all in the Great Hall that the manuscript of 'The
Legend of the Snow Dragon' is a fake!"

Whoa. The tension in the room ratcheted up. Even the
grieving court women fell silent. Every soldier in the room
was at attention, eyes turned to Lucy. The room reeked of
male sweat. Every man realized that there was the makings
of a firefight right here. Royal Guards against the mercs.
And the Royal Guards were outnumbered two to one.

Mike's skin tightened, crawled. There was absolutely
nothing he could do except follow Lucy's lead. Only she
could judge whether to testify to the manuscript's authenticity or not. It was her card to play, and all he could do was
remain on a hair trigger, ready to move.

Lucy looked up, face smooth and untroubled. "Unfortunately the princess is correct, General," she said in her
gentle voice. "I haven't had a chance to tell you yet. While
restoring the manuscript, I came across irrefutable evidence that it is, indeed, a forgery. I'm afraid it would be
quite impossible to testify to its authenticity to the people
of Nhala."

Jesus. That took balls.

Adrenaline pulsed through his system and he felt sweaty
and ragged. Lucy looked like she'd just come in from cutting flowers in the garden.

The general's eyes narrowed. The skin over his cheekbones tightened, his thin nostrils flared. Murderous rage
surrounded him like a cold wind. Two women, two slender,
small women, were standing in the way of his plans to take
over the country.

Two women he could kill with one backhanded blow.

Mike pulled in air, shifted his weight to the balls of his
feet, moved even closer to the Royal Guardsman with the
unsnapped holster.

There was something very bad coming down, the smell
of it even more intense than the smell of the incense.

"I am afraid, Dr. Merritt, that you have misjudged the

situation. Princess Paso will definitely marry me and you"—he snapped his fingers and a soldier handed him a small black case—"you will be imprisoned as an enemy spy. You will be put in our dungeon awaiting trial, and it might take years for this affair to come to trial. Your government will protest, but very soon it will have its hands full with its own . . . problems." He stared at Lucy, then switched that black stare to Mike. "Both of you will rot and die in our prisons underground. Unless you come out into the Great Hall with the manuscript."

"I'm sorry," Lucy said quietly. There was no noise at all in the chamber. "I cannot do that."

"You can," the general growled, "and you will." He walked behind Lucy, face a mask of evil. Mike's hackles rose and he took a step forward, stopping when one of the general's mercs drew his pistol. He wasn't specifically aiming it at Mike, but the pistol was in his hand.

Fuck that. Mike took another step forward.

"Stop!" Changa's voice rang out. He reached inside the black case and pulled out a small, silvery steel object, shaped like a gun.

"I found this in your room, which tells me all I need to know. You are enemy spies."

With a snake-fast move, he hooked his left arm around Lucy's throat and jammed the object against her shoulder. Mike's heart nearly stopped. He froze, hardly daring to breathe. It was an exact replica of the injection gun for the deadly mutant virus.

"Ah." Changa's smile was ice cold. "Mr. Harrington. You know what this is. Say it."

"An injection gun. For a virus." Mike's throat was tight, the words could barely make their way up out of his chest.

"But not just any virus." The general was talking directly to the horrified princess now. "The cylinder will explode in exactly twenty-four hours, releasing the virus, after which Dr. Merritt will die the most horrendous death you can imagine. My men and I will take her to a village along the Indian border where she will die like a dog in the dirt, vomiting up her internal organs. And she will become a carrier, That village and in all likelihood the neighboring villages will be exterminated. That is what I will do, Princess, if you do not agree to come with me into the Great Hall and announce our engagement. If you do not, you will not only be the cause of the painful death of your friend here, but you will also be directly responsible for the deaths of hundreds, maybe thousands, of villagers. What is it to be, Princess? Because the people are gathering in the Great Hall right now."

This was—this was worse, much worse, than holding a gun to Lucy's head. Her face was waxen. She'd seen the CIA operative's death on that tape, too. She knew what the virus did. *Goddammit!* Mike turned to Princess Paso.

"Announce your engagement to the fucker," he said hoarsely. The princess had turned ash white. She was shaking, tears streaming down her cheeks.

"No, Mike." Lucy was looking at him intently. "She can't do that, can't you see? It would betray everything the Royal Family stands for. There's only one way out of this. You must be prepared."

Prepared for what? Lucy was sending him some kind of signal, but what? Mike was ready. Ready for anything, but particularly ready to rip Changa's fucking head off his shoulders. He was really ready for that.

He waited, weight balanced, hands ready, for the opening that Lucy was going to give him.

Come on honey, he thought, bouncing on his toes. *Give me an opening.*

And then—and then Lucy did the bravest thing Mike had ever seen a human being do.

She shot herself with the virus.

*E*IGHTEEN

IT hurt. That was her first thought. It was like a flu shot, only a hundred times worse.

And then her second thought was—*Will you look at that?*

She'd never seen another human being move as fast as Mike. In a microsecond, a gun materialized in his hand from somewhere and then in the next microsecond there was a loud pop and the general fell down to the floor like a puppet whose strings had been cut.

The only thing remaining was a slowly dissipating pink mist in the air.

And one second later, all the rifles in the room were aimed at Mike.

He didn't look afraid, he looked savage. Frightening. Even though he was outnumbered forty to one, she would have put odds on him.

The captain of the Royal Guard stepped forward, doing something unheard of. He put his arm around the princess. In Lucy's day, when she was a child, it was forbidden to touch an adult member of the Royal Family. Only family members could touch each other.

Right now, the captain was guilty of treason and could be shot. Except for the fact that the princess was looking at him with love.

It was clear to all that soon the captain would be a member of the Royal Family.

"*Royal Guards! Arms down! Eyes to me!*" the captain shouted, and all his men stood to attention, rifles down. Changa's mercenary army still stood with their weapons pointed at Mike, eyes darting back and forth because their sponsor, General Changa, was a mass of protoplasm on the floor, blood seeping from his head. They had no commander.

"*We are the Royal Guards!*" the captain shouted. "*Our loyalty is to the Royal Family. Show your fealty to your new queen!*"

The hardwood floors pounded as all the men dropped to one knee, the singing of steel vibrating in the room as swords were unsheathed. They gave the Nhalan battle cry—*hay-yah!*—and with a loud *thunk!* buried their swords point-first in the floor, and bowed their heads.

The Royal Guards were now officially on the side of the angels.

"*Sharmas!*" The captain's voice rang with command. "*Your sponsor is dead. General Changa is dead. He had a plan that would have shamed Nhala until the end of time. But that plan is no more. Swear fealty to the Royal Family, and your contracts will be renewed and your families will continue to prosper. There will be a bonus for every man who swears loyalty to the princess. Men . . . down arms!*"

The slap of hands on rifle butts, the clicking of heels, the Sharmas moving as one.

Nhala was saved.

Lucy's knees gave out. Mike caught her before she fell to the floor.

"Princess! Captain!" he rapped out. "I need to get Lucy to America as fast as I can."

"To Atlanta, Mike," she murmured. She felt weak, dizzy. More a psychological thing than a physical thing. She no longer even felt the injection in her shoulder. It was the knowledge that festering in there, on the other side of acid working its way through a barrier, was a horrific disease for which there was no cure.

She was going to die a horrible, painful death in twenty-four hours if she couldn't get home in time.

"What?" Mike looked down at her, eyes wild. He had been perfectly calm, even cold, as he faced down forty men with guns aimed at him. Now he looked like a wild man. "Why Atlanta?"

She'd thought it out before pulling the trigger. It hadn't been an impulsive move to get them out of a dangerous situation. It had been calculated—and necessary.

"We need to study this virus in controlled conditions, and it has to be surgically removed. But not just anywhere. The doctors have to operate in a biolab, otherwise the virus could get out." She looked up at him, his face inches from hers, and placed the palm of her hand against his cheek. Warm, bristly. The feeling of life itself. A good feeling to have in her hand if she was going to have to die. "Get me to Atlanta fast," she repeated.

Mike helped her to her feet. She stiffened her knees and shook. There was a core of ice in her, numb and unfeeling.

"You're in shock," Mike said. He kept an arm around her and pulled out his cell. No need to keep anything secret now. He punched in a number on speed dial, then waited.

"Yeah," he said suddenly as the connection was made. "I need an emergency exfil. Man down, repeat man down." He looked at her, face grim. "Or rather woman down. We need to get to the CDC in Atlanta within twenty-four hours. Operation Stop Cold. Top priority, over."

He listened, face getting tighter. Lucy's heart sank. Oh God. There were problems. There always were. What had she done? Seared into her mind was the image of the CIA operative vomiting his life's blood out in the snow.

Mike looked at the captain of the Royal Guard.

"There's a C2-A Greyhound taking off now from the

USS *George H. W. Bush* in the Indian Ocean. But its range is fifteen hundred miles, after which it needs refueling. They've got permission to refuel in Goempa, just across the border. They said to meet the plane there. Captain, do you have a helicopter that can take us to Goempa?"

The captain was shaking his head slowly, eyes shifting between her and Mike. "I am so sorry, Mr. Harrington." His arm tightened around Paso. "The situation in the Palace is still uncertain, let alone in the country. The king is dead, General Changa is dead. Our helicopter pilots were under the general's command, which is now gone. It will take time to find the pilots, time to establish a command structure. But I'll send two of my men to drive you down to Goempa. It would take less time than finding the helicopter pilots. If you leave now, you can be there in three hours."

Mike nodded. "Tell your men to wait for us at the Palace entrance, where the welcome ceremony was. We'll be there as fast as we can make it. We need to get things from our room."

Lucy looked up at him numbly. What? A detour to their room? What for? It was just time wasted, time they didn't have. Or rather, time she didn't have.

Paso broke away from her captain and pulled Lucy into a tight, almost painful hug. She was shaking, too. She rested her face against Lucy's for an instant, her wet cheeks cool against hers. Lucy didn't dare shed tears. If she did, she'd never stop.

Mike pulled her away gently, made a fast, sketchy Nhalan bow. "Princess, we must go. Lucy's life depends on speed, now."

"Go." Paso stepped back, wiped at her eyes. "*May the Dragon keep you safe in your journey,*" she said in the Old Language.

Mike tugged Lucy's hand, ran for the door.

Lucy stumbled; her legs could barely hold her up. Mike simply picked her up in one arm and ran. She didn't seem to slow him down any.

"Mike." Oh God, her voice was gone. She licked her lips. "Mike."

They were halfway there. "Yeah?"

"Put me down. I can get there on my own steam. But why do we have to stop by our room? Shouldn't we—" Her voice trembled, she couldn't breathe. "Shouldn't we hurry?"

Mike stopped, made sure she was steady, then took off again, holding her hand.

"We have to hurry, honey. We're going to make it. I promise. But I'm not taking you out into a snowstorm dressed like that. It'd be crazy. You need winter gear. It'll take the captain a little while to muster the driver and the vehicle. I'll feel better if we're all geared up."

They rushed into their room and Mike unerringly pulled out what they needed. He was fast and knew exactly what he was doing. In a few minutes, they were both dressed for the cold, from sturdy boots to warm waterproof headgear. He even put one of his jackets over hers.

But no matter how warmly she was dressed, Lucy was still icy cold inside, where a clock was ticking.

Tick tock. Twenty-three hours forty minutes to go.

Mike's phone buzzed. A text message. He checked it as they rushed out, leaving their suitcases behind. "Greyhound's up in the air, they're going to push it, shave half an hour off their ETA. Oh fuck." He skidded to a stop, looking up at the sky.

It was snowing heavily.

They were outside the main entrance. The instant they were outside the Palace, the temperature dropped fifty degrees. Snow was falling fast enough to coat the huge square.

Mike grabbed her hand and ran to where the vehicle would be waiting. Lucy slid a little, but there was no way she could fall, not with Mike by her side. He didn't seem to even contemplate a possible fall, he just ran flat out, pulling her along.

They rounded the corner, Lucy panting, Mike searching the huge square. They'd only been out a minute or two, and the cold had already penetrated even the warm winter clothing she had on.

A dun-colored military vehicle drove up, the driver buzzing down the window. "Mr. Harrington?"

"Yes. Get us to Goempa fast."

Mike bundled them into the back, and the vehicle took off before he could pull the rear door closed.

Lucy stared out the back window as they pulled away, crossing the huge square, the sight of it already lost in the snow and mist.

Mike was talking into his cell. She didn't have enough neurons to concentrate on what he was saying, though she had an important stake in whatever was being communicated. As in, life or death.

It all felt so far away and yet so crushingly close.

She might not live out the next day. All the emotions thumping around inside her were too strong and sharp to get a handle on. She had to hug herself around the middle so all the sharp feelings wouldn't burst out of her like . . .

Oh God. A keening sound was in the vehicle, louder than the engine. It took her a moment to realize it was her, some kind of noise she was making in her vibrating throat.

She touched her throat to make it stop, but all she felt was her shaking fingertips drumming against her skin.

Mike snapped his cell closed and looked at her closely. Was that—Oh God, was that pity in his eyes?

Lucy was allergic to pity. It had surrounded her like a miasma her first year back in the States, in that horrible boarding school. There'd been nasty little shits and über-nice kids.

The nasty ones tittered behind her back because her clothes were funny, she talked funny, she'd lived in odd places and didn't know any boy bands.

They had been bearable.

What had been awful was the nice kids, the ones whose voices died down when she walked by, the ones who suddenly flashed an insincere smile, all huge white American teeth like Chiclets, so unnatural-looking it was frightening. Inviting her home on holidays because everyone knew she didn't have a family, invitations she'd never accepted because it was easier just to stay in the dorm than to try to fit in with people she barely knew.

And now Mike. If he pitied her, she was done for. If she let even a drop of her fear and panic out, everything would come spilling out and she'd start screaming and crying. She couldn't bear it.

Don't touch me. She sent out the vibes, huddling in the corner of the uncomfortable backseat of the military vehicle. *Don't touch me because I will break if you do.*

He didn't. He simply looked out the window at the swirling snowstorm and gave her information quietly. "We're going to have snow all the way, but I'm told the airfield is clear in Goempa. We're making good time. We'll be there early, and I'm told the Greyhound has good headwinds and will be there on time, maybe even early. They're scrambling a Learjet from Dubai, which will meet us in Mumbai, touching down more or less when we do. Fastest plane they've got. From Delhi it's a straight shot to Atlanta, with a fast refueling in the Azores."

"What—" Her voice came out high and trembling. She waited a second. Swallowed. "What's the timeline? And don't lie to me."

"I won't." Mike met her eyes. "I won't lie to you. Ever. You don't deserve that. Here to Goempa four hours. We'll get there an hour early, and they'll aim to get there as fast as they can, shave as much time off the ETA as possible. Goempa to Mumbai four hours. Delhi to Atlanta fifteen hours, including refueling."

Lucy had always been good at math. "Twenty-three hours," she whispered.

"Tight," Mike agreed. "The pilots say they'll try to gain half an hour over the Atlantic. Everything will be ready for you. Ambulance at the foot of the plane in Atlanta; they'll clear traffic for you all the way to CDC." He watched her eyes, reached for her hand and brought it to his mouth. "Just like a rock star."

"Or the President." Her voice shook. She tried to smile, but it didn't work.

"Yeah. Or the pope. Listen, I'm going to put my arm around you now, Lucy, because frankly, if I don't, I'm going to fall apart."

Startled, she looked at him, really looked. It was a real effort to wrench her senses away from the roiling slithering sickening fear knotting inside her, but when she did, she could see he was telling the truth. Cool, brave Mike Shafer was scared.

He was wound as tight as a drum, muscles tense, tendons standing out in his neck, jaw muscles clenching and unclenching. She could actually hear him grind his teeth.

Lucy had tucked her hands under her arms, trying to comfort herself. Her hand moved across the dark space separating them as if moving through something thicker than air, slowly, pushing against her fears and his. He caught her hand and pulled her gently against him until they were seated hip to hip, her head on his shoulder, his arms around her.

Mike grunted, a sound of relief. As if he'd been in pain and now the pain had stopped. Resting against him, she found it was easier to deal with the uneven ride. The driver was good and had clearly been told to push the vehicle. But snow was piling up, and there were icy patches that had to be negotiated. The vehicle swayed, but Lucy didn't sway with it, because she was anchored to Mike, who was a rock.

He didn't talk and neither did she. What was there to say? They'd either make it or . . . they wouldn't.

It had to be said. Lucy waited until she felt her voice wouldn't betray her. She pulled away, looked him straight in the eyes.

"Mike, if—" She coughed to loosen her throat. "If we don't make it. If we're still over the Atlantic after twenty four hours, you're . . . you're going to have to contain me, or I'll infect everyone on the flight, including you." She met his eyes. "Please don't let that happen. Don't make me hurt other people. Please. I couldn't stand it. Have me put in an airtight container. Tell them to onload something in Mumbai that will contain . . . what's in me until you can get my body to Atlanta. But first—take care of me. Please take care of me . . . before I get sick."

She knew perfectly well what she was asking. If it became clear they wouldn't get to an operating theater in time, she was asking him to kill her and seal her body up.

"Please," she whispered, voice shaking. "Don't let me die that death and don't let me infect anyone." Her entire body was shaking now. She didn't want to die. And she especially didn't want to die vomiting her internal organs, knowing she was going to infect everyone on the flight, including Mike. "Please promise."

He met her eyes, dark pools of stillness in the vehicle. He understood. "Please," she said again, a broken record, because there was nothing else to say.

"I promise." The words were wrenched out of him. Tears welled from her eyes. It would hurt him, maybe break him; she knew enough of him to understand that. But he'd do it.

She could count on him.

She swiped at her cheeks. "Thank you." He'd make sure she had a swift death and that as far as possible she wouldn't infect anyone. It made the whole thing somehow easier to bear.

"So everything better go smooth as fucking cream," he said savagely, "or I'll rip someone a new one."

Lucy gave a half laugh and burrowed her face in his shoulder, inhaling the strong scent of man, knowing her pheromones were mating with his.

GODDAMN!

He'd promised and he'd stick to his promise. They should make it, but if there was one thing Mike knew down to his bones, it was that Mr. Murphy loved fucking with people.

So they might not make it. Lucy might not make it.

She'd asked him to help her die with dignity instead of like an animal, on all fours, wretchedly vomiting her life's blood onto the floor of a plane. He'd promised. He'd . . . take care of her himself before he'd let that happen to her. And it was important to her not to hurt anyone, so he'd take care of that, too.

If anyone had asked him for the very best outcome to the mission, he'd have said—coming back within forty-eight hours having sent vital intel and with a sample of the virus.

Fucking brilliant result, that.

Except, whoops, the sample was in Lucy Merritt's shoulder.

She must have been thinking that when she pulled the trigger. It had been a brilliant move on her part, except, of course, for the minor detail that it would most probably cost her her life.

Because who was he kidding? The flight plan was shaved down to a nothing margin. Everything had to go perfectly for them to make it into the operating theater, and who'd ever heard of everything going perfectly?

He shifted her a little so that she would be leaning more on him. He wanted to touch as much of her as he possibly could. She was light against him, shivering. Not with cold. He took his gloves off, so he could have the feel of her in his hands, cupping her neck. Her breathing was normal, but her pulse was beating rapidly, like a frightened bird's.

Jesus. How could he lose her when he'd just found her?

Life couldn't be that unfair, could it?

Yes, it could. The infantryman with the wife and new baby gets shot in the head on the last day of his last tour in Iraq. The freak accident leaves a healthy young boy a cripple for life. Bad things happened all the time.

One of them wasn't going to happen here. He wasn't going to let it. He'd fucking pull the plane over the Atlantic himself with his bare hands to make it go faster. They were going to make it in time, and they would cut that monstrous abomination out of Lucy, and when she was better, he'd take her to Portland and introduce her to the family, and they'd fall in love with her as much as he had, and then they'd get married. Because he was never going to find another woman like this, ever again. Gorgeous and smart and gentle and brave. Beautiful inside and out.

He was not going to lose her. Just not going to happen.

He looked down at her, shiny hair loose around her shoulders, the curve of her pale cheek elegant in the faint light off the dials of the dashboard. She wasn't sleeping. Her eyes lifted, met his. And it happened again, that electric feeling of both desire and homecoming she roused in him. Unmistakable. Unforgettable. Unrepeatable.

They didn't speak. Everything that needed to be said right now had already been said, and for everything else they had the rest of their lives. He would be with her every step of the way, however long that would be.

His arm tightened a little around her shoulder, and she leaned more heavily against him, her slight weight utterly right.

Mike glanced out the window. It was still snowing heavily, coming down now in sheets. The vehicle was sturdy, though, made for rough mountain terrain and bad weather. The driver was steady. They were making good time. Mike checked his watch. They'd been traveling for two and a half hours. Another half hour to go and they'd be on the tarmac, waiting to be put on the first of two planes that would carry Lucy back to safety.

We're going to make it, Mike was thinking, when a loud crack sounded, a huge black tree fell across the road, and the driver swerved, plowing right through a steep bank of snow, tipping over the edge of a cliff and crashing straight down.

Mike came back to consciousness slowly, the smell of diesel fuel strong and acrid in his nostrils.

His face was crushed against a hard metallic surface. He had a moment of complete disorientation, until he realized he was upside down. In a vehicle, upside down. He frowned, touched his chest. He was bruised, sore, but with no major injuries.

Where was he? His neck was stiff. It hurt to turn his

head, so he did it slowly. In a vehicle. Darkness. Snow. Two bright yellow cones of light with snow falling through them. Silence, except for a metallic ticking noise.

Two men in the front seats, necks at an unusual angle. Softness against his side.

Cold.

His mind was sluggish, making its way through these clues slowly, one by one, trying to add everything up.

Suddenly, reality snapped back into focus.

The army vehicle that was carrying them to Goempa—that was the first stage of getting Lucy to safety—had crashed and fallen off the road. How far had they fallen?

There was no way to tell. Outside the bright cones of light of the vehicle, visibility was about five feet and all it showed was snow and the bole of the huge fir tree that had stopped their slide down a steep slope. A side window had shattered. Snow was piling in, hissing against the still-warm surfaces of the interior of the vehicle. He heard a soft groan at his side and the static in his head disappeared.

Lucy.

He turned to her, pulled her into his arms. There was only the faint backwash of the headlights. He could barely make out her features, but he could see she was paper white.

The snow was coming in too thickly through the smashed window. Lucy's entire side was wet. So were his hands. He looked down at his hands, covered in a black liquid, and his heart nearly stopped in his chest.

Blood. His hands were covered in blood. Lucy's blood.

"Lucy!" He touched her wildly, searching, searching . . .

Lucy lay a hand over his and slowly turned her face to him. "Here." Her voice was low, weak. She brought his hand to her lower right side and he could feel it. A laceration. Deep, still bleeding.

Oh, God.

Mike scrabbled around for something to use as a pressure bandage. He didn't dare use their clothes because it was clear that they'd have to find their way back up to the road and walk. They needed all the warmth they could get.

But the driver and the other soldier up front weren't going to need their clothes. He leaned over the seats, wrestled the heavy jacket off the guy riding shotgun, ripped off a sleeve and pressed it over Lucy's wound. She sucked in her breath sharply but other than that made no noise.

"The men?" Her voice was weaker than before.

"Dead." There was no time to mince words. "Keep that pressed to the wound."

His cell phone was pure static. He called again and again and finally got a weak signal. "Captain Shafer. Dr Merritt and I were on our way to Goempa when our vehicle crashed. Status, over."

It took three tries, but finally he received an answer. The static almost completely overrode the voice, but he knew he was lucky to be able to communicate at all. Normally, comms went down in snowstorms. They'd obviously given him top-of-the-line gear.

The Greyhound was still on its way, an hour and a half from landing. Mike made a quick calculation. They were almost there—only another ten miles to go, but only one way to do it.

"Coming with Dr. Merritt on foot to exfil point," he reported. In decent weather, alone, he could have run the ten miles in an hour, easy. He'd done it before. But carrying a wounded Lucy in a snowstorm . . . "Tell the pilots to wait for us."

"—approaching exfil point. Advise—"

"What?" The signal was degrading. "Repeat, over."

"Storm system moving south, advise speed, Greyhound cannot take off in strong winds, over."

Mike's eyes met Lucy's.

"Roger that. Tell aircrew we're coming as fast as we can, over."

"Mike," Lucy whispered, putting her bloody hand over his. "It's okay—"

He didn't want to hear this bullshit. He knew what she wanted to say. To let her die here.

Bullshit, *bullshit!*

He talked right over her, voice loud. "Okay, here's what we're going to do. We slid down a cliff. I don't know how far, and we don't have time for me to reconnoiter. I'm going to strap you to my back with these guy's belts and we're just gonna climb like we did in the Palace. No problem." He kept talking as he reached over the seats again and stripped off the driver's jacket, his gloves and his heavy-duty fur-lined hat.

Sorry, guys, he thought. *But you don't need this stuff anymore and Lucy does.*

Mike clambered out of the vehicle and rummaged in the back to see what he could raid. A big flashlight. A chemical flare. Two canteens of water. Rope. He used the flashlight to check every corner of the back of the vehicle, but that was it.

What he really needed was mountaineering gear—crampons, ice axe, ice screws—to climb that cliff, but there was nothing.

No time to waste on wishing for equipment that wasn't there.

Mike gently pulled Lucy out of the vehicle. She was trembling, from shock and blood loss. He checked the pressure bandage, which was already almost soaked through with blood. Shit.

He kept his face blank as he made her don the other coat and put the fur-lined hat over her head, pulling the ear flaps down. "There," he said, keeping his tone light. "You look gorgeous. The latest fashion. The Abominable Snowlady look."

Her hand in his shook. Her legs wouldn't carry her much longer, but she raised her head and sketched a smile for him. It nearly broke his heart.

She was twenty-two and a half hours from dying, she was grievously wounded, they were in a snowstorm, and he didn't hear a word of complaint from her.

Mike lifted Lucy's chin on the edge of his gloved hand and looked into her eyes, blue gray and beautiful, full of pain.

"We're going to make it," he told her quietly. "I don't care what it takes, we're going to make it. I am not going to lose you."

He bent down and kissed her, feeling her warm breath. When he lifted his mouth, he saw tears in her eyes.

"Don't, honey," he whispered. "They'll freeze on your face."

"No." She blinked them back. "No tears, I promise."

And he understood what she was saying. She might die, but she wouldn't cry. His heart gave a hard squeeze in his chest.

He turned his back and kneeled. "Put the rope around your back then hand the ends to me. When I stand up, put your arms around my neck and your legs around my waist." He tied the ends of the rope and stood up. She weighed as much as the rucksacks he and his men sometimes had to carry.

The temperature had fallen, or else the cold was starting to seep in. He wanted to shiver, but didn't. He needed for Lucy to have utter faith in him.

He looked up at the sky for a moment. It looked as if it were only a few feet above his head. Strong mountain winds made the snow swirl madly, at times making it snow up. He switched on the powerful flashlight that had belonged to the soldiers, angling it up. The light disappeared into the mist, revealing nothing. He couldn't even get a handle on what his field of vision was.

At least he didn't have to worry which direction to head in. He already knew. Up.

Holding Lucy's legs, he approached the cliff face. His one advantage was the anabatic wind, flowing uphill to surge over the top. It would help him in the climb.

Lucy's head settled on his shoulder. She turned and kissed him on his ear. He hitched her higher and started climbing.

Later, he wouldn't understand how he did it. Part adrenaline, part sheer terror. Parts of the climb were walkable,

barely, a very steep slope. Parts, however, were ice and granite walls, and he simply willed himself up, inch by inch,
handhold by handhold, the wind gusting upward, but also
blowing snow and ice into his eyes, over his hands. Fifteen
minutes into the climb, Lucy was shivering convulsively
against his back, uncontrollable shudders that scared him.

Several times he thought of resting when he found a
strong enough foothold, to check her wound, but in the end
he didn't. There was nothing more he could do for her anyway. The best thing he could do was get her out of there as
fast as possible.

Up—inch by painful inch, always holding on to the cliff
face by three points, only allowing one hand or one foot at
a time to advance. As always, it required absolute and
intense focus, something he usually enjoyed, but now his
attention was fractured. When he realized he was endangering Lucy's life by worrying about her too much and losing his focus, he wiped his mind of everything but the icy
rock face in front of him and the next handhold.

Halfway through the climb, the granite cliff ended and
there was a steep slope, which would be grassy in summer
but now was a snow-covered expanse. He picked up the
pace, almost running, until the cliff face started again,
then he narrowed his focus back onto the ten square inches
in front of his face.

The nature of the changing wind told him he was close
to the top. It was speeding up, an airflow that was finding
its release nearby. Ten minutes later, he reached level
ground and pulled himself and Lucy up and over the top.
He lay on his stomach, panting, mind a completely blank
slate. The wind here was strong, penetrating, icy fingers
reaching to the bones.

Mike allowed himself only a minute's rest. He knew all
too well the siren song of extreme cold. The body wants to
stop and curl in on itself, though that means death.

He stood, Lucy still tied to his back.

He'd climbed straight up, not deviating either to the
right or the left. He checked the rim with his flashlight.

Even through the heavy snowfall, the place where the vehicle had left the road was obvious. Mike turned right, into the wind, on the road to Goempa, ten miles away.

The wind here was his enemy—frigid, unrelenting, pushing heavily at him. The only good thing was that the icy air hit him, flowed around him and protected Lucy. Lucy wasn't bearing the brunt of it because his body was shielding hers.

He was worried sick. She wasn't shuddering anymore. He could only hope the blood loss wasn't making her hypovolemic, because then death would only be a short step away. But her arms still clung to his neck, her legs around his waist. She was weak, but she was alive.

On he trudged, leaning forward into the wind, one foot in front of the other, almost blinded by the snow that was blowing horizontally now. On and on and on.

It was nothing. He knew that. Ten miles was nothing, not even with a woman on his back. He thought of the Antarctica greats. Shackleton and Amundsen and Byrd. Men who'd trekked thousands of miles across icy expanses, sometimes hauling their supplies themselves, sometimes using dog sleds, killing and eating the dogs systematically. They'd spent months on the ice; some had wintered over in darkness without even a dawn to look forward to.

He thought of Joe Simpson, making it down off the mountain with a broken ankle.

He could do this. No question, he could do this. And he would. It was just a question of endurance. He was strong and had immense reserves.

What sapped his strength was crazy worry over Lucy, who might not survive the trek to Goempa and even if she did, might not make it back to Atlanta in time. It drove him a little nuts until he willed himself not to think of it.

It was the secret to survival in extreme temperatures and extreme situations. Think about nothing but the moment. Putting one foot in front of another, taking one breath after another. Living from one minute to the next.

Accepting the cold and the snow and the pain, because

they are what they are. Don't even think about surviving, just think of the now and the fact that you are breathing. He'd often thought there was something very Zen about hardship, about surviving against the odds. You dig into something deeper than ego, something atavistic, into animal roots. Dig in and hold on.

He moved forward, step by step, not daring to look at his watch because time was running out for Lucy and he couldn't do anything about it. She was with him, still breathing, still alive, and that was the most he could hope for.

On and on and on.

Mike sank so deeply into himself it took him time to realize that the wind was no longer blowing so hard that it felt like someone was pushing against him. The snow was letting up. He could see the sides of the road, piled high with drifts. Trees gradually came into view, white, cloudy objects showing up in the cone of his flashlight. The cold hadn't abated. If anything, the temperature had dropped even more, but at least he could see where he was going.

His face was going numb, as were his hands and feet, the prelude to frostbite. What about Lucy? He'd done his best to protect her; at least her face was against his neck and shoulder. But again, there was nothing he could do to help her but plod on.

Whole seconds were going by now without snow. The wind had abated, too. He could hear the scrunch of his boots on the snow. And something else . . . some rumbling noise in the distance. Coming closer . . .

Something glittered in the distance, as if a small sun had risen from somewhere. He couldn't figure it out. The sun was unstable, the light rising and falling. The rumbling grew louder.

He was so exhausted he didn't realize it was a vehicle until it was almost upon him, rounding a corner he didn't even know was there.

Fuck. Mike scrambled to the side of the road. There was political uncertainty back in the Palace. The general was dead, the princess was asserting her power, but no one knew how it would all play out in the end.

Mike had no idea who was coming around that corner, friend or foe. If it was foe, he had no weapons and was carrying a wounded woman. To the left of the road was a completely vertical granite cliff, to the right the road dropped sharply down. Nowhere to hide.

He was contemplating where to find refuge when he heard a noise. An amplified human voice. The wind snatched almost everything except the final "–fer." And then the voice came again, in pure American.

"Captain Shafer! Captain Shafer!"

The cavalry! Mike stood up, scrabbled in his web belt, found a flare, clumsily pounded it on the ice as hard as cement, and it lit up, bathing everything in a hot red light.

The vehicle had a bullhorn on the top. "Captain Shafer, Cap—" The voice stopped when it saw the flare. The vehicle braked. Two men rushed out. Americans. Military. Navy.

One short, one tall. One black, one white.

Mike didn't have the brain cells left to figure out rank; he only knew this part of the ordeal was over.

"Captain Shafer?" The short soldier rapped out. Before Mike could even nod, the other was gently untying Lucy from his back and carrying her to the vehicle.

Short soldier saluted, then held out his hand.

"Petty Officer Reynolds, sir. Man, we're glad to see you. Half the US military is on alert because of you two. I don't know what this is about, sir, but you guys have just become everyone's top priority."

Mike clasped his hand. "Glad to see you, too, soldier. You have no idea."

"Actually, sir, I think I do." He indicated the vehicle. "Gotta get back to the airfield. The Greyhound is waiting, sir. There's a lull, but another weather front is coming. We need to get out pronto."

No shit, Sherlock.

"I know you're on a schedule, that it's imperative to get

to the States as soon as possible." The short soldier was chatty as he opened the driver's side door. "They said Dr. Merritt was wounded. Corpsman Wilson," the tall black one, "is a trained medic. He'll be with you the entire trip." The medic was in the back with Lucy, gently opening both coats, reaching for bandages.

Petty Officer Reynolds made a K turn. Once they were headed in the right direction, he floored the accelerator, driving at the extreme limits of the vehicle's abilities.

"How we doing back there, Wilson?" the driver asked as he shifted into a higher gear.

Mike looked back, saw blood-soaked bandages. He met Wilson's steady eyes and read the message.

Not good.

Reynolds read it, too, his eyes flicking to the rearview mirror. The vehicle leaped forward, the petty officer somehow keeping it straight on the icy road.

Mike met Lucy's eyes in the darkness. The corpsman had taken off her fur-lined hat and the ski mask. Her face was a pale oval in the darkness. She was clenching her jaws against the pain.

"Hold on, honey. We're on our way."

Her lips were pressed together. She nodded.

"Can you give her anything for the pain?" he asked the corpsman.

"Yeah, better to do it now." A swab and a swift injection.

Mike was about to ask him what he meant when he saw lights ahead. Bright spotlights on stanchions. The airfield.

The vehicle cut right across runways, making a beeline for the aircraft. There were steps waiting for them. Mike brushed everyone away, eased Lucy carefully out of the jeep and carried her up the steps, trying hard not to jostle her. He moved into the plane sideways and looked around for a place to lay her down.

A cot had been strapped to the bulkhead. Mike made his way toward it, grateful that Lucy would be lying down and relatively warm. Maybe they could stitch her up here, stop the bleeding.

Everything was going to be so fucking tight. He knew a special operating theater had been set up at the other end. They would be prepared for extraction of the tiny cylinders. But judging from the wound, Lucy would also be needing major surgery on her side.

Mike held her hand. It was cold, clammy. Her skin was deathly, icy white. He smoothed back her hair. "How we doing, sweetheart?"

He was very lucky that Lucy had manners because the answer was clearly *Fucking awful, you moron, what kind of question is that?* Instead, she gave a tired smile. She tried to say something, but it wouldn't come out.

Jesus. Trying to talk would strain her diaphragm, open the wound even more. What the fuck was he thinking?

"Shh." He put a finger across her lips. "Everything's going to—"

He broke off when he saw the corpsman approaching them, dragging something bulky on the ground.

The engines fired—he could feel the vibrations beneath his feet. The Greyhound wasn't built for comfort. The bulkheads weren't insulated. It was going to be a bumpy and cold ride.

"Dr. Merritt." The corpsman held up a Hazmat suit. "I'm afraid I'm going to have to ask you to put this on for the duration of the trip back home."

Mike saw red. He got right into the corpsman's face. There was time for that. "Now, listen here, you son of a bitch. That woman is wounded. You can't ask her to be sealed inside—"

He stopped. He was staring into the barrel of an M9 Beretta, the corpsman's dark eyes steady behind the weapon. "I have specific orders, sir. Right from the top. The Hazmat suit goes on now. I am authorized to use deadly force if you resist, and I am authorized to knock Dr. Merritt out if she resists. That came right from the top, too. Sir."

"Mike." Lucy's voice was barely a whisper. She clutched his hand. "They have to do this. You understand that."

He looked down at her. Her lips were chalk white, deep

bruises under her eyes. Even though the bandage over her side had been recently changed, it was starting to bleed through.

The corpsman was helping her to sit up. He took off her boots and was already putting her feet into the suit.

Jesus. Mike understood, in theory. Lucy was carrying a lethal mutant virus in her body. They had only a terrorist's word that it wouldn't explode for twenty-four hours. She could be infected at any minute and infect the plane, its crew, the pilots. The plane would fall out of the sky. The Hazmat suit was necessary.

But . . . shit. She was already hurting, wounded. The suits were uncomfortable. Nobody could treat her wound while she was in the suit. She couldn't drink, would have to breathe canned air.

Mike had donned the MOPP suit—Mission Oriented Protective Posture—in training. The military version of the Hazmat suit. It was horrible, uncomfortable, claustrophobic.

Lucy gave a cry of pain as the corpsman put her on her feet to get her arms in the suit. Mike couldn't help himself. He moved to stop what was going on and found himself again with a barrel right in his face. The corpsman was on one knee, one arm around Lucy, the gun in his other hand, aimed up at Mike's head. "I'll shoot if I have to, sir. I won't like it, but I'll do it. Our orders are very clear. I'll be court-martialed if I don't obey."

Lucy was swaying with fatigue and blood loss. She'd already been fitted with the mask and hood. "Mike." The respirator made her voice sound mechanical, almost alien. She stopped, coughed. In the unzipped opening, Mike could see that the cough made fresh blood well up.

"Goddammit! At least close up the wound, stitch it or put butterfly bandages or something! Can't you see the shape she's in? She could—" Mike's mouth closed with a snap.

Die. He'd been about to say it. She could die.

Wilson shook his head sorrowfully as he zipped Lucy

up. He'd reholstered his Beretta, but it was within reach. And Mike knew that the whole crew had orders. He could, conceivably, pull Wilson's Beretta and shoot him, but he'd have to kill the whole crew, and then who would fly the plane?

"It's okay, Mike," Lucy said again in her metallic voice. "It's necessary."

"Lie down, please, Doctor." Wilson helped Lucy lie down on the cot. Mike could see her grimace of pain and his hands clenched.

The engines revved, the plane started taxiing.

Wilson checked his watch, looked at Mike. "We're taking off early. The Learjet is waiting on the tarmac at Mumbai. Pilots say there are tailwinds. There's a full medical team waiting on the other end, at Atlanta. You better strap yourself in for the flight. Sir."

Wilson's dark eyes were steady. He was sympathetic, but Mike had no doubt at all that he would do his duty and follow his orders to the letter.

There was a very good chance Lucy might not survive the flight. Something had to be said before he strapped himself in.

He put his face right against the transparent faceplate of Lucy's Hazmat suit and just looked at Lucy. She was so beautiful. So brave. He touched her hand, encased in three layers of gloves.

"I love you," he said.

A faint smile. "I know," the alien metallic voice answered. "Go buckle up."

Five minutes later they were airborne.

An hour into the flight, Lucy lost consciousness.

NINETEEN

TEL AVIV
3 A.M.

IT was a dusty house on a short side street on the outskirts of Tel Aviv. Though it was only ten years old, it looked ancient, the corners of the inferior-grade cement already crumbling.

There was no one about. The soldiers had quietly made sure of that, contacting all the neighbors on the street, quietly evacuating them. There were no nosy insomniac neighbors, no barking dogs, just ten men in Level A Hazmat suits, hiding in the shadows. Waiting.

Two ambulances and three vans with SWAT teams were on a side street.

Two clicks in the leader's headset and he brought his hand down. The go signal.

The soldiers were all brave, technically proficient, had gone over the plan again and again, but a shiver of superstitious terror ran under their skins. They would have had to be robots not to feel it, for inside the crumbling, nondescript house was a plague designed to destroy their country.

These men were the only line of defense against the massacre of their people.

Each man had a moment of atavistic terror, then their

nerves steadied. Each man was a scientist, as well as being a warrior. They were the best of the best their country had to offer.

One of the soldiers held a stethoscope-like device against the walls. There was no question of placing his ear against it. His head was encased in twenty pounds of plastic. The listening device transmitted the sound waves it picked up directly into his headset. Except there was no sound. Nothing, not even the ticking of a clock.

He wanted to wait, but their SCBA respirators only had an air supply of twenty minutes. They needed to do this perfectly, but they also needed to do this fast.

The soldier gave thanks that it was not summer. It was an area too poor for air-conditioning. The windows would have all been open. But it was November, and cold. All the windows were tightly shut.

He gave the sign. The soldiers surrounded the house, half of them climbing ladders they'd brought with them, scrambling up to the second floor.

They all carried tiny precision drills, and at the click, they quickly bored holes through the wooden frames of the windows and threaded tubes into the rooms. Each tube was connected to a canister filled with a derivative of fentanyl, the most powerful narcotic in existence, one hundred times more potent than morphine. The drug was fast-acting for a short duration. Those inside were guaranteed to be unconscious for at least half an hour. It would be enough.

When the canisters were emptied, the men simply broke into the house, uncaring of the noise. Nobody inside was going to wake up.

Moving fast, they carried the bodies outside to the waiting ambulances, where they would be taken to a special laboratory in the desert, to a prison seven floors down, from which they would never emerge.

The men searched the house thoroughly and found ten injection guns and one thousand tiny cylinders, to be dispersed throughout the country. Everything went into a special container, built to withstand an atomic blast.

The contents would be studied for years to come.

Every stick of furniture, every object in the house, was carried out and stored in special vans.

As the sky in the east lightened slightly, they piled into a van that would take them back to Mossad, where they would get out of their suits, have breakfast and then be debriefed.

By midday, they'd be home with their families, having saved their country, sworn to secrecy to the end of time.

MID ATLANTIC
DAWN

Lieutenant Cary Entwiler looked down at the dark ocean, lightening slightly to the east, then looked at his radar.

"There she is," he announced to his squadron. Privately, he thought this was overkill. Six F-16 Fighting Falcons, each with four Boeing Harpoons, was enough to take down a small country, let alone a fishing vessel.

But what was below him was apparently not a simple fishing vessel. He and his crew were not cleared to know what the vessel carried, but they were smart enough to figure it out.

Something really fucking scary, that's what.

Well, the navy was counting on them to eliminate it. and that's what they'd do.

They were cruising at Mach 1.5, at fifty thousand feet. No way anyone on the ship could see them. But the infrared cameras on the lower deck were following every move on the ship. In the sunlight, those cameras would allow Lieutenant Entwiler to see what brand of cigarettes the sailors smoked.

"There it goes," he told his pilots. They were seeing the same image he was seeing. A blue tarp being slowly pulled over the ship. Camouflage. Because they were bringing something deadly to the United States and didn't want to be seen by satellites.

Not today, boys, Lieutenant Entwiler thought. *Not ever.*

He locked in the ship's position, sent it over an encrypted line and a minute later received the message *Proceed.*

"Squadron release," he ordered his men, and the bays of all six F-16s emptied their payload—four Harpoons each, traveling at 500 mph, with two-hundred-pound warheads, arrowing straight to the ship. Each Harpoon cost a million bucks.

Someone wanted every molecule on that ship destroyed.

They watched the massive explosion on their screens, a geyser of water arcing almost half a mile high. The six F-16s remained in a holding pattern for half an hour, watching the sun rise over the calm sea, without any hint that there had been a ship there.

"Okay, guys," Lieutenant Entwiler announced. "Time to go home."

He pulled his plane up, curved around and headed west.

FORTY MILES NORTH OF THE PALACE

The C-130 Hercules lumbered awkwardly across the bright blue Himalayan sky, so clumsy it was almost endearing. Unless you knew what it carried in its hold. A MOAB—Massive Ordnance Air Blast bomb—affectionately known as the Mother of All Bombs, the most powerful non-nuclear bomb ever created. The pilot had his GPS coordinates and so did the bomb itself. It had its own guidance mechanism and was accurate down to an inch.

The ultimate bunker buster.

Only the pilot's screen showed no bunkers, just an endless stretch of snow. But he had his orders and they were absolutely clear. Destroy even the molecules at that particular GPS location.

Well, he had the equipment to do just that.

And he and his crew also had permission from the brand-new queen of the country they were flying over, Queen Paso, to bomb the bejesus out of one corner.

So be it.

When he heard the click in his headset, the pilot calmly pulled a lever and loosed hell on earth from the bomb bay of his plane.

He watched his screens, watched as the equivalent of eleven tons of TNT hit the ground, digging deep, destroying anything living within the blast radius of 450 feet.

There she goes, he thought, as the bomb exploded underground, snow and dirt and rocks flying up with massive force.

There were only fifteen MOABs in existence, and he'd just fired one. It would have made for a good drinking story if he'd had permission to tell it. If he did, though, he'd face a firing squad, so it would just have to be tucked away with the three or four other things he'd carry with him to his grave.

"Heading home," he told the comms officer eight thousand miles away in the Indian Ocean, and veered back south.

His job here was done.

CENTERS FOR DISEASE CONTROL
ATLANTA, GEORGIA
THREE DAYS LATER

Lucy gained consciousness forty-eight hours after the operation.

The doctors had assured him over and over again that she would be fine. They'd made it to the operating theater, sirens screaming, with twenty minutes to spare. The doctors had been waiting, scrubbed and ready. They had operated deep underground in a Level 4 lab with its own self-contained oxygen supply, negative air pressure and a foot-thick steel door.

Mike had waited topside, ready to chew the couches, until four hours later the head surgeon came out, pulling his mask away from his mouth.

Mike wondered how the guy could walk, seeing as how he had two stones the size of refrigerators. The doctors knew that if the capsule in Lucy's shoulder exploded and they were infected, the steel door would never open.

That took cojones.

They had got the capsule out of her shoulder right away and put it into a sealed container and sent it up, then got to work on Lucy.

Who was now alive . . . or not.

"Captain Shafer?"

Mike stood and watched the doctor cross the room, trying to read his face. But all he could see was kindliness and exhaustion.

Mike's heart was thumping heavily in his chest, static in his head.

"Yes," he croaked. "I'm Captain Shafer."

"Pleased to meet you, Captain." The surgeon's grip was strong and dry. Mike's palms were sweating. He'd had to wipe them on his trousers before taking the surgeon's hand.

"So . . . how did the operation go?"

The surgeon gave a gusty sigh and Mike's heart leaped in his throat.

"She lost a lot of blood. It was touch and go. We infused her with three sacks. She lost her spleen, too. But she's young and healthy and we hold out hope for a complete recovery."

Mike's knees nearly gave out. He gasped in air, suddenly realizing he hadn't breathed in over a minute.

"Good—good news." He hardly recognized his own voice.

The doctor nodded. "Yes, indeed." He narrowed his eyes at Mike. "She's going to be weak and recovery could take a long time. Make sure she rests."

Mike nodded, not trusting himself to speak. Oh yeah. She wasn't going to do anything for six months. He'd personally see to that.

"Can I, can I see her?"

"Sure. She's heavily sedated, but you can stay as long as you like. I understand she has no family."

"Not true," Mike said firmly. "She has me."

He sat by her bedside for two days and two nights, just watching her. The nurses came and went and discussed him in a whisper, and he didn't budge except to go to the bathroom.

On the morning of the third day, Lucy's hand fluttered in his. He sat up, all drowsiness gone. Half an hour later, her eyes moved beneath her lids, back and forth, like windshield wipers. An hour later, her eyes opened suddenly.

"Hey." Mike leaned over her, holding her hand. She gripped his hand hard, and he'd never felt anything better in his life. "You're back."

She breathed in and out. Looked at him. "I made it." Her voice was thin and scratchy.

"Yeah." He tried to smile, but it was wobbly. His cheeks were wet. Was it raining in the room? He swiped at them impatiently. "You made it."

Wait, he told himself, *give her time*. But he couldn't. Simply couldn't.

"Do you remember the last thing I said to you?"

She nodded, hair rasping on the pillow. "You said—I love you."

She was still very sick, had risked death. He shouldn't push it. He even told himself not to push it, but then he never listened to himself.

"Well?" he asked impatiently.

Her lips curved in a little smile, and he knew in that instant that she was going to be all right.

"I love you, too," she whispered.

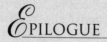

&PILOGUE

THE PALACE
CHILONGO, NHALA
SIX MONTHS LATER

"WATCH that step," Mike said, indicating a tiny imper-
fection in the floor. "Take my arm."

Lucy rolled her eyes and took his arm. She had to watch
it or she'd forget how to walk alone or how to open her own
door or carry her own briefcase.

She straightened the folds of the traditional ceremonial
dress, a brilliant turquoise that matched the silk turquoise
slippers on her feet. A maid had come in and twisted her
hair into the elegant updo of the Nhalan upper classes.
She'd caught a glimpse of herself in the mirror, and really,
except for the shape of her eyes, she could have passed
muster as a Nhalan.

Which, after tonight's ceremony, she would be. Officially. Queen Paso was bestowing honorary citizenship
upon her. Her new name was Tashi Dak, Seeker of Clouds.

She retied the emerald green sash, smoothing her hands
over her hips. She was gaining back some of the weight
she'd lost after the operation. Mike made it his personal
mission to ensure that she ate enough. Her appetite was

coming back, but for the first few months she'd had to choke food down.

Soon, of course, she'd be gaining a lot of weight.

Mike was dressed in a tux, having turned down a Nhalan ceremonial outfit on the theory that he couldn't see himself in a dress. Though he had been badly tempted by the ceremonial dagger.

The doors to their chambers opened and they walked out together, arm in arm.

Lucy breathed in the Palace smell of ancient wood and incense, happier than she had ever been in her life. They walked slowly down the brightly colored hallways, servants lining the walls, bowing as they went past.

Finally, they stood at the top of the stairs leading down to the Great Hall.

Lucy stood in the exact spot where her mother and father had fallen, sixteen years before.

She waited, letting the pain and the pride run through her, and finally let go of the pain. She could almost see the spirit of her unhappiness leave her body and fly away.

Her parents had died heroes' deaths. A whole country revered their memory. They'd lived well and died well and they were gone.

She looked up at Mike and saw that he'd been watching her somberly. He knew. For a jock and a soldier, her Mike was an amazingly perceptive and even sensitive man, though he'd scoff at the thought.

Below, in the Great Hall, a throng of Nhalans awaited them, a crowd dressed in brilliant colors, friendly, happy faces turned up to them. Queen Paso was on a dais at the end of the Great Hall, waiting for her. Her captain, now Prince Consort, was by her side.

"Let's go down," Lucy said to Mike.

She wanted to go forward, into her new life. She'd spent so many years frozen, unable to go back, unable to go forward. If there was an afterlife, she knew her parents were looking down and nodding in approval.

She was going to go forward, in every possible way.

Where before she'd had no family at all, now she was drowning in family. When she was released from the hospital, Mike had taken her to her apartment, helped her pack and then taken her immediately to his family's house in Portland, Oregon, an attractive, rambling building with a huge garden, tailor-made for convalescence.

Mike had opened the door of the house, and waiting for her had been his father, his stepmother, his half sister and two half brothers, four uncles, three aunts, seven cousins and four dogs. All talking and barking at once. All beaming in welcome.

It had been like plunging into a warm, flower-scented ocean.

Uncle Edwin had had a mild heart attack, had retired and—totally unexpectedly—had bought a tiny elegant apartment near Pioneer Square and spent months at a time in Portland, with Lucy.

Mike had retired from the army and was in the process of taking over from his father in the family business. Which was, apparently, blowing things up. Mike loved it.

He loved her, too.

Every day, he asked her to marry him.

And she would. But her new life, however wonderful, had left her unsettled. Every day she said yes but . . . not right now.

They reached the bottom of the stairs, and the people in the Great Hall parted as they walked toward the queen and bowed the deep bow of respect.

"Have I told you how beautiful you look, Tashi Dak, Seeker of Clouds?" Mike murmured to her. "You look every inch the queen, just like Paso."

Now she could see Paso, smiling down at her.

This, this moment was perfect. All the odd jangling strains of her life coming together in a unique whole.

"I haven't asked Tashi Dak to marry me yet." Mike slanted her a glance, dark eyes glowing. "Maybe *she'll* say yes."

"Maybe."

Mike's eyes rounded with surprise.

It was time. They reached the dais, all the Nhalans were behind them, Paşo looking down on them, smiling.

Lucy took Mike's hand, put it against her belly, nudged his shoulder. "We wouldn't want our child to be without a father, would we?"

Mike's deep, delighted laugh rang in the Great Hall. He picked her up and swung her around, her robe billowing.

All the Nhalans around them tittered, the ladies hiding their smiles behind their hands.

Everyone knew Westerners were crazy.

From *New York Times* bestselling author
JAYNE ANN KRENTZ
also writing as
AMANDA QUICK
and
JAYNE CASTLE

Psychic power and passion collide
as a legendary curse ignites a dangerous desire . . .

THE DREAMLIGHT TRILOGY

Fired Up
Burning Lamp
Midnight Crystal

Praise for the trilogy:

"[A] captivating novel of
psychic-spiced romantic suspense."
—*Booklist* (starred review)

"A top-notch performance."
—*Publishers Weekly* (starred review)

"Sharp wit; clever, complex plotting;
intelligent humor; and electric sensuality."
—*Library Journal*

M789AS1010

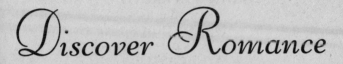